Books by Greg Herren

BOURBON STREET BLUES

JACKSON SQUARE JAZZ

MARDI GRAS MAMBO

Published by Kensington Publishing Corporation

MARDI GRAS MAMBO

GREG HERREN

KENSINGTON BOOKS

KENSINGTON BOOKS are published by

Kensington Publishing Corp.
850 Third Avenue
New York, NY 10022

ISBN 0-7394-6458-2

Printed in the United States of America

You got a lot to learn about life in the Quarter.
     —from Vieux Carré *by Tennessee Williams*

This is for Aunt Julie.

ACKNOWLEDGMENTS

As always, there are any number of people to thank for the support, kindness, and friendship that made the writing of this book much easier. But the difference with this book, opposed to the others, is that it was written in the face of several personal tragedies—and without the support, well wishes, and love, not only of my circle of friends, but also the unbelievable kindness of strangers, I would not have been able to make it through the last eighteen months, let alone write this book. So, to begin with, I would like to thank all of those complete strangers and friends of friends whose kind e-mails and cards helped both Paul and I make it through the horrible summer of 2004. May the Goddess shower you all with blessings.

I would like to single out my editor, John Scognamiglio, and everyone at Kensington. Your compassion and understanding was more than any author could have expected or asked for. Bless you, John—you have no idea how much it meant to me.

Anne Rice, her staff, and her son Christopher also, through their generosity and kindness, helped to reaffirm my faith in the ultimate goodness of human beings.

Julie Smith and Lee Pryor, as always, were there for moral support as well as offering the use of Casa Mysterioso whenever I needed it.

Ellen Johnson, Robin (the best person to stand next to at a party) and Lou Ann Morehouse, Arin Black, Karissa Kary, Steve and Katherine Ecton, Errol and Peggy Scott Laborde, Jane Hobson (who I still owe lunch), Dani Hero, Ellen Johnson, Mark Fernandez, Doug Brantley, Susie Hoskins, Michael Sartisky and Kathy Slimp, Priscilla Lawrence, Denelle Cowhart, and everyone else at the Tennessee Williams Festival also were incredible bedrocks of support.

Pat Brady is not only an amazing talent as a writer, but an incredible friend. I am so proud to know you, Pat. Thank you so much for everything.

Bev and Butch Marshall are two of the most delightful people I've ever had the pleasure of knowing. May the Goddess always be with both of you. I'll have dinner with you two any time.

Mark Richards helps me keep my sanity on a regular basis. Thanks for not only getting me through the last two years, but also for suggesting the ending for this book.

Jean Redmann, Felicia Wong, Heidi Nagele, Noel Twilbeck, and everyone at the NO/AIDS Task Force not only do great work for the New Orleans community, but are also incredible people I am proud to call my friends. Also deserving of mention are the members of the CAN Project staff, who have always been there for me: Roberto Rincon, Eric Johnson, Darrin Harris, Jill Boschini, Tyson Jackson, Chris Rothermel, and James Swire, as well as the volunteers and the Sparq guys. You have always made me smile no matter what insanity was going on in my life.

Also with the CAN office I have to single out Mark Buchseib (Sparqy) and Aika Mongi for special thanks.

Jay Quinn, Ian Philips and Greg Wharton, Carol Rosenfeld, Marika Christian, Trebor Healey, and Victoria Brownworth also deserve crowns in heaven. Thank you so much for always taking my calls—no matter what time of day or night I dial the phone.

David Rosen is one of the most intelligent and kind people I've had the pleasure of knowing. And for his equally wonderful partner, Robb Pearlman, blah blah blah.

Of equal importance are the following people: Darren Brewer, Harriet Campbell Young, my neighbors Michael and John, Val McDermid, Kelly Smith, Marianne Martin, Bill Cohen, Bill Palmer, John Morgan Wilson, Jim Gladstone, Michael Kooiman, Carrie Anderson, Lisa Anderson, Felice Picano, William J. Mann and Dr. Timothy Huber, Dr. Faith Joubert, Nikki and Betty, Jack Carrel, Sheila Wilkinson, Cherry Cappel and Beth Blankenship, Johnny Messenger, Eddie Coleman, Jimmy Carrera, Greg Helmsoth, Drew Zeigler, The Fabulous Deb and everyone at Garden District Books, Philip Rafshoon, Dorothy Allison, Jewelle Gomez, Amie Evans, Jess Wells, Michelle Tea, Katherine Forrest, Ellen Hart, Patrick Califia, Poppy Z. Brite, Dexter Brecht, Terry and Kathy Verrigan, Joy Bollinger, Melinda Shelton, Susan Larsen, Diana Pinckley, Philip Tettleton, M. Christian and Sage Vivant, Karen Kern, Jeffrey Jasper, Steve Soucy, Dan Boyle, Toni Amato, Dawn Lobaugh, Karen Bengtson, Lea Young, Kiki Reineke, Linda Ireland, Margaret Coble, Val McKay, Dix de la Marie, Marda Burton, Kenneth Holditch, Laura Lippman, Chris Wiltz, Ayelet Waldman, Melanie McKay, Lawrence Schimel, Charles Flowers, Patrick Merla, the folks at the Publishing Triangle, Patricia Nell Warren, Betty Berzon, Timothy J. Lambert, Becky Cochrane, all the people who post on my blog, and all the kind readers who have e-mailed me over the years.

A special thanks goes out to Eric Russell and the Gay-Straight Alliance at Manchester High School in Richmond, Virginia. You kids taught me the true meaning of courage in the face of fundamentalist Christian horror. May the Goddess shower you all with blessings, and remember—*no one can make you feel bad about yourself unless you let him or her.* Meeting you kids made me so proud. Never lose sight of who you are.

Anyone I may have forgotten, my humblest of apologies. I'm not as young as I used to be.

I love you all.

PROLOGUE

Last night I dreamed it was Mardi Gras again. It seemed to me I was standing inside an iron gate, watching one of the night parades go by. The sidewalks in front of the gate were crowded with people, all shouting, with their grasping eager hands up in the air. Out beyond the edge of the curb, I could see people sitting in lawn chairs. Still others were up on ladders, with coolers and plastic bags of booty piled around them on the ground. Fathers and mothers were holding up babies, while black kids with the crotches of their pants down around their knees walked behind the crowd, weighted down by the ropes of beads around their necks. Beads were flying through the air, some getting caught and tangled in the branches of the towering, gnarled oaks lining the avenue. The heavy upper branches of those oaks also blocked out the glow of the ancient street lamps, so the night seemed even darker than it should. I could hear a marching band, playing a recent hip-hop hit, and the strange clicking sound of the baton girls' tap shoes on the pavement. The air was heavy with the fragrance of hot grease, corn dogs, and the strange, melted yellowish-orange substance the vendors put on nachos that purports to be cheese—but no one is really sure what it is. A group of flambeaux carriers was passing by, dancing that odd little circular dance they do, their propane tanks popping and hissing, throwing long and twisted shadows that also danced inside the iron fence I was behind. Right behind them a huge float pulled by a tractor was coming and the crowd's shouts became louder, more desperate, more pleading. On the float's front was a huge white clown face, its bright red lips parted in what passed for a smile but seemed to me to be a frightening leer. The masks on the float riders glowed supernaturally at the hordes begging them for generosity in the strange light cast by the moon when it cleared the thick clouds in the cold night sky. I stood inside the black iron fence, my arms wrapped around me against the cold as an increased sense of menace and dread built inside me. Something bad was going to happen—

Oh, get real, Scotty!

If I do have bad dreams, I don't remember them when I wake up. I've certainly never been troubled in my sleep, even though crazy things always seem to happen to me. I'm just one of those people, I guess. For whatever reason, the Goddess has decided to throw some wild stuff at me—she always has, even when I was a kid—and what can you do? I just don't think I am one of those people who is destined to have a nice, normal, quiet life. Maybe it's because I was named Milton Bradley at birth. Yes, that's right. Milton Bradley. My older brother started calling me by my middle name, Scotty, before I started school, and thank the Goddess, it stuck. Can you imagine how cruel the kids would have been to someone named Milton, let alone Milton Bradley? And then of course there's the gay thing. I was lucky—my parents are pretty liberal and are delighted to have a gay son—like it somehow proves how truly cool they really are or something. They are pretty cool, actually.

But I was talking about dreams. Sometimes the Goddess does speak to me in my dreams. I've always had this slight psychic gift all my life—see what I mean about not being normal? Usually I have to read tarot cards to focus the gift and actually see things. But that's been changing over the past year. I've started having visions, which never happened before, and I even communicated with a dead guy a couple of times. But on those rare occasions when the Goddess speaks to me in a dream, I kind of have to pass out first—or be knocked unconscious—rather than fall asleep. (She apparently has a rather bizarre sense of humor.) But I haven't been dreaming about this past Mardi Gras, thank you very much. If I did, I feel pretty certain the dreams would be fricking nightmares. But then again, who knows? I mean, after all, the reality was worse than anything I could dream up—and I've got a pretty vivid imagination.

I was really looking forward to this past Mardi Gras. It had been a while since I'd been able to just kick up my heels, put everything aside, and just party till I dropped. Well, it had actually been since the last Mardi Gras. My three favorite times of year are Southern Decadence, Halloween, and Mardi Gras—not necessarily in that order. Mardi Gras comes first every year, forty days before Easter. Southern Decadence is next, over Labor Day weekend, and I certainly hope I don't need to explain when Halloween is.

Mardi Gras last year had been really fun—I hadn't had to work my wiles as a go-go boy and, frankly, don't remember a whole lot of the ten days leading up to Ash Wednesday. I know that I had gotten a windfall of cash and invested in a pile of Ecstasy, which I started taking the Thursday night before Fat Tuesday. The rest of the weekend is kind of a blur. I know I met a lot of hot guys, danced a lot, and woke up on Ash Wednesday feeling like something the cat had dragged in, chewed up, and spat out. Boy, was that fun!

I didn't get to enjoy Southern Decadence last year. First off, I'd been broke and had to get up and dance on the bar to make enough money to pay the rent. If that wasn't enough, I had to foil a dangerous conspiracy, got kidnapped—it's a long story I won't bore you with right now. Halloween had been fun, but not as much fun as I'd anticipated. My boyfriend Frank had been shot in the arm the week before, and since he was still really not in much shape to party and dance all night long, we'd just costumed, gone out, and come home early. So I was *really* looking forward to Mardi Gras. I wanted to go out in fun costumes, meet lots of tourists, hang out with the locals, and just grin and shake my ass on the dance floor all night long. Things had, actually, been going pretty smoothly. I couldn't complain about anything. I was back living in my building on Decatur Street, my two boyfriends lived upstairs from me, and they had never experienced Carnival before—Mardi Gras virgins. I wanted them to have a great time. I wanted it to be special. But then, I'm getting ahead of myself.

So, I'll just share some facts. My name is Milton Scotty Bradley, but my friends and family call me Scotty. I'm five feet eight, have curly dark blond hair, and weigh 165 pounds, give or take—it depends on my diet. I am in pretty decent shape; I used to teach aerobics and was a personal trainer, and every once in a while I supplemented my income by dancing in a thong in the gay bars. But that was all in the past. Now I'm a private eye in New Orleans. Yes, that's right, a full-fledged fedora-and-trench-coat-wearing private eye. Okay, it may seem like a weird career change for an ex-stripper and personal trainer, but it just kind of presented itself to me. I can't imagine there are a lot of us out there. But what do you do when something drops into your lap without warning? Treat it as a message from the Universe and go along for the ride, that's what. When I got involved in that conspiracy thing during Southern Decadence, I showed a flair for law enforcement. A Fed I met on that case, Frank Sobieski (more on him later), recommended I get a private-eye license. I was tired of being a personal trainer, and that little adventure, although having its scary moments, was kind of fun, so I figured, what the hell? So here I am, licensed and bonded, and working for the Blackledge Agency office here in New Orleans. There are two other dicks (I love saying that) in the office with me, Frank Sobieski and Colin Cioni.

Oh, yeah, Frank and Colin are the two boyfriends I mentioned earlier.

That's right—I have two boyfriends. That's kind of a long story, so I'll give you the short-and-sweet version. I met both of them during Southern Decadence. Colin was working undercover on a case for the Blackledge Agency, and Frank was in town working on getting to the bottom of the conspiracy thing. In one of those things that could only happen to me, Colin's cover was working as a stripper at the Pub with me during Decadence. So we met dancing on the bar, were attracted to each other, and I took him home with me. The next day, I met Frank when he showed up at my apartment, because I'd wound up with an important piece of evidence for his case—it had been slipped into my boot while I was shaking my ass to earn dollars. We also hit it off. I liked them both, and they both liked me. I was going to have to choose between them. I couldn't. Who could? Frank is six feet three of solid, thick, lean muscle. He clips his receding hair, and it's a *hot* look on him. He was a blonde before that, and he has steel blue eyes that seem to pierce your very soul. There's a rather nasty-looking scar on his cheek that makes him look really mean when he isn't smiling. He got the scar early in his career with the FBI but won't tell me how he got it. He also trims the hair on his massive chest (his nipples are *really* sensitive) and ripped stomach. There's no body fat on him anywhere. And he has the most beautiful ass. . . .

Colin is only about five six or seven, but he's gorgeous in a completely different way from Frank. He has 185 pounds of solid muscle packed on his short frame, olive skin, green eyes, and the most beautiful, curly, short blue-black hair. He's pure Italian, the kind who gets that gorgeous bluish black shadow on his face in the late afternoon. He has huge, round, green eyes, and the whitest, straightest teeth this side of a commercial hawking some tooth-whitening cream. When we first met, he told me he was a cat burglar (it's a long story), and although that was just his cover, I know for a fact he can climb up the side of a building. Colin's always full of surprises. He's fluent in Hebrew, for example. I'm beginning to think there isn't anything he can't do.

He's also *amazingly* limber and can contort his body into the most incredible positions.

I couldn't choose—there just wasn't any way.

The really weird thing is it wasn't my idea to have a three-way relationship—the boys came up with it all by themselves with no pushing from me. (My best friend, David, doesn't believe me. He thinks it was my plan all along.) So far, it's been surprisingly harmonious. I live on the third floor of a building on Decatur Street across from the Old Mint, and they share an apartment on the fourth floor. It's kind of cool. We all have our privacy when we need it, or if we want to be together, we can be easily. If Frank needs some alone time, Colin comes down and hangs with me. Of course, we had to set up ground rules. The first thing we negotiated was sex. We decided all three of us didn't need to be present for it to happen without guilt. Sometimes we all spend the night together; some nights we all sleep alone; some nights one sleeps alone. We also decided not to be monogamous. It seemed kind of silly to demand it of each other (things happen, after all—look at the three of us!), but so far no one's strayed out of our arrangement. Goddess, who has time? I do like to go out sometimes by myself, and the bars are always crawling with hot boys, but I am doing it less and less. On those rare occasions when I do go to the bars alone, every time some hot guy gives me the eye I think about what I have waiting for me at home and just smile and look away. No guy is so hot that he would be better than the two I have at home.

So, I guess I've kind of settled down my wayward ways. I worried about it sometimes: Was I getting old? Was I slowing down?

Was I becoming someone I wasn't? I still liked to go out dancing, but if the boys wanted to stay home I found myself staying home with them and doing some kind of crazy thing—when you put together a longtime private eye, an ex-stripper, and a former FBI agent, you can come up with all kinds of interesting experiences.

One night we played "voyeur." I thought it was kind of silly myself at first. I was supposed to climb up the back steps and pretend like I didn't know either one of them. I know I rolled my eyes when Frank was explaining it all to me—role-play has always struck me as kind of silly—but both Frank and Colin thought it would be fun. And they were really into it. So I said, sure, okay, and sat down on my couch. I waited about fifteen minutes after they went upstairs, then followed. As I climbed the stairs all I could think was, "This is stupid, stupid, stupid." As I got closer to the window into their back bedroom, I could hear them. I stopped and listened for just a minute. It was like listening to a porn tape with the picture off. I could hear them kissing, their breathing, the occasional moan, the slap of bare flesh coming together. I found myself getting aroused. I climbed up a few more steps and then found myself peeking over the ledge and into the room. The lights were off except for a few candles burning, and looking at their incredible naked bodies, their mouths pressed together, the urgency of their hands touching and stroking each other, I found myself watching for a lot longer than I thought I would. At first, I figured I'd get so turned on watching I'd be inside joining them in no time. But watching as they got it on, their two sweating and heaving muscular bodies coming together, hands exploring, mouths coming together in kisses both passionate and tender, I couldn't tear myself away. It was like I was seeing something I wasn't supposed to see, and that made it even more intensely erotic and sexy. Once, Frank looked over at me and winked before Colin went back to work on his nipples, and his eyes closed again. It was like interactive porn, almost. And then I realized they were both getting off on me watching, with the window in between us, and it was making them hornier, like they were performing for me, to make me excited, and that was when I couldn't take it anymore and had to join in.

Why on earth would you want to go to a bar when you can do things like that at home?

Suffice it to say, we have a great sex life together.

So, in those days leading to Mardi Gras, life was good. Frank had also gone to work with us for the agency, and we had a small office in the Marigny, in an old building on Frenchmen Street. It was fun—we'd get up in the morning, have breakfast together, and walk over to the office. We'd work all day, and then around five we'd head for the gym. We didn't have anything major to work on at the office; most times it was just doing back-up research for another branch office's case, and the occasional job doing research for a lawyer (my older brother, Storm, had his firm throwing a lot of work our way). I had a regular paycheck and the kind of home life I'd never imagined in my wildest fantasies. We all got along great. About the only real problem had been convincing Frank to try Ecstasy at Mardi Gras. It hadn't been easy, but he finally gave in.

Little did I realize how much hassle we would have been spared if we'd only listened to Frank. You see, there's something about Carnival that affects people. Every day in New Orleans is *anything can happen day,* and Mardi Gras somehow heightens that sense of insanity. Maybe it's the liquor, maybe it's the parades, or maybe it's just the hordes of tourists; I don't know. But Carnival is somehow different, more charged with the craziness that dogs our days here. My mom jokes that during Carnival the city spikes the drinking water, but I don't know if that would do the trick. I think it's something to do with the time of year, the way the planets align themselves or the stars are arranged when the season starts. Crazier things happen than usual. People let down their guard and open themselves to all kinds of bizarre behavior—things they wouldn't do any other time of year. Straight boys go out on Fat Tuesday practically naked, showing off their bodies and actually enjoying the attention from the gay boys. And, of course, as everyone knows, lots of breasts are bared.

I've always called it the Mardi Gras mambo.

And if someone had told me what would happen during this year's Carnival, I would have laughed my ass off at them. *Please*— it was too much for anyone to believe. And Frank has never once, since Fat Tuesday, ever said, "I told you so." Maybe it wouldn't have happened if we hadn't done the Ecstasy, but I have a feeling it was kind of meant to be. Somehow, we would have gotten dragged into it. And if not for the Ecstasy, who knows? Maybe it would have wound up worse than it actually was. You can never question the Goddess and what she has in mind for you. All you can do is take what she throws at you and do your best. There's never any point in thinking, "If we hadn't done this or if we'd done this instead things would have been different."

Things happen for a reason, and it's not our place to question those reasons, right? But sometimes I have to wonder if the Goddess doesn't just enjoy fucking with me for her own entertainment. I mean, she probably *does* have a sense of humor, right? It's not a stretch to think she likes to see how we are all going to react to the curveballs she throws at us. And I usually don't mind the curveballs—that's what makes life interesting, after all, and I can't think of anything more tedious than having a life that is set in stone and completely predictable. Sure, some warning that something crazy is about to land in your lap would be nice—and maybe she could not throw a lot of successful curveballs at me in a row. But I've never been destined for a quiet life, as I've said, and for the most part my life has always been pretty charmed. I've got a great family, a great apartment, and two fabulous boyfriends, so apparently she feels like I need to have some nutso stuff in my life as well. And if that's the price I have to pay for the great life she's given me, so be it. I don't ever want my life to become boring.

And since Ash Wednesday, I've gone over it again and again

in my head. Sure, there were things that could have been done differently, but there was always a sense of the inevitable. It *had* to happen. Maybe I was getting too complacent with my life and the Goddess wanted to shake things up for me a bit. Maybe it was a life lesson she felt I needed to learn. And, ultimately, I did learn a lot from the whole mess. Maybe a bit more than I think I needed to learn, but you never get to make those choices.

And maybe it was just the Mardi Gras mambo getting into our heads and our lives with a gleeful laugh. Mardi Gras is never what you expect, and this last Carnival was nothing like anything I'd ever imagined to experience.

And despite everything, even now, I can hear the music playing in my head, and I can't help but smile about it all.

But from now on, I will always take the Mardi Gras mambo a bit more seriously. . . .

CHAPTER ONE

Nine of Cups

a love of sensual pleasures

Mardi Gras is *not* for the timid. It chews timid people up and spits them out without a second thought.

I'm probably overstating the obvious here. When people think *Mardi Gras* and Are Not From Here, they think about drinking and naked breasts bouncing and utter licentiousness—what the last days of Sodom and Gomorrah must have been like before fire and brimstone rained destruction down on those godless cities of the plain. Certainly there are some Christians who make that analogy, and desperate to save the city and its sinners from that same dreadful fate, they preach from the street corners through megaphones, screaming at the revelers to repent and find room for Jesus in their hearts rather than room for liquor in their livers. No one listens, of course—they just throw beads at them or bow their heads in respect as they walk past. Mardi Gras is a time for frivolity, for letting go of the daily inhibitions that keep people from behaving like, well, uncivilized animals. It's called *farewell to the flesh*, the last chance to sin before Lent, and in New Orleans, we like to do things right. I guess it's all about excess, really. A local performer, who calls herself the world's only "female female impersonator," often claims during her stage shows that the city motto should be "anything worth doing is worth doing to excess."

Of course, the actual city motto isn't that much different, really: *Laissez le bon temps roule.* (Let the good times roll.)

Carnival is all about more: more people, alcohol, sex, fun, dancing, nakedness—more of everything. It's a time when anything goes—well, everything except sobriety. Fat Tuesday is a holiday throughout the state. Any business that doesn't involve serving food or liquor comes to pretty much a complete halt in the days leading up to this final magic day. Mardi Gras is tied to Lent, after all, forty days of piety and prayer leading up to Easter. So, everyone has to get all the fun and frivolity out of their systems before Ash Wednesday. And going forty days without fun and frivolity in New Orleans—well, is it any wonder that Carnival is a nonstop, citywide drunken orgy that lasts up to ten days? We take our fun and frivolity seriously here, and it has to be as much fun as possible to make the somber nature of Lent even more symbolic.

Of course, that's just the story we tell People Not From Here. Nobody *really* takes Lent as seriously as Carnival. The truly devout will give up something—chocolate, maybe cigarettes, some little sinful indulgence like that—but very few people actually give up liquor or sex for Lent. That just ain't gonna happen, folks. Chocolate is one thing, but liquor? Perish the thought. But for most People Not From Here, New Orleans and Mardi Gras are irrevocably linked in their minds—and everyone has his or her own opinion of what Mardi Gras means. For me, it's lots of pretty-boy tourists with little or no morals dancing all night every night with their shirts off with sweat running down their chests, and going to parades with a slight buzz on.

And the most important thing is the throws.

That's right, *throws*, not beads. The krewes don't just throw strings of beads to the screaming crowds, no matter what people might think. They throw plush toys, plastic spears, plastic go-cups, doubloons, and various other things, depending on the krewe. Every krewe has its own unique and special throw. The ladies of Muses, for example, throw red plastic shoes, to add a bit of feminine flavor to the festivities. Of course, the most treasured throw of all is the Zulu coconut. I've caught a few of those in my life. They don't throw the coconuts anymore—too many people have gotten broken jaws or lost a lot of teeth over the years—so now they just hand them off the floats to the lucky chosen few. The hardest thing about getting the Zulu coconut is fighting off all the assholes who seem to think they are well within their rights to try to take it away from you. One year a woman grabbed me by the hair and said she'd yank it all out if I didn't give her my co-conut. I was raised to believe a gentleman never hits a lady, but as she yanked on my hair I realized she wasn't a lady, punched her a good one in the gut, and once she let go of my hair gave her a strong shove for good measure. Bitch won't try that again, I bet.

Throw fever at Mardi Gras is something to see, all right. It can turn into blood sport pretty darned quick.

One of the most fun things is watching people who've never been before catch the fever. I was really looking forward to seeing if Frank Sobieski, reserved retired FBI special agent, could resist the allure of catching throws. I could tell by the look on his face when he'd say things like, "I just can't believe people will make fools of themselves for this stuff," while looking at the big box of beads I keep in my bedroom closet, that he truly believed scream-ing for beads was beneath his dignity. I decided not to tell him that *everyone* thinks that before his or her first Mardi Gras—that it's all just a silly local custom these newbies won't succumb to. *Of course* they won't.

No one *ever* does.

Colin had never been to Mardi Gras either, and he came down firmly on the same side of the fence as Frank. He was just as excited for the season as I was, but he would *never* scream for beads. I just smiled to myself as I listened to them talking about how they would never make fools of themselves for throws. *Just you boys wait,* I thought to myself with a smug grin, *within ten minutes of the first beads flying you'll be whoring yourself for whatever you can catch. Beneath your dignity, my ass.*

I just hoped I could keep the smug "I told you so" look off my face.

There are certain rules about the beads People Not From Here never seem to understand. I've often wished that someone would publish a bead guide for those misguided people who just don't get it. I mean, it's not like it's hard. First of all, *you never buy beads.* The rule is you can only buy beads if you are going to give them away to a total stranger—no exceptions. The second rule is *you only wear beads you were given.* And, of course, the most important of all: *you only wear beads during Carnival.* Every little tourist shop in the Quarter sells beads, and it never ceases to amaze me when I see people walking around with strands of beads around their neck when it isn't Carnival. Nothing screams *tourist* louder than out-of-season bead wearing. You might as well wear a neon sign flashing MUG ME.

And you know those great big beads the size of your fist? Those *never* come from a parade rider. For one thing, they're too expensive. Nope, those are store bought and are almost always worn by really attractive, young, straight college boys in the last full flush of their youthful beauty before the tragic slide into middle age so many of them suffer from. I have a theory about those beads: like a flashy expensive car, the bigger the beads, the smaller the penis. It's just a theory, though. I've never had the opportunity to prove or disprove it.

Of all the parades, my favorite is the Mystic Krewe of Iris. There are several reasons for this. First, Iris is a women's krewe, which means the masked figures on the floats tossing things are not men. Men always look for women (the larger the breasts, the better) and children in the crowd to reward with their largesse. They only throw to men by accident, or if someone yells particularly loud. This sucks if you like to catch throws. However, the ladies of Iris are just as sexist as the male krewe members. They throw to men and children. Flirting with the ladies definitely works. And since Iris rolls on the Saturday afternoon before Fat Tuesday, usually it's sunny and warm. Sunny and warm means I don't wear a shirt. (And a lot of guys don't. It's basically a beefcake bonanza out there on St. Charles Avenue the afternoon of Iris. Did I mention how much I love Iris?)

I get lots of throws at Iris every year.

Carnival so far had been a bit of a disappointment. Mardi Gras was early this year, which meant despite the fervent prayers of the locals, there was a strong possibility that Fat Tuesday itself could be cold, gray, and drizzly. If the weather on Fat Tuesday sucks, it adversely affects the tourist numbers of the following year, so the City Fathers were keeping their fingers crossed and praying just as hard for sunny, warm weather as the rest of us who just want to run around half naked. Unfortunately, every night since the parades started, it had been gray, cold, and wet. The parades still rolled despite the inclement weather, but all the newscasters were despondent about low numbers of people out for the parades. They failed to take into consideration that standing in a slight drizzle on a cold night waiting for a parade isn't fun. You'd think they'd have realized it as they stood out there in their trench coats broadcasting. And, actually, it's better for the businesses. Instead of being out there on the streets, the tourists were in the restaurants and the bars staying dry and warm spending their tourist dollars to support our economy.

Every night after we got home from the gym, I'd ask the boys if they wanted to go out and watch the parades. I *hate* standing out trying to catch throws when it's cold, so I didn't try very hard to convince them. I'd have gone if they'd wanted to, but Frank and Colin weren't into standing around in the cold rain just to have beads thrown at them, so we pretty much blew off the earlier parades. After all, there's always another day of parades, and the Goddess wouldn't be so cruel as to have the weather suck the day of Iris. Regardless, I love the Iris parade, and unless the streets were flooding, we were going. Besides, my sister, Rain, is one of the ladies of Iris, so going was also a family obligation. Actually, most of my relatives are in one parade or another, but Rain's appearance in Iris is the only one I care about.

Fortunately, that Saturday dawned bright and sunny and warm. All three of us had gotten up early, so we could go to the gym and pump up—as I said, the sexist ladies of Iris really notice muscles. We caught a ride with my best friend, David, Uptown, where he managed to find a place to park on Baronne, and walked the two blocks over to St. Charles Avenue.

That's another important thing to remember about Carnival. *Never* watch parades on Canal Street. That's where the mobs of tourists are, drunk and boisterous and pushing and shoving and just getting on your nerves. It's much more fun to go Uptown and watch along the St. Charles route. That's where the locals go. It isn't as crowded, there aren't any breasts being bared, and instead you can see what Carnival really is supposed to be like—or what it was like before the college students found out about it. That's where you see families out with their kids, portable barbecues set up on the streetcar tracks, and coolers full of beer everywhere. Of course people are drinking, but New Orleanians know how to pace themselves—after all, we have to all year long. Drinking might be a city pastime, *de rigueur* for every social event in town, but you don't see people puking or passing out on St. Charles. You don't see men taking a piss in a corner.

Many locals leave town during Carnival. They're sick of the hordes of tourists, the problems getting around the city—St. Charles and Canal, the two main streets in the city, close for the parades, and it's easy to get trapped inside the parade route. I can only imagine how frustratingly annoying it must be to live Uptown during Carnival. There's also the familiarity. If you've been dealing with it your entire life, after a while I guess it can get old for some people, but I am not one of those people. After all, do you get sick of Christmas? And so far, it hasn't gotten old for me. I feel like a kid again every year when the parades roll. I don't believe I would ever get sick of Carnival. I love everything about it. I love the green, purple, and gold decorations everywhere—the huge masks adorning balconies, the beads hanging from the tree branches and the telephone lines. I even love the tourists, even though they do stupid stuff they would never dare to do in a million years at home. I love the parades, catching throws, the nonstop fun atmosphere. I even like the pervasive smell of grease from the vendors hawking corn dogs and French fries and those bizarre sausage sandwiches made with fried onions and green peppers. I love the signs in front of bars advertising BIG-ASS BEER $3.95—40 OUNCES!! Okay, it's not like living in New Orleans is ever boring, mind you—it's kind of like living on a nonstop rollercoaster ride sometimes—but Carnival is different. The whole city is in a festive mood, and everyone is relaxed and just wants to have a good time. What other American city throws such a huge party and invites the whole world to come join the fun?

Is it any wonder I love it here so much?

The first, dull floats had already passed—the ones with the royalty of the krewe. Maids, dukes, duchesses, the court, the captain, the King and Queen—these floats have only a couple of people on them and they can't throw as much stuff. The best ones are the later ones, which have as many as thirty people on them throwing stuff out with one hand while hanging on to their drink with the other. I could tell Frank and Colin were unimpressed so far by their first parade. They still had their shirts on, hadn't yelled once, and were standing back from the crowd with their arms crossed like the sticks-in-the-mud they were being. I'd caught a nice string of red beads from the Queen of Iris, and I had my shirt tucked into the back of my loose-fitting shorts, which just hung off my hips. I hadn't worn underwear, and the shorts had crept down almost to the top of my pubic hair. David had already taken his shirt off, and he'd caught some beads too.

Frank and Colin, though, were just standing there with bemused expressions on their faces, their shirts still on. We were standing on the neutral ground, David and I down on the curb, Frank and Colin standing farther back on the slight upward slope on the other side of the streetcar tracks.

"Just wait"—I nudged David, gesturing back at them—"till they catch their first beads."

David winked back at me. David is the best friend anyone could ever ask for. He's the kind of person you could call and say, "David, I just killed someone," and without missing a beat he'd reply, "Well, the first thing we have to do is get rid of the body." He's in his early forties but is blessed with one of those metabolisms that simply refuses to allow fat to accumulate. We've been working out together for almost three years, and he's managed to put on a lot of lean muscle without gaining a whole lot of weight. His entire body has changed. His reddish hair has gone almost completely white, and he's buzzed it down to the scalp. He has very white skin, which burns easily. He has a massive tattoo of a dragon running down the left side of his body, from the shoulder down around the left pec.

He looks pretty good.

We moved back as the marching band from Warren Easton High School approached. The public school bands are amazing. You haven't lived until you've watched a New Orleans public school band. Even the junior high ones are awesome. They are almost entirely black, and they put on a *show*. They dance and sway as they play their instruments and get into it in a way no predominantly white school band can. And because they don't subscribe to the image that only bone-thin women with huge boobs are sexy, their cheerleaders, drill teams, and majorettes are a mix of different sizes and looks. The girls all have taps on their boots, and they know how to dance in their skintight sequined body suits. And their hair! They have these incredibly elaborate hairdos (what we call "parade hair"); towering masses of curls and curlicues and crimpled hair crowned with rhinestone tiaras. Interestingly enough, the bigger girls—the ones white schools would think too fat and make fun of—are usually the better dancers.

They are *fabulous*.

The band stopped right in front of us and launched into a version of a current hit hip-hop song. The batons started twirling and the pom-poms shaking as the girls went into their dance as the crowd cheered. I looked back at Colin and Frank. They were staring, their mouths open. I walked back to them.

"Those kids are good," Frank said, unable to look away from them.

Colin pointed to a large majorette, stuffed into a tight form-fitting sequined bodysuit. "That girl can *move*."

"She'd be considered too fat to be a majorette in most schools," I said, feeling proud of my city. Our public school system might be one of the worst in the country, but it could produce some amazing marching bands. That has to count for something. "Isn't this fun?"

Frank and Colin exchanged that look I'd come to know fairly well since they'd moved here. It was the "Scotty-is-such-a-cute-little-whack-job" look. I just rolled my eyes. The band was moving along, and the first real float was coming. "Come on, guys, come get some beads. Loosen up already!"

They exchanged the look again. I shrugged and moved back up to David.

Okay, the most important thing about catching throws is to pay attention. You *have* to pay attention. When the throws start flying, you've got to keep your head up and your eyes moving. If you don't, you're likely to get smacked in the face by some beads. Trust me, it *hurts*. (The city council passed an ordinance protecting the krewes from being sued for injuring people. Unfortunately, the riders party just as hard as the crowd, so some of the drunker krewe members will whip beads into the crowd like they're trying to win the World Series. I got a black eye once from a particularly nice string of green, gold, and purple beads. I kept them, and the black eye gave me a kind of roguish, dangerous look. It was kind of cool looking, like rough trade.) As the float got closer, David and I both put our arms up and started shouting. The beads started flying. I jumped up and grabbed a nice string of purple ones, then a couple more. I made eye contact with a woman on the first level, and she tossed me a handful of real beauties, and then the float was gone . . . but there was another one coming up right behind it.

I looked back at Frank and Colin. They had each caught some. Colin had a huge grin on his face and was putting his around his neck. But Frank was just holding his, his arms crossed. *Loosen up, Special Agent,* I thought and turned back to start screaming at the next float.

I'd just caught a nice strand of special beads, red ones shaped like dice rather than round, when I realized Colin was standing next to me, screaming, his shirt stuck into the back of his jeans. I glanced over at him and laughed out loud. He was flexing his biceps and making his pecs bounce! He was justly rewarded for this gorgeous display of masculine musculature with a full bag of beads. He stuck his tongue out at me as he tore the bag open.

Bead fever . . . it's really hard to resist.

After the float moved on, and another marching band—this time the ROTC band from Dillard University—was heading past us, Colin grinned at me. "Okay, this is fun."

I looked back at Frank, who was tucking his shirt through a belt loop. He gave me an embarrassed smile as he looped his handful of beads over his head and walked up to the curb.

"Having fun, Special Agent?" David asked.

He glared at us for a minute, then threw back his head and started laughing. "This is awesome!" he said, in a dead-on imitation of my voice.

And once again, I thanked the Goddess for the amazing life she was giving me. Is there anything better than having two men who love you, who have a sense of play, who can go to a Carnival parade and have a good time in the sunshine? I wanted to kiss them both.

Ah, life is good.

And the sex is even better. Have I mentioned that?

My cell phone rang, so I pulled it out of my pocket and walked to the other side of the neutral ground so I could hear before answering it. "Hello?"

"Hey, Scotty," said a heavily accented voice. It was Misha, my Ecstasy connection. He was originally from Russia, and he has the sexiest accent. "Just wanted to let you know your Avon products came in." Avon is our code for Ecstasy, because when you're on it, you feel beautiful. Hell, everything's beautiful when you're rolling on Ecstasy.

It's such a *nice* feeling.

"Cool. I'll come by around eight. Is that cool?"

"Perfect." He hung up. I closed my phone and grinned from ear to ear as I walked back over to the boys. "That was Misha. Our beauty boosters are in."

"All right!" David grinned, pumping his fists. Okay, one of the bad things I'd done in my life was get him to try Ecstasy for the first time. He went through a phase where he was doing it every weekend, but finally he realized it was better to do it just three times a year, like I'd told him to begin with. *Mardi Gras, Decadence, and Halloween—don't do it anytime in between.*

Frank's smile faded. He sighed. "I still don't think this is a good idea."

Here we go again, I thought, trying not to roll my eyes.

"Come on, Frank." Colin lightly punched him in the chest. "We've been through this already. It never hurts to try something once. No one's going to make you do it again. Just try it once; that's all we ask."

"But it's *illegal*," he growled. "I hate the thought of Scotty taking the risk of getting arrested buying it."

"I've done it a million times." I shrugged. Okay, that was an exaggeration—at least I hoped it was. "And it's cool; don't worry so much. I mean, every time we walk into Mom and Dad's we take that risk." Mom and Dad always have a big supply of marijuana on hand, and they get the best stuff. I don't know how or where they get it—with my parents sometimes it's best not to ask too many questions—but a police drug raid would probably put them behind bars for the rest of their lives.

He held up his hands in surrender. "Okay, okay, I said I'd try it."

I reached over and squeezed his rock-hard ass. "Trust me, honey, you'll like it."

He gave me a guarded smile. "Okay." Another float was coming, and we all assumed our bead-whore positions. He leaned over and whispered, "But I reserve the right to say I told you so."

By the time Rain's float, one of the last, arrived, we were completely buried in beads. My neck was getting a little sore from their weight. Frank was practically hoarse from screaming, and when I recognized Rain behind her mask, I ran up to the side of the float and screamed, "Throw me something, sister!" She threw her head back and laughed. She reached down, loaded up her arms, and began showering beads down on us.

Rain is cool. I couldn't have asked for a better older sister. She prefers to be called Rhonda, but no one inside the family acknowledges that. She's married to a successful Uptown doctor and has a gorgeous house up on Arabella Street. She has a degree from Baylor but has never worked a day in her life. She used to try to fix me up with every gay man she met, which led to a lot of tedious blind dates for me, since she had no earthly idea of what I was looking for in a man. Hell, I didn't know myself back then. Although she had a little difficulty at first wrapping her head around the Scotty-Frank-Colin arrangement, she welcomed my boys into the family without question and treated them like brothers-in-law. Her car had broken down once and Colin, being

Colin, had gone over to her house and in an afternoon repaired the engine. She swore it ran better than it had when it was new. Now, any time her car makes a funny noise, she is on the phone to Colin asking him to come take a look at it. And Frank had taught her how his grandmother used to make brownies, which turned out to be the best brownies ever. "Who knew," she once whispered to me as Frank whipped up another batch in her kitchen, "that a Fed would be such a good cook?" She looked over at him and sighed. "And that ass! My God, he is such a hunk!" Just at that moment Colin came in through the back door, covered with oil and grease from cleaning her carburetor. His shirt was off, and the grease glistened on his muscles, which were flexing as he tried to wipe his hands clean. She looked back at me and sighed. "You have such a charmed life, baby bro."

What could I say? I agreed with her. When she's right, she's right.

And then the float was past. I looked down St. Charles. There were only two more before the police cars and their flashing red lights signaled the end of Iris. We'd already decided not to stick around for Tucks, the parade behind Iris. We had to get David's car back downtown before the cops closed Canal Street down completely for Endymion, which was rolling later that night. Endymion is the biggest parade of Carnival, and it lasts for hours. Crowd estimates for the Endymion parade route numbered in the hundreds of thousands, and people started lining up along Canal Street for it days ahead of time to get a good spot. Endymion doesn't follow the St. Charles route. It comes down Canal Street from City Park, then twists and turns through the CBD on its way to the Superdome. It actually rolls into the Superdome, where the enormous Endymion Ball takes place immediately following the end of the parade.

Besides, it was better to get home and rest up for the evening before putting on our costumes and heading out into the insanity.

Costuming in New Orleans is almost as important as eating.

I'm not sure why we have such a tradition of costuming here—maybe it's Carnival; I don't know—but we all put on costumes every opportunity we get. And heaven forbid you wear the same costume twice! I am always on the lookout for something new and interesting to dress up as, which isn't always easy. That's another way you can tell the locals from the tourists during Carnival—the locals start wearing costumes when they go out at night. Frank and Colin had both been here for Halloween, when we'd all worn harem boy outfits, which looked really hot. We'd even got our picture in the *Times-Picayune*. They still hadn't quite grasped the whole costuming concept, but they good-naturedly went along with me when I said we had to start dressing up on Saturday. Tonight's costumes were pretty simple—black tights and Zorro capes with black sequined masks with black feathers. The tights would show off our legs and butts perfectly, and just wearing a cape exposed our upper bodies to anyone who wanted to take a look—or touch. I'd planned our costumes so that each day they became more elaborate—and sexier. On Fat Tuesday itself, we were going as zebras . . . but I don't want to spoil the surprise of how we planned to pull that off.

I looked over into the backseat, where Colin and Frank were sitting with their legs entwined as David headed downtown. They had so many beads around their necks I couldn't see their chests. "So, did you enjoy your first parade, boys?" I grinned.

"Awesome!" They both grinned back at me, and then Frank added, "We're coming to the parades tomorrow, right?"

I suppressed a grin and the urge to say, *"I told you so."* "Sure, if you want." I turned back around and laughed to myself. *Yeah, you're both waaaay too cool to yell for beads, right? My ass!*

After David dropped us off, we all went up to my apartment and I got out a salad I'd made that morning. It's always important to have food already prepared and ready to eat during Carnival, or you'll forget to eat and fill up on liquor, which isn't good; that's how you wind up as a Carnival casualty. By the time I'd put servings in bowls and walked into the living room, Frank and Colin were already kissing. Their beads were in a huge pile on the floor in front of the couch. I stood there for just a minute. Their shorts were down around their ankles, and the image was like something out of one of the better porn videos.

"Hey!" I said.

They broke apart and grinned at me and beckoned me to join them. I undid the buttons on my fly and sat down right in between them. Almost immediately, they started kissing my neck, which drives me absolutely insane with desire.

Life is so fucking good.

And did I mention the sex is even better?

CHAPTER TWO

The High Priestess, Reversed

a life of indulgence and outward show

At precisely eight o'clock on the dot I rang Misha's doorbell.

The sun had gone down around six o'clock, and the temperature had dropped about twenty degrees. The wind had picked up, too, grabbing hold of my cape and blowing it out and away from my body. I shivered and grabbed hold of the cape, trying to wrap it around my torso as some protection against the wind. It was pretty thin, so I was still cold, but at least my skin was not as exposed. The air also felt damp, which might mean rain later. I looked up at the sky, which was covered with billowing clouds reflecting the neon of the Quarter back down. Yeah, it was definitely going to rain at some point, and I just hoped we were inside the parade and dancing when it started. There's *nothing* worse than being caught in a cold rain when all you're wearing is a cape and tights. I was wearing my mask, and one of the longer feathers was making my left eye itchy. I sighed and shifted it a little bit. That's the problem with masks: the more elaborate they are, the more annoying they can be. I knew I'd probably discard the mask later on the dance floor, after I started sweating.

I'd walked into the Quarter with the boys, leaving them at Lafitte's while I made the drug run. A lot of people were out—a glance down to the straight end of Bourbon Street showed an almost endless sea of bodies—but not as many as there would be later. Endymion was still rolling, which meant at least another 40,000 people would descend on the Quarter after the parade ended. Lafitte's was already packed with revelers—the balcony was crowded full of men leaning over the railing and waving beads at the crowd below, trying to get some unsuspecting guy to whip his dick out or drop his pants and moon them. There were also enough people roaming the streets to keep Frank, Colin, and David entertained until I got back.

Misha lived on Burgundy Street right off St. Ann. I rang the doorbell and looked around. From his front steps I could see Rawhide on the corner. There was already a crowd of leather men out there milling about and drinking. The doorman was precariously perched on a stool checking IDs. Rawhide's management was a lot more cautious and careful than it used to be. The bar had been raided a number of times, which had caused a decline in its popularity. There's nothing like a raid to drive off a bar's clientele. During specialty weekends, a trip down there used to be a requirement of the evening. The place would be packed full of men, and it had always seemed warm and muggy from all the body heat. I hadn't been in there in over a year, and as I watched the long line of men move slowly forward as IDs were checked, I wondered if I should take the boys there later. *Might as well give them the whole Carnival experience,* I thought, grinning as I imagined Frank's reaction to what went on in there. *He really does need to lighten up some.*

My eyes scanned the street, and I noticed a guy standing on the corner on my side of St. Ann, but on the other side of Burgundy. He was casually smoking a cigarette, but he looked out of place. When he noticed me looking over at him, he looked away. He was wearing loose-fitting jeans, a flannel shirt under a black leather jacket, and a black and gold Saints baseball cap. I stared at him. *Why does he seem out of place?* I wondered. He was dressed like most of the guys in line at Rawhide, and the guys just

hanging out in the street. What made him different from everyone else?

He's up to something, a voice whispered in my head. *Better to
keep an eye on him, Scotty, or you might be sorry.*

As I mentioned before, I'm a bit psychic. I'm not sure how it
all works, but sometimes I get messages that I assume come from
the Goddess. I stared at the guy some more, as he crushed the cigarette out under his tennis shoes and lit another one.

That's it, I realized. *He's wearing sneakers, not boots.*

No self-respecting leather guy would ever wear sneakers with
a leather jacket. It just isn't done.

I felt a chill run down my spine that had nothing to do with
the wind.

I had just about decided to go over and talk to him, try to see
what he was up to, when I heard footsteps coming down the hall
toward the door.

"Who is it?" Misha asked through the door.

"It's me, Scotty. Let me in! It's freezing out here!" I replied,
shivering as another gust of wind grabbed the cape out of my
hands, making it billow out around me. Fuck!

I turned to look back at the guy, but he'd gotten into the line
waiting to get inside the bar. Maybe it wasn't anything after all.
Maybe he was just newly into the leather scene and hadn't figured
out all the rules yet.

I heard the deadbolt click back and the chain come off. Then
the door swung open and there was Misha grinning at me. He
was wearing only a pair of green army fatigue pants with the button undone to reveal the waistband of a cheap pair of white
briefs. A pair of dog tags hung around his neck into the deep
cleavage between his massive pectorals. Some razor burn glowed
red just above the dog tags. His skin was milky white and soft
looking. His brown hair was cut short in a military-like style, and
his bright blue eyes sparkled as he grinned at me. He had really
nice straight, white teeth and full red lips. His stomach was flat,

and his broad shoulders narrowed down to a slender waist. He could have been any age between twenty-five and thirty-five. He was about six feet tall and had to weigh at least 230 pounds—all muscle. He's *huge.*

He threw his big arms around me in a bear hug and squeezed the breath out of me. I thought I heard a rib crack, but it was probably my imagination. I swear sometimes he doesn't know his own strength. "Happy Mardi Gras!" He lifted me off my feet without any visible effort.

I gave him a kiss on the cheek as my feet dangled in the air. "Back at ya, darlin'. Now put me down, please?"

"Of course." He set me down like I weighed no more than a feather. "Come in, come in!" He stood aside, and I walked past him into the living room. In one corner a weight bench was set up, with weight plates scattered all over the wooden floor. There was nothing hanging on the dingy yellow walls—they had probably been white originally sometime in the distant past. The room was also sparsely furnished; a coffee table, a couch, and a reclining chair were all pushed into the center of the room, which made it look even bigger and emptier. The furniture all looked new. The last time I'd been there, none of it had matched and it all had looked as though Misha had liberated it from the city dump. A couple of empty water bottles, some change, and a black jock turned inside out were scattered over the coffee table. He walked over to the wall and flicked a switch. I sat down on the couch.

"Are you having a happy Carnival so far?" I asked, shivering a bit. It was almost as cold inside as it was out, but at least I was out of the wind. Being from Russia, this cold was probably nothing to him, but to me it was like being on an Arctic expedition.

"I love Carnival." It sounded like *I luff carny-full.* He beamed at me. "Is so much fun."

I'd actually met Misha two Southern Decadences ago. My then-dealer had sold me a really crappy hit of Ecstasy the night before—it was more like Tense and Bitchy than Ecstasy. I decided not to waste my money on his crap anymore, and I was prowling the bars looking for a new dealer with different—and hopefully better—stuff. I hate looking for drugs in bars; you never know what you're going to get, and there's nothing worse than walking up to happy-looking people with dilated eyes as they bounce in place shaking their water bottles and saying, "Know where I can find some X?" Ugh, I *hate* doing that. I was getting close to deciding just to do without when I'd walked into Oz, pushing my way through all the pretty boys. A bunch of thickly muscled guys were dancing on the bar in white boxer briefs that glowed in the black light. The dance floor was packed with guys in jeans with their shirts off. The stage was also crowded. A great song was playing, a remix of Faith Hill's "Breathe," and I felt like dancing, if I could only shoehorn my way onto the dance floor somehow. I got to the edge of the dance floor and was looking for an opening when I looked up at the stage and caught my breath.

Misha was dancing in front of a bunch of other guys on the stage. His shirt was off, and he was wearing a pair of skintight 501s, damp with sweat. His arms were up over his head as he danced, his lat muscles fanned out and his arms flexing. His pale skin glistened with sweat. He was a big guy, but, unlike most guys his size, he was light on his feet and could move. He obviously was into the music; he was moving to the backbeat, something a lot of guys don't do. My first thought was, "Mary Mother of God! What a stud!" My second was, "Must be a tourist—never seen him before," and the third was, "He's rolling." I pushed my way through the crowd on the dance floor, touching, getting touched, exchanging smiles with sweating, happy boys until I reached the foot of the stage. A couple of muscle guys in their early twenties reached down and held their hands out and helped boost me up onto the stage. I kissed them each on the cheek to say thanks, took off my shirt, and tucked it into the back of my pants. I moved down the stage until I was dancing next to the big muscle god. We looked at each other and I grinned. "Hey." I winked at him.

"Hello," he shouted over the music. "Is good music, no?"

I didn't recognize the accent as Russian then, but I knew he was foreign. "Yeah, it's great! My name's Scotty."

"Is very nice to meet your acquaintance." He started giggling, then danced around so his back was to me. I noticed the acne scars from steroid abuse scattered over the thick muscles of his back but was soon distracted by his beautiful butt. His jeans had crept down a bit so I could see the elastic waistband of his Hanes underwear. There were some great big zits on his lower back, but it was still, all in all, one of the most beautiful backs I'd ever seen. He spun around and winked at me. "Would you like some Happy?"

"What?"

He held his hand in front of my face and opened his fist. A small blue pill inside a tiny baggie was in his palm, and then he closed his hand again. He winked again. "Want some Happy?" He gave me a huge smile. His piercing blue eyes were half shut as his hips swayed back and forth as Faith could feel us breathe, watching over her, and suddenly she was melting into us.

"Ecstasy?" I asked, hoping against hope. *Gorgeous and an X dealer? Thank you, Goddess!* "How much?"

He grinned. "Yes, Ecstasy. Is gift from me to you because you pretty." He stroked the side of my face with his other hand. "You very pretty."

Well, why the hell not? I nodded and took the baggie from him, tearing it open and popping the pill into my mouth. I washed it down with a swig from my water bottle. I kissed him on the cheek. "Thank you!" Nothing ventured, nothing gained, right?

Half an hour later I was practically hanging from the ceiling. It was the best Ecstasy I'd ever taken, and believe you me, I'd taken some good stuff before. I couldn't stand still, and sweat was pouring off of me. Every song the deejay was playing was better than the one before, and I was flying. The music was inside of me, and I was dancing like a maniac. I was waving my arms over my head and flirting with every single guy I could make eye contact with. I kissed a few, touched some bodies wonderingly—apparently the most beautiful men in the world had all converged on Oz that night. Misha and I danced together, laughing and joking and talking some more. He told me he'd just moved to New Orleans from Russia, and if I wanted more Ecstasy, all I had to do was ask. Sexy as he was, though, we didn't kiss or do anything. I touched him a few times, mainly tapping him on the back when he had his back to me. As crazy as it sounds, when you're on Ecstasy that feels incredible. But Misha didn't touch anyone, didn't spoon dance with anyone; he just stayed in his designated spot, dancing and smiling a lot. Sometimes a guy would come along and touch his muscles, and he would smile at him, but after a few minutes he would gently push him away. After a few times, I realized, through my fogged brain, that I wouldn't be going home with him, but I didn't really care. I just liked talking to him, being around him—he had this amazing energy I enjoyed. At some point in the night, Misha gave me his phone number before disappearing into the crowd, never to be seen again that night. I felt a little pang when he left, but before long I was dancing with a tall, lean drink of water from Tampa—at least I think that's where he was from—and I wound up leaving with him later when the drug wore off.

Misha had been my dealer ever since. He never failed me, and he always had good stuff. He was always very affectionate to me, hugging me or giving me a friendly kiss on the cheek, but never in a flirtatious way. At first, this kind of bothered me—I'm not that used to disinterest—but I got over it soon enough. Attraction is a matter of taste, and apparently I wasn't to his taste that way. But I'd never really seen Misha with anyone; he was always by himself, dancing in his own little world. And besides, it's usually not a good idea to have a sexual relationship with your drug dealer. That just leads to problems. Believe me, I know.

In the time since we met, I hadn't really learned much about Misha. I knew he'd grown up in Moscow and had been in the Russian army. Other than that, he didn't like to talk about Russia at all. He would get a weird look on his face and then change the subject. He loved America, he loved New Orleans, and this was his life now, he'd say proudly. Russia was in the past, and he was never going back. I didn't know if he had family back there, but I got the distinct impression sometimes there was a serious reason he'd emigrated. I never pushed the subject—it wasn't any of my business, after all, if he didn't want to talk about it. I also didn't know what he did for a living, although I was pretty sure being an Ecstasy dealer in the gay bars wasn't lucrative enough to pay his rent. But I never asked. The dealer/client relationship automatically puts up some barriers.

He sat down next to me on the couch and patted my leg with a smile. "Is good costume, Scotty. Real sexy. Are boyfriends the same?"

I nodded. "They look better than me." They did; I wasn't just being modest. Frank hadn't been overly thrilled about going out dancing in the tights. Colin and I were both naked underneath ours; Frank insisted on wearing a thong because the tights were "too revealing." Even with the thong you couldn't miss his package, though. He had no idea how popular he was going to be on the dance floor.

He shook his head. "Not believing you."

"Wait till you see them. Will you be out later?"

He nodded, his smile spreading. "Love dancing in crowds. Mardi Gras wonderful." He reached under the couch and pulled out a metal strongbox, which he unlocked. "How many you needing?"

"Sixteen." Frank and Colin didn't know it, but I was buying

enough for us to take one a day through Fat Tuesday. I figured it was a pretty safe bet to assume they'd both like it and would want to do it again. I was also picking up David's for him. David wasn't comfortable around Misha; he always got tongue-tied and said the stupidest things. Misha wasn't even his type; David usually liked small guys, preferably of Latin descent. But Misha had the kind of body that overruled the concept of types. He was *everybody's* type.

Misha whistled. "That many? Is not good for you."

"It's not all for me—" I started to protest, before realizing he was laughing at me. I got my wallet out of my boot, counted out the cash, and put it down on the table. He started placing pills into little plastic ziplock baggies.

His cell phone rang. He had the ring tone set to "Mamma Mia" by ABBA. He reached into his pants pocket and looked at the display. He scowled. "Must take call." He stood up and clicked it on. "Hello?"

He walked out of the room without saying anything, but I could hear someone talking very loudly through the phone. I couldn't make out any words, just that whoever had called seemed to be really pissed off about something. Then he shut the door behind him, and I couldn't hear anymore. I sat there on the couch for a couple of minutes, waiting, then figured I might as well help him out a bit. I started putting my pills into the baggies. I counted out four for David and slipped those into my left boot. I counted out three for tonight and put those in the same boot. The rest I put into one baggie, which I put into the change pouch in my wallet, then slipped it back into the other boot. I glanced at my watch. A few more minutes ticked by, and he still didn't come back. I started tapping my foot.

"Come on, Misha," I said under my breath. I wanted to go, but it seemed rude to just leave without saying good-bye. I looked into the lockbox, which he'd put on the floor. I saw several vials filled with blue pills like the ones he'd given me. There were vials containing pills in different colors—several little amber bottles I recognized as containing GHB—and there were little plastic baggies with white powder (crystal? coke? Special K?) and even a hefty bag of pot. There was a stack of bills that looked pretty thick shoved into one corner of the box; the top bill was a fifty.

Maybe he can *support himself dealing,* I thought, closing the lid and setting it back down on the floor.

Then I heard his voice in the next room. He was yelling, but I couldn't understand anything he was saying. The wall muffled his voice, and he might have been yelling in Russian. Then the noise stopped, the door swung back open, and he walked back into the room.

He looked paler than usual, and as he sat down I realized he was shaking. "Are you okay, Misha?"

He shook his head. "Am fine." He looked at the coffee table and then at me. "You finished bagging for me?" There were beads of sweat on his forehead, despite the frigid temperature in the apartment.

I nodded. "Yeah. You know, you shouldn't leave your strongbox open and alone with someone, Misha. I could have just walked out of here with it."

His eyes narrowed to slits for a minute, but then he grinned. "No! I trust you—you would not do. Not Scotty. Other people I not trust, no, but you?" He patted my leg again. "You I trust. You friend."

I was oddly touched. "Thanks, Misha, that's sweet of you to say."

He looked away and opened his mouth to say something but then closed it again.

"Misha? Are you sure everything's okay?"

"Everything fine." He shook his head. "Um, you mind going? Wish could stay, talk some more, but expecting someone."

"Of course. The boys are waiting for me." He walked me to the door, where he gave me another hug, holding on much longer than he usually did.

"Happy Mardi Gras," I said, giving him a quick peck on the cheek. "And if you need someone to talk to—"

"Happy Mardi Gras to you." He gave me a long look, giving me the impression again that he wanted to say something else, then stepped back and closed the door.

I stood there for a minute. What on earth? Something was definitely bothering him. I debated knocking on the door again to make sure he was okay—and then talked myself out of it. That dealer/client discretion thing kicked in; I wasn't that good a friend of his. If he had a problem, he probably had real friends he could talk to.

You are really getting paranoid, Scotty, I told myself. I stood there on the stoop for a few minutes, trying to pick up the sense I'd had earlier, but it was gone.

I walked up St. Ann to the corner at Bourbon and grinned. I was still cold, but there was a big enough crowd in the street down there to create warmth. I picked my way through the crowd, saying hello and exchanging kisses with friends and strangers alike, and finally emerged out in a less crowded area halfway down the street. It was just a sandbar in the sea of people, though; less than ten yards away the crowd spilling over from Lafitte's began. I'd told the boys to get drinks and we'd meet on Bourbon across from the bar in front of the Clover Grill, so I crossed over to that side and pushed my way through the crowd. The balcony was packed at Lafitte's, and I could tell by the way the crowd was gathered into pockets that someone had to be showing something for beads. Sure enough, a few seconds later the guys on the balcony erupted into cheers and beads showered down to a spot in the crowd.

The boys were standing in front of the newspaper stand. I stood for a minute, watching them. They looked incredible, and everyone walking past was checking them out. Frank had already discarded his mask, and Colin had pushed his up on top of his head. Colin had his back to me, and in the tights his big muscular ass looked like it could crack walnuts without much effort. His broad muscled back tapered down to his narrow waist, and the tights had worked their way down so you could see the top of his crack. *I'm going to have to keep my eyes on them all night so someone doesn't try to take one of them off,* I realized. After all, the gay motto of Mardi Gras was "hold on to your husband!"

Of course, in theory we could all sleep with whomever we wanted whenever we wanted, but *theory* and *reality* are two different things.

David wasn't costuming. His concession to the season was a leather vest and a leather cap pulled down low over his eyes. I slipped David his pills and threw an arm around both of my guys, pulling them in close. "Having fun yet?"

"You were gone a long time." Frank frowned at me. "I was starting to get worried."

Not this again, I thought. *Is he going to be nervous all night long?* "Everything's fine, Frank. Relax already." I reached up and kissed his cheek. "Just have fun, okay?"

Colin handed me a bottle of water and grinned. "Well, we both get nervous when you're out of our sight for a while. I mean, with your history of getting kidnapped—"

"This is true," David chimed in.

"Why does everyone I love get so much pleasure from giving me shit?" I raised my arms imploringly upward and tilted my head back. "Why, Goddess, why?"

They all laughed, the rat bastards.

We watched the crowd for a while, pointing out hot guys to each other for about twenty minutes, then took our pills. Frank hesitated, and then I gave him a reassuring smile. He closed his eyes and washed it down with a big swig of water. I wasn't letting them drink liquor that night. The first time doing Ecstasy is enough of a mind trip without involving booze. I personally didn't like to drink when I was rolling—it made me throw up once—but David always could without a problem. I was Cruise Director Julie McCoy for the evening, so fifteen minutes after we took the pills we walked down the street to the dance clubs.

I could feel mine starting to hit as I led everyone out to the dance floor at the Parade. David's eyes looked bigger, so I knew he was feeling it too. Colin had a big grin on his face. And Frank—he looked like he was going to get sick. He was breathing hard, sweat beading his forehead, and he kept swallowing. *Oh, no,* I thought. "Wait here!" I yelled at Colin and David, then grabbed Frank's hand and pulled him off the dance floor to the front bar area where some couches were placed.

"Are you okay?" I shouted, to be heard over the music.

"I-I-I don't know." He looked at me. His pupils were huge. "I feel really funny, Scotty."

I shoved him down on the arm of the couch and put my mouth on his ear. "Relax, Frank, you're just starting to feel it. Don't fight it—just don't fight it and you'll be fine. Go with it. You'll see." Frank grabbed my hand and squeezed it. His hand was soggy and trembling. "Smile, Frank."

He took a deep breath and smiled at me. "Oh, wow," he said. His pupils were getting bigger, and his legs were starting to shake as well. I grabbed his hands and pulled him back up to his feet. "Bounce, Frank."

He looked at me. "Bounce?"

I started bouncing. It was starting to hit me, and the bouncing felt good. He started bouncing too.

"Do you love me, Frank?"

The smile got bigger, and the tension around his eyes softened. "Yes, Scotty, I do."

A wave of emotion crashed around me. "I love you, too, Frank." And I reached up and kissed him and felt his entire body begin to tremble. Our lips held together, and it was amazing, as though we'd gone into our own little world, and there was nothing else and nobody else in the world that mattered. I pulled back from him. Frank's eyes were half shut, and I'd never seen such a big grin on his face. He looked so beautiful to me then that I wanted to just grab him and hold him tight, press him up against me . . .

Damn, this was *good* Ecstasy!

He was still trembling. "Come on, Frank, let's go dance." I pulled him back to the dance floor.

Colin and David were already out there, dancing and smiling from ear to ear. I could feel Frank starting to dance behind me, and we pushed out to join Colin and David.

"This is fucking awesome!" Colin shouted at me.

Frank just kept grinning.

"Woo!" said David, spinning around with a goofy smile on his face.

Then I recognized the opening notes of the dance remix of Wynonna's version of "I Want to Know What Love Is," and it was like the deejay was playing it just for me. I screamed "Woo-hoo!" and threw my arms up in the air, my cape falling off my shoulders, and I started spinning around, losing myself in the music. I started singing along—my inner drag queen always seems to come out when I'm Xing—and then I felt someone behind me, and I looked over my shoulder to see Frank and felt him grinding against me, and then his arms came around me and he started kissing my neck, and then Colin was backing into me from the front, and I put my arms around him and started playing with his nipples, and he shuddered a bit and the three of us stayed that way for a few moments, our bodies locked together, sweating and trembling and loving the moment, loving each other, and then another wave of joy came crashing through me and I broke free from them and spun away, and then David was tapping me on my back, and I grinned at him, and then Wynonna mixed into Britney Spears's "Everytime," and the dance floor was filled with other guys, and shirts were coming off, and the mirror ball descended from the ceiling, and green laser lights started hitting it, reflecting and bouncing off the steamed-up mirrors around the dance floor, and I grabbed the boys by the hand and dragged them over to the stage and I hopped up, with them jumping up on either side of me, and I stood there, looking out over the heads of the guys on the floor, and I stretched out my arms over the crowd, and it became my crowd, and I started dancing again, the boys dancing on either side of me, and I started performing for them all, letting the music just take me higher and higher and higher. . . .

Three of Wands, Reversed

mistakes may be made through carelessness

We stumbled out of the Parade at five-thirty in the morning.

The sky was starting to lighten, but it was still a dark gray outside. There was a slight rain with a cold wind. There weren't many people still out in the street, but street cleaners had yet to come by, so the gutters were still heaped high with trash. I was drenched in sweat from dancing for almost seven consecutive hours without much of a break. The residue of the Ecstasy in my system was still making my skin hot and sensitive, so when the cold wind hit me as I stepped down onto the damp sidewalk the immediate shiver I felt went right down to my spine. I was in a lull—Ecstasy makes you high in waves. There's an initial high that lasts for several hours, and during those hours the waves take you so high it's almost indescribable; it's like you're flying up in the clouds. You just feel beautiful and happy, and the world is a wonderful place. After that initial high wears down, you're still a little high, but you can stand still without bouncing and can take a break from the dancing—but the waves still come to sweep you up into outer space again. As it wears off, the waves don't last as long and aren't as intense, and the time in between them becomes longer and longer. Sometimes they'll still be hitting you in the afternoon of the next day, and I had a feeling this stuff was so strong we'd still be riding waves well into the next evening.

I grabbed my thin cape and wrapped it around my shoulders in a vain attempt to protect my hot skin from the cold wind. My feet ached and my lower back was sore from the dancing and my socks were soaked completely through. My legs were also exhausted. My boots had rubbed raw spots on my lower legs and a blister had formed on the back of my right heel. Although it was only a walk of about eight blocks, I knew if we tried to walk home, we'd get sick from the cold and the rain—and that would effectively ruin the rest of Carnival.

"Let's grab a cab," I suggested, through chattering teeth.

"Good idea," Colin replied, and he and Frank huddled close to me on the corner as I looked up St. Ann. With a prayer of thanks to the Goddess, I saw a black and white car heading toward us with the telltale United minibillboard on its roof. I waved, and it crossed through the intersection and pulled over. We piled into the welcoming warmth of the cab, and Frank shut the door behind us. I gave the driver the address and she pulled back out onto Bourbon Street.

"You boys have a good night?" The driver was a slender woman with shoulder-length brown hair who looked to be maybe in her early thirties. There was a statue of the Blessed Virgin on her dashboard. She looked in the rearview mirror at us and smiled as she turned up the heater. "Nice costumes."

"Thanks. We had a great time," I replied, rubbing my arms to try to warm them. "You have a busy night?"

"Eh. So-so." She laughed. "Dumb drunk tourists! I wish I had a dime for every one of them who forgot where they were staying tonight."

I laughed with her. Surviving the hordes of tourists during Mardi Gras always forms a common bond for locals in town during the madness. "I hope this rain lets up."

"It's supposed to get up into the seventies and be sunny later." She shook her head. "Y'all are my last fare. I'm going home and sleep as long as I can."

We chatted about inanities as she maneuvered around pedestrians staggering down Bourbon Street. Colin was running his left hand up and down my thigh, and the leg Frank had pressed up against mine on the other side was shaking slightly. I gave him a reassuring smile and he gave me one of his sweetest ones. I wanted to lean over and give him a kiss. When we got home we were going to have some incredible sex, and as far as I was concerned we couldn't get there fast enough. . . .

Damn, that was some *good* Ecstasy!

"Did you hear about the murder up on Burgundy?" the cabbie asked as casually as she had discussed the weather forecast, as she turned right onto Esplanade.

"Murder?" That got my attention. Had I heard that right? On either side of me, the boys stiffened. "No. What happened?"

She shrugged. "At a house up by the Rawhide, on Burgundy. Some guy—I don't know who—got killed. Shot, 'swhat I heard. They had the street closed off for a while." She shook her head. "The crime in this city is really getting out of hand." She started rambling about our ever-rising crime rate, the usual litany all the locals go through whenever something bad happens in our neighborhood or to someone we know.

I closed my eyes, a sinking feeling in my gut. *No, it couldn't be,* I tried to convince myself. *That would be too much.* I tried to close my mind to my external senses and empty my thoughts to try to commune with the Goddess, but she was silent. Unfortunately, I can't summon my gift at will, or even how it will manifest itself to me. It used to be that I just read the tarot cards and she would speak to me through them. But in the last year, the gift had changed. The cards still worked, but recently I started having visions about what was going on, dreams that showed me the path to follow for the truth.

I've even communicated with the dead. Now that was an experience—one I hope I won't have again, at least not for a while.

But if the Goddess isn't willing to talk to me, there's not a damn thing I can do about it.

You can see why I usually keep it to myself. Both Colin and Frank know; they've witnessed it in action. My family knows; my brother Storm refers to it jokingly as my "psycho gift" and teases me about it. But you know how people are about differences— they'd think I was some kind of freak or something if I told them about it, so I generally don't. But this time there was nothing— no sense of anything. I tried to relax, but when we turned the corner onto Decatur I saw the white SUV parked illegally at the corner and knew for a fact I was screwed. The SUV belonged to Eighth District Police Detective Venus Casanova, who I've gotten to know far better than either of us would prefer. Don't get me wrong—for a cop, Venus is incredibly cool, but the only times previously we've come into contact were when I'd found a body. I hadn't found one this time, but it didn't take any psychic ability to figure out Misha was dead, and somehow the police knew I had been there last night. Their presence at my front door made me think they wanted to talk to me pretty badly, probably badly enough to take me down to the station.

And I still had nine hits of Ecstasy in the change pouch of my wallet in my right boot.

This was not a good thing. I was going to have to call Storm and get him out of bed. And I would never hear the end of it.

The cab pulled over in front of the white SUV and I shakily handed the cabbie a ten, waving off the change, saying thanks and "Happy Mardi Gras" to her as Colin opened his door and started to step out. Frank did so on the other side as well. I had just climbed out as Venus and her partner, Blaine Tujague, stepped out of the SUV and started walking toward us.

Not a good sign.

"Detectives," Frank said, folding his arms, "happy Mardi Gras."

I could see that both his and Colin's pupils were still highly dilated.

Which also meant that mine were too.

Fuck, fuck, fuck. Not good, not good at all. I closed my eyes and tried to focus. Fortunately, I was still between waves.

"You guys have a good night?" Blaine asked. He was smiling. He was a great-looking guy of about thirty, about five nine with thick hair the same blue-black as Colin's, but his was straight and parted on the right side. I think he's gay. At least, I think I've seen him around in the bars a few times, but then he could have been working undercover looking for drugs. You never can be sure in the Quarter. He was wearing a thick, wool navy blue trench coat over gray wool slacks. He joined Venus on the sidewalk.

"Yeah," I said. "Quiet night for you, I hope?"

Venus shook her head. She's a tall black woman, quite strik-ing, with smooth, dark skin and almond-shaped eyes, her hair cut close to the scalp. Even in her overcoat you got a sense of coiled muscle and strength. "No offense, Scotty, but I was kind of hop-ing I'd never run into you in a professional capacity again." She was holding a large cup of Circle K coffee and gave me an enig-matic smile.

"Yeah, well." I bit my lower lip. "No offense, but that makes two of us."

"What's all this about?" Colin interrupted. He folded his arms and started bouncing to try to keep warm. "Can't we go in-side and get warmed up? We're not exactly dressed for the weather."

"I need Scotty to come with us to the station." Venus took a sip from her coffee. "You two can go on in."

My heart sank. The nine hits in my sock were burning a hole in my leg.

"You didn't answer his question," Frank replied, coming to

my rescue. "Scotty, you don't have to go with them. He isn't under arrest, is he, detective?"

She shook her head. "Not at this time. We just want to ask him some questions."

Okay, that was a good sign. "Then I'm afraid I'm not going with you," I said. One of the great things about having activist parents is they get arrested *all* of the time. Their rap sheets are probably about a mile long. They've been arrested so many times that it's kind of unusual when they go to a protest and don't wind up behind bars. The New Orleans police department is very well acquainted with Mom and Dad—and I am sure their FBI files would make pretty fascinating reading. Storm, Rain, and I were well versed in what the police can and cannot do, and our civil liberties, almost from the day we learned how to talk. We certainly knew our rights by the time we were old enough to carry protest signs. They used to drill us before protests. In my head, I could hear my mother's voice: "If you are not under arrest, you are not obligated to go with the police. You are not obligated to talk to them about anything, even if you are under arrest. They'll try to make you feel comfortable, like chatting with them will clear everything up and then they'll be on their merry way, but don't fall for it. If you don't talk to them, they'll tell you it'll make you look guilty. Don't fall for that, either. *Looking* guilty and *being* guilty are two entirely different things, and if you've done nothing wrong, there's no reason for you to talk to them unless and until they tell you why they want to talk to you in the first place."

Rain swears her first words were "I want a lawyer." She might not be wrong.

This so totally and completely sucked it wasn't funny. I hadn't killed Misha—then again, I didn't know for a fact it was Misha who'd been killed—but there was also no way in hell I was going down to the Eighth District police station with nine hits of Ecstasy in my boot. Some overzealous ADA could see that as "possession with intent to deal." And that would mean the loss of my private eye license; quite possibly the Blackledge Agency's license to operate in Louisiana, if not some jail time. This sucked! To make it worse, my refusal to cooperate would only serve to make Blaine and Venus even more suspicious of me than they already were. The cops can make your life miserable when they want to, and even when you're cleared they don't have to apologize or correct any of the damage done. It was easy for my mother to say, "Don't talk to the police," but the times she'd been arrested hadn't been for drug possession—or suspicion of murder, for that matter.

I tried again as Blaine and Venus exchanged a glance I didn't really like. "Give me a break, Venus! I'm tired and I'm freezing to death. I sure as hell don't want to go down to the station dressed like this for who knows how long, okay?" I gestured at my tights, boots, and bare chest, for added emphasis. "These boots are fucking killing me! Why don't we all go inside, let me change into something else, and then we can talk in my nice warm apartment, okay? I'll even make coffee. If you still want to bring me down to the station, then I'll come down with you. Deal?" And I'd have Frank or Colin call Storm to meet me down there.

Venus relaxed a little. "That's fine. But we want to talk to you privately." She glanced at Frank and Colin. "No offense, guys."

"No." Frank's teeth were chattering. "Don't do it, Scotty." He was scowling, and I didn't need my gift to know what he was thinking: *I knew the Ecstasy was a bad idea and would land us all in trouble.*

I dug my keys out of my boot and felt my wallet still tucked into my sock. The wallet seemed to be radiating heat against my ankle.

The Goddess smiled on me that time, and I managed to keep my hand steady as I unlocked the gate and led our little party down the passageway to the back stairs. I could hear movement in my landladies', Millie and Velma's, apartment, which meant they were awake. This was both a good and a bad thing. Millie is a lawyer—that was a good thing—but they'd both be pissed about this mess, especially if we'd woken them up. They both hate being woken up early in the morning, and when Millie is pissed at you, it's probably a good idea to pack a bag and leave the country until she's over it. I unlocked my door and stood aside for everyone to troop into the apartment. I turned up the thermostat, and Colin went into the kitchen to start coffee. I started toward my bedroom, but Blaine stepped in my way.

"I'm going to change my clothes," I said, looking him right in the eye. "Do you want to come in and watch?"

"That would be a serious invasion of your privacy, Scotty, not to mention grounds for a lawsuit," Frank called from the living room. Blaine flushed and stepped out of my way. He stopped me as I started to close the door.

"With the door open. I won't look."

If I wasn't so terrified, the thought of a sexy police officer watching me undress would have been more than a little erotic, but that was the last thing on my mind as I walked into my bedroom and sat on the bed, trying to fight off the trembling. The Ecstasy was still working, sending me a tiny wave of highness. I bit my lip and started breathing deep to get it back under control.

"You okay?" Blaine asked from the door.

I looked up. He wasn't looking in but was standing just outside the door. "Just a little nauseous." I tried to keep my voice from shaking. "I guess I partied a bit too much."

"Well, it is Mardi Gras, after all," he said sympathetically from the doorway. His back was still to me.

I slid off my left boot after removing my wallet and placing it on the nightstand. I looked back over my shoulder—Blaine had his back to me, good as his word—and I casually opened the change pouch in my wallet and removed the little baggie. With them in my hand I slid off my other boot, then quickly placed the hits under the crumpled blanket. It wasn't good enough to survive a search warrant, but it would have to do for now. I stood and peeled off my damp tights, tossing them with my socks into the laundry basket. I pulled on a pair of Saints sweatpants and a dirty, black long-sleeved T-shirt from off the floor. I walked past Blaine into the living room just as Colin was pouring coffee. I sat down in my reclining chair and curled my legs up underneath me. I was thirsty and dehydrated, but there was no way I was going to drink any coffee. The caffeine would kick the drug back into high gear. My heart sank as I saw Frank and Colin sip from their cups, but there wasn't any way to warn them.

"Now, what's this about, Venus?" I asked.

"Scotty, where were you this past evening at eight o'clock?" Venus, sitting down on the edge of the couch nearest my chair, pulled a notebook and pen out of her jacket pocket.

"At eight o'clock I was walking up Burgundy Street."

"Where were you going?" Blaine walked over and stood behind Venus, his arms folded.

"To a friend's." I looked him straight in the eye again. His face was expressionless.

Venus sighed. "Scotty, please. You were going to Mikhail Saltikov's house on Burgundy Street, correct?"

"Mikhail Saltikov? You mean Misha?" I'd never known his real name; he'd always just been Misha to me.

Venus put her notebook down and crossed her legs. "Okay, fuck this. I'm going to be up front with you, Scotty, and you know I don't have to be. We know Saltikov was a drug dealer, okay? If you went there tonight, you went there to buy drugs. That's fine. I can see why you wouldn't want to admit that. But I don't give a rat's ass about busting you for that, okay?" She pointed at Frank and Colin. "You've got two witnesses to my saying that." She gave me a crooked smile. "Your esteemed brother could make serious hay out of that in court, am I right?"

I grinned back at her. Storm was a great lawyer. Mom always

said he could argue a nun out of her panties. I felt a little better. Venus might be a cop, but she had always been fair with me in the past, even when she probably shouldn't have been. "Let's just say I went to Misha's for whatever reason and arrived at eight o'clock on the dot. I looked at my watch when I rang his bell."

"And about what time did you leave?" Venus arched an eyebrow up.

"Probably around eight-twenty, eight-thirty maybe. I didn't look at my watch. I got back to Lafitte's to meet the guys about then, right?" I looked over at them for confirmation. Frank was scowling. *Uh-oh,* I thought, *I'm gonna have some "splainin' " to do later.*

"I'd just looked at my watch when he walked up," Colin added. His feet were bouncing on the floor. "It was just after eight-thirty, wasn't it, Frank?"

"Something like that." Frank wouldn't look at me—not a good sign. He was definitely pissed. My heart sank. I was definitely going to hear about this later.

"He was alive when I left," I blurted out.

Both Venus and Blaine turned to look at me.

"Our cabdriver told us someone on Burgundy Street was murdered last night." Frank put his coffee cup down. He was starting to sweat again. "In the same area Scotty's friend lives— *lived*—and you were here to meet us when we got home, and you say you aren't interested in any drug purchases that *might* have occurred." He wiped at his face. "So, it stands to reason that this Saltikov person was murdered, and somehow you know Scotty was there, which is why you're here."

"Very impressive, special agent." Venus bowed her head to him. They'd worked together during the Southern Decadence mess, and I knew she had a lot of respect for his professionalism, even if he wasn't a federal agent anymore.

I have to say I was impressed with both Frank and Colin.

Even high, they were able to say things with—what was it Storm called it?—oh, yeah, plausible deniability.

Venus went on, "Yes, Mikhail Saltikov, Misha"—she nodded at me—"was murdered last night. And as far as we know, you were the last person to see him alive."

"And how do you know that?" Frank wiped his forehead with a Kleenex. His face was getting red, and his feet were tapping up and down. Beads of sweat were forming at the base of his throat.

"Because Misha had a video camera hooked up to his front door with a time stamp on the tape. He recorded everyone coming in and out of the place," Blaine replied. "He turned it off right after you got there. Now, why would he do that, Scotty?"

Oh, sweet Goddess, that's just great. I hadn't seen that one coming. I remembered him flicking a switch without a light coming on anywhere. Why hadn't I thought anything about it at the time? Dumb, dumb, dumb! I could feel a major headache starting to form right between my eyes. I took a few deep breaths—*and remembered handling the lockbox with all his drugs in it.*

My fingerprints were all over it.

Fuck, fuck, fuck!

"I have no idea," I said. *Damn you, Misha!*

"What did the two of you talk about?" Venus picked up her notebook again.

"Nothing really." I thought about it. "We talked about Mardi Gras, how much fun we were going to have, that kind of stuff." Think, Scotty, think! "Oh, he got a call on his cell phone. He left the room to take it and shut the door behind him."

"Do you know who called?" Blaine's voice was just as disinterested as Venus's. I wondered if they were getting ready to go all good cop/bad cop on me.

"No. He just said he had to take the call and walked out of the room. He wasn't happy about it." I remembered the loud voice in the next room. "He was yelling at whomever it was; I could hear him through the door. I couldn't understand what he was saying. I mean, with the door closed and all I could just barely hear his voice, but it did sound like he was yelling in Russian." I thought for a minute. "Well, I assumed it was Russian. It could have been another language, I guess."

Blaine and Venus exchanged glances again. "And when he came back?"

"He was upset—I could tell—and he rushed me out." Maybe I *should* have stayed, made him talk about it. Oh, man. This so totally sucked. But, then again, if I'd stayed, I might have been there when the killer arrived.

Happy Mardi Gras, my ass.

Both Venus and Blaine stood. "And then you walked back to Lafitte's?"

I nodded.

"Did you notice anyone or anything that seemed out of place around Saltikov's?" Venus asked.

"It's Mardi Gras, Venus. Everything looked out of place." I sighed. "There were a lot of people milling about, hanging out around Rawhide, but I didn't really pay much attention. I was in a hurry to meet the guys at Lafitte's."

Venus flipped her notebook shut. "Well, that's all for now." She signaled for Blaine to walk out of the apartment, and she followed, with me right behind them. When we reached my bedroom door, she stopped. "Would you mind if we took your clothes?"

"Why?" I wasn't expecting that.

"If you're innocent, they'll clear you." Venus gave me her enigmatic smile.

With the Ecstasy safely out of my boots, I didn't care they did with my clothes. There wasn't anything on them that would connect me to Misha's murder, since I didn't do it. I walked into the bedroom; picked up the tights, cape, and socks; folded them over the boots; and presented them to Venus at my front door. She shook open a plastic bag, placed them inside, and wrote on the label while Blaine wrote out a receipt for me, and then I shut the door behind them.

I staggered back into the living room, fighting down nausea.

"You shouldn't have given them your clothes," Frank said. "Your sweat—now they have your DNA." His face looked tired. "I am assuming you managed to get the drugs put away first?"

"Appearances to the contrary, I'm not stupid, Frank." It came out a lot bitchier than I intended, but I was beyond caring. I sank down wearily into my wingback chair. Another wave was starting to come over me, so I started taking deep breaths again, and began tapping my hands on the chair arms.

"You need to flush them down the toilet," Frank went on. His face was really flushed. "Right, Colin? There's no safe place to hide them from a search warrant." His scar seemed to darken. His eyebrows came together again. "I *told* you it was a dumb idea."

"Yeah, well, maybe, but we have to deal with it now." I scowled back at him. If he said, "I told you so," I was going to throw something at him—something heavy that would hurt.

"Give them to me," Colin instructed. "They won't have probable cause to search our apartment, Frank."

"Are you crazy?" Frank stood up. He was trembling. Maybe it was just another wave, but it might have been anger. "We just need to get rid of them and be done with it."

I stood up without saying anything, walked into the bedroom, and pulled them out from under the blanket. I stood there with them in my hands and thought about it. *Maybe Frank's right, and I should just flush them down the toilet. But if I do, we won't have any more and Misha's dead.* . . . I walked into the bathroom and stood over the toilet with them.

But I didn't have anything to do with killing Misha, and do I really want to ruin my Mardi Gras?

I said a quick prayer to the Goddess for guidance, but she

didn't answer. I *hate* when she does that. Oh, sure, I know it's because I am supposed to make my own decisions, but a little *help* every once in a while isn't too much to ask for, is it?

I looked at myself in the mirror and started to shake. Whether it was another wave or not, I couldn't tell, but my teeth started chattering and I wrapped my arms around myself. Maybe I should have forced Misha to tell me what was going on. I put the baggie down on the counter and turned on the hot water. Misha was *dead*. I stared at myself in the mirror. He'd been such a sweet guy—always so happy to see me, always so friendly and affectionate, but never in a sexual way. I'd really liked him, and now that he was gone, I was sorry I hadn't made more of an effort to get to know him better. But now that chance was gone, and I felt the tears coming. I had always felt *connected* to him somehow; able to just relax around him and be myself. I stood there for a few moments and let the tears come. As I cried, I said some prayers to the Goddess for Misha. I was going to miss him. I remembered how his big strong arms felt around me as he hugged the breath out of me every time he saw me and spun me around. Why would someone kill him? He was a sweet, kind man. I splashed water on my face and pulled myself together.

I took a deep breath and walked back out of the bedroom. Maybe it would turn out not to be the smartest thing in the world to hold on to the drugs, but Colin didn't seem to want to get rid of them, either. I walked into the living room and handed them over to Colin.

Frank looked at both of us, his head going from side to side. "You know what? You two are fucking crazy!"

"Frank—" I started to say, but Colin cut me off.

"Frank, they aren't interested in the drugs, and you and I both know Scotty didn't have anything to do with this, and Venus knows it too." Colin folded his arms. "*Think* about it. You're not in your right mind right now—"

Frank turned completely purple, his scar almost glowing in

intensity. "And why the fuck am I not in my right mind, huh? I might have known you'd take his side on this—you're just as bad as he is."

"Hey! You're not being fair!" I protested.

Frank stood there for a moment, glaring at us both, his fists clenching and unclenching. "You know what? I think I'm going to go stay at David's for a while." He walked out of the apartment. The door slammed behind him, and I heard him stomping down the stairs.

David is not going to be happy, I thought. David had disappeared from the dance floor a few hours before we left, which generally meant he'd picked someone up. I jumped up to go after him, but Colin grabbed me from behind and kept me from moving.

He is remarkably strong.

"Let him go, Scotty. He needs to work this out on his own. Right now he's not happy, and talking when he's like this will do more harm than good. Trust me on this." Colin kissed my neck. "Part of it's the Ecstasy; you know that. He's upset, and it's amplifying his mood. When he comes down a bit, he'll calm down and feel like a complete ass, and he'll come back." He squeezed me a little tighter. "Our first fight, huh?"

I felt like crying. I *hate* confrontation. I felt another wave coming over me, and I gave into it, leaning back into Colin's bare chest. I closed my eyes. His arms felt so good around me. *At least he loves me,* I thought. *And I guess he's right. Frank'll get over it and come home. Sure, he will. He loves me too—and Colin.*

"I'm sorry, Colin," I said softly and held on to his arms. I started to cry softly. "First Misha, and now Frank's mad at me."

"Oh, baby." He nuzzled my neck. "You didn't do anything wrong, okay? How were you supposed to know Misha was going to get himself killed? Frank knows that, and once he thinks about it, he'll come home." He let go of me and spun me around so I was facing him. "We both knew what we were getting into when we signed up for this ride, you know." He winked at me. "Never a dull life with you around."

I couldn't help myself. I grinned back at him. "Yeah, well, dull would be nice for a change."

"I think"—Colin walked over to the phone—"it's time to call Storm."

CHAPTER FOUR

The Moon

unforeseen perils, deceptions, change

At Colin's insistence, I took a shower while he called Storm.

I was still feeling the drug a bit and was kind of shell-shocked. I couldn't believe Frank would walk out like that, and I felt really confused about what to do next. I kind of thought I should run over to David's and talk to Frank, but Colin was probably right. It was just the overemotional state from the drug talking, and the most important thing was to get myself relaxed and calmed down. I was feeling really, really tired when I climbed into the shower. The hot spray of the water on my slightly sweat-soaked skin felt incredibly good and helped dissipate the chill I'd been feeling since we'd walked out of the Parade into the cold morning air. I closed my eyes and leaned against the wall, letting the water pound into my chest and trickle down my body. *Focus, Scotty, on a happy place and stop worrying about everything,* I repeated to myself over and over again. *Everything will work out just fine, and worrying just borrows trouble. What will happen will happen, and worrying will just make things worse, so let it go.* I pictured myself on a sandy beach, with green waves gently lapping at the shore, and a nice warm breeze caressing my skin as the sun warmed me. The tension knots that had been forming in my back started to loosen up, and I put my head under the water. *Frank will come back, and the police will catch Misha's killer, and it'll have nothing to do with you, because it doesn't. You just were in the wrong place at the wrong time—again. And Misha is in a better place now. Just remember that this life is merely a transition to the next one.* The aches in my leg muscles from all the dancing began to melt away, and I finally began soaping up my body. Damn, the water felt good. After massaging shampoo into my hair, I ducked my head back under the steady flow.

He'll be back—he loves you.

I wasn't sure if that was the Goddess speaking to me, or whether it was just wishful thinking on my part. Sometimes I can't tell the difference.

I climbed out of the shower and began drying myself off. I looked at myself in the mirror. My pupils weren't as dilated as they had been, and I felt about a thousand times better. Colin was right—everything *would* be fine. I walked back into my bedroom, dug out a clean pair of underwear, and sat down on the edge of the bed. I sighed. If Venus and Blaine hadn't shown up, the boys and I would be under the covers at that very moment having a good time enjoying the last vestiges of our high. I picked my robe up off the floor and slipped into it. It had been a Christmas present from Frank. I'd never owned a robe before, preferring to walk around the house naked or just in my underwear, but I loved this robe. It was plush, warm, and comfortable. I walked back out into the living room.

Colin was sitting at my desk, typing away on my computer keyboard. I'd gotten a computer when I first passed my P.I. exam, but after going to work for the Blackledge Agency, the company bought me a state-of-the-art brand-new model that worked so fast it practically had wings and could fly around the room. I still was pretty clueless about how to operate the vast majority of the programs on it, but I could type up documents and use the Internet, which was pretty much all my job had required me to do so far. "What are you doing?" I asked, as I stood behind him, draping my arms around his neck.

"Seeing what I can find out about our friendly local drug dealer." Colin leaned his head against one of my arms, then reached up and stroked my forearms. "Storm's on his way over, by the way. He wasn't really happy about being woken at this hour. Something about staying at the Endymion Ball pretty late last night. He was mumbling so I'm not really sure that's what he said."

"Great." My heart sank. Don't get me wrong; I love my brother, even if he is a horrible tease. There was most likely going to be a lecture involved when he arrived. Although Storm shares the family mentality that the drug laws are antiquated, he's still an officer of the court, sworn to uphold the law. He doesn't see civil disobedience in quite the same way Mom and Dad do. He thinks if a law is unfair, you work to change it, rather than chain yourself to a fence or carry signs. "You're not mad at me, too, are you?"

"No, of course not. Don't be silly. Frank just overreacted, which, given his twenty years as a Fed, isn't hard to understand, is it?" Colin did some more typing, and another window popped up on the computer screen. "Someone would have killed Misha whether you'd gone there or not. It's just bad luck on your part, is all. If you hadn't, we wouldn't be involved in this at all, but those are the breaks, right?" He grinned at me. "Besides, I had a good time last night—and so did Special Agent, whether he wants to admit it or not. You saw him just as well as I did. Did he look like he was having a bad time?"

I considered. At one point, Frank had some pretty guy in his early twenties pinching his nipples while an older muscle guy was grinding on him from behind, and Frank had a big dumb grin on his face. "Yeah, you're right."

"Once you accept that I usually am, you'll be much happier." Colin reached back behind him and stroked my leg. "Don't worry so much about Special Agent, okay?"

"I just hope David was alone." That was wishful thinking. I was almost positive David had not left the bar alone. If he'd brought someone home with him, he wouldn't be too thrilled to have Frank show up unannounced on his doorstep. Neither would the trick—David was too polite and nice to tell Frank to go away. I put it out of my mind. "Find anything interesting?"

"Well, I've hacked into the INS database." Colin really *can* do anything. It's more than a little scary sometimes. Fortunately, he uses his powers for good rather than evil. Well, for the most part, anyway. "And it's searching for his name right now." The computer dinged and a file opened up. Colin leaned in to get a better look. "Isn't that interesting?" He whistled.

"What?"

He pointed at the screen. "He got into the country on a marriage visa."

"Marriage? You mean he was married? To a *woman?*" I tried to wrap my mind around it. Misha was *straight?* Then, come to think of it, I'd never seen him with another guy, and whenever a guy had shown any interest in him, he was very polite but not interested.

"Yup." Colin scrolled down. "He married a woman named Sylvia Overton two years ago. Here in New Orleans—a ceremony at city hall. He originally came in on a tourist visa, then got a green card by marrying a citizen."

"*Sylvia Overton?* You're sure?" I sat down on the edge of the desk, my mind racing. This was getting really weird.

"Says so right there in black and white. Why?"

"I *know* Sylvia Overton." Sylvia Overton was a friend of my Maman, Sophie Diderot. I'd known Sylvia pretty much my entire life. Her husband had been a district court judge for thirty or forty years before dying of a massive coronary a few years back. She was in her late sixties, maybe even older. Why on earth had she married a young Russian immigrant in his twenties? How had she ever come into contact with him in the first place? This didn't make any sense. Aunt Sylvia was married to a *drug dealer?* No, it couldn't be right. There had to be some kind of a mistake. There had to be another Sylvia Overton. "Does it say when they got married?" I remembered vaguely hearing someone say once at a family function that Aunt Sylvia had remarried, but I hadn't paid much attention. I hadn't seen her in a while—come to think of it, not since the judge's funeral. I was about to say as much to Colin when the front door opened. I got up, hoping it was Frank, and was enormously disappointed to see my older brother.

Storm is a tall man, over six feet tall, and loves to tease me that he got the height in the family. He'd been a jock in high school, starring on the football and baseball teams at Jesuit High. He had a big strong frame, but years of eating and drinking well without exercising were starting to show. He was getting a little fleshy—which *I* like to tease *him* about. He has the same dirty blond hair I have, but his is straight with a receding hairline. Fortunately, he keeps it cut short, rather than comb it over. "Is there any fucking coffee?" he asked before plopping down on the couch. He looked tired and hungover and smelled slightly of stale liquor.

"I'll get you some." I walked into the kitchen as Colin clicked to print the file. "You look horrible, Stormy. Hung out with ole Jack Daniels again last night?"

"My old buddy Johnny Walker Red." He rubbed his face. "Thank God Marguerite stuck to mineral water or we'd have never made it home." Marguerite is his wife, a nice Uptown girl who always looks lost at our family gatherings, with a polite smile frozen on her face. "I'm getting too old for this stuff." He always said that when he was hungover, but I knew he'd be drinking again later on. It's Carnival, after all.

"Do you want a sandwich or something to settle your stomach?" I called from the kitchen as I mixed cream and sugar into his coffee.

"No, the coffee's fine." He took the cup from me and sipped

gratefully. "So what kind of trouble are you in now, my Queen?" Even with a hangover of apparently epic proportions, he can't stop himself from teasing me. He really is aggravating.

Colin brought him up to speed while I sat there saying nothing, waiting for the inevitable lecture. Every once in a while, Storm would shoot me a thunderous look. When Colin finished talking, Storm glared at me. "You are so fucking lucky you know Venus. They easily could have dragged your ass down to the station—and you'd be fucked. And I don't mean in the good way, either." He shook his head. "Scotty, when are you going to learn?"

"I know, I know." I held up my hands and didn't look at him. "But without arresting me—"

"Suspicion of murder. Material witness. Drug trafficking. They could have brought you in on any number of charges, you fucking bonehead. Sounds like they already knew that this Misha person was a drug dealer and you were there and didn't even know his real name, so why else would you be there? Obviously, you weren't that good of friends."

"Sex," I replied, sticking out my lower chin. "We could have just been tricking."

Storm stared at me for a moment, then threw his head back and laughed. "Oh, you are a piece of work, baby bro. Sex! That's perfect—worthy of me." But he shook his head. "You shouldn't have given them your clothes. Now they have your DNA."

"What difference does that make? I didn't kill Misha." I folded my arms defiantly.

"Probably also proves you didn't have sex with him."

"Oh." I deflated a bit. I hadn't thought of that.

"Storm, not to interrupt this charming family moment, but this guy got into the country on a marriage visa," Colin broke in.

"And guess who he's married to?" I leaned forward. Storm doesn't shock easily, but I felt confident this would rock him. "Sylvia Overton." I sat back, ready to enjoy the look on his face. I don't get many opportunities to shock him.

Storm's jaw dropped, and his eyes bugged out. His head swiveled back and forth between Colin and me for a few moments before he blurted out, "As in *Aunt* Sylvia? Her husband is—*was*—a drug dealer?"

"You knew him?" I asked. "I mean, I remember hearing she'd remarried, but I don't remember anything about him."

"Yeah, she married some young Russian army guy. I've met him a couple of times." Storm shook his head. "And that guy was your drug dealer?" Storm scanned the printouts, finally setting them down on the coffee table. "I can't believe this. Aunt Sylvia married to a Russian drug dealer?" He shook his head. "This doesn't make any sense." He shrugged. "I mean, I've met this guy and would have never guessed he was dealing—or hanging out in gay bars. At first I thought it was weird she married some guy young enough to be her grandson but then figured, hey, more power to you, Sylvia." He clicked his tongue. "No, this doesn't make sense."

"No, it doesn't," I agreed with him, a little smugly. At least I wasn't the only one who couldn't make sense of it.

"Well, we need to talk to her." He glanced at his watch. "It's almost eight. Probably a little too early to head over there." He looked at the printout again. "Just where did you get this?"

"I hacked into the INS database," Colin replied, with a satisfied smile.

Storm groaned. "I didn't hear that, I didn't hear that, I didn't hear that." He shook his head, but then a sly smile spread across his face. "But that means the police won't be able to get this information for a while. They'll have to go through official channels, so we've got a leg up on 'em." He held up his hands. "Of course, there's no reason for us to pursue this. Maybe we should just call Venus and tip her off."

"So the police can show up at Aunt Sylvia's door?" That didn't seem right to me.

Storm glared at me. "Do you want to be the one to tell her he's dead?"

"Well, no." I hadn't thought about that. When Uncle George had died, it had taken her months to get over it. Maman had spent a lot of time with her, even going on an extended European vacation with her for several months while Papa Diderot drove the rest of the family crazy. But when they'd finally returned home, she'd seemed to have finally made peace with it. They hadn't had any children, so they'd always treated us like we were their kids—like Millie and Velma always had. But how on earth had she wound up married to Misha? How had they met? And how had she *married* my drug dealer? Only in New Orleans could something like that happen.

"I spoke to Angela while you were in the shower." Colin stood up. "She's authorized an investigation—and to retain you as Scotty's lawyer."

"She did?" I felt my face flushing. "I was kind of hoping—"

"That she wouldn't have to know?" Colin looked at me. "Scotty, she had to know. If the police charge you with anything, our entire operation here in New Orleans could be jeopardized." He walked over to me and gave me a quick kiss. "Don't worry— she's completely on your side. She thinks the drug laws are ineffective and useless, and she wants this cleared up as quickly as possible." He turned back to Storm. "And we should go speak with Ms. Overton before the police do."

"Um—" I hesitated. Both of them looked at me. "What are we going to tell her? I'd rather not tell her I was buying Ecstasy from her husband. I mean, I can't believe she actually knew he was dealing, can you? What am I supposed to say? 'Oh, Aunt Sylvia, by the way, your husband was dealing Ecstasy in the Quarter and that's how I met him, and, oh, yeah, he was killed last night?' Somehow, I don't think she'll take that pretty well, do you?"

"She's not made out of glass, Scotty," Storm disagreed. "Aunt Sylvia's a pretty tough old broad."

"We're going to have to tell her, Scotty," Colin replied. "If we don't, the police will, and don't you think it's better to come from you, someone she knows?"

I sighed. "I suppose . . . but Storm, don't you think it would be better coming from you?" It was a last-ditch attempt, but worth a shot. "I mean, you're a lawyer and all—"

Storm started laughing. "Scotty, you're not fooling me. You don't want Papa and Maman to know, do you?"

"I'd prefer that, yes." My Diderot grandparents are extremely conservative. The Diderot family had been in New Orleans since the days when the fleur-de-lis flew over the state. My Diderot grandparents hadn't been really happy when I dropped out of college at twenty. Papa Diderot had looked at me like I was some kind of changeling and said, "Diderots don't drop out of college."

"Good thing he's a Bradley then," Mom had snapped, and we'd walked out of the house. She'd cursed him out all the way back to the Quarter.

Fortunately, somehow I'd kept them from knowing about my days as a go-go boy. How they'd managed to have a radical like Mom as a daughter was beyond my understanding. They were dyed-in-the-wool conservatives, lived in a gorgeous old house in the Garden District that had been in the family forever, and Papa belonged to the old-line krewes, including the ones who stopped parading during Mardi Gras rather than take black members back in the early nineties. No, I couldn't imagine them being thrilled to know I was doing Ecstasy. The fact that I got it from Maman's best friend's husband would make it worse rather than better.

And, okay, if I am going to be completely honest, Papa Diderot scares the bejesus out of me. He's not a big man—he's only a little taller than me, and rather slender—but he has been a heavy drinker all of his life so his face is always a little flushed. He has a thick head of white hair, and bushy eyebrows that come to-gether when he disapproves of something. He has a rather soft, quiet voice, but he can rattle the windows when he is so inclined. He's on several boards, was an incredibly successful lawyer in his own right, and doesn't like to be disagreed with. He's always looked at me like he was ashamed of me and always uses that horrible disapproving tone when he talks to me, like I'm a waiter who's just served him something with a cockroach in it. I don't think he's too thrilled to have a gay grandson, but Mom can be just like him when she wants to be, so he has dealt with it. I wasn't quite sure what he thought about Colin and Frank, but he could hardly approve. Christmas at the Diderots' this past year had been a nightmare. Oh, Papa D had been charming and polite—both Colin and Frank had liked him somehow, which made me wonder a bit about *them*. But every once in a while, I caught him giving me the *look* that I hated when I was a kid.

He's just a mean old man.

"I don't think they'll be too shocked. Mom and Dad pretty much have made sure they're unshockable anymore. Besides"— Storm took a deep breath—"you'd be surprised how cool they are." He saw the look on my face and grinned. "I know, I know, we've been raised to think both sets of grandparents are rigid and intolerant and unashamed capitalists and made their money on the backs of the workers and on and on and on—but think about it for a minute, Scotty. Have they ever turned their backs on Mom and Dad? Ever?" He grinned. "Who do you think used to always bail them out before I got admitted to the bar?"

"Well, maybe you're right." I didn't think he was, but I wasn't in the mood to argue. They'd turned their backs on me, after all. These were the people who had cut off my trust fund when I had dropped out of college. Well, the Bradley grandparents had cut me off from my trust from their side of the family, too, but Dad swore it was Papa Diderot's idea. The Bradley side of the family was also conservative, but not quite as hard-line as the Diderots. Yeah, Storm, they'd be *thrilled* to know my drug dealer had been murdered right after I'd been there. It might even get them to give me access to the trusts again—right around the time pigs sprouted wings and started flying.

Sometimes he can be a bit of an idiot.

"So stop worrying." He snapped his fingers. "I've got to get running. Marguerite's parents are expecting us in a couple of hours for brunch, and you have no idea what a bitch my mother-in-law is when people are late. Well, she's *always* a bitch, but when you give her a reason . . ." He whistled and shuddered. "Can you two handle Aunt Sylvia?"

I swallowed. "I-I guess." It couldn't be any worse than having Christmas dinner with Papa Diderot.

"Great. Give me a call on my cell after you talk to her." Storm stood up and stretched. "Any interruption at Marguerite's parents will be more than welcome, believe me."

I walked him to the door. "Thanks, Stormy."

He gave me a hug. Blech—he did smell of stale sweat and liquor. "Don't worry about anything, Scotty. You handled yourself right with the cops. And Frank—"

"Yeah?"

"You've gotta understand—for a twenty-year veteran of the FBI, our family and the way we live has got to be a little rough on him." He winked at me. "I mean, come on, Mom and Dad break the law on a daily basis."

"Yeah."

He gave me a big bear hug. He's an awful tease, but I couldn't have asked for a better brother. I watched him walk down the stairs, then shut the door.

"I'm going to get cleaned up, and you should put on some clothes if we're going over there," Colin said as he walked into my bathroom. I nodded and started digging through my closet, finally settling on a black pair of jeans and a red sweater while the shower ran. I sat down on the edge of the bed as another tiny wave of the Ecstasy washed over me. Damn, it was good stuff, and it was going to waste. I'd wanted to come home and have sex with the boys while we were still feeling it a bit. And now? Now I had to tell a family friend her husband was dead.

I walked out into the living room and got my cards out. I sat down on the floor in front of the coffee table. I lit a white candle, said a quiet prayer to the Goddess as I held the deck in both hands, shuffled the cards, and then laid them out in the Tree of Life reading. As I turned each card over, there was no mistaking their meaning.

Danger.

Death, with possibly more death to come.

Long-hidden secrets coming to light.

A long journey already undertaken, the result still unknown.

Proceed with caution.

I stared at them for a moment, hoping the meaning would change, that I'd possibly read them wrong. I sighed and got up for a glass of water. I was still dehydrated, and as I was finishing my second glass, I heard the computer ding from the living room.

I walked over to the desk. Colin hadn't signed off-line, and someone had sent me a message. I suppressed a bit of a grin when I recognized David's screen name, then remembered Frank had gone storming over there. *Please, let David have been home alone,* I prayed as I sat down in my chair.

> BUTCHTOP40: Scotty, are you there?
>
> SCOTTYNOLA: Yes.
>
> BUTCHTOP40: What the hell is going on? Frank's sleeping on my couch, and boy was he pissed!
>
> SCOTTYNOLA: Long story—too long to go into on-line. Sorry. I'll call you later.
>
> BUTCHTOP40: Isn't it always? I'm not alone here . . . and I don't mean Frank.
>
> SCOTTYNOLA: Sorry about that. Cute boy?
>
> BUTCHTOP40: Oh, yeah, complete spinner. And a pig. Just the way I like 'em.
>
> SCOTTYNOLA: You go, boy!
>
> BUTCHTOP40: Everything OK?

I stared at the blinking cursor for a minute before typing: *Not right now, but hopefully soon . . .*

"Spinner?" Colin said from over my shoulder. "What the hell's a spinner?"

"A spinner is a little guy. It means someone you're strong enough to sit on your dick and then spin him around—you know, like a top?" I used my hands to demonstrate giving someone a spin. "Hence, *spinner.*" I logged off and shut the computer down. "David really likes little guys."

Colin laughed and kissed the top of my head. "You really are something, you know? Spinners!" He rubbed the top of my head. "Is that what I am?"

"Hardly." I grinned back up at him. "I can't lift you. You might be short, but you're not a spinner."

"Hmmm—but I can lift you. Maybe we can try that later on?" He winked at me. "See if I can spin you?"

"Works for me."

He laughed again. "Okay, come on, Scotty, we'd better get moving."

Colin's black Jaguar convertible was parked in a secure pay lot about a block away from the apartment. Since he'd moved to town, I'd tried to convince him to get a less expensive car—a Jag convertible is just begging to be broken into or stolen—but he loved his car and wasn't willing to get rid of it. I couldn't blame him; it was an absolutely spectacular car. I'd never really understood why or how people could get so attached to their cars until I'd first laid eyes on this one. It had an amazing security system Colin had designed himself, and he claimed the windows were unbreakable. The stereo system was state of the art, and there were all kinds of toggles and switches and things on the dashboard; I had no idea what they were for. If Colin had told me the thing could get airborne I would have believed him. I had no idea how fast it could really go, but one afternoon Colin and I had driven out to Bay St. Louis and on the highway he'd gotten it up to over 120 miles per hour. The engine hadn't even strained. I had a feeling Colin had revamped the car a lot—he's incredible with engines—and that it was a one-of-a-kind car you couldn't just buy at your local Jaguar dealership. David salivated every time he saw it. I have to admit I loved the car myself. It didn't run—it purred. And Colin shifted gears so smoothly you barely even noticed it. And for glamour, you can't beat riding around town in a black Jag convertible. The soft leather seats caressed your skin and were so soft they seemed to contour to your body. He kept it spotless, and the interior still smelled brand new. He'd offered, on more than one occasion, to let me drive it, but I hate driving.

Besides, with my luck, I'd wreck the damn thing.

Somehow, as cool as Colin is, I didn't think he'd be too cool about *that.*

The debris of the Saturday parades was littered everywhere as we headed Uptown. The sun had come out from behind the clouds, and it was going to be a stunningly beautiful day for parade watching. Apparently, the rain was long gone, thank the Goddess. Beads hung from the streetcar wires, the huge old trees along St. Charles, and telephone poles, reflecting the sun into hundreds of colored strings of light. There were already mobs of people settled on the neutral ground and along the sidewalk on the other side of the street, waiting for the afternoon parades to start rolling and the good times to start again. I caught a whiff of charcoal and my stomach growled. *Should probably eat something soon,* I thought as the car shot up the avenue. One of the most important things to remember about taking Ecstasy is you always have to eat something. It cuts your appetite, and if you don't think about it you'll forget all about food, which isn't a good thing—especially if you've been dancing all night long. You *have* to put more food in for energy or else you'll be totally exhausted.

Colin parked the car in front of Aunt Sylvia's house. The yard was immaculately manicured, with bougainvillea growing up the walls of the house itself. It was a big old Victorian with a porch running around the length of the house and a tower in one corner peaking into what had always reminded me of a pointy witch's cap. There were massive oaks towering alongside the driveway, and in one corner of the porch a swing hung. I'd spent a lot of time in that swing when I was growing up. I swallowed as Colin turned off the engine. He leaned over and gave me a big kiss. "Let's go, babe."

"Yeah, okay." I got out of the car and headed up the walk. With a sigh, I pressed the doorbell. Through the wavy glass alongside the oak door, I saw someone approaching, and then it swung open.

Everything went dizzy for a minute and thoughts rushed through my still slightly addled brain. *I can't be hallucinating. Ecstasy doesn't make you see things.* But my reality *was* somehow altered. *Maybe the Goddess is sending me a vision or something.* But I knew that what I was seeing wasn't fantasy, wasn't a vision, but in some weird alternate universe was real, even though I knew it couldn't be. This had to be some kind of cosmic joke. I felt my legs start to buckle.

I reached out and put my hand against the door frame to keep from falling over. I heard Colin climbing the steps behind me. I opened my mouth, but nothing came out. I stood there, stupidly, trying to form words.

Finally, I got a grip on myself and heard myself say, *"Misha?"*

CHAPTER FIVE

Queen of Pentacles

a rich and charitable woman

Whatever else people can say about my parents, one thing they did instill in their children was manners. I knew it was incredibly rude just to stand there on the porch staring at him, but I couldn't, for the life of me, think of anything to say that wouldn't sound stupid. We stood there staring at each other for what seemed like an eternity before he spoke.

"I'm sorry, but do we know each other?" He was smiling at me with a slightly puzzled look on his face. His grayish blue eyes looked from me to Colin and then back again. He was wearing a freshly pressed white button-down shirt tucked into baggy gray wool slacks. The haircut was the same, the face was the same, the build was the same, but there was something different.

The *voice* was different. As I stood there, trying to think of something, anything, to say rather than just gawk like an idiot with my mouth open, I realized that was what was off. There was a very faint trace of an accent, but not nearly as thick and heavy as I was used to hearing from him. And the tone was slightly different too. The Misha I knew had a deeper, almost thicker-sounding voice. This Misha spoke clearly, with a slightly higher pitch to his voice. Then I began to notice other, subtler differences. The chin was maybe a little sharper, the dimples a little deeper in his cheeks, the skin smoother and softer, and the nose a little crooked, almost like it had been broken once and not set completely right. And he stood differently. The Misha I knew kind of slumped as though trying to hide his size. This Misha stood fully erect, with his shoulders up and back.

"I-I don't think we do, after all," I finally managed to get out. But I couldn't stop staring at him. A voice called from down the hallway, "Who is it, Misha?"

That voice I immediately recognized as Aunt Sylvia's. She came through a doorway off the hall and smiled at me. "Why, Scotty! Darling, what are you doing here?" she asked as she put her hands on her hips. She looked genuinely delighted to see me.

There was no way of telling her age from just looking at her. The skin on her face was wrinkle free and tight, although her eyelids were far too smooth and a little sunken—a telltale sign of having had work done. But other than that, you wouldn't be able to tell. Her platinum hair hung down to her shoulders, which were encased in a pink cashmere sweater. Her oval-shaped green eyes opened wide in greeting, and her red painted lips spread in a smile. She was wearing a pair of black slacks, and diamonds glittered at her ears, her neck, and her fingers. She walked toward me and extended her right hand with its perfectly manicured nails. "And this must be . . . Colin? Am I right?" She smiled. "Frank's the taller one, right?" She winked at me. "Sophie's told me all about your arrangement. Somehow I always knew you'd never settle down with just one man."

Oh, great! My cheeks burned with embarrassment. Next, she'd be showing Colin pictures of me when I was a baby or something. Why do older people love to embarrass younger ones?

"Yes." Colin smoothly stepped past Misha into the foyer and extended his own right hand. "Colin Cioni. A pleasure to meet you, Mrs. Overton."

"Scotty, I don't believe you've met my husband." She gave me a quick hug, pressing her cheek against mine. She smelled of an expensive perfume. "Misha, this is Scotty, Sophie's grandson. I just had lunch with your grandmother the other day, Scotty."

Misha smiled and gripped my hand in his, squeezing and shaking it at the same time. His big hand swallowed mine completely, and his grip could break bones with very little effort. "It's very nice to meet you, Scotty. Your grandmother is a fine lady."

"Yeah." I shook my head and glanced over at Colin, my look clearly signaling *help*.

Maybe we'd slipped into an alternate universe or something.

"Won't you come into the drawing room?" Aunt Sylvia said. "We were just about to have mimosas. Won't you please join us?" She hooked an arm through one of Colin's and led him down the hall. "I was just telling Sophie the other day at lunch how much I was looking forward to meeting you and Frank, Colin. . . ." They went into the room she'd just come out of and her voice trailed off.

"You *really* don't know me, do you?" I said to Misha. I shook my head again. There were differences, all right, but at the same time, I couldn't get it out of my head that this was the same guy I'd bought sixteen hits of Ecstasy from the night before.

"No." He shook his head and gestured in the direction of the drawing room. "Please come into the drawing room." I followed him down the hall, watching his butt in the gray slacks. They were built almost exactly the same, but I was right. This Misha walked more erectly than the one I knew.

There were *two* of them.

Or had been.

"Do you have a brother?" I asked quietly as we entered the drawing room. "I mean, the resemblance is uncanny."

Misha and Sylvia exchanged a glance, and then Sylvia said, "Have a seat, Scotty, and have a mimosa. Darling, will you serve?" Her voice was like velvet—but there was steel underneath. She was watching me, and I got the sense she knew this wasn't a social call; but she was a lady and she was going to treat it as such. It's hard to escape your breeding.

I kept watching Misha as he filled four flutes with champagne and then added some orange juice, apparently just for color, judging from the ratios. I sat down in a gold wingback chair and Aunt Sylvia sat down on a green and gold brocade couch. It was a big room, filled with tastefully selected antiques and a number of Audubon prints on the walls. Misha distributed the drinks before sitting next to Sylvia on the couch and crossing his legs. Colin was sitting across from me in a matching wingback chair, and we were facing the two of them across a mahogany coffee table shined to a mirror's surface. Colin made a face as I lifted my glass to my mouth, resisting the urge to down the whole thing in one swallow. Poor thing, he'd only been living in New Orleans for a few months; he hadn't adapted to social drinking in the morning yet. He took a little sip out of his glass and then set it down on a coaster.

"I have a twin brother, yes," Misha said haltingly, looking at Sylvia. "But I haven't seen Sasha in over a year. What is this about? Why are you asking about him?" Sylvia took one of his hands in hers and patted it. "Has Sasha . . . has he done something bad?"

"There really isn't an easy way to do this," Colin said. "I'm sorry to have to tell you this, but your brother is dead." His tone was soft and sympathetic.

"What?" Misha's eyes opened wider, and he looked from me back to Colin then back to me again. He shook his head. His voice shook when he spoke again. "That's not possible. It can't be."

"What is this about, Scotty?" Sylvia turned to me, still patting Misha's hand, his large hand dwarfing her little one. The diamond on her ring finger glinted in the sun streaming through the French doors that led out to the verandah. Her hands were completely steady—steel beneath velvet.

I took a deep breath. I was starting to feel really tired. The Sevres clock on the mantelpiece chimed ten o'clock. "Last night, a guy who looks an awful lot like your husband was shot in a house on Burgundy Street between eight and ten o'clock. I knew him as Misha." I gulped down the rest of my mimosa. "I stopped by to see him last night, and this morning the police came by to question me. That's how I know."

"But . . . I don't really understand," Sylvia said slowly, looking from me to Colin. "This just doesn't make any sense."

"It can't be," Misha said, shaking his head. "It can't be Sasha. It's not possible."

"He looked enough like you to be your twin," I said. Misha just kept shaking his head, not accepting it.

"Sasha," Sylvia said quietly, "I thought Sasha was in Houston."

"He's supposed to be." Misha rubbed his eyes. "This doesn't make any sense."

But a young Russian muscleman in his twenties married to a woman old enough to be his grandmother does? I thought to myself. Fortunately, that was right around when Colin decided to step in and take over. Good thing—I wasn't getting anywhere. "How did the two of you meet?"

Sylvia gave him a dazzling smile. "Several years ago, when my husband died, I decided to do some traveling. We'd always planned on going to Europe, but somehow we never managed to make it. Your grandmother, Scotty, went with me for company. Do you remember that trip?" I nodded. "It was in Munich. I was doing some shopping on my own and stopped into a coffee shop and dropped some of my bags. This handsome young man"—she patted Misha's arm—"came to my rescue and helped me. He was doing some traveling of his own, and we got to talking." She shrugged. "We met a few times after that, and later, we stayed in touch via e-mail. After Sophie decided to come back home, I went to Moscow. I'd always wanted to see Russia, and what better way to see the city than with a handsome young man who speaks the language? Somehow, we managed to fall in love." She leaned over and kissed his cheek and then turned back to me. "Misha came over here about six months later, and we were married."

"And Sasha?" Colin prompted. "You said he was supposed to be in Houston?"

"Sasha came over about a year ago," Misha replied. "We may have looked identical, but we were very different. Sasha wanted to marry a rich American lady, like me. He didn't understand that Sylvia and I are in love, that I didn't marry her for the money; I don't care about the money." He shook his head and sighed. "When his tourist visa ran out, he didn't want to go back, so he stayed."

"So he was here in the States illegally?"

He nodded. "I told him he had to go back, but we argued. He was staying here with us, and I told him he had to go. He went to Houston and started working there."

"How could he work without a green card?" Colin continued.

He shrugged. "I don't know. But after he went there, we stopped speaking. I didn't want him to cause me to be deported. I love it here. I don't ever want to go back." He held up his big hands helplessly. "And now this." His eyes filled with tears, which he wiped away.

He's lying, the Goddess whispered inside my brain.

"So you had no idea he was here, living in the Quarter?" Colin glanced at me.

"I have a house on Burgundy Street," Sylvia said. "In the 800 block. But there's one thing I don't understand."

"What's that, Mrs. Overton?" Colin replied.

"Scotty hadn't met Misha—*my* Misha—until today. So how did the two of you know to come here?" She finished her mimosa and handed the glass to Misha. Without a word he got up and re-filled the glass for her.

"We looked up the ownership of the house he was living in,"

Colin lied smoothly. "It was listed as belonging to you, Mrs. Overton, so we came over here to see if you knew anything. Not that we thought you would," he added quickly.

I played along. "And you can imagine my shock when Misha opened the door." Goddess, Colin was smooth. His tongue was almost as slick as Storm's.

Misha took my glass and refilled it and then sat back down next to Sylvia.

Sylvia took Misha's face in her hands and turned it to face her. "Misha, is there anything you want to tell me? Did you know Sasha was staying in the house on Burgundy?"

"I didn't know, Sylvia. You have to believe me." He looked at her, and she smiled at him, then leaned over and gave him a quick kiss on the cheek.

"Well, that's that." Sylvia stood up. "Sasha knew about the house and probably just moved himself in. I'm sorry we couldn't be of any more help to you."

We had no choice but to stand up as well. "I'm sorry about your brother, Misha."

He didn't acknowledge that I'd said anything. He covered his face with his hands.

The doorbell rang. "That would be our guests. I'm sorry to rush you boys out, but you understand, don't you?" She smoothed her skirt down. "If you'll excuse us?" She walked us over to the French doors, which she opened. "You don't mind going out this way, do you?" She reached up and kissed us both on the cheek. "You must come by for dinner sometime soon." And the doors shut behind us.

But not before I saw Misha sitting on the couch, his head still in his hands. His shoulders shook.

We didn't speak until we were in the car. "He was lying," I said as Colin pulled away from the curb. "He knew Sasha was here, and he knew Sasha was staying in the Burgundy house. I wonder why he didn't want her to know?"

"Why was Sasha pretending to be Misha? That doesn't make any sense." Colin shook his head. "And I didn't buy her story about how they met either."

"You think she was lying?" I went over the interview in my head but couldn't quite put my finger on anything that seemed unbelievable. "Why?"

"I don't know." Colin sighed. "I guess we're going to have to find out. You know her pretty well, I gather."

I shrugged. "You pretty much heard it already." I thought for a minute. Sylvia had gone to McGehee with my grandmother Sophie Diderot; they'd pretty much been lifelong friends. When we were kids, she and Uncle George were always bringing us presents and spoiling us. We didn't really see them that often; sometimes at Papa and Maman's, even more rarely we'd be invited to the Upperline house. What I'd always liked about them was they didn't talk down to us—they talked to us like we were adults. After I was grown, I didn't see them nearly as much as I had when I was young. But I'd always liked them. George had been a judge, very active in local politics and socially, and Sylvia was really involved in charity work. They were just another typical socially prominent and wealthy Uptown New Orleans couple, nothing out of the ordinary about them.

"Any kids?"

"A daughter, Therese. She died young, before I was born. I think it was cancer. Nobody really liked to talk about it much. I guess it was really hard on them both." Whenever my grandmother talked about Therese, she always lowered her voice to a whisper, as though afraid to say things in her regular speaking voice.

"Interesting." Colin whistled. "Isn't Louisiana under the Napoleonic code still?"

"Yeah, I think so. Why?"

"Forced heirship." Colin reached over and touched my leg when we stopped at a light. "Misha will inherit at least half of

Sylvia's estate when she dies—regardless of what her will might say." He shrugged. "It wouldn't be the first time a younger man married an older woman for her money and then killed her."

"Wait just a minute. What are you saying?" My head was spinning. Colin was thinking in circles and I couldn't keep up with him. "You're not making sense. Aunt Sylvia is still alive; it's Misha—*Sasha*—who's been killed."

"I'd be curious to know who stood to inherit her money before she remarried."

"Oh." It dawned on me. "You think someone killed Sasha thinking he was Misha?"

"It's a possibility we need to check into, isn't it?" Colin stopped at the Canal light. "The police probably are operating on the assumption that since he was a dealer, it was a drug-related slaying. But what if it wasn't? What if someone was looking to inherit and had to get rid of Misha first?"

"Then both of their lives are in danger. Shouldn't we say something?" My head was starting to hurt.

"Not yet. We don't know enough yet, and we could be way off base here." Colin made the turn into the Quarter. "So we need to find out who inherits when Sylvia dies. And we need to find out if there's any truth to the story of how they met. Something about it just doesn't sit right with me."

"I don't know why. I thought it was a nice story, if a little weird." I shrugged. "Aunt Sylvia's pretty cool. And she looks pretty good. It's possible he really does love her." I mean, who can explain the inexplicable nature of love? Look at me, Frank, and Colin—that's a hard one for most people with their brainwashed notions of one-on-one relationships to wrap their minds around.

"It's a possibility." Colin opened the gate to our parking lot with the remote clipped to his sun visor. "And Sasha's death could have just been a drug deal gone wrong." He maneuvered the car into a space and turned off the engine. "Of course, we have to be sure that the cops correctly identified the body. I mean, we don't *know* for a fact that Misha is Misha and not Sasha." He shook his head. "Sheesh, I'm even confusing myself. Do you think Misha was lying—was that the guy you knew?"

I shook my head. "They looked a lot alike, but it was two different guys. There were just little differences, you know? Were they enough for me to be sure? Yeah, I'm pretty sure, all right. The guy I bought the X from wasn't the same guy we met this morning. I'm sure of it. But the resemblance is amazing. Like I said, little differences. I mean, I guess Misha spoke better English than Sasha—that would be easy enough to fake, I suppose—but not the way he stood, the way he walked. It would be too hard to keep that kind of an act up, I think." I whistled. "Twins. Who knew?"

"Think, Scotty." Colin got out of the car. "Was it the same guy every time you saw him before?"

I slammed the car door. "No, I can't be sure of that." I shrugged. "I didn't pay attention; there wasn't a reason to. Looked like Misha, sounded like Misha, sold drugs like Misha—why wouldn't it be Misha? I mean, if I'd known to watch for things, yeah, but I didn't, so it's possible that sometimes it was one and other times the other." My head was aching. "Can we just refer to the guy I bought drugs from as *Sasha* and Sylvia's husband as *Misha?* It's all giving me a headache."

Colin pinched my butt. "Anything you want, my queen."

I started to tell him not to call me that—I can't stop Storm, but I'd be damned if the boys started—but I was too tired and figured I'd catch it the next time.

There'd better not be a next time.

We held hands as we walked the two blocks to Decatur Street, occasionally brushing against each other as we made way for tourists and other pedestrians. It was turning out to be an even more beautiful day than the day before. We rounded the corner at Decatur and headed for the gate to the building. The first floor of our building had always been a mom-and-pop grocery store until the fire. Mrs. Duchesnay, who owned the shop, had taken her insurance money and retired to the Florida panhandle. The Duchesnays' shop had been there as long as I could remember, and it always struck me as weird that it wasn't there anymore. I'd always liked Mrs. Duchesnay. The new tenant had opened a coffee shop, and it was already crowded with locals as I unlocked the gate. I debated going in and getting a cup, because I was feeling very tired. I don't know if the X had worn off completely or if there were still some traces of it in my system, but it had worn off enough so that every minute of last night's dancing could be felt in every muscle in my legs. My lower back ached. I just wanted to climb the stairs—each step an agony—and go to bed for a while. I stumbled on the first step.

"Are you okay?" Colin grabbed me and helped me regain my balance.

"I'm just tired. I want to go to bed."

I grabbed on to the railing and started climbing, with Colin right behind me. *What a sweetheart,* I thought. *He's waiting to catch me if I lose my balance again.*

Damn, am I lucky or what?

Finally, I unlocked my door and Colin followed me in.

"There you are," Frank called from the living room. He came bounding down the hall and swept me up into a bear hug, lifting me off the floor. He was still wearing his black tights and had that musky smell of dried sweat I love. "I'm sorry I stormed off. Do you forgive me?"

"It's okay." I kissed his neck. "You had a right to be mad."

He set me down, kissed Colin, and gave him a big hug too. "No, I didn't. I was being an asshole. I was just—" he hesitated. "I was just worried about you, and I channeled it into anger, and that was wrong. I mean, I'm still not comfortable with this whole drug thing, but I did have a really good time last night." He gave me a shy grin. "It was pretty awesome."

What a doll! I put my arms around him and gave him a big

hug. "I love you, Frank." I almost sagged with relief. I hated the thought of Frank being mad at me.

It looked like our first fight was over.

"I love you, too." He grinned at me. "Where've you two been? I was getting worried—and thought maybe you'd gone off to the parades without me."

"We went to meet Misha." I managed to make it into the living room. Every step was torturous; the dull ache in my lower back felt like a bowling bowl was pressing on the bottom of my spine. I focused on making it to the couch—one step at a time.

Frank's jaw dropped. "What?" He looked at me, then back at Colin. "I thought—"

"You explain," I said to Colin, dropping onto the couch. "I'm too tired. I just want to lie down for a while."

"I found out something, too," Frank said before Colin could say anything. "But you go first."

I closed my eyes and listened to Colin explain everything that we'd found out, as well as the necessity for finding out who Aunt Sylvia's heirs were. Frank's a really good listener—the FBI training, I guess—and only interrupted once to say, "*Twins?*" I was just drifting off into sleep when Frank shook me awake. "Come on, Scotty, you've got to see this."

"I just wanna go to sleep," I protested but knew I wasn't going to get anywhere. The boys wouldn't let me sleep until they were darn good and ready, so I dragged myself off the couch and walked over to the computer, certain with every step I was going to collapse. Every muscle in my body felt like jelly, and my eyelids felt like they weighed a hundred pounds each. It took every bit of willpower in my body not to just curl up and go to sleep on the floor.

Frank typed, and then the screen changed. "David showed me this."

A Web page was loading. In red letters on a black screen it said russianstud.com. Farther down, in more red letters, the site

insisted on age verification before allowing access and stated all
the standard porn site disclaimers—by entering the site you were
verifying you were of age, blah blah blah. Frank typed in a code
and clicked "enter."

The screen went white first, then went black again as a picture loaded.

The picture was of Misha, wearing only a pair of skimpy
white bikini briefs, which only emphasized the huge bulge they
contained. I stared at it. I had no idea he was that endowed! He
was smiling at the camera, with one hand held up, as though
beckoning the viewer to join him. His other hand rested on his
lower abdomen, the tips of the fingers inside the waistband of the
underwear. His hairless legs were ripped slabs of muscle. His
stomach wasn't ripped, but it was completely flat, and with the
rest of the definition on his body it seemed somehow sexier that
he didn't have a sixpack. As I sat watching, the picture moved and
turned, so that I was looking at his back, which looked like it was
carved from marble. The briefs barely covered his cheeks, and
they were solid, no fat anywhere. His arms went up and flexed,
and muscles rippled and flowed across his back, and then his hard
butt began to flex and release.

I stared at it. "Oh, my God." How had I never found this before? I was going to kill David for not telling me about this Web
site!

"Wait—it gets better," Frank said, clicking on a link. A number of thumbnail photographs popped up. He clicked on one,
and the screen changed again. A photo of Misha lying naked on a
bed came up, and after a few moments it began to move. He was
stroking himself, and then someone—another man—joined him
on the bed. His back was to the camera, so I couldn't get a good
look at his face. He straddled Misha, sliding down on his erection. After a few moments of this, Misha rolled him over onto his
back and his face came into view of the camera. I grinned. I knew
the guy from my gym, and from seeing him around in the bars.

In fact, I well knew the look of satiated pleasure on his face. I'd gone home with him once, and when we had finished, he'd gone into the bathroom, showered, changed into pajamas, and come back to bed, saying to me as he slipped under the covers, "You can let yourself out, can't you?" He had a nice body, and rather than being offended, I was kind of amused. I'd served my purpose; now it was time to go. That was much better than the tired old game of let's exchange phone numbers, even though we both know neither of us will ever call. No frills, no chills, no damage—everyone gets what he wants and no harm done.

"Every one of these thumbnails is a video clip of Misha having sex with someone," Frank said. "I recognize some of the guys from the gym, some from the bars—almost all of them look familiar. And I seriously doubt every single one of them was willing to be videotaped for a pay Web site, do you?"

Colin whistled. "So, it's not beyond the realm of possibility one of these guys could have gotten pissed off—"

"And killed him. Scotty, do you know any of them by name?"

I pointed at the screen. "Well, this guy's name is Jordan; I don't know his last name. Let me check some of the others."

I took the mouse away from Frank and clicked on another one of the thumbnails.

The picture blew up. It was the same room as the previous one—white walls with unlit candles in sconces, a hardwood floor, and a brass bed. The camera was positioned so that all I could see of the two on the bed was Misha's broad back, which was flexing and moving as he pumped on the body below him, his big white muscular ass shoving and moving back as he worked away. All I could see of the guy he was fucking were his legs, which were up around Misha's shoulders. Misha rolled him up farther onto his back and started pumping pretty fast and hard. I turned up the volume on the computer, and the room filled with the sounds of two people having pretty intense sex. Grunts, groans, bodies slapping together, and the occasional breathy, "Yeah, fuck me man." I couldn't help myself; I grinned, even though it was kind of creepy to be watching a dead man having sex. I'd always thought Misha had the body of a porn star. Apparently, he had thought so too.

"So, Misha—or Sasha—had a porn site." Colin smiled. "He did have a pretty nice body. I wonder how much money he made from the site?"

"Well, David said it cost $19.99 per month for full access. I'm using his access code."

"Not bad. Maybe *we* should think about doing that." Colin laughed. "If we even got a hundred members—"

"That would be two grand—for charging people to watch us do what we would do anyway!" Frank started laughing. "What do you think, Scotty?"

"I think—" I cut myself off just as Misha's whole body stiffened, and his head went back. Then his body began shaking as he reached his climax, and the moans got louder and louder. Then, he let out a deep guttural moan that probably in person would have shaken the whole house. After a few moments of twitching, he pulled back and stood up, getting off the bed and revealing the person underneath him. In his thick accent, he said clearly, "So, you like that big cock, man?"

For a moment, everything in front of me swam, and I heard both Frank and Colin breathe in sharply as the guy's face became clear.

"Oh, sweet Goddess," I gasped. "That's *David*."

CHAPTER SIX

Ten of Wands

one who is carrying an oppressive load

"I had no idea David was a bottom." Colin whistled.

Frank laughed. "Well, from the sound of it, he seems to be enjoying it."

I flushed but somehow couldn't look away from the screen. Don't get me wrong—I enjoy porn just as much as the next guy and have plenty of tapes stashed away in the little cabinet of my entertainment center. Granted, since the boys had come into my life I haven't had much occasion to watch porn—they keep me quite busy, thank you very much—but it is one thing to watch total strangers having sex on tape and another to see your best friend getting pounded by your drug dealer on the Internet.

"What was he *thinking?*" I said aloud. David is a music teacher and band director at a Catholic high school in the Ninth Ward. There had been a big scandal in town a few years ago when a gay teacher at Archbishop Chappelle had been discovered on one of those gay personals sites, with all kinds of naked pictures that left absolutely no mystery as to what exactly he liked to do. (The shot of him tied up spread-eagled on his stomach with his ass cheeks up in the air and spread was pretty self-explanatory.) The teacher had been fired almost immediately, and the letters column of the *Times-Picayune* had been filled with letters from outraged straight people for weeks. David had known him—I'd seen him around in the bars but had never really talked to him—and had just shaken his head. "Well, I don't think people should lose their jobs because of what they do in their free time," he'd said at the time, "but that just seemed to be *asking* for it. What did he think the Archdiocese would do? You never know when one of your students—or the parents of one of your students—is going to run across something like that on-line."

Sure, David had plenty of pictures of himself on various sites, but always without showing his face. I always thought that was kind of silly in a way; the massive dragon tattoo he has running from his shoulder down around his left pec is pretty distinctive, but then not many of his students or their parents had ever seen him shirtless.

"And David actually showed you this?" I scratched my head. That didn't seem like David.

"Well, he didn't show me *this.*" Frank tapped the computer screen. "He just showed me the site."

"I can't believe he never told me he'd been with Misha," I said, unable to take my eyes off the computer screen. David always told me everything. He usually couldn't wait to tell me about the guy he'd fucked the night before.

I'd met David about four years ago on one of those nights when I wasn't in the mood to hit the bars. I'd gone into the Pub, had a couple of beers, and just wasn't in a place where I wanted to do the bar mating dance, that whole exchange of glances, smiles, introducing yourself and chatting for a little while, buying each other a few drinks before finally getting down to business and going home together. Usually I didn't mind, but every once in a while I just got in one of those moods where it seemed like an incredible waste of time. Why did gay men always feel the need to go through these motions? The minute you catch someone's eye and interest is sparked, it would be so much easier—and so much more honest—just to say, "Hi, I'm Scotty. Let's go fuck." I mean, that's what it was all about, no matter how much people liked to pretend they were actually looking for a boyfriend. So, after about half an hour of watching other people do this silly dance, and watching the really young and skinny strippers on the bar that weekend, I walked out and headed down to the bathhouse.

There are some gay men I know who think the bathhouse—bathhouses in general—are disgusting. I've always thought that said a lot more about their own sexual hang-ups than anything else. I mean, come on. What's wrong with a bathhouse? Hell, it's more honest than a bar. At least in a bathhouse, you know why everyone is there and there's no pretense. Everyone is walking around in a towel with his body completely on display, and if you see something you like, you go for it. No talk unless you want it, no exchange of phone numbers, none of that nonsense—just pure animal sex. The place fairly throbbed with sexual energy, and for some reason that always made me hornier than usual—which is saying a lot.

I'd seen David as I was climbing the stairs up to the floor with the "glory hole" booths. He was about my height, and just ripped lean muscle. I smiled at him, he smiled back at me, and then followed me up the stairs. I leaned against a wall, and he brushed past me, copping a feel of my chest. I smiled at him. He took a few more steps, then turned and came back. "You want to go to my room?" he whispered.

I nodded and followed him back down the stairs. He unlocked his room and turned on the light. I dropped my towel and he put his arms around me and we kissed, before lying down on the little bed.

It took about five minutes before we realized we were sexually incompatible.

"That *fucking* figures." David laughed, sitting up and reaching for his pants. "The only hot guy in the whole place turns out to be the only other top here!"

I couldn't help but laugh myself. "Well, I just got here myself, so I couldn't say."

He pulled a joint out of his pants and sparked it. He offered it to me, and I took a few hits before passing it back. It was decent stuff, and we lay down together on the bed and finished, talking and giggling before I finally left his little room. We ran into each other again a little while later and wound up hanging out together—discussing the bodies of the boys as they walked past us until one of us wound up going off with someone. The following Monday afternoon, I was at the gym working out, and I saw him over on the Smith machine. Breaking one of the unspoken rules of the bathhouse (*what happens in the bathhouse stays in the bathhouse*), I walked over to him and showed him what he was doing wrong on the exercise.

And that was the beginning of a beautiful friendship.

David was all about being a top, though. Even his on-line screen name (ButchTop40) proudly proclaimed that to the world. I just stared at the computer screen trying to wrap my mind around this new development in David. It looked like he was enjoying himself.

Well, the heated moans he was emitting every time Misha—I mean *Sasha*—pushed into him were pretty good clues, too.

"I wonder if he knew he was being taped," Frank mused, stroking his chin. "I wouldn't think so, would you? I mean—"

"I doubt it. David's pretty careful about things like this. Besides, he hardly would have showed you this site if he knew he was on it. I mean, if he *knew* he was on here, he would have said something, don't you think?" I grabbed the mouse and clicked the window closed. "I really don't think we need to watch any more."

"I've never gotten any sense from David that he was—" Colin broke off and gave me a grin.

"A bottom?" I glared at him for a minute and then laughed.

"ButchTop40, my ass!" I waved at the computer screen. "I wonder if it was just a situational thing. I mean, you know, Sasha was pretty hot, and if he was a top, maybe—" I buried my face in my hands. "It's not any of our business what David does or who he does, but I wonder why he never told me?" David knew I had a mild crush on Misha—I mean, *Sasha.* Before the boys came along, we had a friendly kind of competition going on when we went out. We always tried to see who could wind up with the hottest guy, and let's face it, Misha, er, Sasha, was definitely a trump card. It didn't make any sense to me. I stood up. I was dizzy—probably an aftereffect of the Ecstasy and being tired—and had to grab the back of Frank's chair to keep from falling down.

"You're going to have to say something to him," Frank said.

"Oh, you can just bet I'm going to." I started to laugh. "Helium heels, your legs have been in the air more times than a ballerina's, you've spent more time on your back than Michelangelo . . . give me time, I can come up with a million of 'em." I'm not Storm's younger brother for nothing, you know.

"Scotty, be serious for a minute." Colin put his arms around me and squeezed. "What if someone who knows he works for the Archdiocese sees this? He could be fired. And it's not beyond the realm of possibilities that some priest would go to this site. . . ."

"Oh, yeah." That sobered me up pretty quick. "Hell, the Archbishop himself probably has this one bookmarked."

"Scotty . . ." Frank sighed. "Look at this." He clicked the mouse again, and the damn tape started playing again. He clicked on the "restart" button on the video player, and there was David on his back on the bed and Sasha climbing up on top of the bed, and he froze the frame. "*Look.*" He pointed with his finger at Sasha's erection. "What isn't there?"

My heart sank.

Sasha wasn't using a condom.

"Oh, sweet Goddess. . . ." I felt sick to my stomach.

I felt myself getting dizzy, my legs started to buckle, and I was falling. . . .

I was falling through a mist, a fog that had come out of nowhere. I could hear the sound of a marching band in the distance, the sound of a crowd shouting and cheering, like a parade was going by somewhere close, but I couldn't see through the fog, couldn't make out anything; there was nothing but fog and more fog, swirling around me and cushioning me somehow, so I wasn't afraid. I didn't know where I was, what was happening . . . but there was a peace there, some kind of energy that flowed into me and made my fingertips tingle a little bit, and I could feel all the tension releasing from my body, the knots in my stomach and back muscles relaxing, and I just went with the feeling, taking deep and cleansing breaths, and the calm seeped into me, slowing my racing heart and bringing me to a place of peace and relaxation, a place where I knew everything would work out, a place where everything would be all right.

And then I glided to a stop, coming to rest on a soft lawn, under the branches of a huge old oak tree, and the grass seemed to shape to me, and my body relaxed further. I could still hear the parade sounds, but they seemed more remote, as though it had passed by. The grass was a little damp, and I climbed to my feet. The fog continued to swirl around me, with the sounds of the parade getting farther and farther away. I could see shapes moving a few feet away from me, almost close enough to touch, but when I reached out, my hands went through them like they weren't there at all, and then the tension came back, my stomach knotting up.

"What's going on?" I shouted, and my voice echoed back to me. "Where am I? What is this place?" I'd been here before, in my heart I knew that I was safe here, but still the fear came bubbling back up inside of me, and I thought about David again, and my eyes filled with tears.

The parade noise stopped, and the silence became oppressive. The fog continued to swirl and move, and then I felt her presence.

"Goddess? Are you there?"

"You are safe here, Scotty."

"Well, great, but where am I and what am I doing here?"

No answer. She's like that sometimes. She only answers what she wants to.

"You brought me here for a reason, didn't you?" There's always a reason, whether she decides to share it with me or not.

"Frank and Colin love you very much."

"I know that!" I was getting impatient. She can be so obtuse sometimes. "I love them, too!"

"They're both in danger, Scotty."

"From what? From whom?" A cold chill swept through me. The boys? In danger?

"You have to be strong. They will be depending on you."

"What about David?" I demanded. I could feel tears swimming up in my eyes, and I wiped at them. "Is he going to be okay?"

"Do you always use condoms, Scotty?" She was using my mother's voice. We'd talked about condoms any number of times. Mom always worried that something was going to happen to me, and I would always tell her "yes" and get impatient, just like I always said "yes" when Rain lectured me, when Storm did, when Millie and Velma brought it up. I'd get impatient and snappy with them, which wasn't fair; it came from love and worry and concern.

I opened my mouth and shut it again. I couldn't answer; the Goddess would know the truth. I bit my lip. No, I didn't always use condoms. I always tried to, I always intended to, I always carried one in my pocket when I went out or availed myself of the ones the bars kept prominently displayed in bowls at various spots, but sometimes when I'd had too much to drink, I didn't have one and neither did the guy, and we'd decide to "play it safe," but somehow once we got into the swing of passion and lust and desire, caution would be tossed aside and we'd blow each other, or the guy would say, "I don't care. I want you to fuck me. You're negative, right?" and I would say, "Yes," because I was, but there was no guarantee that he was, and he really had no guarantee that I wasn't lying, and then I'd wake up the next morning and feel sick to my stomach, sick with fear and wondering, "Was this the time?" So I would always go down to the NO/AIDS office on Frenchmen Street, just a few blocks from my apartment, and get tested whenever I'd been stupid, but so far my luck had held. It was a horrible feeling, knowing I'd done something stupid, put myself at risk because I was too drunk to think things through, and there was always, always, always that chance that this would be the time. . . . "I always try," I said to the Goddess, remembering what the counselors always said, that "condoms aren't 100% effective," and got another cold chill.

"That's all anyone can do, Scotty. Try his best."

"But David—why would he take such a risk?"

"You don't have to worry about David. There are other things you need to be concerned with. Stay focused."

I felt better, somewhat. The Goddess never lies to me. But still—

"The ones you need to worry about are Frank and Colin. They are in danger, and you are the only one."

"What kind of danger?"

"Pray for a brave heart. History cannot be ignored or forgotten, Scotty, remember that. . . ."

"Are you okay? Scotty?"

I opened my eyes. Both Frank and Colin were hovering over me, their faces pale. No matter how many times they've seen the Goddess send me into a trance, it never fails to scare them both shitless. I tried to sit up and sank back down. I had no energy at all, and I was still feeling a little on the dizzy side.

"You need to eat something." Frank walked into the kitchen and started rifling through the refrigerator. I heard the microwave door open, the sound of him pressing buttons, and the hum of it heating something. "You haven't eaten since yesterday afternoon. Your blood sugar's probably too low."

Colin knelt down beside me. "You had a vision, right?"

I nodded. My mouth was dry. I looked into his beautiful blue eyes, so concerned for me. I tried to swallow. "The Goddess"—I wiped my eyes—"she said I didn't need to worry about David."

His face lit up with one of his megawatt smiles, and his entire body sagged with relief. "Oh, thank God." His own eyes filled with tears, and I loved him so much in that moment that I just wanted to hug him as hard as I could. "But you still need to talk to him—or we can. His job's in danger as long as he's on that Web site."

I nodded, took a deep breath, and swallowed. "Um, she also said you were in danger."

The microwave dinged.

"Me?" Colin looked puzzled. "From what?"

"She didn't say." Frank brought in a steaming plate of the chicken casserole Colin had made on Friday night. "Both of you, she said. Both of you are in danger."

They exchanged a glance.

"What kind of danger?" Frank sat down in the reclining chair and crossed his legs. "Maybe of getting arrested for drug possession?"

"Goddamn it, Frank!" Colin exploded. He stormed over to Frank's chair, his fists clenched at his sides. Frank stood up and they stood there, glaring at each other, their chests almost touching. The air fairly crackled with testosterone. As I sat there looking, I could see blue sparks, like little bolts of lightning, popping off their bodies. My vision started to blur again, and I had this eerie feeling I'd seen this before. But that wasn't possible—we all three got along so well we'd never even had much of a disagreement before, certainly not anything where fists were clenched or tempers lost.

History cannot be forgotten or ignored. . . . What's going on here, Goddess? What are you trying to show me?

"Stop it, both of you," I said, taking a bite of the casserole. "And sit down. You're making me dizzy." The casserole tasted even better now than it had on Friday night. Damn, Colin was a culinary genius. There really isn't anything he can't do.

The boys stood there for another second, and then both grinned at each other and wrapped their arms around each other, hugging each other tight and sharing a kiss. I sighed with relief and kept eating. The food was definitely helping. I could feel energy starting to surge through me again.

Frank sat back down in the chair and Colin sat on his lap. "Guys, I'm sorry for being such a dick," Frank said.

"Did you have fun last night?" I asked, changing the subject. No sense going over all that again. Really, the casserole was like a little piece of heaven. What the hell did Colin put in it anyway?

Frank nodded. "Yeah, I did. I've never had so much fun dancing before." He shook his head. "I've never felt so, so free before, you know? I've always been a little self-conscious on the dance floor—and I've never been comfortable taking off my shirt in public before—but it felt right last night."

"You?" Colin grinned at him. "But, Special Agent, you've got a magnificent body. When you took your shirt off last night"—he winked at me—"angels sang, the planets aligned, and"—he ran his hand down the center of Frank's chest—"everyone wanted you."

"Yeah, right." Frank's face reddened. "I don't think so."

"Oh, come on, Frank." I scooped the last of the casserole onto my spoon and swallowed it down. I felt much better. I leaned back into the couch and couldn't resist teasing him a little bit. "There were boys hovering around you all night long."

"I guess I just always think of myself as being skinny."

"Skinny?" Colin stared at him. "Lean, maybe, but not skinny." He grabbed one of Frank's arms and made him flex. "I mean, look at the size of that baby! No, I don't think anyone would think you were *skinny*, Special Agent. You are porn star material for sure."

"I was skinny in high school." Frank looked away from both of us. "They used to call me Ichabod Crane."

It's funny how high school keeps haunting you no matter how long you've been out—if you let it. "Frank, high school was over twenty years ago." I leaned back into the couch. "You've got a great body. And all those assholes who made fun of you for being skinny are probably all fat out-of-shape blobs who look like hell now."

"Yeah, well, whatever." Frank shook his head. "We're getting off the track here."

Every muscle in my legs moaned as I stood up and walked over to the chair. I knelt down in front of them. "Frank, you're a dreamboat. Stop worrying about that stuff. You were one of the hottest guys there last night."

Frank smiled at me. "You're so sweet." He stroked my cheek. "But we need to focus. Tell me about your meeting with your aunt."

I sat down with my back against his legs, and he started massaging my shoulders as Colin and I filled him in. When we finished, he whistled. "There were two of them?"

"Misha was lying; I'm sure of it. I'm not sure about what, though." Colin stood up, stretching and yawning. "Can we go lie down?"

All three of us got up and walked into my bedroom. Colin pulled off his shirt and dropped his pants and jumped up onto the bed in his white boxer briefs. Frank and I grinned at each other, then hurriedly undressed and climbed up on either side of him. Colin put an arm around each of us and we cuddled into his warmth. "What did *you* think, Scotty?" Frank asked.

"He was definitely not telling us everything." I started stroking Colin's leg. "So, apparently, the guy I knew as Misha was really his brother, Sasha, which doesn't make a lot of sense to me. Why wouldn't Sasha just *be* Sasha? Why pretend?"

"Do you think Venus knows yet?" Frank was stroking Colin's other leg.

"Probably not. It'll take days for her to get cooperation out of the INS." Colin shrugged, leaning his head back with his eyes closed. "You know, we have to think about the possibility this was drug related."

Not this again, I thought, tensing up. "I can't imagine he was that big time a dealer." I pictured the strongbox, the roll of cash, the baggies filled with pills, the vials of liquid. *Well, maybe it was possible.*

"But you don't know that," Frank said calmly. "For all you know, Scotty, he could have been the city's biggest dealer. And we can't rule out the Russia connection, either."

"The Russian mob?" Colin mused. "That's another possibility." He laughed. "But I don't think we have anything to worry about from the cops anymore. We've got any number of more logical suspects for them to check into. Our work here is done, and now we can enjoy the rest of Mardi Gras." He leaned over and kissed my neck. "Are we agreed on that? Now that our little Scotty boy is pretty much in the clear, we can focus on having fun again."

That was a huge relief. It was all just a little Mardi Gras mambo, and our part of the dance was over.

"It would be nice to make it through Fat Tuesday without Scotty being kidnapped again," Colin teased. I resisted the urge to punch him.

Like it's *my* fault I've been kidnapped twice? But still . . . "I think we can rule out the Russian mob." I yawned. I was really tired, and the bed felt so soft, and their body heat was so comforting and soothing. There really *isn't* anything like cuddling with two guys you love.

"I mean, the thing that bothers me the most about all of this is the coincidences." Frank kissed my shoulder. "I mean, what are the odds that your drug dealer has a twin brother who married an old friend of your grandmother's? And your dealer is sleeping with David?"

"It's New Orleans." I shrugged. "Everyone in this city is

about one degree of separation from everyone else." It was true; for a big city, New Orleans was really just a small town. Everyone knows everyone else—and their business. There are *no* secrets in New Orleans.

"Okay—enough talk!" Colin commanded. "We're done with this, agreed? We're just going to relax and enjoy Carnival, agreed? And if Venus shows up again, we'll give her what we found."

"Shouldn't we give it to her anyway?" My entire body felt like dead weight. I leaned back into Frank's hard chest.

"Probably not. Cops don't really like it when people interfere with their investigations. I've learned that the hard way." Colin yawned and nestled down farther into the bed. "Damn, I'm tired."

"We've been up all night," Frank pointed out. "Maybe we should take a nap." He pinched my butt. "And if we're going out dancing again tonight—I mean," he hesitated, "I mean, shouldn't we rest up before we take X again?"

"I know that wasn't the Special Agent talking." Colin laughed. "I mean, surely that wasn't an ex-FBI agent suggesting we do drugs again?"

"You really had a good time last night, huh, Frank?" I reached back around him and stroked his back.

"Yeah."

"Then we definitely need to get some sleep." I yawned. "Our costumes tonight are going to look great—so everyone be quiet and let's sleep, okay?"

They both mumbled assent.

"Works for me," I replied and closed my eyes. Venus was a good cop. I didn't have anything else to worry about . . . and I could talk to David after Fat Tuesday about the Web site thing—and the condom issue. It wouldn't be fun—it would be pretty fucking awkward—but it could keep until Ash Wednesday. Why ruin his Carnival by worrying him? I could cross that bridge when I came to it. My breathing started coming more steadily.

My entire body relaxed, and I could tell by his even breathing that Frank had drifted off already. He felt so good pressed up against me, and Colin's heartbeat and body heat were lulling me.

"Love you, Colin," I muttered as I pressed my head up against his shoulder.

"Love you too, Scotty." He kissed the top of my head.

And I drifted off to sleep.

CHAPTER SEVEN

Four of Swords

there will soon be a return to the active life

I opened my eyes just before four—bright eyed, bushy tailed, and raring to go.

I lay there for a couple of minutes, listening to the boys breathing. They were dead to the world, and I didn't think it would be cool to wake them up. Frank's arm was draped over me, extending past me and over Colin. Barely breathing, I carefully moved my own right arm from underneath Frank's and off of Colin. It worked, so even more carefully I lifted Frank's arm off me and slid slowly down to the end of the bed. Colin groaned a bit in his sleep, and I froze, but then Frank, still asleep, moved forward a bit until he remained against Colin. I managed to stand up without the bed bouncing and remained there looking at them. *I'm so lucky,* I thought, as a smile crept across my face. *Any guy would consider himself lucky to have either one of them, and I've got them both—and they love me.* I walked over to the window and looked out into the courtyard. The sky was overcast and it was kind of gray, but I could see Millie and Velma and some of their friends braving the inclement weather, sharing a joint and drinking mimosas. Just then, Millie looked up and saw me and smiled, waving her hand. I waved back. Millie and Velma were incredibly cool. Velma went to McGehee with my mom (and I'd be more than willing to bet that the best friend combo of baby dyke and social activist had caused many a sleepless night for the staid administration of that fine rich kids' school in the Garden District), and she and Millie were more like aunts than family friends. I debated going down for a mimosa, then decided that coffee was probably a better idea. My mind was still a little fogged from the Ecstasy hangover, and the last twenty-four hours *had* been a little on the intense side, even for me. I let the curtain close and walked into the bathroom.

I looked at myself in the mirror and almost screamed. There was snot in the corner of my eyes, my hair was standing up in what best could be described as a Medusa-like fashion, and there were bags forming under my eyes. "You could scare small children," I said to my hellish reflection in the mirror. I was also very dehydrated, and before brushing my teeth I gulped down several handfuls of water from the tap. I took a deep breath and looked in the mirror. It hadn't been an optical illusion or my mind playing tricks on me. I looked pretty hellish. I badly needed a shave, and—what in the name of all that's holy was *that?* I leaned closer to the mirror and stared. Yep, I was right the first time. A big old, angry, nasty, red zit was starting to form on my chin. "Sheesh," I said, running my finger over it. "I'm almost thirty—what the hell am I doing getting zits at my age?" I turned on the hot water spigot and soaped up my face before scrubbing it thoroughly with a rough washcloth. I splashed water onto my face, dried it, and looked again. Not quite so bad, but the hair was still a disaster area. *Oh, well,* I thought and walked into the kitchen. I ate a banana while starting another pot of coffee.

I sat at my desk while the coffee brewed and stared at my computer screen. I debated turning it on but finally decided not to. *I won't let Mardi Gras be ruined for me,* I said to myself. *The boys are right. Let Venus track down Sasha's killer; I'm out of it. And David can wait until Ash Wednesday. So, Mardi Gras is ruined only if I let it be ruined,* I decided and leaned back in the chair. The boys both wanted to go out dancing tonight, so there was absolutely no reason we couldn't put on our costumes for tonight and go out into the crowds again. And who would have ever thought taking Ecstasy again would be *Frank's* idea?

It *would* be a shame to waste the costumes for tonight.

I'd planned every night's costumes very carefully. To follow up last night's sexy Zorro outfits, tonight we were all going as Mercury, messenger of the gods. We'd gotten gold square-cut bathing suits, masks, and cheap boots. We'd painted the boots gold and sprinkled them all over with glitter. Colin had made these cute little wings for the boots we'd painted gold to match and, of course, glittered up. We also had gold body paint. That was our entire costume. Square cuts, boots, masks, and body paint. Well, and glitter, too. When we'd tried on the suits—I'd insisted on a dry run on all of our costumes—the boys looked like a million bucks, even without the body paint. *Everyone* was going to notice us tonight, which was the main point of costuming. If no one noticed, why bother?

Of course, wearing body paint had its drawbacks. For one thing, it comes off to the touch, so if—*when*—we got groped on the dance floor, everyone who touched us would have gold fingers. It also has a tendency to run, so once we started dancing and sweating, it would start streaming off of us in little rivers, leaving zebra-like streaks. By the time we made it home tomorrow morning we would look pretty shitty, but by that point who'd care? We'd also have to shower before getting in the bed to avoid ruining the sheets, but I also figured part of the fun would be the group shower to get cleaned up. Events had conspired this morning to keep us from having fun after we got home, but surely the Universe couldn't be so cruel as to have that happen two mornings in a row.

And the best part of the Mercury costume, easily hands down, was how much fun it would be applying the body paint to the boys. Just the thought of squeezing the body paint out of the tube onto their bare skin then spreading it over their muscles had been getting me excited for days. What can I say? I love to rub on the boys. Who wouldn't?

I rolled a joint and lit it, blowing the smoke up at the ceiling. I willed myself to relax. Angela had authorized us to investigate, but Colin and Frank both seemed to feel we'd done what she'd wanted, which was simply to clear me, not find the actual killer. I wasn't really sure how I felt about that. Weren't detectives not supposed to stop until they solved the case? Colin and Frank both always made fun of my "notions" of what being a detective meant. "It's not wearing trench coats and fedoras and following people around," Colin had said once when I'd groused about spending so many hours on the computer looking things up. "Nowadays its mostly computer work, and making phone calls. It's not a Humphrey Bogart movie." For Christmas, Colin and Frank had actually gotten me a nice black trench coat with a thick, warm red lining; a matching black felt fedora; and an antique magnifying glass. They were great gifts, expensive too, but I still got the sense that in a way they were kind of laughing at me. Oh, sure, they both loved me so it wasn't in a mean-spirited way by any means, but there it was. Frank had twenty years with the FBI; Colin had been working for Angela for a while; and I was the rookie, with no real experience in detection. And if I was being completely honest, I wouldn't have survived without the boys' help. As for any detecting I'd done, well, in all fairness again, it was just pure dumb luck and some help—a *lot* of help—from the Goddess. No, I wasn't a *real* detective. I was just the office mascot—and a lightning rod for trouble.

"Lighten up," I said out loud. "So being a detective isn't what you thought it would be like. It beats dancing on the bars and training people, doesn't it?"

No, I didn't miss whoring myself for dollar bills from drunks. I didn't miss training clients who couldn't understand why they weren't losing weight or getting huge muscles overnight, who didn't feel the need to pay me on time. I didn't miss teaching aerobics classes, doing the same monotonous routine ten to twelve times per week until I knew it so well I could do it asleep. It was nice getting a biweekly paycheck that was way more than enough to cover my expenses. I'd managed, in the few months I'd been working for the Blackledge Agency, to pay off most of my credit card debt, and that was a really good feeling.

But it wasn't as *exciting* as I thought it would be.

Oh, sure, I never thought it would be one thrilling case after another. But here we were with a murder investigation practically fallen into our laps, Angela's permission to investigate, and just when it was starting to get really interesting, we were backing off.

Maybe the boys think partying is more important to you than solving the case.

Now *that* was an unpleasant thought.

I walked back down the hall and looked at the two of them sleeping. I couldn't help but smile. They really were two of the sexiest guys I'd ever seen in my life. Frank had his arms around Colin, and their bodies were so close together a playing card wouldn't have fit in between them. *No, I was wrong,* I decided, as I watched Colin shift a little in his sleep, and Frank snuggle him a bit tighter. *They are both professionals, and they wouldn't back away from a case just because I want to have a good time. If they've decided we're done, then we are done.*

On the other hand, it wouldn't hurt anything for me to put some more thought into it, would it?

I walked back into the kitchen and watched the stream of coffee filling up the pot. *Okay, Mr. Detective, think about it.* I certainly hadn't killed Sasha. My connection to him was tenuous at best—the old "wrong place at the wrong time" thing, which was certainly beginning to seem like my stock in trade. The porn site, the connection to Aunt Sylvia, even the drugs—all were viable motives pointing in directions away from me. Sure, it was strange that my dealer had a twin brother who was married to an old family friend, and even stranger that one of them had slept with my best friend. It was an awful lot of coincidences—but these kinds of coincidences happened in New Orleans all the time. The only other explanation was that me, my family, and our friends were being targeted somehow—but, no, that was just stupid. What would be the reasoning behind that? Yeah, both sides of my family had money—the Diderots more than the Bradleys—but why on earth would anyone target *us?* Papa Diderot still was chairman of the board of the bank the family had owned since the Spanish flag flew over the city, but Papa Bradley was a retired corporate lawyer. No, that just didn't make any sense at all. It was coincidence, that's all. Like that time this really hot guy picked me up one night at Oz, and I went home with him. As he pulled into the driveway of a house in the Garden District, I realized in horror that I had been there before, only a few weeks earlier—picked up by a different guy. They'd been a couple for about twelve years and had an open relationship, as it turned out, but at the time I'd been terribly embarrassed.

I sighed. My head was starting to hurt from all this circular thinking. The boys were right, no doubt—it was probably best that we leave it all to Venus and the cops from now on. I wasn't totally comfortable with the idea of not turning over what we'd found out to the police unless they came after me again, but then again, why implicate David and the other guys on the Web site even slightly if it wasn't necessary? Besides, that was the cops' job, not ours. Maybe I should tip David off that Venus might come knocking on his door . . . but then why worry him unnecessarily? I didn't *know* she would—she might not ever find the Web site—and David did know about it. Weird that he'd never seen himself on it. *Stop it, Scotty! You're obsessing.*

I sighed. Nope, no reason I could see not to enjoy the rest of the holiday. We had our costumes, we had our drugs, and we were safely out of it.

But my mind, damn it to hell, just wouldn't let it go. We were detectives. Wasn't investigating what we were supposed to do? Okay, Frank had been a longtime Fed, and Colin, well, I didn't know how long he'd been in the business, but certainly longer than me. Look at everything they'd been able to find out, while all I wanted to do was go to sleep! Some detective I was. What exactly did I have to contribute to this team, anyway?

The Goddess speaks to you; that's what you bring to the team.

I got myself a cup of coffee and spiked it with Bailey's Irish Cream and headed into the living room. My gift isn't exactly a science: sometimes the Goddess talked to me in dreams, sometimes I could focus on my tarot cards and get answers. Sometimes the messages that came to me through the cards didn't make sense—until it was too late to matter. Sometimes I misread them and realized it later. Sometimes they didn't tell me anything. It could be annoying, but you can see why I didn't set up a table in Jackson Square and take money for it.

I sat down at my coffee table, lit two white candles, and got out my tarot deck. I took another hit off the joint and pinched it out. I started shuffling, thinking about how cool it would be if I could solve this case without any help from the boys, prove to them I was a valuable asset to the agency. Not that they ever made me feel like I wasn't, but sometimes, like I said before, they would give each other that annoying Scotty-is-such-a-cute-little-whack-job look.

I closed my eyes and held the deck in my hands. I said a quick prayer to the Goddess. *Please, Holy Mother of us all, please tell me through the cards the answer to my question and help me to see the truth.* I opened my eyes and laid out the cards, then started slowly turning them over.

Overindulgence, in food or drink.

Perpetual Peter Pan, a refusal to accept adult responsibility.

A dangerous journey, possibly across water.

I stared at them. Nothing like getting bitch slapped by the Goddess—*perpetual Peter Pan, my ass!* I swept the cards up and wrapped them back in the blue silk cloth, then shoved them into the old Cuban cigar box I kept them in, and slid it under the couch.

Apparently, the Goddess didn't want to help.

I got up from the table and walked out onto my balcony. The sun was struggling to shine through thick clouds. It was probably going to rain again. The air was thick with moisture. Decatur Street was full of people carrying go-cups with their necks weighted down with beads. They were all laughing and joking, shouting at others, as they staggered around. Every once in a while someone would shout drunkenly, "Happy Mardi Gras!" and a cheer would go up from one end of the street to the other. I stood at the railing looking down and watching. I smiled involuntarily. The tourists were annoying, sure, but I always thoroughly enjoyed watching them. Most of them probably spent the rest of the year weighted down with the mores of their communities, doing the nine-to-five thing, being responsible adults. Coming to New Orleans for Mardi Gras was their chance to be kids again, to act crazy and do things adults weren't supposed to do, let off steam, and just go nuts before returning to their straightlaced world of work, kids, and church.

A group of what were probably college kids caught my eye, and I turned to watch them. There were six of them; three guys, three girls, most likely couples down from maybe Baton Rouge. The girls were dressed in tube tops and low-waisted jeans that looked like they were going to walk out of them at any minute. Two of them showed tattoos on their shoulders, and all three had their navels pierced. The boys were wearing football jerseys tucked into baggy jeans, and one of them was Abercrombie-and-Fitch-catalogue handsome, with clear skin, thick hair hanging down into his eyes, and wiry muscles. They all had huge plastic cups about half full with beer. They were laughing and joking and hanging on each other, just giving each other shit and having a great time. I watched them cross Barracks Street and walk in front of the black iron fence running around the old Mint. *Probably frat boys from LSU,* I thought, and as they got closer I saw that the other two were just as good-looking as the catalogue model guy, just not as flashy. Their walks had that straight-boy swagger to it, that particular wide-legged gait with their pelvises thrust oh so slightly forward, conveying the sense of privilege that automatically came with being straight white boys from well-off families. All six of them were drunk, which meant they'd either all pass out or puke (or both) before the night was over. The girls walked behind the guys, and then they stopped in front of a guy leaning against the fence almost directly across the street from my building. One of the girls pulled a string of beads over her head and tried to give them to the guy, but he just brushed them off. The girl shrugged, her friends laughed at her, and then they moved on down the sidewalk.

I turned my attention to the man who didn't want beads.

The guy against the fence was wearing a black and gold Saints baseball cap pulled down low over his forehead, so I couldn't see his face. Despite the warm mugginess and stickiness, he was wearing a black leather jacket zipped shut over black slacks and boots. He stood there, staring across the street, every so often turning his head and gazing up and down the street before turning back to stare at the building on the other side of Decatur from where he was standing. I stood there, staring. I'd seen some-one else act like that. . . .

And then I remembered. It had been hot, and I'd been tired, and the guy across the street had been Frank, before I knew him and he was still with the Feds. He'd been watching my front gate, trying to blend in and not be noticeable, but still watching every-one coming up and down the sidewalks.

Which was exactly what this guy was doing.

A cold chill went down my spine, and I realized I was still in my underwear. My first instinct was to wake up Frank and Colin, but then I gave myself a mental slap across the face. *You're a licensed private eye now,* I told myself. *Quit expecting them to do all the dirty work. Not five minutes ago you were thinking about trying to solve the case on your own to prove yourself to them, and at the first sign of trouble, you're going to run and wake them up? Sheesh—some private eye you are!*

I went into the bedroom—the boys were still sleeping, still twined together—and pulled on a pair of jean shorts and a dirty Tulane sweatshirt that didn't smell too bad. I shoved my wallet into my pocket and grabbed my keys and went down the back stairs. The courtyard was deserted; Millie and Velma had either taken their guests inside or moved on to whatever party they were going to. By the time I got to the bottom of the steps, I had my plan of action. He hadn't been watching the balconies—he'd been watching the gate. I would go in through the back door of the coffee shop—one of the privileges of living in the building—so he wouldn't know I'd come out. I'd get a copy of the paper, some coffee, and sit in a window seat and watch him, see if I could find out what he was up to out there. If he was watching my building, he had to be trying to keep tabs on us. I doubted seriously anyone would be trying to keep an eye on Millie and Velma. But why, and for what purpose? He could be a cop—Venus trying to make sure we didn't skip town or something—but during Mardi Gras, the police force was stretched notoriously thin for parade duty. Locals always joked that during Carnival was the best time to commit a crime because the cops were all tied up with the tourists. Could they afford to spare the manpower to watch us?

I opened the back door to the coffee shop, which opened into a narrow hallway with the bathrooms and various offices and storage rooms opening off it. I walked up into the main room. There was a young guy with multiple tattoos and facial piercings typing away at a laptop in a back corner, but he was the only customer in the place. Darcy, a multitattooed, pierced, and dreadlocked lead singer for a local Goth band was working, and I got an iced mocha at the counter, grabbed a copy of *Gambit Weekly*, and sat down at a window table. I glanced out. He was still there. The same routine—eyes locked forward on the gate, every few minutes looking away to scan the street, and then back to the gate. I started flipping through the paper, trying to glance out the window every few seconds without being obvious. I felt kind of silly trying to hide behind a newspaper and be inconspicuous, but he didn't seem to notice me. I was about a third of the way through my drink when he glanced at his watch and turned to walk back up Decatur deeper into the Quarter.

I got up and walked out, spotting him turning the corner to walk up Barracks into the Quarter. I ran to the corner, dodging the festive partyers, and caught sight of the ball cap crossing to the other side of Barracks near the parking lot of the Richelieu Hotel. I tried to dodge around a crowd of drunks wearing those ridiculous hats that hold beer cans with tubes running down to the wearer's mouth, and by the time I finally got around them and looked again I saw the cap going around the corner at Chartres, toward Jackson Square. I started running, drawing some stares, and slowed down to a stop when I reached the corner of the Richelieu Hotel and peered around to see up the street. There was no sign of him. I jogged down the block and looked up and down Governor Nicholls Street, to no avail.

I'd lost him.

Nice work, Sherlock, I thought, as I stood there, scratching my head. How had he disappeared so completely? I hadn't been that far behind him; he must have ducked inside somewhere. I walked back down to the corner of Barracks and Chartres. All the houses were closed up and quiet. The balconies were deserted. The corner across from where I was standing was a private house and still. The other corner was an art gallery, also closed—which left the Richelieu Hotel. I walked back to the entryway of the big reddish brown building and went into the lobby. I looked around. There were people all around, talking and laughing. There were plenty of ball caps—Yankees, Dodgers, Alabama, Ole Miss, even Michigan—but no Saints.

I walked up to the front desk. "Um, excuse me?"

The young uniformed black woman gave me the big smile of a service employee who took pride in her job. She was slender, and her hair was cut very short. "Yes, sir? How may I help you?"

"Did you see a guy come in here"—even as I spoke, I realized how silly I sounded—"wearing a black leather jacket and a Saints baseball cap?"

Her smile faded a bit for just a moment as she assessed whether I was crazy, but it was probably not the strangest thing anyone had ever asked her. One of her eyebrows went up, and amusement danced in her eyes, and I realized I'd probably become one of her cocktail party "crazy Mardi Gras" stories. "No, sir, I don't believe I did. Should I keep an eye out for him?"

"Thanks, but no need." I gave her my best smile and walked away. There was a man sitting in a wingback chair wearing black jeans that looked kind of like the ones the guy had been wearing, but he had no jacket or cap, just a white T-shirt that read *Fuck you, you fucking fuck.* I sighed and walked back out onto the sidewalk. I looked up and down Chartres. He couldn't have known I was following him, so . . .

I stopped at the corner to toss my coffee cup into the garbage can, and that's when I saw it.

The cap was sitting on top of the pile of garbage inside. Looking around to see if anyone was watching, I reached in and grabbed it. I turned it over and over in my hands. It was just a Saints ball cap, one that could be bought anywhere in the city. There was no name written in magic marker on the inside—that would have been too much to hope for. It seemed relatively new. In fact, the price tag was still on the underside of the bill, but it didn't tell me anything, just the price—$12.95—and the tag was from one of those pricing guns any number of small stores in the Quarter use. I sighed.

Well, he might not have been watching the gate, I reasoned as I walked back home, feeling kind of stupid about the whole thing. *He might have just been waiting for someone, and that's just where he was standing. But he looked like he was up to something—and I lost him.* Stupidly I'd keyed in on what he was wearing. Some detective I was! I had no idea what he looked like and couldn't even really describe his physical stature. He was taller than those young girls, but that didn't mean anything. The jacket was kind of shapeless. *Stupid, stupid, stupid,* I berated myself as I climbed the stairs and unlocked my back door.

Colin was pouring himself a cup of coffee when I walked back in. "Where'd you go?"

I didn't answer at first, conducting an internal monologue about whether or not to tell him I thought someone had been watching us. Then I imagined the Scotty-is-such-a-cute-little-whack-job look he'd get on his face, and I made up my mind. "I just wanted to get some air." I shrugged. "Where's Frank?"

"Still sleeping." Colin yawned. "You want some coffee?"

"Sure, let me get my cup." I got my cup from the living room and refilled it while Colin splashed the liqueur into it. I took a sip and smiled at him.

"You sure you're okay?" Colin asked.

"I'm fine," I said, and we walked back into the living room, where we sat down on the couch together.

He draped a leg over mine. "You ready to have fun again tonight?"

I grinned at him. "Yeah." And then I thought, *Yeah, not saying anything was the smart thing to do. It was nothing, just my over-active imagination playing tricks on me again—it has been a rather rough twenty-four hours.*

"I just hope the cops aren't here waiting for us when we get home," Colin teased.

I stiffened. "Colin, that wasn't my fault."

"Easy there, bud!" He held up his hands defensively, a big grin on his face. "I knew when I signed up for this there'd never be a dull moment with you around, darlin'."

"Yeah," I said crossly. I looked into his face but could tell he was still in a teasing mood, and I didn't want to hear it. I pushed his leg off me and stood up. "I think I'm going to go lie down for a little while."

"Scotty—"

"Don't worry about it." I stalked down the hall, pulling my sweatshirt over my head and sliding under the covers on the bed. Frank was still sound asleep, and I lay there beside him for a moment, staring at the ceiling, and then Frank moaned a little bit and rearranged himself so that our bodies were entangled. I felt his warmth and relaxed a little bit. After a few moments, I felt myself getting a little drowsy. I closed my eyes.

I'll apologize to Colin later, I thought as I drifted off. *And everything will be fine. We'll have a good time tonight. . . .*

You'd think I'd have learned by now.

CHAPTER EIGHT

The Wheel of Fortune

the ups and downs of fate

"There." I stepped back from Frank's back. "You're done."

He turned around, looking down at his body. He looked incredible, even more so than usual. From the top of his head to where his legs disappeared into his boots, every inch of exposed skin was covered in gold body paint. The glitter I'd mixed into the paint sparkled and shimmered in the light from the chandelier overhead. Every muscle seemed to jump out with even more definition than usual. Oh, yes, I had been right to pick out these outfits. We were going to stop traffic. I stepped back and gave him a good, long, appraising look. The paint covered his scar, which gave his face a more benign look. He's a very handsome man with the scar—it gives him a rugged, masculine, testosterone-driven don't-fuck-with-me look—but he must have been amazingly gorgeous before he had it, when he was a young man. For a brief moment, I tried to picture him as he must have looked at eighteen.

Frank tugged at his swim trunks a bit in the crotch and gave me a sheepish look.

"I don't know if I can go out in public looking this—this *exposed*." He sighed. The trunks were a lycra-cotton blend and covered us like another layer of skin. Not much was left to the imagination—which was the whole point. "I feel like I'm practi-cally naked. What if, you know, I get *excited?*"

"You'll be even more popular," I teased.

"It's Mardi Gras," Colin said as he handed Frank a go-cup full of orange juice and vodka. The glitter on his shoulder caught the light and flashed red, blue, and yellow at me. "You look *fabu-lous*"—he was imitating my voice again—"and everyone's going to want you."

The crap I have to put up with! Why does everyone always like to tease me?

"Yeah, whatever." Frank looked at himself in the mirror, tugged at the crotch again, then reached inside and adjusted himself a bit. He took a drink and grinned at Colin. "Good drink."

"Thanks." Colin saluted us both with his own cup. "I have to say, we all look pretty good."

He was right; we did look hot. I didn't grow up in New Orleans for nothing, after all. I definitely know how to pick cos-tumes that worked. I picked up my own gold-painted hat with the two lightning bolts sewn on the sides and placed it on my head. I looked over at the boys. Damn, they were absolutely gor-geous. I said so and said another prayer of thanks to the Goddess. I am so blessed.

They looked at each other and grinned. They turned their backs to me, and each struck a double biceps pose. Their arms seemed to double in size, their lats fanned out, which made their waistlines seem to shrink by inches until they were almost nonex-istent. Definition carved deep canyons into their backs, and the snug trunks seemed to barely cover their round butts. The trunks also rode a little low, barely covering the top of their cheeks. If they slipped down even the tiniest fraction of an inch, tan line and butt crack would be exposed for everyone to see—and drool over. That would happen later, I knew, on the dance floor. There's nothing sexier than a shirtless man on the dance floor showing a bit of marble-white cheek. The low-riding trunks were definitely tantalizing and hard to look away from. They were going to be incredibly popular again tonight. Finally, I got my camera and snapped a picture. "Now turn around," I said, and they obliged, putting their arms around each other and mugging for the camera. We did the whole camera-costume thing—individual pictures, then me with Frank, then with Colin, before setting it on autosnap and taking some group shots.

"All right, are we ready?" I checked the little camera bag I had painted gold and tossed over one shoulder. I took inventory: house keys, ID, cash, joint for maybe later to relax a bit to help the descent from the drug heights. I had everything I needed. "You guys got everything? Check again to be sure." They both rolled their eyes and checked their own little camera bags and gave me a thumbs-up. "Okay then." I handed the boys their pills. "Okay, ready for blastoff?"

I usually don't like to take Ecstasy before leaving the house, but Frank had made that a condition of doing it again, which made perfect sense. No sense risking carrying it around, in case something happened and we got stopped and searched. Better to carry it on the inside. I could still remember the feeling of those pills burning into my leg while Venus and Blaine questioned me that morning. Better safe than sorry wasn't a bad idea. The joint was my little secret for later, and besides, it was just a joint; nobody gave a rat's ass about a little pot in the Quarter. There was always someone smoking pot on the balconies during Mardi Gras.

Frank looked at his pill for a minute, before popping it into his mouth and washing it down. He gave me a weak little grin. "All righty then."

"It'll be fun." I kissed his cheek. "Remember how much fun it was last night? Tonight's going to be even better." I touched his ass and went on. "Everyone is going to be so jealous of me with my hot guys." Sunday night was always fun on a nonholiday weekend—and during Carnival it was even better than Saturday night. Traditionally, Mardi Gras continued to build every night until Fat Tuesday. Every night the crowd got larger, louder, and more festive. Mardi Gras and New Orleans was working its magic on the tourists. Each day, they would be less and less inhibited, more relaxed, and even friendlier. That was the thing I loved the most about New Orleans. People for the most part were just out to have a good time and be friendly. It wasn't like that in other cities, but that, I guess, is just part of the magic of New Orleans. Guys who, in other cities, went out dancing with a major attitude and looked down their noses at everyone else came to New Orleans and seemed to leave the attitude back home. The crowd of gorgeous men out last night in the gay bars certainly hadn't seemed inhibited, and there would probably be even more of them out tonight. And we were definitely dressed to be noticed. I took my pill and washed it down with some of my screwdriver. "Let's go, boys."

There was just a hint of chill in the damp night, and I shivered as I closed the gate behind us. It wasn't uncomfortably chilly, probably in the high sixties—the tourists from up north would think it springlike—but I would have preferred a few more degrees of warmth. The night sky was filled with clouds, and I could hear the dull roar of Bourbon Street seven blocks away. Bacchus was rolling down Canal Street about now, which made this the perfect time to get to the bars. Later, after the mad crush of the thousands on the parade route descended on the Quarter, the lines would be around the block to get in.

We started walking up Barracks Street, and some drunk girls in their late twenties whistled and cheered at us from across the street. I grinned, and Frank turned and gave them a bodybuilder pose, which led to more cheers, and Colin and I joined in. All four of them ran across the street, slopping their drinks out of their cups, and bestowed beads on us, each one reaching up to kiss us on the cheek as she placed her bounty around our necks. "You boys gay?" one of them drawled drunkenly. I placed the accent as Southern Alabaman.

Colin cocked his hat to her. " 'Fraid so, ma'am."

"Well, that's a goddamned shame. If you change your minds we're staying at the Wyndham. Room six fifty-seven." She winked, then grabbed Colin's butt and gave it a good squeeze, and then they scurried off, laughing and hooting.

We looked at each other and started laughing, then kept walking. Several times we got stared at, but never in a look-at-those-freaks-Martha kind of way. Most people smiled, others yelled "awesome costumes!" and still others threw beads. Every time we passed a crowded balcony of partyers, we got requests to show more skin than we already were and got beads anyway after we declined. Some were more than happy to let us flex for them instead, before raining down beads on us. Both of the boys had these great big happy grins on their faces. It was like, somehow, they had no idea just how handsome and sexy they really were before tonight and all this appreciation for their oh-so-tender flesh. I watched them, returning smiles and saying "Happy Mardi Gras" to strangers like they'd lived here their whole lives. They were having a great time, like I knew they would, and we hadn't even gotten to the bar yet. And they were gorgeous men, and I loved them and they loved me right back.

I knew they'd get the true spirit of Mardi Gras, and I couldn't have been prouder.

We met David in front of the Clover Grill. He'd chickened out on the Mercury costume and was just wearing jeans and a white tank top. He just shook his head at us. "Look at you *whores.*" He shook his head again. "Once again, showing your-selves to be true representatives of the gay community—putting your best face forward. Is it any wonder people think we're all going to hell and are out to seduce their children?"

"Fuck you, David," Frank said, winking at me, and I knew what he was thinking. I laughed.

Obviously, the Ecstasy was starting to hit him—and he was awful cute and sweet when he giggled like that. He really was a handsome man, and so was Colin, and I was so lucky to find these two guys to share my life with. A big burly bear walked by wearing just overalls with one strap down to reveal his massive hairy chest, and he smiled and I smiled back and said, "Happy Mardi Gras," and he reached out and touched my chest and said it back to me. He moved on, and the crowd on the balcony at Lafitte's cheered. I looked over and saw beads raining down on a drunk fraternity boy holding his open pants up with one hand while he held a big cup of beer in the other and his girlfriend was catching the beads for him, and then a breeze came along, and the overpowering smell of frying grease from the Clover washed over me, but it smelled good, and I smiled at David and . . .

Okay, Frank wasn't the only one it was hitting.

We started up Bourbon Street, pausing under the balcony of the AMBUSHmag office. The fabulous drag queens up there cheered and tossed beads at us, and we waved and flexed for them, and a gaggle of hot shirtless guys in jeans walked by and grinned at us, and then we kept walking up the street, and there wasn't a line, so we paid our cover and went inside. When we got to the top of the steps I recognized the song playing, "Easy as Life," by Deborah Cox, whom I just loved, and I dragged the boys with me out onto the dance floor.

"Nothing in life is ever easy, nothing in life will ever run true," I sang along with Deborah, throwing my arms up in the air with joy. We started dancing, and then Deborah Cox mixed into another song. We climbed up on the stage and I stood next to a guy wearing jeans that were so low his big, hard dick was the only thing keeping them from dropping to his ankles, and we danced together. At some point he kissed me, and I just smiled back at him. The songs kept melting into each other, and I kept dancing, no track of time. This was some *fucking* awesome X. At some point, Frank made a signal that he was going to get some water, and I watched his head bob through the crowd on the dance floor. He kept getting stopped so people could grab his butt or pinch his nipples or stroke his chest and he had this huge smile on his face.

Then the next song was "I Want to Know What Love Is," by Wynonna, and I went into performance mode.

"It's gonna take a little time," Wynonna and I sang, and I raised my hands up toward the ceiling as the drum beat began, and the crowd down below me let out a cheer. I noticed Colin was dancing with some pretty young Hispanic boy who looked like he'd never eaten a French fry or cookie in his life, and I didn't know where David was; this Hispanic boy was totally his type. I kept dancing . . . and as the chorus crashed into gear, smoke flew out from the ceiling and the crowd cheered again and I was bouncing, jumping up and down. "I want to know what love is. . . . I want you to show meeeeee-ee-ee-ee-ee-ee!!"

And I gave myself to the music and the dance.

The high stopped rather suddenly, as it is wont to do sometimes, but I was still dancing, moving my feet but not as crazed as I had been. I realized Frank still hadn't come back. I looked at my watch and was stunned to see it was two-thirty; we'd gotten to the Parade around eleven. *That's strange,* I thought, and turned to ask Colin if he knew where Frank was.

Colin was nowhere to be seen either.

I kept moving but started looking around the dancing bodies to my right, in case I'd missed them. No, they weren't on the stage, and I looked to the left. Not there, either. I squinted and peered through the flashing lights at the dance floor. It shouldn't, I figured, be hard to spot them, even if they'd taken the winged caps off. I mean, how many people in the place were painted gold?

But they weren't on the dance floor either.

Okay, this was beyond strange—this was fucking *weird.*

They wouldn't have just left me, would they?

Of course not, I reasoned. They probably just went to get

water or something, ran into some hot guy, and were probably in a darkened corner of the bar making out. I couldn't believe that both of them would just take off with someone without telling me, though. They never had before, after all, but other than last night, they'd never been on Ecstasy before, either. Maybe I should get down and go look around. But then what if they came back and I was gone? It had never occurred to me that we might get separated, so I hadn't come up with a contingency plan. That was, sadly, a real rookie mistake. You *always* have a contingency plan in case you get separated. It was entirely possible they'd hooked up with guys and were gone for the night.

Which made me feel like an ugly stepsister.

I pulled away from the guy who had his arms around me and was grinding on my ass. I turned and gave him a smile. "I'm going to get some water." As soon as I said it I realized how dehydrated I was.

He gave me the lazy grin of the happily drugged. "Coming back?"

I nodded, knelt down, and stepped off the stage. I made my way through the crowd and stood on the edge of the dance floor. The bar section was crowded, but not so bad I wouldn't be able to get around it. I walked around and saw no sign of them. I ordered a bottle of water and asked the bartender if she'd seen two guys dressed like me.

She gave me my change and shook her head. "You know the rules—hold on to your husband, honey!" she shouted over the music.

I gave her a sardonic grin and walked to the other bar in the back. Not there. I checked the bathrooms and then went out onto the balcony. It was packed, and I had to fight my way through, but they weren't out there either. I managed to fight my way to the railing and glanced down into the crowd in the street. They weren't there either.

Another wave started to wash over me as I stood there, and I started bouncing a bit on my feet, dancing in place. Where the hell could they have gone?

I finally turned away from the railing, took a big drink from my water, and walked back inside. I walked over to the dance floor, but there was no sign of them. *Ditched by my boyfriends,* I thought, starting to get more than just a little bit pissed off. *They could have at least had the decency to tell me they were leaving, the rat bastards!* I considered going out onto the dance floor, but somehow, the joy of the evening was gone. I was still high, but I wasn't in the happy place anymore. I bummed a cigarette from a leather man even though I don't smoke, but I didn't want to just stand there looking deserted either. I looked at my watch again. Just past three. It was just so not like them to do this.

I decided to go down to the street and look around a bit for them, hoping against hope they'd be coming up the stairs when I descended, but no such luck. I walked out the exit and looked into the mob of people on the sidewalk and street.

My heart stopped for a brief second.

Misha was standing across the street. He was standing by the NO/AIDS table, which was abandoned for the night. He was smoking a cigarette and scanning the crowd at the intersection. He was wearing sand camouflage army pants and no shirt. *What the hell was he doing down here in the gay section? Did Aunt Sylvia know he was down here? What was he up to?*

I took a swig of my water and started walking across the street. Someone in a group of guys reached out and pinched my nipple. I grinned at him and kept walking.

"Misha?" I asked, as I got close.

He peered at me for a second. Then his eyes grew wide and he started backing away from me.

"Misha, it's me, Scotty."

He turned and ran.

What the fuck?

I took a deep breath and started running after him.

He wasn't going as fast as he probably could; he was wearing those big, thick army combat boots. He headed up St. Ann toward Dauphine Street. *Was he heading toward the house on Burgundy? I wondered.* But when he got to the corner, he turned to the right. Every running step was agony. I was in a lull from the drug, which meant that I was now fully aware that, in my feet, calves, and lower back, I'd been dancing nonstop for hours. But I kept going. Why was he running away from me? Why had he reacted so strongly to me? He hadn't reacted like this when Colin and I had seen him at Aunt Sylvia's house this morning.

Or had he? I wondered, trying to dig through my drug-addled brain to remember how he'd acted.

He *had* seemed ill at ease and uncomfortable, now that I thought about it. But I'd just assumed it had been the news about his brother, and having us show up unexpectedly the way we had.

But he hadn't acted afraid—which was exactly how he was acting now.

Afraid of me? Why?

It didn't make any sense.

I got to the corner at Dauphine and saw he was halfway down the block on his way to Dumaine. The street was fairly deserted, and I sped up, my feet and calves begging for mercy.

He turned right onto Dumaine, heading back toward Bourbon Street.

When I reached the corner he had made it to the crowd spilling into the street in front of Lafitte's. *Great, I could lose him there.*

I took a deep breath and kept running.

I slowed down, trying to catch my breath when I reached the corner at Bourbon. He was still running, now heading down Dumaine toward Royal Street. I took a moment to take another drink of water—I was dehydrated—and started running again.

He slowed when he crossed Royal.

I don't fucking believe this.

He stopped at the gate behind the Devil's Weed and pulled

something out of his pocket. He unlocked the gate and stepped through, slamming it shut behind him.

Another coincidence? How the hell did he have a key to my parents' back gate?

What in the name of the Goddess was going the fuck on around here?

There was no need to keep running, so I stopped and tried to catch my breath. I took another gulp from my water bottle, emptying it and putting it on top of a full trash receptacle. I walked casually down to the gate, using my own key to let myself in. I climbed the steps and unlocked the kitchen door and walked into the kitchen. I could hear voices coming from the living room. The light was on in the kitchen, and several empty wine bottles were lined up on the counter. Mom and Dad were night people, always had been, and stayed up every night until almost dawn, sleeping in till about noon every day. My mother likes to say, "No truly civilized person gets out of bed before noon." They stayed up all night, smoking pot, drinking wine, and talking politics, sometimes just the two of them, and sometimes they had friends over. As a kid, I'd gotten used to going to bed to the sound of voices passionately arguing in the living room. I always thought it was kind of cool that my parents weren't like other kids' parents, but right now I wasn't exactly so sure how I felt. I was in another lull, so I could think a little more clearly, but as cool as my parents were, it was still kind of weird to show up in their house practically naked and covered in gold body paint following a Russian.

A Russian they knew, apparently.

Misha was standing with his back to me, talking wildly.

Mom and Dad's living room is a huge room with high ceilings that opens out onto the wraparound balcony. They've never really cared about expensive furniture, and the art on the walls is primarily protest posters mixed in with Bob Marley, Che Guevara, and Franklin Roosevelt. Mom and Dad's politics were leftist just stopping short of communism. "Communism is good in theory," Mom once expounded over dinner, "but unfortunately human beings are easily corrupted by power, and once that corruption sets in, the system fails. Just like any other system of government. They're all good in theory, but most humans just don't live up to the ideals their government sets for them."

The room was full of pot smoke, and there were two open bottles of wine on the coffee table. Mom and Dad were sitting, listening intently to whatever it was Misha was saying.

"Then he chase me!" Misha said, gesturing wildly with his hands.

Mom looked up then and saw me. She got a big smile on her face. "Scotty! This is a pleasant surprise!"

Misha turned, and his face drained completely of color. His eyes got wide again, and he put his hands up in the air, backing away from me. "No, no, no! Please!"

"What is your problem?" I stared at him. "Why are you acting so crazy?" My cell phone started ringing in my camera bag. I grabbed for it. "Hello?"

"Scotty, where the hell are you?" It was Colin; in the background I could hear the music blaring. "I've been looking everywhere for you!"

"I'm at Mom and Dad's. You need to grab Frank and get down here." I hung up the phone and shoved it back into my bag. "Now, what the hell is going on around here?"

"Don't kill me!" Misha begged.

"What are you talking about?" I felt really tired. I sank down into a chair and looked at Mom and Dad. "Do you have any idea what's going on around here?"

Dad took a hit from the bong and blew the smoke out. "Sasha, this is our youngest son, Scotty. He's not going to hurt you."

Sasha?

"Wait a minute—hold on for one damn minute." I held up my hands. "Sasha? I thought Sasha was dead."

"Because you kill him," Sasha said, his jaw set, his eyes glaring.

Whoa. "Look, bud, I didn't kill anyone."

"Sasha, Scotty didn't kill anyone," Mom said, her eyes flashing. "That's just not possible. You're mistaken."

"I *saw* him," Sasha insisted.

"Wait a minute." My head was starting to hurt. "I am fucking confused here. If Sasha is alive, who the hell was killed last night?"

"My brother Pasha." Sasha was still glaring at me. "And you killed him."

Pasha? What the hell?

"Stop saying that! I didn't kill anyone."

Sasha looked at my mother. "Cecile, I call Pasha last night. He tell me Scotty there. He wearing Zorro costume—cape, tights, mask. Then when I came back to the house, I *see* man in same costume leave house. I go inside and find Pasha—dead." He pointed at me again, his hand shaking. "Because you kill him!"

I sighed. "Yes, I was wearing a Zorro costume last night. But I didn't kill . . . Pasha?" My head felt like it was going to explode. "Who the hell is Pasha?"

"There were lots of men out last night dressed like Zorro, Sasha," Dad said. "I saw quite a few of them. It's not like it's a really original costume or anything."

Sasha looked at my parents, and then back at me. "Maybe," he said slowly.

"Yeah," Mom chimed in. "There're always lots of Zorros." She looked at me. "That wasn't very original, Scotty." Her tone indicated disappointment, and the look on her face clearly was saying, *Didn't we teach you to be more original with your costuming than that?*

"I wasn't trying to be original; I was trying to be sexy," I said, through gritted teeth. "Now, will someone please tell me who the hell Pasha is?"

"Pasha my brother," Sasha said, seeming to relax a little bit. He peered at me. "Maybe not Scotty after all." He didn't seem completely convinced, but at least he wasn't calling me a murderer anymore. That seemed to be a step in the right direction.

"Hey, everyone!" Colin walked in, looking a little the worse for wear. His gold body paint had streaks in it, and his trunks had slipped down a bit, revealing a line of white skin and some pubic hair. He stared at Sasha. "Misha?"

"Sasha." He thumped his chest. "Me Sasha."

Colin stared at me. "Scotty, what the—"

"I have no fucking idea." I waved my hand. "Where's Frank?"

Colin grinned. "Um, he left with this hot guy from San Diego. I think he's staying at the Place d'Armes."

"What?" I felt a pang of jealousy. Sure, we'd always agreed that we didn't all have to be faithful to each other, but this was the first time any of us had strayed, and Frank was the last one of us I would have expected this from. Then I got over myself. Frank looked great; he was a sexy guy, and I'd dressed us all up in skimpy, sexy costumes. It was a wonder it hadn't happened last night.

But I still didn't like it—and I didn't like *that* feeling. It said something about me I wasn't sure I liked very much.

"He'll be home in the morning." Colin winked at me.

I let it go. I'd deal with it later. "Back to the subject at hand, will someone please explain to me who the hell Pasha was?"

"Scotty"—Mom took a hit off the bong—"there were *three* of them. Identical triplets."

"And just how do you know that?"

"Maybe it would be best if we let Sasha explain," Dad said, taking the bong from Mom.

Sasha sat down in a wingback chair and started talking.

CHAPTER NINE

The Magician Reversed

plans are poorly constructed

The room was silent, with only the occasional shout from the street downstairs breaking the quiet. I was twitching and about ready to scream when my mother poured a glass of wine and handed it to Sasha. He took a drink, gave her a smile, and she patted his shoulder. "Go ahead, Sasha. Tell him the truth."

Sasha gave me a shy smile. "It started when my mother died," he said, taking another sip of his wine. He flicked his eyes over to my mother, and she just nodded. He seemed to draw some strength from her, and something seemed to pass between them, but that could have been my imagination. "Five years ago. We live in Moscow. We never knew father. She always say he die before we born but would have loved us very very much. She teach ballet. In her day she prima ballerina with Bolshoi, but she injure knee and not able to dance anymore." He smiled sadly, remembering. "Apartment filled with posters of her. She was quite beautiful. Strict but beautiful—she tough, but always knew she loved us. She good mother."

"I'm sure she was," Mom said, sitting down on the arm of the couch and stroking his arm. She pushed a stray strand of hair out of her face and smiled at him. "I'm sure she loved you all very much."

"We all three big boys." Sasha gave me a rueful look, and that shy smile again. "But clumsy. She say she never understand how she could have such clumsy boys. But she want us to have good life. In Russia," he paused, "under old *Soviet* system the only way was sports or ballet. We too clumsy and big for ballet, she decide, so she decide we be in sports. She take us all the time to sports camps, to see if we could be Olympic athletes for Soviet. We wind up in wrestling camp. We naturals, coach say, and trainable."

"I was a wrestler," I said, without thinking. Colin slipped his hand into mine and squeezed it. I gave him a half smile.

Sasha smiled at me. "You have body for it, I think. Very nice body, compact and strong."

"Thanks." I *had* been a good wrestler, until I'd given it up my senior year. I got into wrestling because it was a socially acceptable way to roll around with another guy. Once I discovered the joy and easy accessibility of gay sex, I didn't need it anymore.

"So we train all time, go to school, far from home. Camp was in what now St. Petersburg. We not see her much, but all the time she write letters. Every day, she write letters. She tell us to work hard, do our best, and she proud of us. We exercise; we train hard; they give us shots to make us bigger and stronger. We get better and bigger all time. Then system collapse. No more money from Soviet. Some wrestlers go back to families. It hard for Mother to keep us in camp. She have hard time keeping students too. Terrible times, lots of troubles, no money. But she manage to keep us in camp. We keep train. We get bigger." He pointed to his chest. "Get big, like now. We all identical, look same, built same." He smiled. "Coach used to never know which was which. We play tricks on him, tricks on other wrestlers. We compete, but," he fumbled for words, "never good enough. We never make international team. Coach tell Mother put us in army; we better off there, never win Olympic medal. Then Mother get cancer." His face clouded. "Was terrible time. She dying, worry about what happen to us. So join army. Army makes us wrestlers again. Not much different as army wrestler than Soviet wrestler. Give us shots. Make us lift weights. We get bigger and bigger. Then she die." His eyes filled with tears, which he wiped away.

"I'm so sorry." Mom rubbed his arm again. "That had to be hard on all three of you."

"That when things change, when Pasha and Misha change." He gave a bitter laugh. "That when we find out Father not dead, still alive." He rubbed his eyes. "Father live in America. We find old letters. Life in Russia now bad. Barely enough money to eat. Had to have other family move into Moscow apartment, share with us, eight of us then in three-room apartment. Not enough heat. Not enough room. Terrible, terrible. Misha get idea to write Father ask for money. He rich American, Misha say. Maybe come to America, have new life for us. In America with Father. Me, not think such good idea." He sighed. "Mother always make sure we learn English. We never know why. Now we know. Misha say she have us learn so we can someday go live with Father, so he be proud of us. I tell Misha bad idea. If Mother wanted us to go to America why she never say? Why she say Father dead? But he not listen. Misha determined. So he write letter. Months go by, no answer. Misha work in information at army, so he start finding out on In-ter-net." He pronounced the word carefully, pausing between each syllable. "He find out Father have wife, other family. He say wife maybe not like that Father have sons in Russia, maybe Father not want her to know, that why he not answer letter. He say maybe Father pay us to not tell her."

"Blackmail," Colin interrupted. "Sasha, that's a crime in America."

"I tell him bad idea. If Father not want us, so be it. He forgot about us all these years, why things change now? But Misha not listen. Misha think he should pay." Sasha shrugged. "So, he write again. No answer. Then he decide that if Father not want to help us he write wife."

"I don't understand," I interrupted. It was a sad story, but what did this have to do with anything?

"Tell them, Sasha," Mom said, giving me a look that made me close my mouth. I hadn't seen that look in years. "Tell them who your father is."

Sasha wouldn't look at me. "Father name George Diderot."

"What?" My jaw dropped. I looked at my mother, then to Sasha, over to my father, who just shook his head sadly. My head started spinning. *"Papa Diderot is your father?"*

No one denied it. I closed my eyes and tried to wrap my mind around it. It just didn't compute. It didn't make any sense. That would make Sasha, Misha, and Pasha my mother's younger brothers—and my uncles. I felt sick. "I don't believe this. It can't be true—it *can't.*" Papa Diderot, that fine upstanding Uptown gentleman who believed in good, conservative family values, was nothing more than an adulterer with three bastard sons from a Russian ballerina?

Hell was surely freezing over.

"Scotty, it's true. I know it's a lot to take in, but it is true," Mom said. She got up and walked over to me, kneeling down right in front of me, taking my hands into hers. "It was a shock to me, too. But we"—she inhaled sharply—"had DNA tests done. Sasha and I have the same father. And if Sasha is my brother, then Misha and Pasha are too."

"Why am I just now finding this out?" I exploded. "How long have you known? Why didn't anyone tell me . . ." My voice trailed off, my anger starting to be replaced by something even worse. I remembered that first time I'd seen Sasha at Oz, the powerful attraction I'd felt for him, and my stomach began to churn.

The only reason I hadn't slept with him, hit on him, was that *he* hadn't been interested.

I had come this close to having sex with my uncle.

I wanted to throw up, to get up and run out of the room, down the back stairs and out of the house, screaming all the way.

This was too much to be borne . . . this couldn't be true . . . the one constant in my life had always been the family, and now . . .

"Scotty, you have to listen to me," Mom was saying. "We didn't want to tell you because we wanted the whole thing resolved before we said anything." She swallowed. "I know, it was wrong, we should have told you, but I didn't want you to be upset—"

"Does Papa Diderot know?" I choked the words out. I pictured him sitting at the dinner table, smug and fat and complacent, lecturing me on how I needed to go back to school, make something out of myself, and all the time he . . .

"It's complicated," Dad said, from the other side of the room. I turned my head and looked over at him. His face was grim, his lips compressed into a straight line.

"Misha wrote Maman Diderot." Mom sighed. She got up and walked over to the mantel, where she picked up my senior picture, looked at it for a moment, then set it back down and turned back to me. "When she got the letter, she called me in hysterics. I had no idea what was going on. She wasn't making any sense. She was just screaming and crying and I'd never heard her like that before. You know how she is, Scotty, always calm and quiet and gracious and never raising her voice. She was breaking things and screaming—I could hear things crashing in the background—and I had to go over there. This was three years ago. She was crazed, Scotty. I'd never seen her like this before. She was completely out of control. She'd just, I don't know, snapped. I didn't know what she was going to do. I tried to talk her down. I was afraid to leave her alone, even for a minute. She was threatening to kill herself, to kill Papa. . . . You remember when she went away for a few months?"

"I thought she—" I stopped. "You told us she went to visit a sick friend in Florida." I hadn't given it a second thought when Mom had casually told me over dinner one night, while spooning stir-fried vegetables out of her wok. Maman Diderot was always doing that kind of thing; that was the kind of thing ladies of her generation did. If a friend needs you, you go for as long as it takes. "You lied to me. You lied to me about it."

"Yes, Scotty, I did, and I'm sorry about that. You have no idea how sorry I am." She hugged me, getting gold paint and glitter all over her T-shirt. "I didn't want to—it was a strange situation, and I didn't know what to do." She shook her head. "I didn't handle it well. Hell, apparently I haven't handled any of this well."

I resisted the urge to push her away. "So where did she really go?" I said, in a quiet monotone. I wanted to scream. All of my life my parents had been so big on truth. And she'd lied to me. They'd both lied to me.

I could hear her telling me when I was a little boy, "Always remember, Scotty, that the truth shall set you free."

Yeah, right.

"She went—" she took a deep breath and her eyes shone— "she had a bit of a breakdown, Scotty, and I thought it was better if she stayed in a convalescent hospital for a while and got the help she needed." She stood up and picked up the bong, inhaling the smoke deeply. "I made some mistakes, Scotty. I didn't know what to do. I was furious—*furious*—at my father. How could he have cheated on her, had children with another woman, and *never* told her, never acknowledged them, just abandoned them to their fate that way? What kind of *parent* does that, can do that? It was like he was a complete stranger to me. And at the same time I wasn't sure, you know? I didn't *know* these guys were my brothers. Maybe it was all just an attempt to get money out of us."

"So what did you tell him?" Colin tried to put his arm around me, but I shook him off. I wasn't in the mood for being comforted.

She bit her lip. "I didn't tell him anything. I wanted to find out for myself. So, I wrote to Misha, asking for proof that he was who he said he was. At that time, I only thought, you know, that there was only one." She tugged on her long braid and laughed.

"I probably would have been right there with Maman at St. Rose's if I'd known there were three. He never mentioned in the letter to Maman that there were triplets. He sent me letters from Papa to his mother—love letters—but that was just proof of an affair, not of parentage." She took another hit, holding it in, then blowing it out in a plume slowly toward the ceiling. "The times made sense. I checked it out, you know? Put on my Nancy Drew hat and started sleuthing. I remember that my parents separated—"

"*What?*"

"You were a little boy; you don't remember." She shrugged. "Storm and Rain remember. They separated for a few months. I never knew the reason they separated was that he was having an affair. Maman never told me that. All she would ever say was he needed to sort some things out, and when he did, he'd come home. That's all. Turns out when the Bolshoi performed here— you know he's on the ballet board—he met Svetlana at a reception, and that was how it started. He followed her around the country on their tour—I gathered that from his letters—but when the Bolshoi went back to Russia, he came home, begged Maman for forgiveness, and she took him back. And that was the end of it." She reloaded the bong and took another massive hit. "They got back together. I never knew there was another woman until Maman showed me Misha's letter. Then it all came spilling out of her. She was like a crazy woman. I really thought she was going to harm herself, so I called Dr. Langdon and he came over and sedated her. Papa was out of town then—he was in New York—so I called him and told him Maman was going away for a while."

"You had her committed." It was like she was a completely different person from the mother I'd always known.

She ignored that. "And when she came back out, I told her that"—she bit her lip—"I told her the story wasn't credible. I figured I could buy Misha off, you know? I sent him money and asked him to stay away from us." She waved her hands. "You know we have more money than we'll ever spend. I told Misha I would send him a check every month as long as my mother was alive, *as long as he never contacted her or Papa ever again.*" Her eyes filled with tears. "Oh, Scotty, you have no idea how much I hated myself. I was no better than Papa, you know? I was *buying* them off. But I didn't know how Maman would ever be able to handle it, you know? But lies are always, *always*, a mistake."

"We thought it was all settled," Dad said. "But what we didn't know was that Maman was writing him too, and also sending him money."

"And you had no idea this was going on?" I turned my attention to Sasha. Colin was squeezing my leg, and I shoved his hand away. I didn't want to be touched. I know he was just trying to be there for me, and be a comfort, but I just wasn't in the mood. "Your brother was soaking my mother and my grandmother and you had no idea?"

"No." He shook his head violently. "Misha acting strange, but he never say anything to Pasha and me. And then Pasha start getting in trouble."

"This just keeps getting better," I moaned. My head was starting to hurt. I could feel another wave of the Ecstasy trying to take over, but I fought it off. *Deep breaths, Scotty, deep breaths. Hold it together; don't lose it.* "What kind of trouble?"

"Film company come to Moscow, look for actors. Easy money, Pasha say, but I not trust them. He want to meet them, so I go with him." He made a face. "They make sex movies, want muscular Russian boys have sex with each other to sell to people. Not for us, I say. Pasha say if people want to pay for his body, that fine with him. Why else have big muscles if not make it pay, he say? I tell him no better than whoring. He say our mother just a whore, why not him? No different than being athlete for state, he say. It not for me—especially when they want Pasha and me have sex together." He shuddered. "It *fine* with Pasha, he say. He out of control since we find out about who father really is, like he different person. He used to be such nice kid, but everything changed now. I beg Misha talk to him, but Misha want nothing to do with him."

"That's disgusting." Gorge rose in my throat, but I forced it back down.

"They pay us lot, Pasha say. I say no, but he make movies for them. They give him drugs. He start using drugs all time." Sasha covered his face with his hands. "And then Viktor Kafelnikov notice him, like him."

"Viktor Kafelnikov?" Colin sat bolt upright. "Not *the* Viktor Kafelnikov?"

"You know this guy?" I turned to Colin.

His face was grim. "Oh, yes. He's one of the head honchos of the Russian mob. An incredibly dangerous man."

Better and better. My head was really hurting now.

"He give Pasha money. Car. Furs. Jewels. And more drugs. Pasha get worse and worse. Pasha not seem to care what happen to him anymore. I beg Misha to help me with him, but Misha say he want nothing to do with Pasha—he not brother anymore."

"Then Aunt Sylvia and Maman decided to go to Europe." Mom sighed. "If I'd only known what she was up to, I would have stopped her. But she wanted to meet Misha, see for herself if he was really a Diderot. She and Sylvia cooked the whole thing up . . . the reason they were going to Europe was to help Sylvia get over Uncle George's death, but the real reason was so that Maman could meet Misha."

"I don't know that I want to hear anymore," I mumbled. I closed my eyes and leaned back in my chair.

"She was convinced once she laid eyes on him." Mom sighed. "There's something about the eyes—" I glanced over at Sasha and realized, with a start, exactly what she meant. *Sasha had my grandfather's eyes.* "And to make matters worse, Sylvia fell for him."

"Misha quite charming." Sasha nodded. "Ever since teenager, able to get women to do what he want. I not even know he went to Germany to meet them. He not talking to either me or Pasha by now. We not brothers anymore, he say, when I try to talk to him. Then he brag about how he get rich American woman to marry him, and he leave Russia and have wonderful new life in America, leave Russia far behind and pretend like he never from there to begin with. I not know why he act this way, like Pasha and me he ashamed of."

"So, just how exactly did you end up in New Orleans?" My head no longer hurt. *Shock,* I thought. *I am going into shock. That must be what this is. My mind is shutting down because I can't handle it. This is too much.* I shivered a bit, and Colin put his arm around me again. This time I didn't push him away. It felt warm, heavy, and comforting, and I leaned back into his bare chest.

"I find out about rich woman Misha marry." He smiled smugly. "Misha not smart as he think. I find letters. I get addresses. Then we have to leave Russia." His eyes filled with tears. "Pasha get bad, get worse. He no like Viktor anymore. Viktor make him do things he not like, then threaten him. Pasha tell him he going to leave, he want to get away from him, he want to have life back, but Viktor not let him go. He tell Pasha he kill him if Pasha try leave him—he kill me too. Pasha come to me, crying, scared. Viktor going to kill him, he say. He say Viktor make him do things—make him come on to men, then film them together and Viktor use movies to force them to do as he say. I did not know what to do." He looked at my mother. "I turn to sister."

"Sasha wrote to me," Mom said. She reached for the bong again. "You can only imagine how I felt when I found out that there were *three* of them. And then Sylvia comes home from another trip to Europe *married* to one of them." She exhaled. "Thank the Goddess for marijuana."

"But what about—" I rubbed my forehead. This was really too much, even for me. I've sort of gotten used to my life being insane, but this? "How did Maman feel when her best friend married—I can't even say it; I can't even fucking *think* it."

"Betrayed. She felt incredibly betrayed. I still can't believe Sylvia did it." Mom walked into the kitchen and came back with another open bottle of red wine. "I thought she was going to have another breakdown. They haven't spoken since then, not that I can blame Maman, I'm absolutely furious with Sylvia myself. How could she do that to her so-called best friend?" She refilled her glass and shakily took a sip. "Then Pasha and Sasha arrived . . . and it's not like I could confront Papa with them yet. Maman was about to go off the deep end again, and now I was going to spring two more kids on her? That she didn't know about? Her reaction to one was bad enough. . . . It's been hell, Scotty, you have no idea."

"Really." My tone was very sarcastic. I knew I was acting like an ass, but I couldn't help myself. How could they have kept this from me?

She gave me a wounded look. "So, I went to Misha, and you can only imagine how he reacted when I told him that I knew about the others, and that he'd been lying to us all." My mother got a grim look on her face. "I was ready to blow the lid off then—but I . . ." She stopped and started to cry—my incredibly capable, always together mother. I had never seen her cry before—and I stared at her, my mouth open. Dad walked over to her and put his arms around her and held her for a few moments until she got control of herself again. "I *couldn't* do it to Maman, so I made sure Misha put Sasha and Pasha up in the Burgundy house. I mean, Sylvia never used it anymore, and she'd never know . . . while we figured out what to do next."

"Stop for just a minute." I held up my hand. "Okay. I think I'm getting this." I wasn't, really. My head had stopped trying to grasp everything a long time ago. "But how did you turn out to be my drug dealer?" Something else occurred to me. "And I met you a year ago." I looked at my mother. "*Just how long has this been going on?*"

"We met accident." Sasha shrugged. "One night in bar. I not looking for you, but when I see you I know who you are." He pointed to my senior picture on the mantelpiece. "Recognize from picture. You come dance by me, and I think, *this my nephew,* so I friendly to you." He gave me that damn shy smile again. "I wanted you like me."

"Why didn't you ever say anything to me?" I glared at him. "I mean, we're family, and you never said anything. Ever. Not even a hint."

"I asked him not to," Mom said. Her voice was miserable. "Scotty, I know I handled this really badly, but I didn't really know what to do; you have to believe me."

"Yeah, and I'm too *fragile* to handle the truth, right?" I snapped. I was starting to get really angry, and I struggled to keep it down, keep it under control. Losing it wasn't going to change anything. I took some deep breaths and looked back at Sasha. "And why were you dealing drugs anyway?"

Sasha drew himself up proudly, puffing out his big chest. "I *not* sell drugs. I gave you drugs, but *Pasha* sold drugs."

"Like there's a difference?" I was starting to sound like Frank, but I was beyond caring. "So, when I was buying drugs, I was buying them from Pasha, but you were the one I met first? And why were you all calling yourselves Misha?"

"Um, that's another thing," Mom said. "Sasha and Pasha aren't exactly in the country legally. They came in on tourist visas . . . and just kind of, well, *stayed.*" She sighed. "I had Misha get duplicates of his papers, so that Sasha and Pasha would have legal papers. If they were ever asked, they were supposed to say they were Misha."

Okay, now I didn't want to hear any more. I stood up. "And I think that's about enough." I held up my hands as my mother opened her mouth to say something. "I've heard enough for right now, okay? Let me just recap, make sure I'm up to speed, okay? Let's see. My grandfather had an affair with a Russian ballerina. He knocked her up with not just a baby, but triplets. My grandmother knows there's one child, but not three. One of them married her best friend. My grandfather doesn't know they exist at all. The other two are in the country illegally—and my mother has helped them defraud the INS. One of them is my drug dealer, and the other one was murdered last night by someone we don't know. Have I missed something?"

"Well, there's more," Dad said, avoiding my glance.

"More." My legs buckled and I sat back down on the couch, hard. "Of course there's more." I buried my head in my hands.

"Viktor sent people after Pasha," Sasha said softly. "He said he would never let Pasha go. I see strange men watching house the last week. And Pasha"—he closed his eyes—"Pasha, he *stole* from Viktor before we left Russia."

"He stole from a Russian mobster." I heard myself saying the words. "I can't fucking *believe* this. It was the goddamned Russian fucking mob, right? That's who killed Pasha last night, right? Russian hit men, hired by some psycho gangster back in Moscow." I struggled to my feet. My legs were incredibly tired, and it took all of my strength to remain standing." I gave a bitter laugh. "Thank the Goddess Frank is off tricking." He would be *furious*.

"Scotty"—Mom gasped—"are you all right, honey?"

"No, I'm not all right. How could you possibly think I'm all right?" But the words didn't sound right. They sounded slow, like when I used to play my parents' old records on a slower speed. The words sounded muted and slow and deeper than my usual voice sounded, and I could feel the darkness starting to form on the boundaries of my vision. The room was starting to spin around me, and the colors of the curtains and the walls seemed to begin to bleed into each other. I tried to grab hold of the arm of the couch to balance myself. I was dimly aware of my mother lunging for me; of Colin starting to get up; of a strange look on

Sasha's face; and of a crash as my dad knocked the coffee table out of the way, sending the wineglasses, the bong, and the wine bottle crashing to the floor. Out of the corner of my eye I could see the green bottle falling, the label side up, as reddish purple liquid came spewing out of the neck in slow motion. Everything was in slow motion, and I knew I was losing it, I knew I was blacking out, I was tired and my mind was overtired and overstressed, and I felt Colin's arm go around my waist just as my legs gave way, and then the room started spinning, and as though from a million miles away I could hear people saying my name, as I tried to keep my balance, before it became a lost cause and I knew I was going to fall, as my dead weight sagged against Colin's arm, and in the distance I could hear drunken shouts from the street, and horns, and music was playing, and I crazily tried to recognize the song for a moment, and I kept falling, and then I knew the song—the song was "If Ever I Cease to Love," the Mardi Gras theme song—and I wondered if I was going to make it. . . .

Then everything went dark.

CHAPTER TEN

King of Swords

a man with the power of life and death

I had just stuck my head under the shower jet when Colin said something I couldn't hear.

I pulled my head back, wiping water out of my eyes, and said, "Huh? Sorry, I didn't hear you."

The hot water felt incredibly good as it streamed over my body. The water pressure was almost strong enough to knock me down, tired as I was, but he was standing right behind me. I leaned back into him for just a moment before balancing on my own feet again. The water pooling in the bottom of the tub was gold with flecks of glitter floating on the surface. Colin was scrubbing my back with a bar of soap. It felt really good.

"I said, it's really scary when you go into one of your trances," he repeated, as he massaged soap into my butt cheeks. "I mean, you're not out for very long—thirty seconds, maybe, tops—but it scares the piss out of me still, you know? Your whole body twitches, your eyes roll back in your head, and you mutter a lot. It's almost like you're having an epileptic fit. I don't think I'll ever get used to it."

"Really?" I hadn't given it much thought. Of course, I'd never witnessed one of my trances, just experienced it. It's been happening to me for almost ten years; I had the first one when I was nineteen. I was by myself when it happened, in my apartment in Nashville, when I was going to Vanderbilt. It *had* been scary for me; when I came out of it, I had no idea what was going on or what had caused it. I'd been reading the tarot cards for years, since a friend of my parents' had told me I was psychic and had sent me a deck, but that was the first time I'd ever had a direct communication of any kind with the Goddess. For a while, I'd been afraid that I might have one of the trances in a public place, but the Goddess was far kinder than that. She always managed to wait to talk to me until I was either alone or in the company of friends or family.

This time had been different, though. It was the first time I'd ever gone into a trance and come out of it not remembering anything—but I felt a lot calmer. "I don't foam at the mouth or anything, do I?" I asked. That would be all I needed.

This provoked a laugh. "No, you don't." He turned me around so the water was rinsing the soap off my back. "But it always gives me a jolt—I mean, what if something was seriously wrong with you and we just assumed it was another trance? How would we know?"

I'd never thought about that and shivered, despite the hot water. "I don't know. . . . Everyone always says they last less than a minute, so if I'm ever out for longer than that, better get me to the emergency room."

"Okay, you're paint free." Colin stepped back and grinned at me. "My turn."

I moved aside and let him step past me into the stream of water and brushed against his side as we switched places. He winked at me as he handed me the bar of soap and faced me. He leaned back and let his head go under the water. Streams of steamy water cascaded down his torso, leaving tracks in the gold paint I'd spent so much time putting on him. I soaped up my hands and started rubbing on his chest. The body paint washed off, exposing his olive skin, but I kept kneading his chest. Colin's body is thickly muscled, but he isn't ripped the way Frank is. When Colin flexes his muscles, the muscle cords become defined and the veins pop out, but when he's relaxed, his skin and muscles are smooth as silk. His muscles are hard and don't give when you push on them or squeeze them. It's like trying to squeeze a rock in your hands. I ran the soap over his smooth, flat stomach, and then down the legs. The soapsuds on my hands began to take on a golden, frothy hue, so I rinsed them off and started again. Colin moaned a little bit, and then I turned him around and started working on his back.

"Can you believe this?" I asked, as I slipped the soap into the crack between his cheeks and then out and down the back of his legs.

"That feels nice," Colin said, half drowsily. "Believe what?"

"This whole crazy triplet thing. Isn't this insane?"

He turned around and looked me in the eyes, laughing. "I think there's never a dull moment with you or your family, is what I think."

"I know. I cannot believe Papa Diderot—" I stopped myself.

"I think there's more to this than we think," he interrupted me and pulled me close so that our bodies were pressed up together, the water splashing into my eyes. "But we're better off out of it. If it's the Russian mob we're dealing with, we're better off leaving it to the cops. You don't know what they would do." He shuddered.

"How do you know what the Russian mob would do?" I reached around him and turned the water off.

We stepped out of the tub, and I handed him a towel. I started drying off my legs. "I've dealt with the Russians before." Colin shrugged, wiping the towel across his chest. "They aren't— they aren't nice people, Scotty. They kill first and ask questions later. If they even think you've betrayed them, they kill you. Bim, bam, boom." He rubbed the towel through his curly hair. "And I don't quite believe Sasha's story."

"Join the club." I pulled on a pair of gray sweatpants and tied the drawstring. "If Mom hadn't had the DNA test done, I'd be willing to bet the farm every single word he said to us was a lie. I mean, it was a good story and all, but I don't know. . . ." *He has your grandfather's eyes, Scotty. You know he's family.*

Colin put on his black sweatpants. "I don't trust him either. He knows more than he's letting on. Come on, let's go to bed."

We'd decided to stay at Mom and Dad's and take a nap before heading home. I hated the thought of Frank out with someone else—but I just needed to get over that. We didn't own each other, after all.

Sasha was being put up in Rain's old room for the night. The sun was just starting to come up as we walked out of the bathroom into my old room. The rest of the apartment was dark and silent. I switched on the overhead light. Mom and Dad had kept my room exactly the way it was when I'd moved out, which always kind of creeped me out a little. It was like a Scotty shrine—which was just plain weird.

But whenever I had to sleep there, it was kind of comforting.

Well, Mom had cleaned it, so it wasn't *exactly* the same. It had *never* been tidy when I'd lived in it.

On one wall was a poster of Mark Wahlberg from his Marky Mark days, wearing just a pair of Calvin Klein briefs and a big inviting smile. Over my desk was a poster of Scott Madsen, the original Soloflex model. My high school wrestling trophies and medals were scattered over the top of the bookcase holding all the books I'd read as a kid—everything from the blue spines of the Hardy Boys to Patricia Nell Warren's *The Front Runner.* Sleeping in my room was like stepping back in time. I turned down the covers and slid underneath. "I can't believe Frank didn't have the decency to tell me he was leaving," I said, pouting a little. *Grow up, Scotty!*

Colin reached into his little shoulder bag and pulled out his cell phone. "You weren't there, Scotty. We looked for you, but we just couldn't find you, and Frank did tell me, you know. I never knew you were so jealous."

"I'm not jealous!" *Liar.*

He dialed a number and just gave me that infuriating grin. "Hmmm. He's not answering. Obviously, he's otherwise occupied." He lay down next to me and put his arms around me. "Guess you'll just have to settle for me tonight." He nuzzled my neck. "Am I not enough for you?"

I pushed him away. "That's not it; you know that. But I'm not in the mood, okay? This has been a really weird night."

"Sure. Okay." He shrugged.

"Colin—" I stopped, not really knowing how to say it.

He put his hands behind his head. "What?"

I hesitated, trying to think of the right way to say it, and then plunged ahead. "How do you . . . how do you *know* the things you do? I mean, you said you've dealt with the Russian mob before. You know how to fix engines, you can hack into the INS computer, you can . . ." My voice trailed off.

He gave me a sad smile. "I also speak five languages fluently: English, French, Hebrew, Arabic, and German."

My jaw dropped. "How?" I grasped for words. "I mean, you never talk about your past, your family, anything." It was true. When he'd moved into the apartment upstairs from mine, there was nothing really personal there. No pictures of family—Frank had plenty. You couldn't turn around up there without bumping into Frank memorabilia. Photos of his dead parents, his sister and her family, his graduation picture from Quantico—there was no escaping it. But Colin had nothing—no college diplomas, nothing of a personal nature, like high school yearbooks and photo albums or anything. It was like he'd never existed before he came to New Orleans. He'd just moved in with his clothes, some CDs, and some books, but other than that, nothing. I'd noticed it—Frank had even said something about it to me once—but we decided to let Colin open up to us about his past in his own time.

"I wondered when you were going to ask. With your curiosity, it must have been driving you crazy."

"Actually, no." I shrugged. "I figured you'd talk about your past whenever you were ready to. But I really want to know."

He leaned back against the headboard and closed his eyes. "Are you sure you want to hear this?"

"Yes, I do." I sighed. "I mean, this whole thing with the triplets, I mean, I can't believe Mom and Dad kept this from me. I don't want *us* to have any secrets, okay?"

He sighed. "Okay. I was born in San Francisco. My parents were Jewish—Italian Jews whose families had gotten out of Italy before, well, before the war. I had an older sister and two younger brothers. When I was ten, my dad was killed in a car accident. My mom's brother had relocated with his family to Israel right before I was born, and my mother decided to move us there too after Dad died. She couldn't take all the memories in San Francisco, I guess." He gave me a sad smile. "I was fifteen when they all died."

"They died?" I felt a knot forming in the pit of my stomach.

"It was my brother Noah's birthday," he went on, his voice an emotionless monotone. "I had a test the next day, so Mom made me stay home. I was furious. They were all going to a movie and then out for pizza after. I was so angry I yelled at her, but she wouldn't budge. School was the most important thing to her, you know? So I stayed home to study and off they went. When it was time for me to go to bed, they weren't home yet—which was odd. It was a school night, after all, and Mom was always adamant about making sure, you know, that we all got a good night's sleep before school. After a while, I started to get worried. I called the pizza place they were going to but couldn't get through. I turned on the television. There was a special news bulletin." He closed his eyes. "A fourteen-year-old Palestinian girl had strapped explosives to her chest and detonated herself in the pizza place. And I *knew,* I just knew, they were all dead. A little while later, the police showed up and told me."

I opened my mouth but nothing came out. Anything I could say seemed so trite, so foolish. "I'm so sorry, Colin," I finally said, patting his leg.

A single tear spilled out of his right eye and down his cheek. "She was flirting with Noah, witnesses said, at the counter, and then she came right over to their table and just . . . blew herself up." He shuddered. "And I was angry, Scotty, so fucking angry. I hated them all—the Palestinians, the Arabs, all of them. And I wanted to make them pay. So I trained. I studied hard in school, worked out, studied self-defense and martial arts. After I got out of school I was in the army for two years. The Mossad saw something in me—I didn't care if I lived or died, and I was smart and I was skilled, so they recruited me as an agent. I went undercover, infiltrating their terrorist cells, killing when I had to. . . ."

"How could you go undercover?" The horror he was telling me—the only way I could handle it, digest it, was to keep my mind blank. I couldn't imagine how it must have felt . . . how I would have felt if Mom and Dad and Storm and Rain had been killed. "You don't look . . ."

"Arab?" He laughed a little bitterly. "I told you—I am fluent in Arabic. Yes, I have blue eyes, but contact lenses can change that. A little base make-up, grow out my facial hair a bit, and speaking the language . . . oh, yes, Scotty, it's very easy to pass. For seven years, I was the Mossad's best agent. I took the toughest assignments, the ones where the odds were so against my surviving, because I just didn't care whether I lived or died. I kept hoping that one day they'd find out and just kill me . . . so the pain and the hate would go away. But I was too fucking good at my job. I kept thinking, *'If I succeed, I'll be saving Israeli lives.'* I was dead inside, not capable of feeling, and then one day I was caught—and I had to kill or be killed." He closed his eyes again.

"I was caught talking to my superiors on a cell phone. My cover was blown . . . by a fourteen-year-old boy . . . and I had to kill him. As I held my gun on him, all I could see was Noah's face . . . and the boy was so frightened . . . and I couldn't do it, Scotty. I just couldn't do it. All I could see was my brother's face. He was such a bright kid, so sweet and kind and loving, and to die the way he did . . ." He wiped at his eyes again. "I couldn't kill this kid. I couldn't. So, I just knocked him unconscious and got the hell out of there."

"Of course you couldn't do it." I was taking deep breaths as emotions washed over me. I felt nauseous. My eyes were filled with tears.

"His eyes haunted me," Colin went on, like I hadn't said anything. "I took a leave and went away. To Greece. I hadn't felt anything in so long, Scotty. I'd been dead inside . . . but that kid . . . all I could think of was Noah, and my mom, and Rachel, and Abram. What would they think of the way I'd turned out? Would they be proud of me? And I knew. I *knew* they'd be ashamed. *I* was ashamed. I thought I was avenging them, protecting other families from what had happened to us, but the truth was I'd turned into a killer—and my job required me to kill *their* children. There was so much blood on my hands . . . I knew I couldn't go back. I knew I couldn't keep doing my job. I couldn't. Where was it all going to end? Hatred breeds hatred, violence only breeds more violence, and you just keep piling hate on violence and it can only end in a bloodbath, with everyone on both sides dead. On Mykonos, I met a Greek boy, nineteen, named Alexandros. I always knew I was gay, you know, but I'd never ever acted on it." He laughed. "I was a twenty-six-year-old virgin, if you can believe that. All I'd ever done was jack off when I got horny, but this kid . . . he was beautiful and he was very aggressive . . . wouldn't take no for an answer . . . and I wound up spending a couple of weeks with him. He taught me how to live again, how to feel—that life was something to be cherished and enjoyed. I called my superiors and told them I was resigning my commission and staying forever on Mykonos. I wasn't going back to Israel . . . and it was on Mykonos that Angela Blackledge approached me."

My head was spinning. I couldn't absorb it, take it all in. Colin, my sweet, loving boy with the big smile and the devilish sense of humor, was a killer—had killed. This same guy, who could make awesome brownies and always fixed my sister's car, in whose arms I'd lain and slept, whose warmth I'd cuddled up to in bed at night, and always, somehow, managed to make me feel safe and protected, had killed mercilessly—who knew how many people? How many innocents?

I remembered David once mockingly saying to me, "You know, you're the fag most likely to sleep with a serial killer."

He'd meant it as a joke, but he'd been right.

"So I went to work for Angela," Colin said. "And it was great, you know? Being a private eye, righting wrongs, and you know what? I'm good at it—and I can be proud of being good at it—but I could never really be proud of myself before. Oh, sure, I could always tell myself about all the lives I'd saved, but I was a killer—that was the bottom line. But all the skills I'd learned, to survive, actually came in handy for this line of work. And I never killed again, Scotty." His voice broke. "And then I met you . . . and Frank, and I found that I was capable of loving again, of falling in love and having some kind of normal life. And your family . . . taking me in and treating me like a member of the family without question . . . it was almost as though it were *meant* to be, you know?"

"Why didn't you tell me any of this before?" My voice was hoarse.

He looked at me. "Because . . . I never wanted you to look at me the way you are right now—like I'm some kind of monster." His voice broke, and he started to cry. He put his hands over his face and his body shook.

I sat there for just a moment and then threw my arms around him and pulled him in close, kissing the top of his head, my mind racing. I didn't say anything because I couldn't think of a single thing to say. He put his arms around me and we just sat there for what seemed an eternity in silence. *He's a stranger; you don't know him at all,* kept going through my head. *This man you've loved, you've made love to, been intimate with, has killed Goddess knows how many people, the hands that have explored your body have blood on them, and how many of them were innocent?*

And then a kind of calm came over me. *Imagine yourself in his place. Imagine being a teenager and finding out that your entire family was killed, blown up, for no other reason than being in the wrong place at the wrong time . . . that you could have been with them, but for the random choice of fate. How would you feel? What would you have done differently? Yes, he's killed, but is it any different from him being a soldier? Can you love someone who's served in a war and killed? Of course you can. Try to be a little more understanding. He's suffering, and he is a good person. He's proved that to you over and over again, and you couldn't have loved him if that were not the case. He needs you. He's just revealed himself to you, opened himself up the way you've wanted him to, and you can't just reject him—after everything he's been through in his life, you can't do that.*

I turned his face up so he was facing me. I reached over and wiped the tears off his face and gave him a smile. "Colin . . . how awful for you. How absolutely awful."

In a small voice, he said, "I do love you, Scotty."

I leaned in and pressed my lips against his and smiled. "I love you, Colin." I brushed my hand against the side of his face. "How horrific it must have been." I struggled to keep my voice steady. "How you must have suffered . . . it breaks my heart."

And once those words were out of my mouth, I knew I was right. He didn't need judgment; he needed compassion and love; he needed me.

One of the basic tenets of my belief system is that love and intimacy are the ultimate healing power. And if anything, Colin needed that healing.

"I love you so much," he finally said, stroking my hair.

"I love you too," I said. "I'll always love you, no matter what." I kissed his cheek again. "You can always count on that."

We lay down and I slid my arms around him.

I held him until he fell asleep.

And then I allowed myself to cry for him.

CHAPTER ELEVEN

Page of Swords, Reversed

an impostor about to be revealed

I woke up in the late morning.

The light coming through the windows was grayish, like it was going to rain at some point. I hadn't slept well—no big surprise there. I didn't feel completely rested but was wide awake—that horrible middle place where you know you're really tired but you won't be able to get back to sleep. I lay there for a few minutes more, hoping I was wrong, that sleep was still possible, but finally just gave up and got out of the bed.

Colin was still sleeping, his mouth open, his breath coming softly and a look of complete peace on his face. I stood there for a moment, watching him almost in wonder. Some glitter still glinted in his hair in the dull light. I don't know why I watched him. I still loved him. Was that crazy, knowing what I now knew? My mind kept darting back and forth, arguing with itself. I wondered how soldiers' wives did it; how they coped when their husbands came home from war. Obviously, they had to know that their husbands had killed people. Maybe they pretended to themselves that their husbands hadn't actually, that it was someone else who had done the killing. I couldn't pretend to judge Colin. I didn't know how I would have reacted in the same situation. He was a good person. My family wouldn't have taken to him so strongly otherwise; we may be a family of nutcases, but we're usually pretty good judges of character. I remembered, standing there, one afternoon when we'd dropped in on my parents and had lunch. I could picture it so vividly, he and my mother standing in the kitchen making a salad together, how easy they were with each other, just talking and laughing and having a good time. No, in spite of what he'd done in the past, he was a good person. No one was good enough of an actor to fool my mother, which also gave me pause about the whole Sasha situation. I was pretty sure he wasn't telling us the whole truth; but Mom seemed to believe everything he said. So, maybe I was wrong about him.

I walked down the hall to the kitchen and started grinding beans for coffee. The entire house was silent. There wasn't much noise coming from the street. Lundi Gras, Fat Monday, wasn't as crazy as the weekend. Even the tourists seemed to take the day off, until the parades started again that night. A lot of locals have cocktail hours around five for friends, and everyone usually winds up wandering home around nine to rest up for Fat Tuesday. The locals, from years of experience, know that it's best to turn in early and not overindulge on Lundi Gras. Fat Tuesday starts early in the French Quarter. Some people get up early to head down for Zulu and Rex on the parade route. Others get up as early as four to start putting on their costumes and make-up. The Society of St. Ann, a foot parade of celebrating people in costume, begins its bar-hopping route through the Quarter somewhere between eight and ten—one of its great traditions is its unpredictable start time. By eight, people in costume are everywhere—heading to breakfasts with mimosas, Bloody Marys, and Irish coffees, cheerfully toasting those up on the balconies, wishing each other a happy Mardi Gras—and it lasts all day until the bells of St. Louis Cathedral begin to toll at midnight, announcing the end of Carnival, and the streets empty. That's why the locals try to retire early on Lundi Gras. So, on Lundi Gras night, the vast majority of people out are from out of town, the ones who don't know that the best part of Fat Tuesday is the morning, which is fine with the locals, because that means the morning still belongs to us—well, us and the tourists who've stayed out all night.

I poured myself a cup of coffee and took it out to the deck after spiking it with Irish crème. There was a bit of a chill in the air, but it was also damp, the air heavy. The sky was full of gray clouds, but here and there the sun's rays shone brightly through holes, like the image of God in a religious painting. My parents' deck is a rarity in the Quarter. A door in the kitchen opens out onto it, and they have deck chairs and a table with a rainbow-colored umbrella. The deck can't be seen from the street. The house rises up all around it on every side. In the summer with direct sun, it can be completely unbearable out there. But on a cool morning, it is a little piece of heaven. There are ferns and plants in pots scattered everywhere; my father created a misting system for when the sun is strong to keep them from frying to a crisp. I sat down and sipped my coffee, trying to will myself to relax.

Last night hadn't been the first night I'd slept alone with Colin since the boys had moved to New Orleans, but it had felt strange. I didn't know if that was because of what Colin had told me—and I was still processing that—or if it was because Frank had voluntarily left with some guy last night. Something about that didn't feel quite right to me; somehow I'd never thought that *Frank* would be the first one to stray. Maybe I was arrogant, but it felt like I'd been betrayed. I guess I'd always thought I was the slut most likely to. Frank was such a stand-up guy, so committed to both Colin and me. Sure, he'd been on Ecstasy, which threw everything out the window. I guess I'd figured that Frank would never do it.

Which was incredibly self-centered and selfish of me.

"Get over yourself, bitch," I said out loud.

The door opened, startling me a bit. "Do you mind if I join you?" Colin asked. He was holding a cup of coffee in his hands. His hair was tousled, and there was still sleep in his eyes. He was bare chested with a pair of my old gray sweatpants covering him from the waist down. He looked tired, like he hadn't slept well.

"Of course not," I replied. "You have to ask?"

Colin pulled out a chair and sat down on the opposite side of the table with me. He wouldn't look at me, keeping his eyes down on his coffee cup. An uncomfortable silence began. I took a drink out of my coffee and Colin finally said, "About last night, Scotty . . ."

"Colin." I put my cup down and reached over, curling my right hand over his. I took a deep breath. "Thank you for telling me, for talking about something really painful. It was very brave of you."

"Oh, Scotty." His voice was quiet. "I was so afraid to tell you—and Frank. I mean, I *knew* I was going to have to at some point, but I just kept hoping I would never have to." He gave me a sad smile. "In a way, I feel better now . . . like a burden's been lifted off me."

"I love you, Colin." I meant it. "About Frank—"

"Scotty, I know how you feel." He gave a sad little laugh. "I know it's wrong, that we all agreed we could pretty much do whatever we wanted to, no explanations needed, no questions asked, but I really didn't like seeing Frank with that guy last night. I didn't like it one bit."

I stared at him. "I know what you mean. I've been sitting out here slapping myself around for being bothered by it. And this whole thing with the uncles . . . I don't know what to think of all this."

He gave me a lopsided grin. "Well, we can always do some more investigating." He finished his coffee and got up, rubbing at his eyes. "You want some more?"

I stood up, shaking my head. "No, honey, I think I want to go home. Let's grab some clothes and get out of here."

On the way back to the room, I opened the door to Rain's old room. Sasha was sleeping on his stomach, snoring softly, wearing nothing but a pair of green-and-yellow-checked boxer shorts that reached down halfway to his knees. I stared at his back. Yes, there were the scars from the steroid-induced acne I'd noticed before. *My uncle,* I thought and then closed the door back again with a sigh. *Why did you tell me your name was Misha?*

It was a *fucking* lot to take in. No wonder I was feeling tired.

We found some old LSU sweatshirts of mine in the closet in my old room, and we put on our gold-painted shoes. We looked completely ridiculous, but we washed our faces and combed our hair before climbing down the back stairs to Dumaine Street. But one of the nice things about living in the Quarter is that no matter how disheveled you might look, no one even looks at you twice. After all, it's not like it's not a common sight. We're so used to seeing strange sights we don't even blink. You see someone wearing what they were wearing the day before and you just assume they haven't been home yet. During Mardi Gras it's also not unusual to see a man walking back to his hotel in just his underwear, having lost his pants sometime during the night. It's never happened to me, thank God, but I've seen it a few times.

We held hands as we walked home, and his hand felt nice in mine. There were a lot more people out than I would have thought, but they were carrying plastic shopping bags rather than big-ass go-cups. Their necks were still adorned with beads, and every once in a while we'd pass a balcony with people out drinking and tossing beads down. The damp air got thicker as we walked, becoming almost a mist, not quite rain but wet enough to dampen my hair and form beads of water on the back of my neck. My legs ached from all the dancing and the blister on the back of my right heel had burst at some time, and it stung with every step I took. Finally we turned the corner at Decatur, and I got out my keys. I unlocked the gate and we headed for the back stairs. Millie was picking up trash in the courtyard, and she just gave us a wave as we started climbing the steps. She also gave us a bemused smile as she took in how we were dressed. I knew that look—she'd want details later, assuming we'd been on some sexual escapade.

The first thing I did when I got inside my apartment was check for Frank to see if he'd come home yet, but the place was empty and still. I stood in the living room for a minute, looking at the empty glasses we'd left and the empty tubes of gold body paint. Just over twelve hours ago we'd been getting ready for a fun night out on the town. I choked back a sob and then noticed the answering machine light was blinking. *Maybe he had called.*

The only message was from Venus, unfortunately.

"I don't care what time you get in, Scotty, I want you to call me as soon as you hear this message. Do not, I repeat, do not go to sleep without calling me."

Colin was starting another pot of coffee in the kitchen. "There's a message from Venus," I called to him as I dialed her cell number. He nodded as her line started ringing.

She answered on the third ring. "Casanova."

"Venus, this is Scotty Bradley." Colin brought me a cup of coffee and sat down on the couch. "You called me?"

She let out a long breath. "Scotty, are you at home?"

"Well, yeah."

"I'll be there in five minutes." She hung up before I could say anything.

I put the phone down. "She's on her way over."

"Did she say why?"

"No." I shrugged. "Who knows what's going on anymore?"

"Scotty"—he kissed me on the neck—"I know you're upset about all this family stuff, and I don't blame you. They shouldn't have kept it from you. But that wasn't your choice, you know."

I was getting really annoyed. "That doesn't make it right— and one of my uncles I didn't know about is dead."

He gave me a big hug. "It'll be okay, baby."

Venus was wrong. It was closer to fifteen minutes before I opened the door to let her and Blaine in. "Do you want some coffee?" I asked as we walked down the hall to the living room.

"I'll have some. Just black is fine," Venus said, taking off her jacket and sitting on the couch.

I went into the kitchen to get it, and Blaine followed me in. I got down a cup and started pouring while he watched me. I put the pot back and looked at him. "You don't have to watch my every move, you know." I knew it was procedure—they had to know where everyone in the apartment was at all times—but it wasn't like I was going to pull a gun on him or anything.

I was about to say that when he half smiled. "You *really* don't remember me, do you?"

"Of course I remember you." I rolled my eyes. "You're Blaine Tujague. You're a homicide detective. Sure you don't want any coffee? It's no trouble."

He shook his head. "And all this time I thought you were just being an asshole."

"What are you talking—" I broke off and stared at him. He'd always looked sort of familiar to me, but I'd never really given it much thought. Everyone looks familiar in New Orleans, and I knew I'd seen him in the bars a couple of times. I kept staring at him, and I got a sudden mental flash of him naked. "I've seen you naked," I blurted out.

Okay, I have to admit, I've seen a lot of men naked. I am even willing to admit that fact sounds pretty bad. I will even go so far as to say, yes, I am a slut. But just because I've seen a man naked doesn't mean I've slept with him. I was a personal trainer and aerobics instructor for years. I've spent a lot of time showering in gym locker rooms. One night, when I was at the Pub with David, I looked around the room and realized with a start that I'd seen almost ninety percent of the men in the bar naked. But I've seen more straight men naked and in their underwear, I would dare say, than gay men.

Which is truly a frightening thought.

"You remember?" Blaine had a huge grin on his face now.

"Well, kind of." I shrugged. It was weird. Despite the high number of men I'd slept with, I always remembered them. It was something I took a certain amount of pride in. I wasn't one of those people who fucked someone and then forgot that they ever existed or that it had even happened.

Blaine reached over and patted my arm. "You *were* pretty wasted that night." He shrugged. "I was, too."

I just gave him a lame smile, hoping that I wasn't blushing with embarrassment, and walked past him with Venus's coffee. I handed it to her and sat down. "So, why did you want to see me?" Blaine followed me in and leaned against the wall, watching me with that weird half smile on his face.

She took a sip from the coffee and then set it down on the table. "Something really weird came up in this case, and I was wondering if you knew anything about it."

I glanced over at Colin, who gave an almost imperceptible shrug. *Weird* didn't come close to describing my last couple of days, so I was curious to see what she thought was so strange. "Okay."

"We ran his prints—the victim's. Misha's." Venus looked from me to Colin and back again. "And there wasn't a match in the system."

"So?" I shrugged nonchalantly. "Why is that weird?"

"So we ran them through all the databases, and still nothing." She was watching me pretty closely.

"I don't get it." I looked at Blaine, who'd stopped grinning at me at this point, then back at Venus. "What's so weird about that?"

"He should have been in the INS database," Colin interrupted. "The INS fingerprints applicants for resident alien status now. Isn't that right, Venus?"

She nodded. "And what's weirder is we pulled up his info in

the INS database. The picture on file matches the victim's face, but his fingerprints don't. It doesn't make any sense." She rubbed her eyes. "Unless—oh, Lord, I don't even want to say it out loud; it's so crazy."

"Go ahead." I waved my hand. "I'm getting pretty used to crazy." I gave Colin a half smile. "You might be surprised."

"The only thing that makes sense, crazy as it is," she paused again, as though trying to gather her nerve to say it out loud, cleared her throat, and went on, "is if there were *twins*." She covered her face with both hands, dropping her head down. "I know, I know—it sounds crazy, but it's the only thing that makes sense. That's the only way the two sets of prints wouldn't match. The victim wasn't Misha Saltikov."

It was all I could do not to laugh. *If only it were just twins, Venus,* was what I wanted to say. I could sympathize—it wasn't going to be easy explaining this all to her lieutenant—but if the notion of twins freaked her out this much, what was she going to say when she found out it was actually triplets? That they were my uncles? And so on and so on and so on. Sheesh, what a fucking mess. I wasn't even sure I could keep the whole thing straight.

She went on. "It would be pretty simple, I suppose, for Misha to come over here, get all of his immigration paperwork put together, and then mail it or courier it out of the country so his brother could get through Immigration completely under the radar . . . but why would they want to do that?" She shook her head.

"Unless the brother wouldn't have been allowed to enter," Blaine said. He pulled out a pack of cigarettes. "Do you mind if I smoke?"

I shook my head. "Feel free." I don't smoke, but growing up over the tobacco shop as I did, smoke doesn't bother me. Yeah, there's the whole secondhand smoke thing, but as long as the air we breathe anyway isn't clean and pure of toxins, I don't worry about cigarette smoke. I got an ashtray out from one of the end tables and handed it over.

Blaine shook one out and offered the pack to Venus. She took one and gave me a guilty look. "I quit a couple of years ago, but—"

"Have you checked with the Russian authorities?" Colin asked. "Maybe it wasn't so much that the U.S. would have denied him entry; maybe he was trying to get out of Russia without *them* knowing."

"Yeah, I've got someone working on that." Venus inhaled and blew the smoke up toward the ceiling. There was a look of pure pleasure on her face, and then she regretfully stubbed the cigarette out in the ashtray. "And the house—the crime scene? It belongs to Sylvia Overton, if you can believe that. And even weirder, Misha—the one who's in the country legally—is here on a *marriage* visa . . . married to Sylvia Overton." Venus shook her head. "Do you know who Sylvia Overton is? Christ, this just keeps getting crazier and crazier."

I started to say something but Colin gave his head a little warning shake, so I kept my mouth shut.

Blaine took over at this point. "My mother knows Sylvia. Let's just say she's socially prominent and leave it at that. We've tried reaching her, but she doesn't return our calls. We've stopped by her home a few times, but there's never an answer when we knock and ring the bell."

"Really?" I sat up. "That's not good. I mean, we just saw Sylvia—when was it, Colin? I can't keep track of the days anymore."

Colin gave me a pained look. "We were there yesterday morning."

Venus's eyes narrowed. "And what were you doing there?"

"She's an old friend of the family," I replied. "She's my grandmother's best friend." Venus and Blaine were looking at me, both with that suspicious cop look on their faces. I looked over to Colin for support, but he had a sour look on his face. It was perfectly apparent that he hadn't wanted me to tell them anything about Aunt Sylvia and her husband. But I couldn't exactly stop now and pretend I hadn't said anything. "We were invited over for brunch. We just made an appearance; we were tired and wanted to get to bed, but I didn't want to just blow it off."

"And you didn't think it strange that her husband looked just like your drug dealer?" Venus started tapping her fingers on her knee.

"We didn't meet her husband. He wasn't there," Colin interrupted smoothly. "We only stayed for a few minutes, had a mimosa, and left. Did you even know she had remarried, Scotty?"

"No."

"Don't try to bullshit me, you two." Venus pointed a finger at me. "Scotty, you expect me to believe that the guy you got your drugs from is murdered, and you just happen to show up for brunch at the home of the woman who owned the house the murder took place in the next morning, and she just happens to be married to the twin of the victim? And you didn't meet him? Come on. How fucking stupid do you think I am?"

"I don't think you're stupid," I said carefully, my mind racing. "Come on, Venus! Be fair. Blaine just said his mother knows Sylvia. She's an old friend of my family's. I didn't know she'd remarried." It sounded lame, even to me—even though it was true. "I mean, I never pay attention to stuff like that. . . ." Why had Colin said we hadn't met Misha there? I was stuck, couldn't think of anything else to say that wouldn't dig me in deeper.

Venus shook out another cigarette from Blaine's pack, her hand shaking a bit. "You two are investigating this, aren't you?" She frowned. "And where's Frank?" She looked from Colin to me, and back again. "What's going on around here?"

I started to say something but Colin cut me off. "Frank met a guy last night and left with him and his friends. We're not sure when he'll be back."

Friends? This was the first I'd heard of this. I frowned at Colin, but he avoided my eyes.

"Yes, we decided to do some checking," Colin went on. "Wouldn't you have? You two had basically come over here yesterday morning and all but accused Scotty of killing his dealer. We found the same things you did, Venus—that there were two of them, and one of them had married Sylvia Overton. We'd been invited over there for brunch, so we went. Her husband wasn't around, and there wasn't any way to talk to her alone—she had too many guests—so we decided not to say anything to her. We didn't want her tipping off her husband. And we didn't know until yesterday morning she'd remarried. Scotty was just as shocked to find out as you were, Blaine. It didn't make any sense to us either." He spread his hands out in a gesture of confusion. "So we decided to leave it all up to the police to do their usual fine job." He gave her a winning smile. "Now, I don't understand why Mrs. Overton isn't returning your calls, or answering the door when you drop in on her, but it's also Carnival, so I doubt if it's anything sinister." He stood up. "Now, if you'll excuse us, we haven't been to bed yet, and we're kind of tired."

Venus and Blaine stood. I walked them to the door. Venus stopped. "I don't believe for a minute you three aren't looking into this," she whispered to me at the door. "And I don't think you're being honest with me about other things. I should run you in for interfering with a police investigation, but I know your goddamned brother would be at the precinct in five minutes screaming." She sighed. "So, I'm asking you to keep me informed of anything you find—and to be fucking careful."

"Cross my heart and hope to die." I smiled.

She just glared at me and then followed Blaine down the

stairs. I shut the door and walked back into the living room. I plopped down in a chair. "What next, chief?"

"I think we need to head back over to Sylvia's and have a little chat with Misha." Colin flipped his cell phone open. "I'm going to call Angela again." He walked into the bedroom to make the call.

I stared after him for a moment, a sharp retort on my lips. I got my cell phone out and called Frank's phone again. After a few rings, the voice mail picked up. I hesitated, wondered what to say, and then just hung up. Anything I might say would probably sound jealous or angry, and I didn't want to upset him. He had just followed the rules the way we'd spelled them out, and who was I to be jealous?

Feeling really ashamed of myself, I sat down on the floor in front of the coffee table and got my cards out. I cleared my mind of everything, all the doubts and fears, and said a quick prayer for strength, trust, and courage, then began shuffling the cards. I closed my eyes and tried to focus. I spread the cards out and began turning them over.

History repeats.

Pray for a brave heart.

The need for strength to do what is right.

Danger at every turn.

I stared at the cards and sighed. It wasn't as reassuring as I'd hoped. What the hell did they mean? I remembered that strange moment the other night when Frank and Colin had confronted each other—the blue energy that had crackled off the two of them, the feeling I'd seen that happen before, that the scene had once played out before.

Maybe I was wrong to trust Colin.

No, that was just stupid. Where did that thought come from? It didn't make any sense. . . .

He's lied to you before, more than once.

But why would he lie to me about Frank leaving with some guy?

No, I was just unsettled about things—that was all it was. The whole situation with the triplets had thrown me off my usual course.

But Colin had lied before.

We'd first met during Decadence. We'd both been dancing on the bar at the Pub. I'd felt a strong attraction to him almost immediately, and when we were done with our shift, he'd come home with me. Then, when I started stumbling over dead bodies, he took great pains to avoid the police. He'd explained to me then that he was a cat burglar, and was wanted. It wasn't until he turned up again in October that he told me the truth—that he worked for the Blackledge Agency, as an undercover operative, and he'd lied so his cover wouldn't have been blown. He'd sworn then he'd never lie to me or Frank ever again. I'd believed him, and so had Frank. Now we all worked for Angela Blackledge . . . and I supposed he hadn't really lied. He just hadn't told either one of us about his past. I could understand it, given how painful it was, but still, it was possible he was lying again.

Colin walked back in, holding his phone and frowning. "Angela's waiting to hear back from one of her contacts in Washington. But she agrees with me—she thinks there's more to Sasha's story than he's letting on—and she's not happy about it." He barked out a laugh. "And Angela is not someone to get on the bad side of."

"Yeah." I swept the cards up and wrapped them back in the blue silk I kept them in, then placed them back in their cigar box and slid them back under the couch. "So what do we do now?"

"Like I said, I think we need to have another little chat with Misha." He shrugged. "I'm going to jump in the shower real quick." He gave me a lazy little wink. "Want to join me?"

"I'll just wait till you're done." I waved at him.

He frowned. "Are you okay?"

"I'm worried about Frank!" I shrugged. "I know it's irrational but—"

He crossed the room and massaged my shoulders. "Scotty, what's wrong with you? You're not the jealous type. I told you—he just went off with this guy. He's okay. I'm sure I'm right."

I pulled away from him. "Then why isn't he answering his phone?"

He flinched. "Maybe he's sleeping?" He rolled his eyes. "I'm getting in the shower." He walked out of the room, leaving me staring after him.

CHAPTER TWELVE

The Chariot, Reversed

uncontrolled passion leading to one's downfall

It started raining on our way Uptown. The skies literally opened and water came flooding down in a deluge. Lightning crashed and thunder roared, shaking the windows of the car and sending some kind of subsonic sound to my nervous system, putting my teeth on edge. Colin still hadn't spoken to me, which didn't help my nerves.

Why was he acting so weird? Yeah, maybe I was being irrational, but I couldn't help it. I just had this feeling something was wrong. . . .

He'd turned the radio up loud in the car to preclude talking as soon as he'd started the car. After he'd gotten out of the shower, he'd gone up to his apartment to get clothes without saying a word, leaving me alone in my apartment with my thoughts. I got the sense I'd hurt his feelings, which bothered me, but I couldn't really think of anything to say to him that would make him feel better. I felt bad about it, but I couldn't help it. Sure, I could apologize, but I wouldn't mean it. Sure, I was sorry if I'd hurt his feelings, but . . .

Fucking get over yourself, Scotty.

It didn't help that I was emotionally fried and physically tired, which was definitely not me at my best. But listening to the loud music on the car radio was making me feel oddly better. A new

local station had debuted a few months earlier, all dance music—
and not the crap they played all the time in the straight bars on
Bourbon Street every day. I'd yet to hear Billy Idol's "Mony
Mony" or "Paradise by the Dashboard Light" on the station; the
people there played the kind of music the deejays in the gay bars
played, which was incredibly cool. Oh, every once in a while they
had to slip in one of those so-called sports jams straight people go
crazy about when they hear them at an NFL game or a NASCAR
race so that nobody would think it was a gay station, but I could
put up with that as long as it wasn't all the time. Dance music has
always connected with me; listening to it always improves my
mood and makes me feel better. That was why, I think, I always
did so well when I was a go-go boy. I could actually dance, as opposed to most of them, who just climbed up on the bar and
moved their feet in this weird zombie-like way or moved their
hips back and forth so their dick would just flop around. I *performed* when I was up on the bar. Then again, I also had never
had to use a vacuum pump to make my dick look bigger or the
cock ring. Getting up on the bar and having people look at me
with lust in their hearts was all it took for my dick to get semi-
hard and noticeable in my thong. I might not have been the
dancer with the biggest dick or the most ripped muscles, but I almost always got the most attention and, most important, the
most money. I missed it sometimes; it was fun being up on the
bar and having everyone's eyes on you.

Almost against my will, I started tapping my fingers on my
knees as the station played a dance mix of Celine Dion's "A New
Day Has Come," and by the time we turned onto Upperline
Street, I was singing along with the chorus. Colin pulled up in
front of Sylvia's house but didn't turn the car off. He smiled at
me, and I couldn't help smiling back. When the song ended, he
shut the car off.

"I didn't mean to hurt your feelings," I said, putting my hand
on his leg. Lightning flashed nearby, followed by a roll of thunder

so loud my ears rang. Car alarms started blaring. "It's just a lot to handle. . . . I'm really overloaded. I feel like my circuits are fried, you know?"

He put his hand on mine and squeezed. "I know, Scotty, you're dealing with a lot. And I'm probably being oversensitive myself. It's just—" He hesitated for a moment and looked out his window. The rain was coming down hard, thumping on the roof and spilling down the windows. "It's just that every time, you know, you act different around me now I think it's because of what I told you last night." He laughed. "Kind of self-absorbed of me, huh? No, Colin, Scotty's world doesn't revolve around you."

I couldn't help myself. I laughed. "Well, it kind of does—you and Frank, really. But all this crap about my grandfather, and Frank not coming home, and"—I pounded my head against my window softly—"why can't my life ever just be *normal?*"

"It'll all be over soon enough," he said softly. "Believe me." He undid his seat belt. "Come on, let's make a run for it."

"Okay." I leaned over and kissed him softly on the mouth. "I trust you, Colin—and I love you. Nothing's ever going to change that."

His face softened. "I love you, Scotty." He looked through the windshield at the sheets of rain cascading down it. "You ready to make a run for the front door?"

I nodded and opened my door at the same time he opened his, took a deep breath, and climbed out into the rain.

It had gotten colder since we'd gotten in the car. The wind was blowing hard, branches bending and waving, leaves being blown off and swirling in the wind. The gutter was full of water, and the rain just kept coming down. The lights were on in Aunt Sylvia's house. Even though I ran as quickly as I could up the walk, I still managed to get soaked. I rang the doorbell, wiping water out of my eyes and shivering a bit. My jeans were completely wet. Colin reached over and pushed a wet strand of hair off my forehead and grinned. "You look like a drowned rat."

"I feel like one." I shivered again and leaned on the bell again. I heard the loud chime ring through the house. "The lights are on, so somebody has to be here." My teeth started chattering.

I was about to reach for the doorbell again when the door opened, and Misha scowled as he looked at us. "What do you two want?" He folded his arms, blocking the doorway as though daring us to try to get past him. His eyes were icy, and his lips were compressed into a tight line. A nerve in his cheek twitched.

"Just to talk to you for a bit, *Uncle* Misha." I smiled. "Won't you let us in? I mean, since we're family and all." I stared at his face. Yes, those were Papa Diderot's eyes all right. Funny how all three of them had gotten his eyes—none of the rest of us had. We all had brown eyes, like Maman.

His entire body sagged, and his arms dropped to his sides. He looked down at the floor. "Oh." He stepped back and held the door open wide. "Come in." He gestured with his hand. I didn't waste any time getting into the warmth. "Could I have a paper towel or something?" I asked, dripping on the marble floor in the entryway.

He wouldn't look at me, but he gave Colin a once-over and then said rather curtly, "Wait here," before heading down the hall. He returned a few moments later with a pair of fluffy white bath towels, which he wordlessly handed to us. He stood there watching us, his arms folded, that same impassive look on his face.

"Where's Aunt Sylvia?" I asked, rubbing the towel over my hair and wiping the water off my face and neck.

"Today is the day she plays bridge." He folded his arms again. "So now you know the truth." He stood there, staring at me, as though daring me to say something.

"Can we go into the living room and sit?" Colin suggested, giving Misha his most winning smile. "I think we'd be more comfortable there, don't you?"

Misha stared at him for a moment, then shrugged. He turned

on his heel and stalked down the hallway. We followed word-lessly. I glanced over at Colin, who gave me a broad wink. I wasn't sure what we were supposed to be accomplishing here—but we were at least a step ahead of the cops. I was still a little cold but spread the towel out on the couch before sitting down and cross-ing my legs. I stared at Misha. His face was a little flushed. He was wearing a tight white T-shirt that strained as it tried to stretch across his chest. There were yellowed sweat stains under his arms and a spot of grease on the front. His jeans were also tight and faded, hugging his legs like lycra. He remained standing, arms folded, the muscles bulging. "So you know?" he finally said to me again. "How do you like the truth?"

"Why didn't you say anything yesterday?" I asked. "You sat there and lied to me, to us."

"It wasn't my choice." He shrugged, walking over to the desk and opening a drawer, pulling out a pack of cigarettes and light-ing one. "I didn't want to keep all these secrets. How do you think it feels not to be acknowledged by my family? Not good, I can tell you that. I hate all this deception, all these lies. All to pro-tect your precious grandmother." He spat the words out at me. "Like it's my fault her husband slept with my mother. Like it's my fault she's not emotionally stable enough to handle the truth. No, I didn't choose this." He stabbed at the air with his cigarette, dropping ash on the floor. "You Americans! You can't handle the truth. You coddle each other and pretend that life is wonderful, life is just great, and don't want to rock the boat, pretend every-thing is fine. Well, life isn't great. Life is hard. Bad things happen, and the sooner you all recognize that the better off you'll all be." He pounded his chest. "In Russia, you learn that life is hard. You have to be strong. You have to be tough."

The good feeling the music had given me in the car began to evaporate. I started to get a little mad. "How do you think your brothers feel about *you* pretending they don't exist?" I snapped. "Talk about secrets and lies!"

He made a contemptuous noise. "I do not pretend my brothers don't exist, although there are times I wish they didn't." His face reddened. "They are shameful, a disgrace to our mother's memory."

"That's not what Sasha says," I replied. Animosity was radiating off of him. I didn't like him at all, uncle or no. It was easy to believe what Sasha had said about him.

He stubbed the cigarette out viciously in a crystal ashtray. "Sasha is a liar. They are both liars. They always have been. They wouldn't know the truth when it slaps them in the face."

"Why don't you tell us the truth, then?" Colin said smoothly.

Misha sat down on the couch facing us. "Are you ready for the truth, Scotty? The truth about your precious family?"

I bit my lip and counted to ten. "Tell us." I forced a smile on my face. "I'm trying really hard to understand all of this."

Misha looked at me. "All right. We never knew the truth about our father until my mother died. Going through her things, I found the letters he wrote her." He rolled his eyes. "Till the day she died, she believed he was going to come for her, for all of us. She was a fool—a romantic fool pining away for a man who didn't want her." He looked away from me and lit another cigarette. Lightning flashed again, and the thunder rattled the entire house. "I have the letters, if you want to read them, if you don't believe me. All those years she waited for him, her rich American lover. Waited for him to leave his wife, come to Moscow and marry her, bring us back to this country. She wasted her entire life waiting. Although anyone could tell by reading his letters that he was finished with her. She was a regrettable episode in his life; he was never going to leave his precious family. Yet still she clung to that hope, when she should have just forgotten him and gotten on with her life, found another man. She was beautiful, you know. So very, very beautiful. And gentle." His face softened. "She could have had any man she wanted just by crooking her finger at him. Instead she chose to throw her life away on a man who wanted nothing to do with her." His face hardened again. "So, when she died and I knew the truth, I wrote him." His tone was bitter. "I wanted him to know she was dead. That she died waiting for him."

"The fact he was rich had nothing to do with it, did it?" My voice shook. "I'm sure you wanted nothing to do with his money, right?"

"My mother never took a cent of his money," Misha snarled, his eyes shooting daggers at me. "There we were, in Moscow, starving and struggling, while over here he was living in a mansion, not wanting for anything. None of you were. It was sickening. She wouldn't ask him for what was rightfully hers. And ours. So of course I wrote to him. Of course I expected him to take care of us. He should have. It was his responsibility. He owed it to us." He made a nasty sound. "And of course he didn't answer my letter."

"So you wrote my grandmother." I tried really hard to keep my voice from shaking. Mean-spirited as he was, he was right. Papa should have taken care of the triplets—they *were* his sons. And how could he have ignored the letter?

I always knew he was cold, but this was even colder than I'd ever thought him capable of being. He'd cut off my trust funds without a second thought when I dropped out of college, and although he'd never admit it, I was positive he'd convinced Papa Bradley to do the same. Not that it mattered; sure I'd been poor and there'd been times I couldn't pay my bills, but ultimately I was glad I didn't have that money. Sure, when I was living on ramen when clients didn't bother to pay me, I cursed at him as the water boiled and I added spices to the tasteless noodles to try to make it more edible, but now that I had a regular paycheck I was glad I'd gone through those poor periods. I'd had to make my own way, and there was some satisfaction in that.

But to just ignore the letters? To pretend that they didn't exist? What kind of man was my grandfather?

Misha stared at me. "No, who told you that? That isn't true. *She* wrote me. She told me she was coming to Europe with a friend and sent me a ticket to meet her in Munich. And so I went to Munich to meet her." He sighed. "I didn't know what to expect . . . but she was not what I was expecting. She was nice. Once she saw me, she said she knew it was true." He looked off into the distance and smiled a little, his face relaxing a bit. "She said I had his eyes. I was expecting maybe she'd create some kind of scene, call me a liar, but she was kind. She was upset, but she was kind to me. I had dinner with her several times, her and her friend Sylvia." He smiled at the memory. "She told me she would help me, but I couldn't ever come to this country. She would send me money, help me get out of Russia if that was what I wanted, but I couldn't come to the U.S. Maybe sometime in the future, but not then, she said. The time wasn't right, but one day it would be. And Sylvia . . . Sylvia was wonderful. I found myself caring for her, and after I went back to Moscow she wrote to me—such wonderful letters."

"Why didn't you ever tell Mrs. Diderot there were three of you?" Colin interrupted.

"I think one was a big enough shock for her." He shrugged. "There was time later to tell the whole truth." He shrugged again. "If the time was not right for me to come to America, then the time wasn't right for her to know there were three of us."

I bit my tongue. I was getting mad, and from past experience, I knew it was better to just not say anything. It was apparent to me that he didn't want to share in the sudden American wealth with his brothers. He didn't care about my grandmother's feelings. That was just bullshit, a way of justifying his own bad behavior in his own mind. Hell, I didn't believe anything he was saying. I glanced over at Colin. He had a skeptical look on his face.

"Maybe you just didn't want to share with your brothers," Colin suggested, smiling.

Misha's face darkened and he scowled again, the thick eyebrows coming together, his eyes narrowing. "Pfah." He waved at the air. "Sasha and Pasha—like they were anything someone would be proud to claim! Pasha, whoring himself out on films, taking drugs, sleeping with gangsters! Yes, I was ashamed of them. Is that what you want me to say? Pfah. But what can you do? They are still my *brothers*." He turned back to me. "You know your grandfather. Do you think he would be proud to have such men as sons? Do you?"

He had a point, although I said nothing. There was no way in hell I was going to admit to *him* he was right. For a brief moment I felt bad. I didn't like him at all, and the last thing in the world I wanted was to have him as a relative. He was nothing like Sasha.

"What was wrong with Sasha?" Colin went on.

"You met him, didn't you, Scotty?" Misha sneered. "You saw for yourself what he was like."

"Yeah, I met him," I shot back. "And you know something? I thought he was a really nice guy, sweet and kind—someone I'd be proud to claim as a relative." I was coming dangerously close to losing my temper, but I couldn't stop myself, couldn't rein it all back in. "I can see why you'd be ashamed of that."

"You know nothing!" he said, with a weary wave of his hand. "You know nothing of what life was like for us back in Russia. I may not be proud of my brothers, but what can you do?" He shook his head again. He tapped the side of his head. "Pasha was never all there, what you would call *slow*. I was oldest, then Sasha, and then Pasha. Such a sweet little boy—he would do whatever we told him to do. So, when Sasha wanted to make some money off Pasha's body, Pasha would do whatever he was told."

Colin apparently thought he might attack me, because I saw him tense out of the corner of my eye. Then Misha took some deep breaths, the redness faded from his face, and he shook his head. He turned his back to us and walked over to the mantelpiece and bowed his head. His entire body slumped, and then it slowly began to regain strength visibily. When he spoke again, his voice was calm. He didn't turn around, keeping his back to us. "Sasha is a liar, Scotty. From the time we were little boys, he always lied. Even when he didn't need to, when there was no reason to lie. Anything Sasha might have told you was a lie." He turned and looked at us both. His face was resigned. "You think I like saying these things about my brothers? You think I would say this if it weren't true?"

I wasn't convinced. I didn't like him and I didn't believe a word he was saying.

Colin shrugged, but his body was still coiled and ready to spring. "Sasha told us all about Pasha and the mobsters."

Misha sighed. "I don't suppose Sasha told you it was he who first gave Pasha the drugs?" I gave a bit of a start. Misha looked over at me and smiled smugly, shaking his head. "I didn't think so. Of course Sasha would never tell you something bad about himself. No, Sasha is a saint, watching out for poor dumb Pasha, and greedy selfish Misha wants nothing to do with his brothers." He snorted. "Yes, it was Sasha who first gave him drugs, got him hooked and needy to the point where he would do anything to get more. *Anything.* It was Sasha who started taking Pasha around to the clubs, introducing him to rich men with disgusting tastes. And when people would offer them money for sex—and there were a lot of them—Sasha would take the money and send Pasha off with them. Did Sasha tell you that part?" He laughed coldly. "Did Sasha tell you about how he would make Pasha strip down to a jockey strap and pose for the men? And Pasha was so desperate for the drugs he would agree to anything, anything at all to get his next fix. He used to let people burn him with cigarettes; there was a nice government official who liked to burn his muscles, to see how much he could take without crying out. Did Sasha tell you about him? No? And then there was the foreign diplomat who liked to tape electrodes to Pasha's nipples and balls and shock him. Did he tell you that?" He shook his head again. "And after the drugs, Pasha, never quite right to begin with"—he tapped the side of his head again—"he was just *gone*. Simple, like a child again—but worse than before."

I was so sickened I couldn't speak. *He's lying,* I told myself. *Sasha would never do something like that to his own brother. Not the Sasha I knew. It couldn't be an act—so Misha has to be lying.*

I wanted to throw up, to just jump up and run out of the room, out of this house, go back in time three days before I knew the Saltikov brothers existed, back to a time when all I knew of any of them was that one was my Ecstasy dealer and kind of a nice guy.

"Sasha was what you call a pimp, right?" He waved his hand at me. "What do you think of a man who pimps his brother for money?" He walked around until he was standing in front of the sofa facing Colin and me. "Is that someone you'd be proud to know, to call uncle? Tell me, Scotty! Is that someone your grandfather— *my father*—would be proud to call son? To introduce to the rest of the family?" He ran his hands over his head. "And you wonder why I wasn't proud of them? You wonder that I was ashamed of what they had become?"

These people are my relatives, I kept saying to myself as Misha continued with his rant about his brothers, and I gripped the arms of the sofa until my knuckles turned white. I looked over at Colin, but he wasn't paying any attention to me. His eyes were narrowed, and he was watching Misha. *No wonder Maman didn't want them to come to America.* I kept watching Colin. Something wasn't—

The French doors behind where Misha was standing exploded, sending glass fragments everywhere.

Misha pitched forward onto the glass coffee table, which shattered. His head hit the floor with a dull thud.

I just stared down at him. His head was inches away from my feet.

"Get down, Scotty!" Colin shouted, hitting the floor himself and rolling over to the wall.

I just stared at him stupidly. "What the hell—" I started to say.

There was a weird little ping sound, and then the lamp on the end table next to me went flying backward, crashing onto the floor and shorting out. The entire room went dark.

"Get down!"

I slid down to the floor and flattened myself out on the carpet. My heart was pounding, and I could feel vomit threatening to come up. My whole body was shaking. *Someone was shooting at us. And Misha . . .* I looked over to where he lay, not moving. A puddle of dark red blood was starting to spread under his head, soaking into the carpet. *That'll never come out,* I thought rather stupidly. *Aunt Sylvia's going to have to have that replaced.*

Something hit my hand, and I was startled to see it was a cell phone. "Call Venus," Colin hissed at me. I looked over at him. He was on his knees crouched down behind a reclining chair. He was fitting a gun with a silencer. "I'm going to go see if the coast is clear." He gave me what was probably meant to be a reassuring look, but it wasn't. His face was a rigid mask, and his eyes were cold, almost lifeless.

It was the expression of a man who was about to face death without fear.

This was the face the people he'd killed in Palestine had seen before he'd pulled the trigger.

"Are you crazy? You can't go out there!" I started to crawl over toward him, but he held up his hand, stopping me from moving. I gaped at him. *Where the hell did the gun come from? Where the hell did he get a silencer? What the hell is going on around here?*

"Stay put and call Venus and the paramedics." His voice was like cold steel. "Venus is speed dial ten." He rolled over to where the French doors were swinging in the wind. He peered out and then was out the door before I could say another word. I watched him until he disappeared out of my line of sight. My teeth started chattering again. The wind was blowing in through the open doors, picking up loose papers and blowing the ashes out of the ashtray Misha had been using. The curtains around the other windows began to dance as the wind grabbed hold of them and billowed them out.

Maybe I should go after him.

But I didn't have a gun.

My hands shaking, I turned the phone on and called Venus. I don't remember what I said, or what I did, but there must have been something weird in my voice. She told me to stay down on the floor, not to move, and to take deep breaths. She would take care of calling the paramedics and she would be there as quickly as she could. I said sure, that would be fine, everything was fine, I was fine, not to worry about me.

That accomplished, I closed the phone and looked over at Misha. I crawled slowly over to where he lay, and remembering my CPR training, I reached for his neck to feel for a pulse at the carotid artery.

Nothing.

He was still warm, but he was dead.

In the distance, I could hear sirens wailing over the sounds of the storm.

When I pulled my hand back, it was covered in blood. I looked at it for a few moments. It was dark red.

I just stared at him. He was dead. My uncle was dead. Another one of my uncles was dead. Three days ago I didn't even know they existed, and now two of the three were gone. But I wasn't feeling anything. Shouldn't I feel something? It didn't make sense to me. He was my *uncle,* for crying out loud. Why didn't I feel anything?

The pool of blood was spreading.

I felt eerily calm.

The French doors kept swinging in the wind. There was

another flash of lightning nearby, and then a roar of thunder that shook the entire house for a couple of minutes. All the car alarms that had stopped braying started up again. From my spot on the floor, I stared out into the gray rain, squinting. Where was Colin? What was he doing? Was he okay? Was the shooter still out there, waiting for me to stick my head up?

Finally I gave up trying to see him out there. The grandfather clock in the hallway started chiming the half hour. The rest of the house was still, no sound at all—nothing but the rain and the wind and the occasional bang of the French doors slamming against the side of the house.

I closed my eyes and prayed for my uncle.

CHAPTER THIRTEEN

Knight of Wands, Reversed

discord, suspicion

Colin never came back.

After what seemed like an eternity—but according to my watch was actually only about five minutes—I decided it was probably safe to get up off the floor and away from Misha's body. I slid up onto the couch, poised to dive back down if I heard another *ping*, but there was nothing. I sat there, trying to get my heart rate to slow down. *Deep cleansing breaths,* I kept repeating over and over again to myself, keeping my eyes closed as the sirens got louder. I flipped open the cell phone again and made sure not to look where Misha's body was. I dialed Storm's cell phone. I quickly explained what had happened and that the police were on their way already, and he told me, as I expected, to keep my mouth shut.

Like I didn't know that already.

The rain had stopped, and I kept my eyes focused on the French doors, expecting Colin to come back through at any moment. The cold wind was making me shiver again. I thought about getting up and closing the door, but that was a dumb idea. The cops wouldn't like me messing with their crime scene, and besides, it wouldn't help. The glass had been shot out. I could see the jagged pieces lying scattered all over the floor. I wrapped my arms around me and started rubbing them to try to get the blood flowing again, but I couldn't stop shivering. My teeth were chattering. My clothes were still damp, so I grabbed the towel Colin had left behind and wrapped it around me. It was no help; it too was damp. I heard a click as the central heating clicked on, and I checked around for a floor vent. I spotted one over by one of the windows and walked over to stand on it. Before long warm air was blowing up my pant legs and I wasn't shivering anymore.

Where are you, Colin? Are you okay? What's happening out there?

Car doors slammed out front. I didn't want to leave the warm air, but I was glad the cops were finally here. I breathed out a sigh of relief and crouched down, making my way out of the room, all the while listening carefully for more shots. Once I made the hallway, I quickly shut the door behind me and took a big, deep breath. Of course it was silly—shutting the door wasn't going to make the reality of what happened in there go away, nor was it going to make me any safer—but somehow having that door shut behind me made me feel somewhat better about everything.

Colin was fine—he had to be.

He's okay, I told myself as I wandered to the front door. *You didn't hear any more shots from outside, so he's probably perfectly okay, trying to figure out who was doing the shooting. He knows how to take care of himself. If nothing else, the little story about his past as an Israeli commando should make you aware of just how good he is at what he does.*

I opened the front door as Venus and Blaine came running up the walk, their guns out. I held my hands up. Some other cops in uniform were creeping around the side of the house, guns drawn, in their navy blue NOPD rain slickers. "I think the coast is clear." My voice was shaking. I swallowed and took a deep breath. "There hasn't been any more shooting. Not since, you know . . ." I let my voice trail off. "The body's in the sitting room, third door down the hall on the left."

Venus gave me a funny look. "Are you okay?" She was holding a cup of PJ's coffee in her gloved hands.

I turned my head. It seemed to take a really long time, but then her face swung into focus. "Fine. I'm fine, Venus." I gave a brittle laugh. "Colin—he went out after whoever it was. He hasn't come back." I swallowed. "I don't know what happened to him." I gave her a weak smile. "But I'm sure he's okay. Really. Colin knows how to take care of himself."

A young black cop stuck his head out the door. "The house is cleared, ma'am."

Venus and Blaine exchanged a look, and she said, "Stay here with him, Blaine. I'll go check things out." She went into the house and shut the door behind her.

Blaine smiled at me and touched my arm gently. "Why don't we sit down here on the steps, Scotty? You look a little green. You might feel a little better once you sit, you know? Just keep taking deep breaths. You're okay now. We're here."

"I feel a little green, but mostly I'm cold. I feel like I am never going to be warm again." I laughed. It was weird, the laugh seemed to echo in my head. I frowned, and it stopped. There was a strange buzzing sound in my head, and I shook it to try to get it to stop. Blaine was watching me, like I was an exhibit under glass or something, and it was bugging me. I was just about to ask him to stop staring when an ambulance roared up, followed by a fire truck. Blaine grabbed my arm and we moved back to the porch and off to the side from the front door and sat down in a porch swing. I sat and watched as uniformed personnel rushed past us. I felt like telling them that there was no need to rush, that Misha was dead and nothing they could do was going to change that— not unless they had the power to regenerate life—and somehow I doubted that. "Do you ever get used to it, Blaine?" I asked idly as the stretcher went by. "He's dead, you know. They won't need the stretcher. They're just going to pronounce him dead on the spot." *Dead, dead, dead.*

He looked at me strangely. "Get used to what, Scotty?"

"Watching people die." I pushed against the porch with my feet, and the porch swing began to swing a bit. "Do you ever get used to it?" I stared at him.

That weird look again, then he looked away. "I hope I never do."

"Huh. This isn't the first time for me, you know." I knew I was babbling but couldn't stop myself. He was sitting right next to me, our knees almost touching. Somehow it seemed that if I could just keep on talking, it wouldn't be real, that Misha hadn't been shot and killed right in front of me, that he wasn't lying in a pool of blood inside. *My uncle,* I reminded myself. *My uncle, my uncle, my uncle. Two of my uncles are dead and two days ago I didn't even know they were alive. Ain't life funny?* "Every time it happens I keep thinking, you know, this will be the last time, you know? But then it happens again, and it doesn't get easier. . . ." I shook my head. I felt that weird numbness I now knew to associate with shock. I started shaking a bit. The wind was starting to blow stronger and colder, and the air was heavy with moisture. "And usually when someone dies right in front of me they were trying to kill me, so I guess this time is different somehow . . . but it's the same, you know? So, yeah, I was wondering if it ever got any easier the more it happens. I mean, will there come a day when someone can get his brains blown out right in front of me and it won't bother me at all?" I was babbling out of control now.

"Hang on." He got up and walked over to Venus's white SUV and rooted around in the back for a few moments, as my teeth started to chatter. The thickening mist turned back into rain just as he stood back up, clutching a thin blue blanket triumphantly in his hands. He ran up the walk as he unfolded it and sat down again, wrapping it around my shoulders. For a thin blanket, it was surprisingly warm. He smiled at me. "That should help a bit."

The rain started coming down again in torrents as a van with the NOPD logo with the quarter moon and stars on its side drove up.

That was when I realized Colin's car was gone. I looked at Blaine. "Was a black Jaguar parked where that van is when you drove up?"

Blaine's eyebrows knit together. He thought for a minute. "No, should there have been?"

"That's where Colin's car was parked." My heartbeat slowed down a little. That was a good sign. Colin must have followed whoever had done the shooting. That meant he wasn't lying in the back of the house or in the side yard with a bullet in his head. Relief flooded through me and I relaxed, to the point where my body sagged and I almost fell into Blaine. I sat back up and gave him a sheepish smile. "Sorry about that."

"It's okay." He gave me a big smile. "You've been through a lot today. It's okay. Are you feeling better?"

"Yeah, I am." I shuddered again. "Damn. It was so sudden, you know? We were just talking and then the next thing I knew . . ." I closed my eyes and remembered the lamp exploding, the glass in the windows breaking, the look on Misha's face when the bullet hit him . . . and leaned over the side of the verandah and puked into the bushes.

I sat back up and wiped my forearm across my mouth. My stomach was still cramping, and I bent over at the waist to try to relax the muscles. "Sorry about that." I gave him a weak smile. "Couldn't help it." My mouth now tasted sour and I could feel a headache starting right in between my eyes—one of the blindingly painful ones that make you wish you were dead.

"It's okay." Blaine's voice was soothing. "Is there anything I can get you? Anything at all?"

"A toothbrush and toothpaste would be nice," I said, with a broken laugh as I pulled up my shirt to rub on my teeth. "And aspirin."

He handed me a stick of chewing gum. "Will this do? There's aspirin in the SUV, I think. I can go look."

I took the gum from him, unwrapped it, and popped it into my mouth. Almost immediately the saliva glands reacted to the sugar or the artificial fruit flavoring, taking away that wretched cottony feeling. My teeth, though, still had that raw after-puke feel to them. Blech. I looked out on the lawn. It was pouring, and the wind was picking up again. *Parade's going to be cancelled tonight,* I thought. "No, that's all right. You'll get soaked." I gave him another weak smile. "And if you caught pneumonia I wouldn't be able to sleep at night."

"I don't mind. It's no big deal." He stood up and gave me that high-wattage smile again. "Besides, I never catch cold." He turned up the collar of his trench coat and ran across the lawn.

He's awfully sweet, I thought, as I watched him jump into the front seat of the SUV and pull the door shut. *Why have I never noticed that before? I can't believe I slept with him and don't remember it.* I'm usually pretty good about things like that, especially when it's someone as cute and sexy as Blaine—and nice, too, for that matter. I tried to remember as the rain started coming down harder and water began to swirl around in the street gutter. I got occasional flashes of memory—Blaine dancing at Oz with his shirt off with a bunch of other shirtless guys; Blaine hanging out on the corner at St. Ann and Bourbon with a group of other guys; Blaine dancing onstage at Oz in a black jock, winning the Calendar Boy contest one Thursday night—but as for he and I interacting other than on murder investigations, my mind was completely blank.

Blaine climbed back out of the SUV and opened an umbrella but still moved pretty quickly to get back to the porch. He closed it and sat down next to me again. He offered me a small bottle of generic ibuprofen and a small bottle of water. I shook out four pills and washed them down with the lukewarm water. "Does

Venus, like, have everything you could possibly want in that SUV?"

Blaine laughed. "Actually, I bought that water yesterday and never opened it, left it in there. But, yeah, she's pretty much prepared for everything."

"Cool."

"It never gets easier, you know—when someone dies in front of you?" He shrugged. "It doesn't. The first time it happened, it was a little black girl in the Irish Channel. I'd been on the force for about six months. We responded to a call about a shooting, and it was a five-year-old-girl. Drive-by. Best we could figure, they really wanted her uncle, who was staying with them. She was playing in the front yard, and he was on the porch when they opened fire." He looked down at his hands. "Of course, they didn't get him. Just her. She died right in front of me." He gave me a sad look. "That was the hardest one, you know. But it doesn't get easier, ever. You think you'd get hardened to it, but you don't. It's always hard. It's worse when you're the one who shot them, though."

"So you've killed in the line of duty?" It was a morbid conversation, but I didn't want to think about my uncle lying in his own blood in the sitting room less than fifty yards away from where we were sitting.

He just smiled at me. "Can we change the subject?"

I shrugged. "Sure." I pulled the blanket tighter around me.

"So, when you and Colin got here, was Mrs. Overton here?"

That gave me a start. "Um, no, she wasn't." I thought back. Had Misha said anything about her? I couldn't remember to save my life. For all I knew, she could have been upstairs or in the kitchen when we were talking to him. I'd been so focused on getting him to talk, to tell us the truth, it had never even entered my mind that she wasn't around. I frowned and tried to remember. "You don't think—"

"Think what?" Blaine looked at me, his eyebrows lifted. He

had emerald green eyes, just like Colin. In fact, his coloring was very similar to Colin's. The same olive skin tone, the bluish tint of his cheeks when his beard was growing in as stubble, the reddish thick lips, the strong jaw—they could pass for brothers.

Brothers. Just the thought made me bark out a nervous laugh. I definitely had brothers on the brain. I took another swig of water. There was a thought trying to take form in the outer reaches of my mind, something to do with brothers, yet it was just out of reach.

"Think what?" Blaine pressed again, and the thought was gone.

"I don't know." I shrugged, frustrated. "I'm just wondering where she is, that's all." I looked out into the rain. "I mean, she's probably okay, right?"

"I'm sure she is. You must have been really shocked to show up here and see this guy, right?" Blaine went on. "I mean, you thought he was dead."

"Well, no. I mean, I knew they were twins. When we came by yesterday—"

"You came by before?"

I stood up, using the railing to help me to my feet. I was still wobbly. "Well, yeah. I mean—" I stopped myself. I could hear my mother's voice in my head: *Rule Number One is you never talk to the police, no matter what they say, unless you have a lawyer present. They will always try to get you to talk, to incriminate yourself, even if you haven't done anything wrong. They don't care; they're just trying to make a case no matter what, and if it means going after the wrong person they don't care. All they want to do is make their case and move on to the next one. It shouldn't be like that but that's how it is. They aren't bad people, after all, but they have a terrible job and they are overworked and underpaid. So, never, ever under any circumstances talk to the police without a lawyer present to look out for your best interests. The police aren't interested in helping you. They just want information.*

Sitting there, holding my bottle of water, I looked at Blaine, who was looking at me with that innocent half smile.

He seemed so nice, so accommodating. Running out into the rain to get me water and aspirin, being so friendly, telling me we'd slept together, establishing a bond—

Getting me to talk.

This was a crime scene. Misha was dead. I was here, on the scene. Two nights ago his brother was murdered, and I had been there as well.

I was prime suspect number one, and I was talking to a cop without my lawyer present.

"You're very good," I said, reaching into my pocket for my cell phone. "You almost had me convinced."

He gave me an innocent look. "What are you talking about?"

"Drop it," I said, a little sharper than I'd intended. "This conversation is over." I flipped the phone open, cursing myself for almost falling for the oldest trick in the cop book. Sure, I hadn't done anything wrong—all I'd done was, once again, be in the wrong place at the wrong time—but I had no idea what they were looking for, what Blaine and Venus were trying to figure out. I doubted they were trying to prove that I'd done anything, or had anything to do with Misha's shooting, but better safe than sorry. I hit the speed dial button and punched in three. Storm answered on the second ring. I walked away from Blaine. "Storm, I'm at Aunt Sylvia's and the police are questioning me." I took a deep breath. "Someone shot Misha, and I have no idea where Colin is. Can you get over here now?"

"Scotty, are you crazy?" I heard him take a deep breath. "I'm already on my way. I'm stuck behind the parade lining up—I'm trying to get around. Don't you remember calling me?"

"Oh, yeah." What was wrong with me?

"Don't say a word to anyone. I'm on my way."

I closed the phone and walked back to the stairs. "My lawyer's on his way over."

Blaine shrugged. "I don't understand. Why do you think you need a lawyer if you haven't done anything wrong?"

Now that I knew what he was up to, it was almost so predictable to be laughable. "Drop the act, Blaine. I'm not saying another word about anything until Storm gets here." I sat down next to him. But I couldn't resist. "So, when exactly did we sleep together?"

He looked away. "It's been a couple of years."

"How did we meet?" I pressed him. "And where?"

"At Oz. It was a Saturday night. In the summer."

"How did we meet?" I pressed, ninety-five percent positive he wouldn't be able to give me any details.

"On the dance floor. You were dancing with that friend of yours, the one with the dragon tattoo, and our eyes met and I came out on the dance floor and we started dancing together."

Oh, could he be any more generic? I rolled my eyes and gave up. He was going to keep sticking to that lame story, apparently, and I wasn't in the mood to trip him up. I was annoyed at myself for almost falling for it, but to give credit where it's due, he was very good. I stared at him, searching the recesses of my memory. Yes, I'd seen him naked, and then it came to me exactly where. I'd seen him naked in the locker room at my gym, more than once. If he hadn't thrown me by claiming to have slept with me, I would have remembered right away. No, we'd never had sex. I blew out a sigh of relief. At least I wasn't going completely crazy. In all fairness to Blaine, I would definitely have remembered having sex with him. He was too sexy to forget.

His face was almost cherubic in its innocence. He was definitely good-looking, and a charmer. He could probably get women to open right up to those eyes, those sweet facial expressions, never letting on to them that he was gay, just charming the confessions right out of them. Yeah, he was good at what he did, all right. If I hadn't almost fallen for it, I could admire his skill. Instead, it just kind of made me mad.

Venus came out onto the porch. She smiled at me. "You guys have a nice chat?"

I gave her a weak smile. "Storm's on his way."

She gave Blaine a quick glance and then turned her eyes back to me. When she spoke again, the friendly tone was gone from her voice. "All right, Scotty, you want to tell me what happened here? And what you were doing here?"

"I'm not saying a word until Storm gets here."

"Scotty—I know you didn't shoot him," Venus said. "I found the shell casings outside." She shrugged when I didn't answer. "The shooter was outside, just off the side verandah. I just want to get your recollections while they're still fresh in your mind. Did you see anything?"

I kept silent.

"Why were you and Colin here?" she tried again.

I turned and walked away from her, down the verandah to where it turned and ran down the side of the house. I heard her swear, something like "goddamned Bradleys, anyway." I stood there for a moment, staring, trying to remember everything that had happened. It bothered me that my memory was so sketchy. I supposed it was posttraumatic stress disorder or something. Yellow crime scene tape blocked off the area just outside the French doors to the living room and also fluttered in the wind and rain in the yard, where it connected some of the verandah columns with a couple of trees. Some guys with umbrellas and NOPD rain jackets were taking pictures out in the yard and others were sifting through the grass.

I narrowed my eyes. The shooter must have been near the tree where the techs were working, but that didn't make any sense. The house was raised; the verandah was at least three feet higher than the ground around the tree, and we'd been inside the house. I closed my eyes and tried to remember if the curtains on the doors had been open. I'd been sitting on the couch facing the doors, but for the life of me couldn't remember if the curtains had been open or not. I hadn't paid any attention to that, and once the shooting had started I'd dived for the floor. So, if the shooter had been out by the tree, he would have been shooting up at Misha, and that angle didn't seem right somehow.

I took a deep breath, closed my eyes, and tried to remember it exactly as it had happened.

I remembered the lamp on the table shattering.

The sound of the glass in the windows of the doors breaking—*had the curtains been open?*

I remembered the look on Misha's face as he was hit, the way his eyes rolled up as his body fell forward into the table just as I dove to the floor, Colin yelling at me to get down, and everything kind of moving in a weird slow motion.

I opened my eyes. The curtains *had* to have been open.

Because how else would the shooter have even known that Misha was in the room? Surely he wouldn't have just started shooting blindly into the room, with no idea of whom he was going to hit.

I shivered. Had it been the Russian mob? Just opening fire blindly through the French doors and hoping to take out everyone in the room?

But there had been only two shots.

The curtains must have been open but I couldn't remember.

And if the curtains had been open, Colin must have seen the shooter.

He wouldn't have gone outside after him otherwise. He was too smart and well trained to just run outside when someone was shooting unless he could see that the coast was clear. He wouldn't just run out into the line of fire. Colin was incredibly observant; he noticed things that most people didn't.

So, if the curtains had been open, he had to have noticed the shooter. But before or after the shooting started?

I shook my head. It didn't make any sense. He must not have seen anyone until after the shooting started.

Please be okay, Colin. I couldn't stand losing both you and Frank—

I stopped that thought dead in its tracks. *Frank is fine. He is just out tricking. That is all.*

Storm's silver Mercedes drove up, and I let out a sigh of relief. He opened an umbrella as he got out and had a big grin on his face as he walked up to the house. He nodded at Venus and Blaine as he walked past them and gave me a broad wink as he approached. "So, what fine mess have you gotten yourself into this time?"

I started whispering, filling him in on everything that had been going on since I'd last talked to him. He whistled several times—I left out the part about the triplets being our uncles. I knew he'd get pissed, and I needed him thinking clearly. I hadn't done anything wrong—at least I was pretty sure I hadn't—but there would be time to deal with all of the family nonsense later. I paused when the morgue guys brought the body out, and we watched in silence as they loaded it into their van. I felt like throwing up again but put that out of my mind and went back to my story.

Storm looked over at Venus and Blaine. "You haven't done anything wrong that I can see." He shrugged. "I mean, outside of maybe obstructing justice. And that's a stretch; you aren't required by law to keep the police informed of anything you find out in the course of your own investigation." He scratched his chin. "I don't like that one bit."

I hadn't told him about Colin's confession—no telling what the family would think; *I* still didn't know what to think about that—and just said, "And I'm starting to worry about Frank."

Storm laughed. "Come on, baby bro, how many times have you caused someone to do the same thing? Mom and Dad used to be terrified all the time when you didn't come home at night." Storm leaned on the railing and looked down into the rosebushes.

"It really surprises me that the Feds haven't turned up around here, to tell you the truth."

"The Feds?" I stared at him. "What the hell are you talking about?"

"Scotty—Russian mobsters?" He shook his head. "The Feds should be all over this, you know. And the triplets, well, they're Russian—foreign nationals. Who knows what they may or may not have been involved in back home. Pasha—it was Pasha, right? I can hardly keep them all straight—was involved with a Russian mobster. The Russian government has been trying to prove that the Russian mob has ties to the Chechnyans—and that just screams *terrorism* to me. Come to think of it, Homeland Security should have turned up by now." He shook his head. "Come on, let's talk to them." He reached over and rubbed my head. "I love you, little bro, but sometimes I swear I don't know how you get caught up in these things."

CHAPTER FOURTEEN

The Lovers

choice between vice and virtue

They say that confession is good for the soul, but I've always dismissed that as a ploy by priests to get people back into the church. All those years I spent in Catholic schools I never really took the confessional all that seriously. Besides, my parents weren't Catholic; they were pagans, and every day when I got home from school they spent a good hour "deprogramming" (their word) me from what the priests had spent all day drilling into my head. Rain, Storm, and I were sent to Catholic schools because their schools were better than what the city had to offer; however, my parents suffered tremendously with liberal guilt for doing it. (Mom and Dad did set up a scholarship fund for deserving students from poor backgrounds to go to private schools; that probably helped their consciences somewhat.) I never really minded the religious lessons we were taught; I learned the catechism and all of that stuff—I was even consecrated in the church (it was necessary for me to stay in the schools). Although I didn't really believe in what I was learning, I did find some comfort in the rituals. I liked listening to Mass, especially in the original Latin. I liked the cool outfits the priests and higher-ups in the church wore; all those rich vibrant colors and great fabrics. Of course, when the Pope came to New Orleans we all were let out of school to go catch a glimpse of His Holiness; same thing whenever one of the reliquaries came to town to be venerated. Mom always called those occasions "The Great Holy Tour," but I was always amazed at how the devout reacted: crying, swooning, and going into hysterics as the gold-plated box with this or that saint's finger or jawbone or toenail went past them. I also saw the merit of the confessional; you went in, admitted to your sins, and then the priest gave you acts of contrition and God forgave you. As I got older, I became a little more cynical about it. *How great was it to be Catholic? You could be a mass murderer as long as you went to confession and said a few "Our Fathers" and "Hail Marys."* But every once in a while, I would go to Mass at St. Louis Cathedral in the Quarter and lose myself in the pageantry and ritual. It was soothing.

The confessional was never really a problem until I hit puberty and started having feelings for other boys. Obviously, I knew what the Church's position on homosexuality was, so what was I supposed to say? I *knew* the priests, no matter how cool, would never approve or forgive my sexual attraction to other boys. By the same token, how was I supposed to explain my parents? How could I go in there and say, "My parents are pagans and every day tell me that everything I learn here about God is sexist, misogynist, racist crap and that the Catholic Church has been the single biggest instrument of repression in history?" No, that wouldn't go over too well with even the coolest of the priests. So I'd go into the little booth, ask forgiveness, and then recount minor things—swearing, yelling at my brother or sister, not honoring my parents, making fun of my teachers—those sorts of things. I just wanted to get it over with, get my assignment of "Our Fathers" or "Hail Marys" or whatever the priest wanted me to say and be done with it so I could get the hell out of there. In real life, I found that confessing to other people sometimes might make *me* feel better, but it didn't always have the same effect on them. Confession is not about the other person; it's about you.

So, I figured, it's just easier never to do anything wrong or hurtful to someone else so you won't ever be put in that position of having to clear your conscience.

Answering Venus and Blaine's questions about the shooting, on the other hand, wasn't making me feel much better about anything. I wanted to try to call Colin's cell phone, find out where he was, make sure he was okay, but I couldn't do that until I was done with them. At first, it was easy answering their questions. They just wanted to know about the shooting—how it happened, what we were doing, where everyone was when the shots started coming—those kinds of things. When they asked about Aunt Sylvia, I didn't know how to answer. I drew a complete blank. I just shrugged. "I don't know where she is."

"I know," Storm interrupted. "She's playing bridge at my grandmother's."

Of course, it's Monday—and Misha had *told us that right when we arrived,* I remembered. *How strange that I'd forgotten that.* Every Monday Maman's bridge club met at the big house on Third Street. They had brunch, drank mint juleps, gossiped, and played bridge until about three in the afternoon—or whenever they got too drunk to keep track of the game anymore. Even on Lundi Gras, they still got together. Papa Diderot always called them "the hen pack" and made himself scarce whenever they gathered in his house. "I can't stand the sound of their cackling; it cuts right through me," was what he'd always say when asked. What making himself scarce usually meant was heading down to the Boston Club and drinking Wild Turkey until he was poured into a cab later that afternoon. He always timed it so he arrived after the hens were gone; then he and Maman would stagger up to their bedroom and pass out until it was time for dinner and more drinks.

Blaine wrote down the address and phone number of Maman's house and walked down the verandah to make a call on his cell phone. I assumed he was getting someone to go over and let Sylvia know she was again a widow. *Better a cop than me,* I thought, shivering again. How exactly would Maman react to the news that her husband's bastard was dead? I tried to imagine it and couldn't.

"So, Scotty, what brought you and Colin over here this morning?" Venus asked, knitting her brows together. Blaine rejoined us.

"Well, as I said before, Aunt Sylvia—Mrs. Overton—is an old family friend," I said carefully, looking over at Storm, who nodded. "And yesterday morning, we figured out that Aunt Sylvia owned the house where—" I stopped. How could I say this without confusing everyone? They all looked at me, and I swallowed, took a deep breath, thought "fuck it," and plunged ahead. "Where who we *thought* was Misha was killed. And we found out that Aunt Sylvia had actually *married* him, which was kind of a shock, so we came over here to tell her. You can imagine my shock when Misha opened the door." It wasn't entirely untrue; I just switched out why we came by today for why we came by yesterday.

Venus and Blaine exchanged a glance, then Venus said, "And that's when you found out that there were two of them?"

I nodded. "And that's when we—" I paused and looked over at Storm, who was frowning. There was no getting out of this now. I was going to have to let him in on the family secret—if he didn't already know. I had to tell the cops—they were going to find out sooner or later—but I didn't want Storm to find out at the same time. "Can I have a minute alone with my brother?"

"Fine." Venus threw her hands up in the air. "Take as long as you want."

Storm and I walked back down to the corner of the verandah. I swallowed. *How much did Storm know about the family connection? It was possible he already knew, but better safe than sorry.* "You might want to sit down."

Storm made a face at me and leaned against the railing. "Nothing that comes out of your mouth is a shock to me anymore, little bro." He lit a cigarette and blew smoke out of his nose. His eyes narrowed. "Is this going to be one of those things that made me sorry I'm a lawyer?"

I gave him a faint smile. "Oh, maybe. This may come as a surprise to you, Storm—I know it did to me—but Misha is— *was*—our uncle."

Storm goggled at me. "What?"

One of the things I've always admired about Storm is his even temper. He never gets mad—about anything. He's always calm and rational, which is why he's such a good lawyer. Even when he was a kid, he never got angry—no matter how much he was provoked. So, I was hoping he would be able to keep cool about this. I explained everything Mom had told me the night before. As he listened, though, I began to get nervous. First, his eyes narrowed and his lips practically disappeared. Then his face went white, then red, and I found myself talking faster and faster. By the time I was finished I could tell he was about ready to blow his stack. He crushed his cigarette out with a vicious stomp of his foot. He turned and walked away from me for a second, then walked over to the railing and slammed his fist down on it. He turned back to me. "I. Don't. Fucking. Believe. This," he said in a low voice. He ran his hands through his hair. "You mean to tell me Mom's known about this for fucking *months* and never said anything to us? Ever?"

"Stay calm, Stormy," I said, shaking my head. "I know, I know. I was shocked—still am, in fact. It was quite a bit to take in."

"And there's *three* of them." He pulled a crumpled pack of Marlboros out of his pants pocket and lit another one with a shaking hand. He puffed away at it for a few moments until his head was half hidden in a cloud of smoke. But his face relaxed as he kept puffing, and I could see him pulling his head together. "Jesus Christ. I can't believe Mom kept this from us. So much for openness and complete honesty within the family, like she's been preaching to us since we were fucking born. Hypocrite." He started pacing again, flicking ash from time to time. "Well, you can't tell them *that*—about the family connection." He made a jerking motion with his hand in the general direction of Venus and Blaine. "That's all we fucking need." He leaned against the railing. He buried his face in his hands. "No, that's not right. Focus, Storm! You *have* to tell them about Sasha. If we don't tell them about all of this, they'll just find out some other way and it'll look bad for everyone—the whole fucking family. Shit, shit, shit. Christ, they could think Maman did this."

"Maman?" I stared at him. He had to be insane. I mean, sure, I guess there was a motive there—but Maman? I tried picturing it in my head. Maman was one of those old-school Southern ladies—white gloves, her hair always perfectly coiffed, shoes and accessories all perfectly matched, soft-spoken and gentle. It was next to impossible to picture her standing out in the rain with a rifle. "That's just crazy."

"Scotty, Maman is a crack shot." He gestured toward the crime-scene tape. "Shooting someone dead through a window? She could do it with one eye closed and a hand tied behind her back backward with a mirror and not even blink."

"Maman?" I stared at him. "No fucking way."

"Don't you ever pay attention at those interminable family gatherings?" He rolled his eyes. "I swear to God, if I have to fucking hear one more time about how her father used to take her shooting and hunting when she was a kid—Scotty, they used to go on safaris when she was growing up. She's hunted *lions*, for Christ's sake. Her and Papa Diderot used to take *their* kids shooting. Haven't you ever heard Mom bitch about how horrible it was that they killed wild animals all the time, and that's why she's a vegetarian? You can't tell me you've never heard *that* story. She tells it all the fucking time. It's practically a goddamned Thanksgiving tradition."

"Um, I always kind of tune Mom out when she's talking about Maman and Papa." It was true—I did. I'd heard the stories about how awful they were so many times that I stopped listening before I hit puberty, and pretty much erased them from my memory. The stories might have been different, but they always boiled down to the same theme: Maman and Papa were horrible, repressive capitalistic tools of the government who'd tried to brainwash their children into becoming card-carrying conservative Republicans like themselves. "But, of course," Mom would say, throwing her hands up in the air, "they're my parents and Goddess help me, I love them."

"Jesus, Scotty, Maman carries a *gun* now! A very ladylike pearl-handled revolver that will fit in any size purse. She never leaves the house without it, you know, in case someone tries to carjack her or mug her, she can blow a hole through him. She can also shoot a rifle, and, like I said, she's a dead shot." His eyes began darting back and forth as his mind worked. "And the other one was shot Saturday night?"

"Yeah." My head was spinning. The thought of my grandmother blowing someone away with the pistol she tucked neatly in her purse was something I couldn't quite wrap my head around.

"Shit. Pasha, Sasha, and Misha? Sounds like Donald Duck's nephews." He shrugged. "Well, she couldn't have done that. I can alibi her for Pasha. We were all at the preparty before the Endymion Ball, and there's no way she could have slipped out of there in her evening gown, gotten down to the Quarter and shot someone, then slipped back in without being noticed." He sighed. "Listen to me: I can alibi my grandmother. Those are words I never thought I'd have to say." He threw back his head and barked out a laugh.

"So, what should I tell them?" I leaned against the railing. My headache was coming back with a vengeance.

"Well, you have to tell them there's three of them—or were, at any rate." He puffed madly on his cigarette. "You know what? Leave the family stuff out of it. They might not ever find out about it and, hopefully, by the time they do, we'll know who was behind all of this." He tossed his cigarette out into the grass. "And as soon as we can, we're heading over to Maman's and we're getting to the bottom of this."

"You don't really think—" I stopped myself. I couldn't even bring myself to say it out loud. *Someone in the family could have done this. Why hadn't that occurred to me before?*

But then, of course, Sasha had thought I *had killed Pasha. . . .*

He glared at me. "I don't know what to fucking believe anymore. Come on, let's wrap this up so we can get the fuck over to Maman's."

To say that Venus wasn't happy to find out that it was actually triplets as opposed to twins would probably be an understatement. It looked like steam was going to start coming out of her ears, and, for a minute, I thought she was going to punch me really hard.

Actually, she was so mad she couldn't speak for a few minutes. She got up, paced around, and spluttered every time she opened her mouth. She even scared Blaine a bit. Finally, after smoking a cigarette and grinding it out under her shoe like she was pretending it was me, she calmed down enough to sit back down and smile at me. "Were you planning on reporting this triplet thing at any time, say, in the near future?"

"Well—" I stopped talking because I knew she was right.

Her eyes glittered dangerously. A vein in her forehead was pulsing. "So, let me get this straight. Pasha Saltikov was the one shot Saturday night. Misha Saltikov was the one who was just shot here. And the final triplet is Sasha?"

"Yeah." I thought for a minute, sorting them all out in my head. "Yeah, that's right. At least I think so."

"And where can I find this Sasha?"

Out of the corner of my eye, I saw Storm give his head an almost imperceptible sideways shake. "Um, in all the excitement last night, he just kind of took off." I shrugged. "I'll tell him to call you if I see him again."

"Great. Just great." Venus stood up. "Come on, Blaine." They started down the stairs. "I need you to stop by the station to give a statement. Feel free to bring the shyster with you." She turned back to me and got right in my face, jabbing me in the chest with a well-manicured nail. "And don't get any funny ideas, Scotty. I'm not convinced you're telling me the truth. I ought to run your ass in."

"On what charge?" Storm challenged her.

"Annoying the hell out of me." She turned on her heel and stormed off down the walk.

"Okay," I called lamely after her. I turned to Storm once they were safely in the SUV and on their way. "Any particular reason you had me lie to her about where Sasha is?"

Storm already had his cell phone out and up to his ear. He held up a hand to shut me up. "Hello, Mother, dear. Can you, Dad, and dear, dear *Uncle* Sasha meet Scotty and me over at Maman's? We're heading over there right now." His voice dripped with sarcasm. He clicked the phone off. Almost immediately it started ringing. He glanced at the caller ID and grinned before turning the phone off completely. "They'll be there." He turned it off.

We ran through the rain to his car, and he turned the heater on full blast. "We're going to Maman's?" I asked, through chattering teeth. I still had the police blanket but it was wet. Shivering, I tossed it behind the seat and turned the vents so they blew hot air right at me. I wasn't looking forward to this.

"Oh, hell, yeah." Storm made a U-turn and floored the accelerator, spinning the tires on the wet pavement. "Time for a fucking family meeting."

I chose not to point out that Rain wouldn't be there, so technically it wasn't a real family meeting.

Maman and Papa Diderot lived on Third Street in the Garden District. The house had belonged to the Diderots since they built it just before the Civil War, with what my mother always disdainfully referred to as "slave money." It was gorgeous, a raised three-story Greek Revival American "cottage" with a wide front porch, set back behind a circular drive with lush bushes surrounding the house on every side. Huge old swamp oaks shaded the big expanse of lush green grass to its left. The entire yard was closed in with a black wrought iron fence that tilted and leaned in some places. The house itself was painted white, with window shutters a dark emerald green. There was a brass plaque mounted in the fence next to the front gate, describing the original owners and naming the architect who built it. The plaque, from the National Historic Society, honored the house as a historic landmark. I've loved the old house, with its high ceilings and hardwood floors and massive rooms, since I was a little boy, even though it was always dark inside. The thick, heavily brocaded curtains were always drawn, shutting out the light. We weren't allowed to act like kids inside the house; all the furniture was old and valuable and Maman was deathly afraid we'd break something. We also weren't allowed to play in the side yard where anyone could see us; we were only allowed in the backyard, with its high bushes shielding us from the view of any wide-eyed tourist driving past. The house always seemed to me to cry out to be allowed to live again—for the rooms to be filled with the light the windows were designed to let in. It always kind of seemed like a museum inside. If I lived there I would open all the windows and let in the light and fresh air.

The round drive at Maman's house was practically empty of cars when Storm made the turn into it almost on two wheels. But I recognized Rain's Range Rover parked under the awning, and Storm almost hit it from behind when he slammed the car into park. He was out of the car and climbing the steps two at a time before I could get my seat belt off. He unlocked the front door and left it open for me as I scrambled to catch up. I could hear voices coming from the ladies' sitting room, as Maman liked to call it, up ahead and down the hall to the left.

"I should have gone with her," I heard Maman say as Storm and I walked through the door. She was holding a highball glass in her hand, and she finished the amber liquid in it with a skilled toss of her head. She was wearing a gray silk dress, pearls at her throat. Her face was perfectly made up, every white hair in place on her head. Rain was sitting, her legs curled underneath her, on the green and gold brocade couch.

"Hey guys," Rain said, a strange look on her face. "You wouldn't believe what just happened—"

"Aunt Sylvia's husband was shot and killed, and she's on her way to the morgue to identify the body." Storm's voice was harsh. He jerked a thumb at me. "Guess who was there when he was shot?"

Maman's glass dropped, shattering on the floor. Her hand went to her throat and her face went pale. "Scotty, darling, are you all right?"

"A little shaky, but okay." I sat down in a wingback chair.

"Storm, what the hell—" Rain started, but Maman interrupted her.

"Language, young lady." She pressed the buzzer on her desk that summoned Helga, the housekeeper. "Do you need a drink, darling? Storm?"

"Bourbon, please," Storm replied, and when she turned to me, I nodded. She filled two glasses with ice and bourbon just as Helga walked in. She handed us our glasses and she turned to Helga. "Helga, dear, I broke a glass. Would you be an angel and take care of it?"

Helga had worked for my grandparents as long as I could remember. She was originally from Sweden, and she was a little shy of her heavily accented English, so she didn't speak much. When we were little, she used to take us in the kitchen and give us chocolate milk and sugar cookies. She looked pretty much the same as she had when I was a kid, except for the gray in her hair and the telltale wrinkles and the thickening of her waist and hips.

She glanced at me and gave me a little smile before nodding and silently disappearing back down the hall. We sat there in silence until she returned, swept up the wreckage, and vanished again.

"Now," Maman said, sitting down next to Rain on the couch, "what is all this about?"

But before Storm could say anything, my parents stormed into the room. "Storm, I did not raise you to be rude to your mother!" Mom snapped. "I—"

"Where's Sasha?" he interrupted her.

My mother is seldom at a loss for words. I've seen her debate Christian protestors on the spot, scream at cops, and argue with politicians—and they always come off the worse for wear. There's never been any doubt in my mind where Storm's arguing skills came from. But this time, her mouth opened and closed, as her eyes went from me to Maman to Rain to Storm and, finally, Dad.

"He went out a little while ago. We were just starting to get a little worried about him when you called, son," Dad said, putting his arm protectively around Mom. She leaned into him. They were both wearing jeans and T-shirts.

"You just let him walk out?" I said. "Knowing full well there are people out there trying to kill him—"

"Enough!!!" Maman roared.

We all turned to look at her. In all of my twenty-nine, almost thirty years, I have never once heard Maman raise her voice. In fact, I've never seen her anything but calm and gracious. But now, her face was mottled red with fury, her eyes shooting flames. Her hands on her hips, she stalked over to my mother. "Cecile, sit down and shut up. You, too, Douglas." Meekly, my parents sat on the sofa facing the one Rain was on. She turned to me. "And you, young man, you do not talk to your parents that way in *my* house as long as there is breath in my body." She glared at each of us and then added, in her usual pleasant speaking voice, "When you say *Sasha*, do you mean Alexander?"

We all just stared at her in shock.

She waved her manicured hand. "Listen, it's bad enough that Mikhail was killed this morning—I am still reeling from that news—but now you say someone is trying to kill Alexander as well?" She turned to my mother. "And he was at your home, Cecile?"

Mom nodded numbly. I've never seen her eyes that wide open before in my life. Well, I've never really seen her speechless before, for that matter.

"This is terrible, just terrible." She shook her head. "This is going to kill your father. Just kill him."

"Maman—" I cleared my throat. "Maman, you mean you know there were three of them?"

"Unlike what some people think, I'm not some stupid old woman who can't handle the truth." She shot a glance at my mother. "Nor am I going to have a nervous breakdown."

"But Maman," my mother finally said, "you did have a breakdown."

Maman rolled her eyes. "I was *upset,* Cecile, when I found out about Mikhail. Who wouldn't be? To find out that my husband had a child with another woman? I just needed to get away for a while, get my head together, figure out what to do next. Obviously, divorce was out of the question." She sat down in the matching chair to the one I was in. "What would be the point of throwing all these years of marriage down the drain because the affair I forgave him for years ago produced a child he had no knowledge of? That 'sanitarium' I went to, Cecile, was actually a very nice spa. While I was there, I hired a private eye to find out if this Mikhail was indeed my stepson. Sylvia helped me."

"Aunt Sylvia?" Rain replied. She looked over at me for help. I just shrugged.

"Yes, Aunt Sylvia," Maman snapped. "Anyway, to make a long story short, I contacted Mikhail and arranged to meet him in Munich. He seemed like a nice enough young man, and the story was true—my investigator turned up the birth certificate."

"So that's how you knew there were triplets," Storm said.

"I already said I knew there were triplets!" She waved a hand. "Honestly, does *everyone* in my family think I'm a *moron*?" She sighed. "Of course, I tried to find the other boys. But I had no luck. It was like they had just disappeared into thin air. Mikhail claimed they were into drugs, pornography. You name it, Mikhail said they were into it. He obviously loved the idea that they were gone. I never pursued it with him much, but I tried to find them . . . for your father's sake. And then Sylvia fell in love with Mikhail. Of course, he was after a marriage visa and her money, but he's been good to her." A tear escaped her eye. "She's going to be devastated, just devastated."

"For my father's sake?" Mom choked the words out. "What are you saying?"

"They're his *sons,* Cecile." Maman stared at her. "Of course, he'd be delighted to know about them, to find them, to welcome them into the family. Do you really think your father is such a monster that he—that *we*—would turn our backs on family?"

"I—" Mom choked, "I was just trying to protect you."

"That's very very kind of you, Cecile, but I don't need protection." Maman got up, walked over to Mom, and gave her a big hug and kiss. "You have no idea how much it means to me." Her voice was heavy with emotion.

"But Papa didn't know about Mikhail?" This was from Storm. He looked completely bewildered—pretty much how I was feeling.

"I didn't—oh, God forgive me—I didn't tell him Mikhail was his son. I wanted to find the other two boys first." She wiped tears away. "He'll never forgive me . . . all this time he could have had with his son, and now it's too late. Secrets, secrets and lies, this is what comes from not telling the truth. You say two of them are dead?"

I nodded.

"Well, then we have to make sure nothing happens to Alexander—make it up to him somehow." It was a command.

My cell phone rang. I walked out into the hall, leaving them to talk. "Hello?" I answered.

"Scotty? Is Sasha."

"Where are you?"

"Meet me at your house. Have bad news for you."

"Sasha—" I struggled for a minute. "Bad news? What do you mean?"

"The bad guys—they have Frank."

And the line went dead.

CHAPTER FIFTEEN

Four of Cups

a time for reevaluation

I just stood there in the hallway, staring at my cell phone in disbelief.

The bad guys have Frank?

Pray for a brave heart.

Everything started to get a little fuzzy and my vision swam. I don't know how to describe it, really. My entire mind and body went numb, and there was this awful buzzing in my ears. Somehow, I could hear my heartbeat over the buzzing. Then I couldn't seem to catch my breath. My lungs seemed determined to gasp every last molecule of air in my lungs out and didn't seem to want to take any back in. My eyes filled with tears. My legs wobbled and I grabbed for a Louis XVI decorative chair to keep myself from falling. I held on to the chair with all my strength, but my arms seemed to be made of limp pasta, and I kept sinking toward the floor until I was somehow able to take a deep breath. Finally, my blood started flowing again and I was able to right myself. My stomach clenched and unclenched, spasming with cramps, and I started gasping for air again. Spots began to dance before my eyes. This time I realized I was hyperventilating and bent over, putting my hands on my knees and consciously trying to slow my breathing. Tears were flowing out of my eyes uncontrollably as I huffed and puffed and tried to get control of myself again. With a conscious effort I shut down my mind and focused. I closed my eyes and thought about my happy place—one of the beautiful beaches of the Florida panhandle, where the sand is as fine as sugar and just as white, where the warm waves are a beautiful clear emerald green, turning blue as the water gets deeper farther away from the shore. I focused on the warm sun; the gentle, cool salty breezes blowing over me; the cry of the gulls; and the slightly fishy smell of the gulf. Finally, after a few moments, when I wasn't completely sure I was going to be able to pull it together, my breath started coming more evenly and my heart rate slowed down.

All those years of teaching aerobics *finally* paid off.

I swallowed. *The bad guys have Frank.*

How in the hell had that happened?

My hands still shaking, I pressed the callback button, but it just clicked over to voice mail, a toneless voice telling me to leave a message. I dialed Colin's number, but after one ring it too went to voice mail.

Okay, I have to get home, I thought crazily. How did Sasha know where Frank was? How had the bad guys known how to get him?

I *knew* something was wrong with Frank leaving. I'd been right. It wasn't like Frank to run off with someone. I *knew* it. Wait till I saw Colin again. . . .

I walked, a little shakily but okay, to the door to the parlor. Voices were still going—not arguing, but it was definitely a heated discussion. I don't think I'd ever seen Maman quite so animated and passionate, so alive. If it weren't so important I get the hell out of there, I would have just enjoyed watching. Of course, when my family gets going, you can't just sit there quietly; you eventually get pulled in. There's no such thing as passive observation. You can just be sitting there, minding your own business, trying not to be noticed as the conversation rages and boils around you, not saying a word, just enjoying yourself, and then someone sees you out of the corner of his or her eye and will turn on you. You can't beg off, pretend not to have an opinion. No, there's no avoiding it; they're all looking at you then, and there's not a damn thing you can do but join in.

As much as I would have loved to have voiced my opinion on all the secrecy and lying that had been going on within the family circle for just over two years—Storm was making that very point, and doing a very good job of it, judging by the redness of my mother's face—I didn't have time for that now. I managed to catch Rain's eye and motioned for her to join me in the hallway. She rolled her eyes, got up, and walked out without anyone batting an eye.

"What?" she whispered once she joined me, her eyes still focused on the room. Mom was now defending herself passionately, jabbing her finger in the air as she made her points, Dad backing her with an occasional "Yeah" and by tightening his grip around her waist.

"I need you to take me home like five minutes ago," I whispered back. "But I don't want anyone to know. You up for it?"

"Sneak out of a family meeting?" She giggled like she used to when she was a teenager. "We haven't done that in years." She considered it for a moment. "I don't know, Scotty. I hate to miss this." She gestured back at the room, where now Maman was making the point she was hardly a delicate orchid who needed her family to protect her from the world. As she spoke, some of her hair worked out of place and I saw, for the first time, the strong resemblance my mother bore to her. Hell, Mom had to get all that spirit from someone; I just never dreamed it was quiet, ladylike Maman. Rain listened for a little while longer before giving me a broad wink. "Looks like Maman's got everything under control." She giggled again. "Let me get my purse."

It's relatively easy to sneak out of family meetings. The secret was to wait till the discussion got so heated and focused that the participants were completely unaware of anyone in the room who wasn't participating. Of course, you ran the risk of being noticed as you made your escape and getting dragged in, but Rain was a master of the trick. I don't know how she did it. I never could manage it without her assistance. She once told me she walked out of a particularly virulent one and not only got fifty dollars out of Maman's purse, but had Dad give her his car keys without a second thought. As I watched her slip back into the room, grab her purse, and soundlessly walk back out, I believed it.

It was like she was invisible.

"Is this one of your little adventures?" she asked as she slipped the Range Rover into gear and we pulled out of the driveway. "I've always been so jealous of them." She sighed. "They must be so much fun."

"Well, in a way it is—but they're hardly fun." I closed my eyes as she pulled out way too fast in front of a cab to be able to stop and waited for the impact. When none came, I opened my eyes to see the cab swinging around us, the driver angrily giving Rain the finger as he honked his horn. She gave him a big smile and flipped him off with both hands. "I mean, being kidnapped and tied up isn't all it's cracked up to be, you know." I sighed. *Which is what's happening to Frank right now.* I didn't say it out loud, although I was about ready to have a complete meltdown. "Did you know Misha was our uncle before today?"

"Well, yeah," she said. "Maman told me after he married Aunt Sylvia. She didn't tell me there were three of them, though." She shook her head. "That was kind of a shock to find out. I mean, wow, it's like something out of *All My Children*—you know, how long-lost relatives you never know you had show up? She got a thoughtful look on her face. "They've never done triplets, though."

"Why didn't you tell me?" I looked out the window. "Why did Maman tell you?"

"Looks like the rain is letting up, so maybe Orpheus will roll after all," she said absently. She was silent for a moment and then said, "Scotty, I'm sorry. Maybe I should have said something . . .

maybe Maman should have. I don't know. In hindsight, yeah, keeping these secrets maybe wasn't a smart idea, but it's easy to say that now. Maman had her reasons for keeping it quiet, and I had to respect that. She asked me not to say anything to anyone else, so I didn't. I didn't think it was that great of an idea, but it wasn't my place."

"What other secrets are there?" I sounded like a pouting little kid, but I couldn't help myself. "What else don't I know?"

She shrugged. "Hard to say, baby bro. I think that's everything—but it's a pretty big one, don't you think?"

My mouth opened and closed. I braced my hands on the dashboard as she slammed on the breaks as the light at Louisiana turned red right in front of us. She glanced over at me. "You look pretty upset, boo."

"Well, considering the fact that I just found out I have three uncles and two of them have been murdered in the last two days—one of them right in front of me—I'd say, yeah, I think I am a little upset," I said crossly. "I mean, I know I don't pay much attention when the family's together so I miss things sometimes, but still. . . ." I tapped my hand on the window.

"Yeah, well." She gave me a little smile. "We're hardly a normal family, are we?"

"Define normal," I grumbled. "I mean, really. Mom and the grands can't stand each other, the grands are ashamed of me, Papa had an affair *and* triplets with a Russian ballerina—just your typical American family."

A horn blared behind us. The light had turned green, but Rain ignored it. The car honked again, and Rain rolled her window down and waved it around her, putting on her flashers with her other hand. She turned back to me, frowning. "Where on earth did you get the idea that Mom and the grands hate each other?"

"Um, Rain, do you mind driving? I'm kind of in a hurry."

"We're not moving until you tell me."

"Rain, the guys who shot Misha and Pasha have Frank, and I *need to get home now!*"

She looked at me for a moment, put the car in gear, and said, "Why didn't you just say that?" She floored it and the Range Rover's back tires spun with a loud squeal and the stench of burning rubber permeated the vehicle. The car leaped into the intersection after fishtailing a bit. I winced. "So this is one of your little adventures?" she asked, not taking her eyes off the road and passing a slow-moving Toyota with Oklahoma plates on the right. "What are you and Colin going to do? Go rescue him?"

I flipped open my cell phone and dialed Colin's number again, but it still went to voice mail. "Damn it!" I swore, slamming it shut. "I can't get hold of Colin. I don't know where the hell he is. He went after the guys who shot Misha. . . ." I couldn't help myself—I started crying. Anger, frustration, and helplessness flooded into my mind, taking turns controlling my mind, and my heart started beating faster again. I put my head down, knowing that the gasping would be right behind.

Rain started petting my head. "It's okay, boo, don't cry. I hate it when you cry."

Rain had always hated it when I cried when we were kids. She was always trying to make me feel better, stop crying. Sometimes she would pet me and talk softly to me, telling me it was all right until I stopped; other times she would try to make me laugh. She's a great sister—you couldn't ask for a better one.

I heard another horn blare as she ran the light at Martin Luther King. She ignored a stop sign, then swung into a vicious left turn onto Calliope that I wasn't sure she was going to make. She swung into the right lane and flew up to St. Charles, where the light was green, and she sailed through. Then she slammed on the brakes to avoid rear-ending a Porsche at the Carondelet light. "Okay, I'm not crying!" I held up my hands. "I've stopped, look! Now I am just in terror of my life!"

She looked at me and then grinned. "Frank'll be okay, Scotty, you'll see. He's trained for these kinds of situations. And you'll get hold of Colin, and you know he can do anything."

I took some deep breaths. *Stay calm and focused. Getting killed on the way home isn't going to help Frank. Just be patient and you'll be there soon enough.*

Pray for a brave heart.

I closed my eyes and said a quick prayer for strength and patience, and when I opened my eyes we were moving again. I felt somewhat calmer. Of course Rain was right. I had to stay calm. Frank would be fine. If I panicked, I wouldn't be any use to anyone. I tried calling Colin again, but no luck.

He can't just be on the phone this whole time. He must have just shut it off.

Why would he do that? I wondered, and then realized Rain had said something I hadn't heard and was waiting for me to answer as she turned onto O'Keefe. "I'm sorry, what did you say?"

"I was asking you again why you think Mom and the grands hate each other," she replied. "I mean, that's just crazy."

"Well, I think it's pretty obvious the way they talk to each other—"

She waved her hand. "Please. They just like to argue. Papa and Maman adore Mom. And Dad, too. They may not always agree—well, they never agree—but the grands are really proud of them."

It was my turn to stare. I'm sure my jaw had dropped too. "You aren't serious?"

"Scotty, who always bails Mom and Dad out of jail?" She laughed. "Maman and Papa, that's who—and they never just send someone or a lawyer. They go, every time, and sit there in the waiting room until Mom and Dad come out, and then they all go out for dinner and drinks." She gave me a wink. "Like you said, just your typical American family."

"But Papa is always just so *mean*."

"That's just how he is. He's like Storm. You don't think Storm's mean, do you?"

"Well, no. He's just annoying—on purpose." Storm was the most horrible tease. Sometimes he drove me absolutely insane. At least he'd stopped calling me "my queen." But he still called my psychic power my "psycho gift."

"Well, Papa is the same way. That's how he shows affection. Is it how I'd prefer he be? No. I don't particularly like being quizzed on a regular basis about why I'm not pregnant, but hey." She shrugged, turning onto Esplanade. "Now, do you need my help with rescuing Frank?"

She was so completely earnest that I had no doubt she would be willing to strap a dagger to her leg, and I had this mental image of her in a commando outfit. I couldn't help myself. It was all so absurd that my Uptown Mrs. Doctor sister was eager to help in a rescue mission that I started snorting with laughter.

"Don't laugh at me! I'm *serious*." She punched me in the leg as she pulled over at the corner of Decatur and Esplanade.

"You have no idea how much I love you right now." I leaned over and kissed her on the tip of her nose.

"You sure you don't need my help?" She frowned at me. "I never get to have any fun."

She'd always said that when we were kids. I grinned back at her. "I know, it's not fair."

She laughed then and gave me another hug. "Oh, Scotty, don't you remember?" She pointed her index finger at me and did a dead-on impersonation of Faye Dunaway in *Mommie Dearest:* "Ah, but nobody ever said life was fair, Tina."

That made me laugh, and she laughed with me. She reached over and wiped the tears off my cheeks before planting a big, wet, sloppy, slurpy, noisy kiss on me. "I love you, little bro."

"I love you, Rain."

She twisted her face into her best grimace and rolled her eyes.

"Even now you can't call me *Rhonda?* What does it take in this family to get a little respect anyway?"

"I will *never* call you that." I grinned back at her. "Rain was the little girl who always pulled me out from in front of cars."

She gave me a long look, her eyes shiny with fresh tears, before blowing me a kiss. "Frank's going to be fine." And then I got out of the car.

I watched her negotiate the U-turn at Frenchmen and waved as she drove past. I kept watching—and waving—until the trees shielded the Range Rover from my sight. I took a deep breath and started walking up the sidewalk to my front door. *I've got to find Frank,* I thought, and felt the tension starting to build again. I started looking around for Sasha on the street. He wasn't in front of my gate. Maybe he'd gone into the coffee shop to get warm; it was still a bit damp and chilly.

I glanced across the street and my blood ran a little colder.

The guy who'd been watching the house was there again.

I stopped dead in my tracks and took a better look.

I wasn't sure if it was the same guy. They seemed to be of the same size, and the outfit was similar—baseball cap pulled down low to mask the top of the face, a grayish trench coat with the collar turned up, jeans and athletic shoes beneath. If it wasn't the same guy, it was two guys with the same sense of style, at the very least. The street wasn't as crowded as yesterday; some brave souls had ventured out from cover since the rain had stopped, although the sky was completely hidden by clouds running every shade of color between gray and black. I didn't know if he was watching for me, per se, but if Frank had been kidnapped, they might have tracked him back here. They might be looking for the rest of us, if they didn't have Colin. I casually pulled out my cell phone and dialed Colin again. Nothing. My heart was racing.

It wouldn't be too hard to track us down; we were all three listed in the phone book with our addresses there for anyone to find. Even if he wasn't watching for me, I didn't like the looks of this. It was definitely not a good sign.

I waited for a crowd of tourists to walk across Esplanade and then fell into step alongside them as they headed up Decatur. They were jabbering and chatting away and didn't notice me on their outer edge. My mind was working. The guy who'd watched the house before had reminded me of Frank. Frank had been a government agent. The plot of every single spy movie I'd ever seen rushed through my head. Maybe Frank had information on someone or something that made him dangerous from his days with the FBI. Frank never talked about his days with the FBI; his cases, the people he worked with, what kind of inside information he'd been privy to that certain people in the government might not want to be public knowledge. My imagination was certainly not helped by the mistrust my parents had sown into me my entire life about the Big Brother in Washington, watching and monitoring our every move. When we reached the door to the coffee shop, I ducked inside, worked up to a fine emotional turmoil of terror and paranoia.

And I wasn't even stoned.

Nor was Sasha inside the coffee shop. Where the hell was he?

I walked over to the counter and casually ordered an iced mocha from a clerk I didn't recognize. I gave her a good hard, long look. She was maybe twenty and everything about her screamed poor college student working her way through college— the dreadlocks dyed blue and scarlet, the exposed pierced navel, the row of posts running up the outer lobes of her ears, and the surly attitude. I kept watching her—the paranoia again—but finally decided she was exactly what she seemed. She was also pretty efficient at quickly making an iced mocha. Darcy, the usual daytime girl, was actually pretty slow, which sometimes was annoying if I was in a rush. I paid her, threw a dollar in the tips jar, took my drink, and headed to the hallway to the courtyard. I unlocked the door and slipped through, pulling it shut and locking it again. *It's nice,* I thought, *having a secret entrance into the house.* I took a deep breath and felt relief flood through me. Once inside, of course, the paranoia left, like it was never there, and I felt kind of silly.

But the guy is watching the house. Again. You didn't imagine that, Scotty.

Velma was sitting at the table, sparking a fat joint. She gave me a big grin and waved me over.

I glanced at the stairs and thought about just waving and heading up, but Sasha wasn't anywhere to be seen, and there was nothing to do but sit there and wait for him. Besides, my aunts Millie and Velma aren't the kind of women you can just ignore. They're not really my aunts; they're lifelong friends of my mother's, and a long-term lesbian couple. They've been together longer than most straight couples I know. Velma was more than capable of getting pissed if I blew her off and storming up the stairs behind me. She once beaned Frank with a frying pan, something she now regrets terribly, but he's never really been comfortable around her ever since. In her defense, he was holding a gun on me at the time, but still. . . . His head ached for days. So, if Frank had just escaped from abductors, the last thing he needed was for Velma to come storming into the apartment. Besides, she was not, despite my age, beyond grabbing me by the ear and twisting. Not to mention the great deal she and Millie had given me on the rent.

Basically, I'm pretty much their bitch.

I walked over and she offered the joint. I shook my head. I could still remember the self-induced paranoia; the last thing I needed was to enhance it with marijuana. "No thanks, Aunty."

She shrugged and took another long hit. "Your loss, buddy. This is some primo shit."

"Where's Millie?" It *was* some strong stuff; I could tell by the smell of the smoke. I looked at it longingly, then at the stairs, then back at her. *No, Scotty, it's not a good idea,* I told myself. *Be strong.*

She gestured upstairs and then the smoke exploded out of her in a racking cough that doubled her over. She kept coughing for a few seconds more before finally straightening up, her eyes red and watering, and said, "Whew," as she reached for her bottled water. "She's up there with some of her lawyer buddies—you know, the power dykes." She winked at me. "There's only so much of that talk I can stand. Where've you been?"

"At Maman's," I said. It wasn't a lie; it *was* the last place I'd been. No sense in telling her what was going on, I figured. She'd tell Millie—Millie is a lawyer in the sharkiest sense of the word; she's Storm's role model—and I'd have to deal with that. Like I said, they aren't the kind of women you can just trifle with. They'd want to help somehow, and if I was even able to convince them there was nothing they could do, they'd both worry themselves sick. Or drive each other crazy.

"Why're you coming in through the coffee shop?" She narrowed her eyes a bit.

"Because the walkway roof drips," I said, without even having to think. It does, badly. During a storm you have to keep your umbrella up or risk getting soaked. You'd think when the house had to be rebuilt, they'd have replaced that roof. Sometimes I think they didn't because they enjoy listening to me bitch about it. I know it's caused them amusement on more than one occasion to see me get soaked.

She rolled her eyes. "It wouldn't have anything to do with the guy watching the house?"

"You know about that?"

She sighed. "Listen, pal, your aunt and I aren't stupid people. And after what happened with the arson last summer"—that was when the house burned down—"we keep a close eye on what's going on in the street. I don't want to be uprooted again. Sooo, what's going on?"

I looked at her and then sat down with a sigh. "It's real complicated. Let's just say two people are dead, I don't know where

Colin is, we think it might be the Russian Mob, and Frank—well, Frank is missing. I think the Russians might have him. I have no idea who the guy outside is."

"You want me to get my frying pan?" Her eyes gleamed.

What is it with these women? I wondered. "No, I don't think so. And the bad thing is, the guy who told me the Russians have Frank was supposed to meet me here, and he's nowhere to be found."

She got a weird, guilty look. "Um, there's a guy in your apartment. Hot, all huge and muscular. I figured there was a story. . . ."

I kissed her on the cheek; said, "Save me some of that stuff"; and ran upstairs. I got progressively wobblier as I climbed, finally having to grab hold of the rail tightly. My hands were shaking so hard I could barely fit the key in the lock, but finally the door opened and I ran down the hall to the living room. I could hear the television on. "Sasha?" I shouted.

He was sitting on the couch, slouched down in his jeans and a tank top I recognized as one of my dad's—and it was waaaay too small for him. His face lit up when he saw me. He flicked off the television with the remote, jumped up, and came bounding over to me. He threw his arms around me, practically squeezing the breath out of me in the process. He picked me up off the ground and kept holding—until I finally was able to squeeze my hands in against his chest and push lightly. He didn't let go, so I pushed harder. Finally, I had to say, "Sasha, I—can't—breathe."

"So sorry!" He set me down. "So glad to see Scotty!"

"Yeah, so I gather." I gave him a weak smile. "How'd you get in here? And where's Frank?" As I stared into his face, it dawned on me that he didn't know Misha was dead, and my entire body sagged. Someone was going to have to tell him, and I had this horrible feeling it was going to have to be me. It was just a bit too much for me. He grabbed me before I could fall and propped me up.

"Parents gave spare key." His ice blue–gray eyes examined me carefully. "Scotty all right?"

"I'm fine." He let go of me and I looked at him. "And Frank? Where's Frank?"

"I know where Frank is." He gave me a big smile. "Now we have to go get." He nodded his head happily. "Be easy—what you call piece of cake?"

"Piece of cake," I said, nodding.

And everything went spinning and gray.

CHAPTER SIXTEEN

Ten of Wands

one who is carrying an oppressive load

"You must pray for a brave heart."

I heard the Goddess's soft, gentle voice through the fog as I drifted downward. The light sound of her voice seemed to wrap around me as I floated down, the gray mist swirling around me but nevertheless caressing my skin, as though slowing me as I moved ever downward. Down below me I heard a marching band's drums being pounded, the blast of the tubas, and the cheers and shouts of a crowd. It was a night parade, and through the mist I could see the flickering torches of the flambeaux carriers. Even though I was drifting, weightless, I felt calm and at peace. My worries and stresses had been taken from me. My body no longer felt sore and tired and exhausted. My feet landed on something solid. Now I could just barely make out the shapes and sounds of people shouting at the riders on a float, and the throws were flying. A string of green, gold, and purple beads landed at my feet, with a medallion attached. I bent down and picked them up off the damp ground, and the medallion leered at me. It was a harlequin's face, all white with a green and purple cap with gold trim. There was a heart-shaped mole on one of its cheeks, and the bright red lips were pulled back in a leering grimace. Around the edge of the medallion, rather than the name of a krewe, were the words MARDI GRAS MAMBO. *I turned it over and over again in my hands.*

And the voice came again through the mist.

"You must pray for a brave heart."

"What does that mean?" I asked, looking around me. I never saw her, no matter how close I could sense her presence at times—yet I always tried, squinting my eyes and peering through the damp, cool air. I know intellectually that she is ethereal, that she doesn't have to take shape, probably only takes shape when the human she is speaking to cannot understand or comprehend her unless she is in human form, but I still look. "I don't really understand. You say it to me all the time but I never really know what it means." I sounded like a pouty child not getting his way, but I couldn't help myself. She'd thrown quite a few curveballs at me in the last couple of days, and without meaning any disrespect, I kind of wanted some straight answers from her.

I mean, what's the point of being able to communicate with the Universe if its meaning doesn't make sense to you?

"You will understand when the time is right. It means what it means. Pray for a brave heart," she said, her words like the wind around me.

"But that doesn't help me—and that doesn't help me find Frank!!" I kicked at the ground angrily, clutching the medallion in my hands.

"Frank is fine for now. You will do what needs to be done."

I stood there, the medallion in my hand. So many questions, so many possible answers—I didn't even have the slightest idea of where to start, where to begin. I turned it over in my hand. It was heavier than plastic, and I brought it closer to my eyes. It was made of metal, not plastic. I'd never seen anything like it.

"Life is testing you, Scotty. Nothing comes to you that you cannot handle. It is how *you handle what life presents you that matters."*

"That's a load of crap!" I shouted, waving my arms to try to part

the mist, make it go away so I could see better. "I don't want to be tested!"

"The only choice is how to handle what life presents to you." Her voice was fading now, she was going back to wherever it was she went, and I would be returning to my plane. The medallion burned in my hands, and I dropped it, and the ground beneath me began to dematerialize, and I began to fall again, slowly, the mist wrapping itself around me, and as the mist and the grayness began to give way to light again, I could hear her words echoing in the distance.

Pray for a brave heart. . . .

"Scotty?" I looked up into Velma's gray eyes. Her face was concerned at first, but then as my eyes began to focus better, it dissolved into a huge grin. "Just another trance, then. Thank God." She stood up with an enormous sigh of relief. "I swear you scare the shit out of me sometimes."

"What are you doing here?" I asked, trying to sit up, but I got dizzy and collapsed back onto the back cushions of the couch. Well, at least I was sitting up. The room wasn't spinning or anything, and everything was slowly coming back into focus. Out of the corner of my eye I saw Sasha come back into the room, a soaked paper towel in one hand, folded tightly into a pad. His face also lit up with a smile and what looked like relief. He sat down on the sofa.

"This one came out on the balcony and yelled for help." Velma looked into my eyes. "No, you seem fine." She looked over at Sasha, then back to me with a wink.

"Oh, my God! Sasha, where's Frank? We've got to go get him." I tried to get up but got dizzy again.

Velma shot a glance over at Sasha and then looked me in the eyes. "I don't think you should be going anywhere for a while, young man. You just passed out—"

"Oh, for Pete's sake, it was just a trance. I was talking to the Goddess. It happens all the time—"

"Why don't you try calling Colin again?" she suggested.

I glared at her but tried again. I flipped the phone closed when the voice mail picked up. But then an idea came to me. I could use some help. . . .

I walked over to my desk and got Angela Blackledge's business card out of the top drawer. Colin had given it to me when we'd opened the office, with strict instructions never to call her unless he was unavailable and it was an emergency.

I think this definitely qualified as an emergency.

I called. It rang twice, and then a disembodied voice came on the line: *"We are sorry, but the number you are calling is no longer in service. Please check the number and try again."*

What the fuck?

I tried again, with the same result. I handed the phone to Velma with the card. "You try."

She dialed, then held up the phone so I could hear the message again.

I sat down hard in my desk chair. Had the whole world gone completely insane?

There had to be some rational explanation. Maybe Angela had just had her phone number changed. But why didn't I have the new number?

Sasha walked over to me and put his big hands on my shoulders. "Is going to be okay, Scotty. Did you see Misha?"

And then, as I looked up into his face, his bright eyes, the smile on his face, I realized that I wasn't the only person with problems. "Oh, Sasha," I whispered, and I started crying. "I'm so so sorry."

His entire body went rigid and he stood up completely straight. He bit his lower lip. "Misha dead?"

He stood there, not moving. His shoulders didn't shake. He was completely silent. But tears flowed out of his eyes.

Somehow, this silent, unmoving grief was the saddest thing I'd ever seen.

I stood up and threw my arms around him. He grabbed on to me, and I braced myself for the rib crushing that was to come. But he held me loosely, and he still didn't shake—nothing. The only way I knew he was crying was from his breathing.

Finally, he let go of me and stepped back.

"Sasha, what exactly happened in Russia?" I asked gently. "You didn't tell us everything last night, did you?"

Sasha nodded but didn't say anything. He reached up and wiped the tears off his expressionless face. He walked back into the living room and sat down on the sofa. Velma and I followed, and we sat down on either side of him, taking his hands.

Looking straight ahead, Sasha said, "Kafelnikov is very bad man, Scotty. He tied to Chechnyan rebels—and Middle Eastern terrorism. And he trying to move operation out of Russia and into United States . . . which big problem for your country." Sasha tilted his head up and looked at me. "I was approached by an American agent, yes." His English was no longer broken. I stared at him. He sounded exactly like Misha had. The accent was barely discernible. But then, the facial resemblance was so uncanny; they all three had looked so much alike.

"They wanted me to take Pasha's place with Kafelnikov," he went on, shaking his head. "I owed it to Pasha. You don't understand. Pasha wasn't a bad person."

"What!?" I exploded. I stared at him. "Our government asked you to take his place? But that's not *right.*" In the back of my head I could hear my mother tsking. "The government isn't supposed to do a lot of things, Scotty," she was saying inside my head, "but that doesn't mean they don't do it. That's why we always have to be vigilant."

"They promised me to bring Pasha to America and get him off drugs," Sasha continued. "They trained me for weeks—very intensive training on self-defense and weaponry and so forth. I already was proficient from my days with the Russian army, but they trained me well, and they didn't want to take any chances.

The only problem was Kafelnikov—he was an animal. He couldn't get enough of Pasha." He shuddered. "I put him off as long as I could. Repulsive as I found him, somehow I managed to do it. For Pasha. They smuggled Pasha into America—Houston—and put him in a drug hospital, and I took his place." He closed his eyes. "Viktor was a monster." He shuddered again. "It was horrible, the things he liked to do. He liked to—no, I don't want to say." He looked at me. "I don't want anyone to ever know." His eyes were pleading.

More secrets, more lies.

"There's more, isn't there?" I asked, although I didn't really want to know.

"No." Tears again silently began to leak from his eyes. He looked at me, pleading.

"Tell me," I insisted softly.

"I"—he swallowed—"Pasha was never"—he tapped the side of his head—"he was never *smart*. He was a simple boy, really sweet and kind. But the drugs *changed* him. He didn't care about anything anymore. He was more than Viktor's lover."

"He was part of it, wasn't he?"

Sasha nodded. "You have to understand—it was all my fault; I had to save him. . . ." He started to sob. "Pasha was not a monster. He was such a sweet little boy. Sasha and I always had to watch out for him."

"Sasha?" I let go of his hand. "*You and Sasha had to look out for him?*"

I stared at him. My head was starting to hurt again.

He stared at me, and then his jaw clenched.

"You're Misha, aren't you?" I couldn't help myself, the absurdity of it all was too much for me. I started laughing, but then I started crying too. "So, why are you still alive?"

"What the *fuck* is going on around here?" Velma held up her hands. "I'm not following this."

"You do need a scorecard," I sighed, wiping my face. "Okay,

let me see if I have it right, okay? Correct me if I'm wrong." I started ticking things off on my fingers. "Papa Diderot had an affair with your mother and got her pregnant. She went back to Russia without telling him she was pregnant. She gave birth to identical triplets—Pasha, Sasha, and Misha. After she died, Misha wrote to Papa Diderot for help. By this time, Pasha had gotten mixed up with drugs, porn, and a really bad Russian gangster. American agents approached Sasha about getting Pasha to turn on the gangster Viktor Kafelnikov."

Sasha—*Misha*—nodded.

"Okay, then Maman Diderot responded to your letter. She came to Europe with her best friend, Sylvia Overton, who then fell in love with you and you two were married. You came to the United States, and then the American agents swapped Pasha out for Sasha and brought him to the States and put him in rehab. When Pasha got out of rehab, he came to New Orleans and started dealing drugs—I'm assuming Pasha was the one I bought my X from?" He nodded again. "So, when did Sasha get here?"

Velma still looked confused.

"His cover was blown a couple of weeks ago," Misha said, "so they brought him here."

"Well, our government did a really shitty job of hiding you all," I replied. "And how did Pasha find *me?* Was that a setup?"

"No, just blind luck. . . ." He ran a hand over his cropped hair. "I knew there was a nephew who lived in the Quarter—a dancer boy. Your grandmother had shown me pictures of you. I saw you leaving Pasha's once. I couldn't believe he was selling drugs to his own nephew." He shook his head.

"Oh, I left out the part, Velma, where Mom found out about them and wrote to them. Did you look them up?"

"I looked them up." He sighed. "It wasn't hard to find them. Douglas and Cecile, very welcoming and nice, but they told me not to tell you, so I didn't. Cecile said when the time was right everyone would know, but she didn't think your grandmother was ready."

"She knows now." I was so tired of the whole mess I just wanted to scream. "In fact, she knew from the beginning there were three of you." And to myself, I added, *And if everyone had just been honest with everyone, maybe Pasha and Sasha would be alive right now. Fucking secrets and lies. When exactly did my life become a plot borrowed from* All My Children *anyway?*

There would be time for confronting the family later—once Frank was safe and whoever was killing off my uncles was behind bars.

That was going to be one hell of a family meeting.

"So, where are these Russians? Did you recognize them?" I asked.

"At the Devil's Weed. I went down the inside staircase and heard someone talking on a cell phone in Russian. I figured, how many Russians can there be in New Orleans? I took your spare keys from your parents."

I sighed. Mom and Dad had my keys hanging on their kitchen wall with a sign over it that says "SCOTTY'S SPARES."

He continued, "So I followed him. He kept speaking in Russian on his phone; it didn't make any sense to me. He didn't see me, so I followed him into the hotel, the one there on the corner. That's where they are staying."

"The Bourbon Orleans?"

He nodded. "That must be where they have Frank. I know the room."

Velma rubbed her hands together. "So, I say we go get him."

"Velma—" I didn't know what to say. I was incredibly touched she wanted to go help rescue Frank, but at the same time it would be dangerous. I wasn't even sure I was up for it. When it came to rescuing, it was usually Frank or Colin rescuing *me*.

I decided to try Colin's cell phone one last time. I said a quick prayer as I dialed, but I knew even as I said the words in my head that it wasn't going to work, that there wasn't going to be an answer.

Sometimes I hate being right.

It was up to me, and me alone.

I was going to go get my man. Or die trying.

"Stop thinking like that," I said out loud, shivering. I rubbed my arms to get the goosebumps to go down.

I walked over to the French doors leading to my balcony. I peered through the curtains. The guy was still there, leaning on the fence watching. I narrowed my eyes.

"Misha, Velma, come here for a minute," I said, turning to them. They joined me at the window. "See that guy down there? The one leaning against the fence?"

"In the ball cap? Yes," Misha replied. Velma nodded.

"Want to ambush him? He's watching the house, and I don't like that one bit."

Misha frowned. "Why is he watching the house?" He gave a low growl in his throat.

"I don't know, but there's not a single good reason I can think of, so he must be up to no good. I say we go down and get him."

Misha bared his teeth in a savage grin. "Sounds like fun." He popped his knuckles. "You think he's maybe one of the people who killed Pasha and Sasha?"

"Misha"—I put my hands on his shoulders so we were looking into each other's faces—"we aren't going to *hurt* him, or anything. We just need to overpower him and get him up here. He might have some answers, some information we need."

"If he killed my brothers, I will get answers out of him," he said grimly, rubbing his big hands together.

I started to say we couldn't break the law by hurting the guy, but I stopped myself. I couldn't blame Misha for how he felt; the reality was if they'd hurt Frank in any way, I might not be able to stop *myself* from inflicting some damage on him. I smiled back at him. "And then we're going to go get Frank—you want to help me with that?" *Fuck* you, *Colin. I don't need your help—or your permission—and we are going to have a serious chat later,* I added under my breath.

Colin always said that the more complicated the plan, the more likely things were to go wrong. Bearing that in mind, I kept the plan very simple.

The tricky part was going to be getting Misha out of the apartment without being noticed. This is where Velma came in handy. She quickly explained something I didn't know—that in the shed at the back of the courtyard was a door that opened out into a small alley that came out in a parking lot on Barracks Street. We decided that Misha would go out that way, solving that problem. Velma and I would go through the back door into the coffee shop. Once we saw Misha on the opposite corner of Barracks and Decatur, Velma would go back out into the courtyard and come out through the front gate. She would cross the street and distract the guy, which would be the cue for Misha and me to make our move and subdue him. Velma was a little disappointed I wouldn't let her use her frying pan on him, but I promised her if he wasn't willing to talk after we dragged him back upstairs, I'd let her.

Simple, right? I said a quick prayer, we had a group hug for success, and put our plan into motion.

After Misha went out the shed door, Velma and I casually entered the coffee shop through the back door.

"This is kind of fun," Velma whispered. I shushed her.

The coffee shop was pretty empty. The college girl who'd been working earlier looked at me funny when I came out of the hallway but didn't say anything. I headed over to the window tables and sat down at one right next to the door and peered out. I didn't see Misha, and I felt my blood start pumping a lot faster. *Come on, Misha,* I said to myself. *Where are you?* The guy didn't seem to have noticed anything; he was still standing there, every once in a while scanning the people walking up and down Decatur Street. A few eternal moments ticked by, and then I saw Misha across the street. His eyes met mine, and I nodded. "Velma—"

She'd already gotten up and was heading across the street. I sat there, barely breathing, hoping against hope she'd be okay, and then she was there, right in front of him, shielding the coffee shop door from his line of sight.

"Attagirl!" I grinned.

I got up from my window table and ran out the front door. Just as I did, Misha shouted. *That wasn't part of the plan,* I realized, and started running across the street. Velma threw herself at the guy. She pressed him back into the fence just as the guy turned his head and stared at Misha, eyes widening in recognition. He shoved Velma away and she fell into the street. Then he started to reach inside his coat—it all seemed to happen in slow motion. I ran across the street just as the guy's hand came out . . . and I saw that he was holding a gun, and he was aiming it at Misha . . . and without stopping to think, or even being aware of what I was doing, my heart pounding in my ears, I leapt into the air and kicked him in the wrist. I wasn't even aware that I was yelling. His wrist slammed into the iron fence and the gun flew into the grass on the other side. A jolt of pain went up my leg, and I fell, landing on my side on the ground, all the breath being knocked out of me, and I felt even more pain. *I hope I didn't break a rib or something,* I thought, wincing a bit, still not able to believe I had actually kicked the gun out of his hand. He crumpled to the sidewalk clutching his wrist, his eyes staring at me in shock and anger as Misha came running up. I got to my feet and stared at him, rage coursing through me.

"Shut the fuck up," I said crossly as Misha grabbed his arm and locked it behind his back. I reached through the fence and my fingers closed around the barrel of his gun. I slipped it into the back of my pants after making sure the safety was on. I helped Velma to her feet. "You okay, Aunty?"

"I'm fine." She got right in the guy's face. "No thanks to you, asshole. Is that any way to treat a lady?"

"Fuck you!" he spat at her.

Misha threw a good, hard punch to his jaw, and his entire body went limp and he sagged back against the fence.

"That's for not treating the nice lady with respect, asshole," Misha said, rearing his fist back for another punch.

People were staring, I realized, as I grabbed Misha's arm. "Stop, Misha, no!" Misha was too strong, and for a moment I was afraid he would throw me aside and keep beating on the guy. But then the rage in Misha's eyes faded, and he dropped his arm.

"Help me," I said. "We need to get him inside, remember?"

Misha nodded, knelt down and picked the guy up like he didn't weigh anything, and threw him over his shoulder.

A small crowd had gathered, watching us across the street. They parted for us, their faces white with shock, their mouths open as we walked across the street, and I unlocked the gate. "Happy Mardi Gras, y'all." I gave them a smile. "Nothing to see here. Have a great time!" I stood aside as Misha carried him past. I gave them all a brief nod and then shut the gate behind me.

CHAPTER SEVENTEEN

The Devil, Reversed

removing the chains of bondage

The guy moaned all the way up to the apartment.

I led the way, hoping he wasn't moaning loud enough for Millie and her guests to hear. I wasn't quite sure how I'd explain this to them. I can usually think pretty quickly on my feet, but what on earth could I say about having a Russian carrying a man with a swollen wrist up the back stairs? *Excuse us, ladies, sorry we bothered you, but it's nothing to be concerned about. Oh, his wrist is swelling up? He's a little drunk is all and fell on the sidewalk. Call an ambulance? Um, no, I think he's going to be okay. Just some ice and ibuprofen and he'll be right as rain.*

Yeah, right.

All I could do was pray they wouldn't hear us. By the time we'd gotten him inside my apartment and Misha had set him down on the couch, his wrist was swelling up really bad. Looking at it made me queasy and also made me feel bad. I still couldn't believe I'd leapt through the air like that, let alone maybe broken this guy's wrist. I *hate* violence. Even though I know it's sometimes necessary, I tend to avoid it whenever humanly possible. I left Misha to tie him up while I dashed into the bathroom to look for the pain pills prescribed for me when I'd had my wisdom teeth out the year before. I'm a pretty quick healer, so after the first day of misery and swelling I hadn't had to take any more of the pills. I said a quick prayer as I dug through the medicine cabinet, asking the Goddess to forgive me for resorting to violence. I couldn't remember exactly where I'd put the little brown bottle of pills, but I knew I hadn't thrown it away; you never throw away perfectly good prescription pain pills. After a few moments, I found it hidden behind a half-used can of shaving cream. I shook two out into my hand and filled a glass with water.

The guy glared at me when I walked back into the living room. Misha had done a good job of tying him up with an extension cord—maybe too good of a job. The cord looked a little tight and painful to me. "Here, open your mouth. This is Demerol."

He just kept glaring and kept his mouth closed. "Look, I'm sorry about your wrist, but you were pulling a gun and it looked like you were going to use it, okay? This isn't poison or anything. It's Demerol. To lessen the pain in your wrist."

He just kept glaring.

I shrugged. "Suit yourself, bud. If you'd rather be in pain, that's your call."

"I'm not taking anything!" he spat the words out.

"Okay, whatever." I put the glass of water and the pills down on the coffee table.

He swallowed. "You three are in a lot of trouble," he said, with a snide grin. "You've got no idea how much trouble you just bought yourselves."

"Won't be the first time," I shrugged, "nor the last." I looked at his swollen wrist and felt a pang of guilt. I hadn't had to kick him so hard. I walked back into the kitchen; dumped some ice into a rag, which I knotted; and brought it back and put it on his wrist. "Now, you want to tell me why you were watching my apartment?"

He didn't reply.

"Okay, fine, be that way." I reached inside his jacket and felt a wallet inside an inner pocket. I worked it free and flipped it open. My heart sank. "Oh, fuck."

"What's wrong?" Misha asked.

"He's Homeland Security." I tossed Misha the badge. "Special Agent Vince Clay." I sank down on the couch and buried my head in my hands. This was not good, not good at all. Yes, we were definitely in for it now. Why the hell was Homeland Security watching the house? I could understand *today*, but they'd been watching the house since Sunday, maybe earlier.

I gestured to him. "Velma, how long have they been watching the house?"

She thought for a moment. "I first noticed on Saturday night, before you guys went out. I wasn't sure, and when I checked again there wasn't anyone there."

Saturday night, before Pasha was killed.

What was going on?

And then I remembered. That night when I'd picked up the drugs, someone had been watching Pasha's house. I thought I'd been wrong—the guy had wound up going into Rawhide—but maybe I had been right. The Feds had to know the triplets were in New Orleans, and they were under federal protection. That would explain why someone had been watching the Burgundy house—although they'd done a pretty shitty job of protecting Pasha. But why had they started watching *my* house on Saturday night? They would have had no idea who I was after I showed up at Pasha's. I looked back over at Special Agent Vince Clay. He had a really weird look on his face, a kind of smirky grin. "How's the pain?"

"Better," he mumbled.

"Why were you watching my house?" It couldn't hurt to ask, even though I was pretty sure he wouldn't answer me.

He goggled at me a little bit and then looked away. "Wasn't watching for you."

"Then who were you watching for?" Someone had been watching the house before I'd even known about the triplets, which sent a stab of fear through my heart. *None of this made any sense. . . .*

Then it came to me, and I sat down hard on the coffee table. *Colin. What if* Colin *was the one they were after? He'd said he'd been an agent with the Mossad—Israeli commandos. What if Colin hadn't told me everything? What if . . .*

My head really was starting to hurt again.

Okay, then. I stood back up. I needed to get him to a hospital to get that wrist looked at, but how to do it? As soon as he was out of our power, he'd get people to come after us. I dialed Venus's cell phone, but the voice mail clicked on after one ring, so I hung up. He was tied pretty securely—maybe it would be okay to leave him for a while—and if Colin should *finally* come back and find him, well, good enough for him. Let *him* figure out what to do with Special Agent Vince Clay of Homeland Security. But, on the other hand, I couldn't just leave him there, injured. He should have the wrist looked at, at the very least. Finally, with a sigh, I called 911. As I waited for someone to answer, an idea came to me. I grinned. When the operator answered, I said, "Hi, I think we need an ambulance." I gave her the address. "There's some guy passed out drunk in front of my house and his wrist is all swollen. I think he might have broke it when he fell down."

"Ambulance is on its way, sir."

"But he isn't passed out, Scotty." Velma said.

"I'll take care of that," Misha said, slipping one of his forearms around and under his chin. The guy's eyes goggled, then his face turned red, and then he went limp. "Sleeper hold." He grinned at me. "I learned in Russian army."

I knelt down and untied him. "Come on, Misha, help me get him downstairs. Velma, you're going to have to stay with him until the ambulance comes."

She went into my kitchen and came out with a frying pan.

She gave me a grim smile. "I'll keep him quiet; don't you worry about that."

Misha reached down and swung him up into his arms effortlessly, without even grunting from the exertion. I gaped at him. It's not like Special Agent Clay was a small man; I figured he had to weigh at least 180 pounds.

Wow, he's really strong. But then all of them were.

Someone had shot Pasha from the inside of the house, but he'd had that place locked up tight, and he wouldn't have let just anyone in.

He had to have known his killer.

Venus would have said if someone had broken in—and she wouldn't have really needed to question me; obviously, I had been let in. They had it on tape.

Who would he have let in?

I shook my head. It was crazy, what I was thinking. I had to focus on Frank.

And if I was right, it didn't solve the problem of who'd killed Sasha. I was inclined to think it was the Russians—maybe they didn't know Pasha was dead and mistook Sasha for Pasha. It was an easy mistake to make; I myself had trouble telling them apart without looking closely, and the shooter had been outside and at some distance. Yes, it could easily have happened that way.

Sasha died because he was pretending to be Misha.

Wait a minute. There was no reason for the Russians to want Misha dead. Sasha and Pasha, yes, but not Misha.

I sighed. What a fucking mess.

We headed down the stairs, down the passage, and then out the front gate. Misha wasn't even breathing hard. He gently placed Special Agent Clay face down on the sidewalk. I have to say, if you didn't notice the swollen wrist, he looked just like any other passed-out drunk on a Quarter sidewalk. A couple of people stared as they walked by, but I just grinned and shrugged.

"Doesn't know his limits, I guess." They nodded and kept walking.

I turned to Velma. "Okay, you know what to do."

She showed me the frying pan again before hiding it behind her back and leaning against the gate. "I'll konk him a good one if he comes to." She nodded. But I heard the siren, and then the ambulance came around the corner and rolled to a stop. As the paramedics climbed out, I pointed to the guy.

One of the paramedics, a chunky girl in her early thirties, took his vitals. "Yes, he's probably just drunk." She sighed. "I am so sick of Mardi Gras." She looked at his wrist, prodded it a bit, and then shrugged. "No, it's not broken but it's pretty badly bruised." She barked out a short laugh. "Good thing he's out like a light; otherwise he'd be in some major pain."

I nodded and watched her and the other paramedic strap him onto a gurney and run him over to the back of the ambulance. I waited until he was inside and it had started moving down Decatur, its siren blaring, before I walked into the coffee shop and joined Misha.

I glanced over at the counter. The college girl was staring at me—but then she'd seen quite a bit of me over the last hour. I smiled and nodded, and she turned away. I looked back at Misha. "Okay, let's go."

We walked back outside and headed down the sidewalk, pushing our way through the crowds. It was after five now, and although the air was thick with moisture, it hadn't started raining again—and the crowds were coming back to the streets. I heard someone say that Orpheus was going to roll after all; they'd just made the decision to brave the rain. And the costumes were coming out. We passed a couple dressed like Glenn Close and John Malkovich in *Dangerous Liaisons,* a Cleopatra, some cave people, and a guy dressed as an old K&B drugstore. At the corner at Royal there was a group in black tie and masks, their women dripping with sequins, their masks incredibly elaborate with huge feathers. I was walking so fast I was almost running. The closer we got to Bourbon Street, the thicker the crowds became, until I was dodging around people, bumping into others. I cut up Royal Street, ignoring the drunks on the balconies yelling down and tossing beads to other drunks. I stopped at the corner of Royal and St. Ann and stared down the street at the Bourbon Orleans. The second- and third-floor balconies were packed with people. The street was also packed. I turned to Misha. "You're sure the Russians are there?"

Misha nodded. "I'll show you."

The Bourbon Orleans is a historic hotel and might even be a national landmark. It's been there forever, standing at the corner of Bourbon and St. Ann. It was originally built as a convent and served as a soldier's hospital during the Civil War. Sometime after that, it had become a hotel enormously popular with gay tourists, because it stood at the corner of the big gay section of the Quarter. Its long wraparound balconies on the second and third floors helped—people love our balconies, standing up there above the crowd and partying while looking down at the hordes of people in the streets. It was pink for many years until it was painted a kind of grayish green, when the Wyndham chain bought it. It had recently undergone an extensive renovation and now had two bars on the first floor on Bourbon Street. One of them, Napoleon's Itch, supposedly was a gay bar but I'd never gone inside. It was on the wrong side of St. Ann for me; I hated crossing that invisible barrier between gay and straight Bourbon Street.

Misha walked down St. Ann with me right behind him. We pushed through the crowd in front of the doors of Oz and fought our way inside. It was dark inside, Donna Summer was wailing, and hugely muscled guys in glowing thongs were dancing on the bar. The dance floor was packed, and so was the area surrounding the bar. Straight women were pushing dollars at the go-go boys. Misha pushed his way to the staircase and I followed him up and out onto the balcony. The St. Ann side was not nearly as crowded as it was closer to the corner and over on the Bourbon Street side. We made our way out to the railing and Misha pointed across the street. "That room." The balcony doors were shut, as were the curtains; it was the only room on the floor with its doors shut. The lights were on, though. I counted the doors. It was the third room from the corner.

My mind worked quickly. "Okay, we need to get on the balcony."

"How?"

I grinned. "Leave that to me." I hadn't lived through twenty-nine Mardi Gras, Southern Decadences, and Halloweens without figuring out how to get on the balcony at the Bourbon Orleans. "Come on." We fought our way back downstairs and through the crowds and down to Royal Street. We turned at Orleans and walked in the front doors of the hotel, and I headed for the elevators, acting like I belonged. No one would challenge us during Mardi Gras—for that matter, any time the hotel was jam packed with tourists and the streets were full of people. There were always so many people around in the lobby, coming and going, that the staff had no idea who wasn't supposed to be there. We rode up to the second floor, and we walked around to the Bourbon Street side. It didn't take long to find a door slightly ajar, just as I expected. I pushed the door open and looked in. The room was empty and the French doors were wide open; the residents were out on the balcony. On party weekends, you could always find a room door open—and the guests out on the balcony. The trick was getting out the balcony door without being noticed, or without having someone walk back into the room for a drink or to use the bathroom while you were inside. But even then, it was easy to brazen it out, pretend you had friends out there and you thought this was their room, apologize for the mistake, all the while continuing to walk toward the balcony doors and escape. There was always the possibility you'd run into some anal asshole who thought you were stealing stuff, but it hadn't happened to me yet. There's always a first time though, so I motioned to Misha and we walked quickly across the room and out onto the balcony. No one said a word; none of the people at the railing even looked back at us as I softly closed the French doors behind us. Misha grinned at me. I winked at him and said, "Follow me." We headed down to the St. Ann side. It was much more crowded at the corner. The people were standing two or three deep at the railing there, and even on the St. Ann side there were a lot of people standing around drinking. All of them were focused on the street and the balconies across the street. Taking a deep breath, I found the third set of French doors and knelt down to peer through the crack in the curtains.

Two men were sitting in chairs, facing the television, in suit pants and ties. One was wearing a blue dress shirt, the other a white shirt. Guns hung in shoulder holsters at their sides. I gulped. But at least there were only two of them.

And in a chair, also with his back to me, was Frank. At first I wasn't sure if it was him or not; then I realized he was still covered with glitter and gold body paint. It *had* to be Frank, I realized. Our Mercury costumes had been unique, unlike the Zorros. He looked okay; of course, I couldn't see his face, but he wasn't slumped down or anything. He was also tied up. Seeing that made my heartbeat start to race. I was relieved he was okay—hell, alive, for that matter—but seeing him tied up and helpless made me angry.

I stood back up, my mind working. "Okay, Frank is in there."

Misha nodded. "Okay, how do we get him out?"

I narrowed my eyes as I looked at him. "Can you create a disturbance in the hall, but get away without being seen? Something loud that would make them come out?" I moved closer to the doors again and looked down the space between them. They were probably locked, but the latch wasn't fastened. That made me grin. This was going to be almost too easy. *Hang in there, Frank, help is on the way.*

"Yes, I can do that." He nodded. "I know what to do."

"Okay, then, create a distraction and get the hell out of here. Head back to Mom and Dad's. Frank and I will meet you there." I said a quick prayer to the Goddess as Misha disappeared around the corner. I wasn't completely sure how I was going to get into the room, but I knew somehow I was going to, even if I had to break a window. I started praying, repeating the prayer over and over again in my head as I waited, sweat dripping down my forehead. "Come on, Misha," I muttered. "What's taking you so long?"

Seconds passed. *Come on, come on.*

There was a sudden *crash* and the suite's door swung open, slamming into the wall and swinging back almost shut. Misha stood in the doorway, sticking out his tongue and holding up both hands, his middle fingers distended. Then, he turned and ran to the right.

Both men jumped to their feet, pulling their guns, and headed out the doorway.

Here goes nothing, I thought, stepping back and kicking at the French doors. The doors flew open with a big crash.

"What the fuck?" someone said behind me.

I turned around and saw a group of people, beads around their necks, drinks in their hands, staring at me openmouthed. I raised my hands and shrugged, giving them a sheepish grin. "Locked myself out."

They all nodded. One said, "Right on, dude," toasting me with his cup, and then they all turned back to the street.

Ah, Mardi Gras.

Hoping that Misha had managed to lose them somehow, I dashed across the room and knelt in front of Frank and pulled out my keychain with its Swiss Army knife. I cut the ropes at his feet and around his wrists, before pulling the duct tape off his mouth.

"Ouch!" he said, before adding, "about fucking time."

"Come on. We've got to get out of here," I urged him. "Can you stand?"

I helped him to his feet and maintain his balance. He was a little wobbly but seemed fine. He moaned a bit. "My legs are asleep."

"Come on. We've got to hurry." I ran to the door and checked both ways. The hallway was empty. The upstairs at the Bourbon Orleans has a big rectangular hallway, and if Misha hadn't gotten either back out onto the balcony or down the fire stairs, they would be coming around the left corner. I ran down there, checked and saw no one other than a maid, and ran back to the room. "Can you walk, honey?" I asked.

His jaw clenched. "I need to tell you something." His scar looked like it was on fire—he was furious.

"Not now, Frank—later when we're out of here." I helped him to his feet. He leaned on me as his legs buckled. I half pulled, half dragged him out through the front door into the hallway.

"Come on!" I grabbed Frank and dragged him down the hallway. There was a set of fire stairs just around the corner. I was sweating and breathing hard; so was Frank. When we reached the corner, I looked. Even the maid was gone. With a sigh of relief, I grabbed Frank by the hand and led him to the stairs. He seemed to be able to walk on his own. Once inside the stairway, I asked, "Can you handle the stairs?"

He nodded. "I think so." He did a couple of kneebends. "They're not asleep anymore."

"Then, let's get the hell out of Dodge, okay?" I smiled at him. There was a huge bruise on the side of his face, and he was pale. His eyes were bloodshot. The bruise pissed me off. *Someone's going to pay for that,* I decided. "Come on, babe." We started down the steps, Frank walking behind me just in case he lost his balance. I wasn't sure I would be able to catch his dead weight, but I figured I'd find the strength somehow. Frank stumbled on the stairs a couple of times, but I was able to catch him and keep him from falling. "Do you need to rest for a minute?" I asked when we got to the bottom of the stairs. I bit my lip, hoping he'd say no. Every second we stayed in the hotel, the better the chance of being caught. "Are you okay?"

He gave me a weak smile. "No, let's get the fuck out of here." He grimaced. "I don't ever want to see the inside of this hotel again."

"Attaboy." I gave him a big hug, and he wrapped his arms around me tightly. "All right, then; let me see if the coast is clear."

I opened the door and looked. The lobby was crowded, but I didn't see either of the goons anywhere. Then it hit me. Frank was going to stand out like a sore thumb with his little gold swim trunks and gold-painted boots—not to mention the now streaky gold paint and glitter all over his body. *"Fuck.* Wait here a minute." I slipped out into the hallway and whistled as I walked out to the pool area. Sure enough, just like I remembered, there was a towel stand out by the pool—and praise be to the Goddess, someone had left a pair of sweatpants there. I grabbed two towels and the sweatpants and ran back inside. "Here, put these on." I tossed him the sweatpants and started rubbing at his skin with the towel. All I managed to do was smear the paint some more. Frank leaned on me as he put on the sweatpants, pulling them up as high as they would go. He grinned at me and grabbed the other towel, which he draped around his shoulders.

"Hardly incognito, but it *is* Mardi Gras." He shrugged. "Scotty, we really need to talk. You've got to hear what I have to say. . . ."

"Later, Frank—we've got to get out of here."

"But, Scotty—"

"I know; I love you, too." I grinned. "Come on, then." We slipped back into the hallway. We ran into the lobby, slowed down and walked naturally to the front doors, but once out on the sidewalk started running again, heading for Royal Street. Frank's legs obviously weren't working yet, as I had to slow down a few times so he could catch up. People stared at us as we went by, and I kept scanning the crowds of people for the thugs but didn't see them anywhere. We didn't slow down until we got to the Devil's Weed. We walked to the back door and stood there for a minute to catch our breath. Frank put his arms around me and gave me a big kiss. "I knew you would come for me," Frank said, between gasps for air. "What took you so long?"

"Who were those guys, Frank?" I changed the subject.

He shook his head. "I don't know. I don't know anything about *them*. But they were Russian; that I know. What they are up to, I don't know, but I do know—" He hesitated. "Scotty, this is going to be hard for you to believe, but you've got to listen to me."

"I mean, how did they get you? That's the part I don't understand. I mean, you left with a guy, right? Was that a setup?"

Frank's face turned red and his eyes narrowed. "Is that what you think? You think I left with a *trick?*"

"It's okay, Frank. It bothered me a bit at first, but it's okay now." I was babbling and didn't care. "Come on, let's get inside and in the house."

I unlocked the door to the back steps, closing it once we were inside. We started up the stairs, Frank behind me and holding my hand. Every once in a while he squeezed it. I unlocked the back door and called, "Mom? Dad? You here?"

"In the living room, Scotty," my mother replied.

With a sigh of relief, I turned and threw my arms around Frank. I held him like I never wanted to let go. "I'm so glad you're okay," I whispered.

"I knew you'd come," he whispered back, kissing my cheek. "I knew it, but we really have to talk, Scotty. *Please*, it's important."

"Come on, let's go into the living room." I grabbed his hand. "We have a lot to talk about—you wouldn't believe what's been going on the last couple of days. We'll get Mom to look at that bruise, and then we can talk, okay?"

"I think I know more than you think I do." He rubbed his chin ruefully. "I could stand to sit down." He didn't go inside the door. "You mind if I come in a little later?" His eyes looked a little glassy. "I'm feeling a little woozy."

I kissed the top of his head. "You just stay here. I'll go get Mom and Dad to help me bring you in."

I could see the living room was dark when I walked in, and automatically I reached for the light switch. "Why are the lights—"

As the room flooded with light, I saw in horror that my parents and Misha were tied up. Only my mother wasn't gagged.

And the kidnapper with the white shirt was standing next to her, a gun against her head, a nasty smirk on his face.

CHAPTER EIGHTEEN

Justice

*justice will be done; balance is required
in all things*

Until that moment, I would have said there's nothing more horrific than looking down the barrel of a gun.

I've unfortunately looked down more than my fair share of them. And just like the dead bodies thing, every time I find myself on the wrong end of a gun, it's just as rough as the first time. It never seems to get easier. *But this was worse,* I decided in that split second as my eyes scanned the room and took it all in. *It's much, much worse when the gun is held to your mother's head, and all you can do is stand there helpless.* I stood there in the doorway from the kitchen, frozen in complete shock. I didn't know what to do; I couldn't move or speak. My mother's eyes were wide open and she was moving her eyes rapidly back and forth, trying to signal me—or maybe she was just having a seizure of some sort. My father's eyes were also wide open; Misha's looked resigned. "What the hell? What is going on here?" I said loudly as Frank came through the back door. I hoped that White Shirt hadn't heard two sets of footsteps on the stairs, or heard Frank and I having our little chat out there. Out of the corner of my eye, I saw Frank stop dead in his tracks when I spoke. I couldn't turn my head or anything without tipping White Shirt off that I wasn't alone—Frank was our ace in the hole. I just took a deep breath and, feeling like an idiot, said loudly, "Why are you holding a gun on my family?"

I took a step forward, willing Frank to go back down the stairs and go for help. I couldn't take my eyes off the gun pressing against my mother's temple, even though her eyes were still moving back and forth. *What the hell is she trying to tell me?*

"Sit down." He gestured to a vacant chair with his free hand. His white dress shirt was wet at the armpits, and his forehead was wet with sweat. "Or I'll shoot her." He pressed the gun tighter against her skin. She closed her eyes. His eyes glittered. "Believe me, I would love nothing more than to shoot this bitch." That was when I noticed the scratches on his face. Mom, apparently, had not gone down easily. *Attagirl,* I thought to myself.

I've always been raised to believe that *hate* is the worst emotion possible for humans. The very basis of my religious beliefs, my spirituality, is that hate is a destructive force that will eventually consume the hater with its negative energy and rot his or her soul. Everything evil that humans do springs originally from hate. Evil is not possible without hatred. Murder, rape, war, and violence all are symptoms of hatred in the soul. Evil and hate are vile, despicable twin sisters who should be reviled and avoided at all costs. If all humans could turn their backs on hate and evil, the world would become a paradise where we could all live together in peace and harmony. I've never allowed myself to let hate into my heart or my mind. Even when it flashes into my consciousness, I've always managed to take a deep breath and step away from it, turn my back and return myself to a balanced state of peace. I never let my anger, at those moments when it takes control, sink roots in my psyche and deepen. I never wish ill on another human—after all, the basic karmic principle of the Goddess is that whatever energy you send out into the Universe returns to you threefold. So, I pray for the haters of the world. I pray for the fanatics who shoot doctors who perform abortions and blow up Planned Parenthood. I pray for the haters who masquerade as Christians and pervert the religion of the Prince of Peace into something Jesus Himself would regard with horror. I pray for the monsters pretending to be humans who attend the funerals of AIDS victims with signs that read GOD HATES FAGS and AIDS KILLS FAGS. I always pray that the rapists, the killers, and the violent will somehow find the grace to let go of their hatred and make peace with the beautiful, magical, wondrous Universe with which we have been blessed.

Yet as the barrel of the gun pressed against my mother's temple, I wished in that moment that my psychic gifts were a lot more powerful than what they were. I wished that I had the ability to move objects with my mind. I wished that I could shoot laser beams out of my eyes. I wished that I could unleash some kind of power or magic that would disintegrate the white shirt–wearing gunman into ions, as slowly and painfully as possible. I felt the anger, the power of rage and hatred coursing through my body as I carefully raised my hands up in the air over my head and walked slowly over to the chair, all the while hoping, with each step I took, that Frank was at that very moment on his way down the back steps and going for help. "You are never going to get away with this," I said, knowing I sounded trite, trying to keep my voice from shaking. I didn't want him to know how terrified I actually was.

Pray for a brave heart.

It made sense to me now.

I sat down, placing my hands on my knees so they were visible. I willed my hands not to shake. I wasn't armed, but he didn't know that, and I wished I'd brought the gun I'd taken off the Homeland Security agent with me. As soon as I was sitting, he turned the gun away from my mother and pointed it at me. I closed my eyes and said a quick "thank you" to the Goddess. At least for now my mother was safe. I opened my eyes and watched as he walked toward me. His face was twisted with hate. *You're a dead man, Scotty,* I thought to myself, but then wondered why Misha was still alive. *Wasn't that the whole point—to kill all three of them?*

I weighed my options and tried to clear my mind. As powerful as the rage and the hate were, I knew they would only cloud my mind. I needed to be calm, to clear my mind. I took some deep breaths and felt calmer, tried to force the anger out and let the peace in.

Could I possibly kick the gun out of his hand when he got close enough?

Pray for a brave heart, Scotty.

I let go of the anger. I closed my eyes and prayed for strength and wisdom. As I prayed, I felt the darker emotions drain from my body and a sense of peace and serenity slowly sweep over me, blanketing me with a sense of calm. I felt energy radiate through my body, coursing through my veins, filling my muscles with a kind of power I'd never known or felt before. My tiredness, the aches I'd been feeling, were gone and I felt refreshed, and I knew I could do it—somehow I just knew I could get the gun away from him and save everyone. I opened my eyes.

He was getting closer to me, that sick gloating smile on his face.

I coiled my legs, getting ready.

I closed my eyes again and prayed again for the strength, for accuracy, for the ability to somehow save my family.

I opened my eyes. He was close enough. I took a deep breath and kicked out with my right leg.

I managed to catch him in the wrist and his arm flew up. The gun went off with a deafening roar as it flew out of his hand, and plaster rained down from the ceiling as I launched myself out of my chair and at him. I caught him in the midsection with my shoulder, and we fell backward, landing on the coffee table, which collapsed beneath our weight. I wrapped my legs around his to immobilize them and squeezed mine together as tightly as I could as I slammed my right hand into his stomach over and over again, knocking the breath out of him as he tried to hammer blows down on my head and shoulders. I didn't feel them, felt nothing at all except the urgency of finishing him off, rendering him helpless and impotent. Adrenaline raced through my body and I kept slamming my fists into his ribs and stomach while my eyes glanced around the room, trying to locate where the gun had fallen when it flew out of his hand. I saw it—lying on the floor just beside where Misha was tied up. I reached up with one hand and shoved his chin upward. He clawed at my hand, which gave me the opening I was looking for. I released his legs and grabbed his Adam's apple with my other hand, giving it a tight squeeze with all the strength in that hand, then shoved him aside and rolled across the floor to the gun. I grabbed it and stood up, pointing it at him.

Oh, thank you, Goddess, thank you.

I gestured to the chair. "Have a seat." I smiled at him as he wheezed for breath. The Adam's apple is incredibly sensitive. Hitting someone there or just giving it a good squeeze is just as effective as doing the same thing to the balls: it's equally immobilizing. He was coughing and gagging, his eyes watering. I felt a brief rush of exhilaration, which I quickly squelched. "I said get in the fucking chair *now*." I gestured again. "I will shoot you," I said, in a very pleasant tone, hoping he had no idea I was bluffing. He glared at me and climbed up into the chair. "I want to see your hands. Keep them where I can see them, okay? My trigger finger is kind of itchy." Okay, so I was borrowing dialogue from B movies, but I didn't know what else to say.

Okay, now what, Scotty? I asked myself. I couldn't very well take the gun off of him. I glanced around for something to tie him up with, but the only thing I could see was the extension cords he'd used on my parents and Misha. They were knotted pretty tightly, and I didn't dare take my eyes off him long enough to untie one of them to use on him. *Maybe the best thing was to just hold the gun on him and stall for time until Frank got back with the police.* I walked over to him and pressed the gun to his temple. He whimpered a little bit.

"I want some answers," I said. "Start talking."

He spat at me.

"Nice." I shook my head. "Didn't your mother ever teach you that's not very nice?" I prayed to the Goddess to forgive me, and I smacked him across the face with the gun. A bruise started to form on his cheek, and I remembered the bruise on Frank's face. Anger rose inside of me, but I forced it down. *Stay calm, stay calm. Help will be here any minute.* He just kept glaring at me, without saying a word. I sighed. I just don't have it in me to be an interrogator. I don't have the stomach for torturing people, I realized. Maybe I don't have what it takes to be a private eye if I can't beat a confession out of someone.

But somehow, I couldn't think that was a bad thing.

I heard a noise in the kitchen, and with relief looked up, expecting to see Frank and maybe reinforcements—and my heart sank when I saw a gun pointed directly at me.

It was the other guy from the Bourbon Orleans, the one with the blue shirt.

"Drop it," he ordered, cocking the trigger.

I bit my lower lip. *Might as well try to keep bluffing.* I put my gun against White Shirt's head. "I'll kill him."

Blue Shirt gave me a pitying look and shrugged. "Go ahead. Then I will shoot you." He raised his eyebrows. "It doesn't matter to me. Go on then. Shoot him." He smiled the coldest smile I had ever seen. It sent chills down my spine. His eyes were unlike anything I'd ever seen before. I've often heard that the eyes are the windows of the soul. If that was true, then this guy had no soul. His eyes were completely dead and empty. They were the eyes of someone who had killed before and would kill again—a man who *enjoyed* killing people. He would kill me without a second thought and then turn his gun on my parents and Misha just for the sheer joy of killing. "And then I will shoot them all."

I was in the presence of something almost inhuman, a killing machine, someone with the morality of a shark, a predator who killed merely for the pleasure of it.

I dropped my gun and raised my arms yet again over my head and walked backward away from White Shirt.

White Shirt picked up the gun and turned it on me, a malevolent grin on his face. "I knew you hadn't the stomach for killing. Americans never do," he sneered at me.

He's going to kill me. Ah, well, it's been a pretty good life. I've pretty much enjoyed my every day. I had wonderful parents and truly great friends, not to mention the last few months with Colin and Frank. I've been happier than anyone has a right to expect, and I've had lots of good times, and I am not afraid—

"You let this boy disarm you?" Blue Shirt said, his voice almost wondering. "Can't I leave you alone for a moment? Are you so worthless? So incompetent? You let a weak American boy take your gun away from you? You are a disgrace."

A gun fired.

My entire body tensed. But I felt nothing. I opened my eyes in time to see White Shirt topple over backward, a blooming red rose expanding in the middle of his chest, a look of complete surprise on his face. I stared in horror as his body hit the floor, and the blood began to pool and spread across the shiny hard wood. My legs felt weak, and I leaned against the wall to keep from falling. Blue Shirt was now pointing his gun at me. I prayed again—*Goddess have mercy on White Shirt's spirit, and please protect me from this maniac, protect us all*—and tilted my chin up defiantly. "Well, go ahead and shoot me then. But why did you do that?" I tried not to look at White Shirt, just nodded with my head.

"He's a fool. He needed killing. Now I don't have to share fee with him." He shook his head.

"Well, go on, get it over with. Shoot me."

"That is not the plan."

The plan? What the fuck?

Yet it was still a relief to hear him say it. I hoped Frank was on his way with the cops or Colin or anyone. I swallowed.

"So, what exactly is the plan?" I asked, keeping my voice steady. It wasn't easy.

He frowned at me. "Shut up."

Behind him, in the hallway, I saw the door to the staircase leading to the shop slowly start to open. It had to be Frank, back with the cops or someone. *Thank you, Goddess.* I smiled at Blue Shirt. *Keep him distracted; keep him talking; keep him from turning around and seeing that someone is coming.*

"Are you the one who killed Sasha and Pasha?" I asked, willing myself not to look at the door to the staircase. "Why? Why did you do it?"

"I said shut up." He glanced quickly at his watch, an annoyed expression on his face, waving the gun at me again.

Frank stepped through the door, and I almost fainted with relief. He was holding a gun. His face was grim and twisted with anger.

That didn't bode well for Blue Shirt.

Keep him talking, Frank seemed to say with his eyes.

"What I don't understand is why," I went on. "I mean, why does Viktor Kafelnikov want them all dead so badly? I mean, is he really that crazy that he can't stand being rejected?"

He gave me an odd look. *"Kafelnikov?"*

There was a little pop, and he got this surprised look on his face before pitching forward onto the floor. He fell in slow motion, seeming to take forever. The gun fell out of his hand and went clattering across the floor. I watched it go, bouncing until it started spinning around and around before finally coming to a rest.

My legs gave out and I sat down on the floor with a bone-jarring thud that shook the room. *Thank you, Goddess, oh, thank you.*

Frank picked up the gun and ran across the room to me. "Are you okay?" He knelt down, his eyes concerned. He cupped my chin in his hand and examined my face. "He didn't hurt you, did he?"

"No." My mouth was incredibly dry, and I started to shake a little. "I'm okay." I nodded and gestured to everyone else. "Untie them . . . make sure they're all okay." I looked at White Shirt and felt gorge rise in my stomach and looked away. Frank was untying my mother. As soon as my mother could stand she threw her arms around Frank and squeezed him with a death grip, showering his face with kisses, and then was on her way across the room to me.

"Um, Mom, if you don't stop squeezing me you're going to break a rib," I said, but I was squeezing her just as hard.

"Oh, Scotty." She wiped tears out of her eyes. "When he had that gun on you—oh, dear Goddess." She let me go and walked over to where Blue Shirt's body was lying. She launched a hard kick into his ribs. "May you burn in hell for all eternity, you monster."

I couldn't help it. I laughed.

After everyone was untied and we were all talking a million miles an hour to each other and making sure we were all okay, Frank shouted, "Attention!"

We all shut up and turned to look at him. "Venus and the cops are on their way." He waved his cell phone. "I just called them, so we need to get our stories straight."

I stared at him. *Get our stories straight? What the hell was he talking about?*

"Let's go out on the deck, okay?" He turned and walked through the kitchen. Dumbly, we all followed him. Once we were all gathered out there and seated, I said, "Frank, what are you talking about? Why do we need to get our stories straight?"

He turned to Misha. "What do you think, Misha? Do we need to get some things straight?"

"Misha?" My mother stared at him. "But why—I don't understand. I thought—" She looked at me for help.

"I know, I know, Mom. You need a scorecard," I said. "He's been pretending to be Sasha."

"Please understand, Cecile. I was trying to help my brothers." The tears started coming out of his eyes again. "It was so horrible being in Russia. And seeing what was happening to Pasha. I knew we had to get out of Russia. That is why I wrote to our American family. But I couldn't tell Mrs. Diderot the truth, the *full* truth. We had a plan, you see. My brothers and I decided that the best way to save us all was for me to come to America. We pretended that we'd fallen out, to protect *me* from Kafelnikov . . . and by then, Pasha was so deeply involved with Kafelnikov we knew he could never get away alive. Kafelnikov forced him to kill, to bind him even closer to him. He forced him to be involved in the drugs, the gun smuggling—so that there was nothing he could do to get away. So, I wrote to Mrs. Diderot. Everything else just went from there."

"Did you marry Sylvia just to get out of Russia?" my mother asked.

He shook his head. "Americans," he said with a smile. "It was her idea—so I could stay in the country. At first, we tried to keep it a secret, but people would wonder why Sylvia had a Russian man in her house. I do love Sylvia. She is sweet and funny and kind, and she has been very good to me."

"So, you aren't gay?" I asked. Not that it mattered. I felt stupid after I'd said it.

He gave me a look. "Yes, but because I love men does not mean that I cannot love a woman."

"Amen." My mother nodded. When I looked at her, she

shrugged. "Scotty, no one can control who they love. You of all people should know that."

I nodded. When she's right, she's right.

"When I came to America, I came to the FBI and told them I have information on Kafelnikov—and that my brother wants out; he had even more information. They were interested . . . but by then Pasha was too addled with the drugs. He was useless to them as he was, so they came up with the idea to switch Pasha for Sasha, and bring Pasha to the United States to get cleaned up . . . and then Sasha would be brought over later. So Pasha got cleaned up but he doesn't want the protection program, so Sylvia and I brought him to New Orleans and set him up in Burgundy house." He turned to me. "Pasha was your dealer, Scotty. I didn't know about the drugs again, or the Web site, but he used my name. I was here and not hiding, so we figured it easier for him to pretend to be me, that nobody know there were two of us. Then a few weeks ago Sasha's cover was blown, and they had to bring him to the United States. I didn't know what to do; they brought him to New Orleans. I don't know what they were going to do . . . they were trying to convince them to change names and disappear." He shuddered. "Saturday night the FBI called me. They told me two of Kafelnikov's killers were in New Orleans, were seen skulking around Burgundy Street house, so I called Pasha to warn him."

The phone call that upset him so much, I remembered.

"He told me that I was paranoid, that everything would be okay, so I called Sasha. I tell Sasha to switch places with me—had to go to party but I was worried." He sighed. "I didn't tell Sasha why; he was just happy to go with Sylvia. I came down to the French Quarter and see—" he stopped, looking at me.

"What did you see?" Frank prodded.

"I saw man in Zorro costume. I thought it was Scotty because Pasha told me what Scotty was wearing when I called." He looked away from me. "I go in and find the body. I call the cops and came here, pretending to be Sasha." He held up his hands. "And that's all."

I swallowed. "I have to ask you something, Misha, something really important." Every eye turned to me. I took a deep breath. *"Was Zorro wearing a shirt?"*

The door opened, and Venus stepped through with an irritated look on her face. "Ah, the Bradley family. With corpses in the living room, no less." She sighed. "All right, might as well all head down to the station to clear this mess up. Any objections?"

No one said anything. She looked at Misha, shook her head, and looked at me. "And this time, Scotty, you've managed to raise the dead. I can't wait to hear this story." She walked over to me. "You need to stand up."

"Why?" I looked at her in bewilderment.

"You have no idea how much I hate doing this." She pulled my hands behind my back gently and placed handcuffs on me. "Scotty Bradley, you are under arrest for assaulting a federal agent. You have the right to remain silent. . . ."

CHAPTER NINETEEN

Seven of Wands

the ability to hold one's own against adversaries

I waited forever for Storm to show up at the police station—it seemed to take hours.

Of course, getting from Uptown to the Quarter while the Orpheus parade was rolling is a nightmare. He finally came into the interrogation room, mopping his face with a handkerchief as he sat down heavily in a chair. He was wearing black tie, and I realized I'd pulled him yet again from a party. "Um, sorry," I said.

He looked at me. "Don't be. The party was at Marguerite's parents'." His wife's parents threw the *worst* parties. I'm not sure what it was. There were always interesting people, really good food, and lots of liquor, but they were interminable bores. I'd finally stopped going after the third time I was invited. He sighed. "Okay, baby bro, you're in some deep shit now."

I nodded tiredly. I *had* assaulted Special Agent Vince Clay. Several times since Venus brought me in, some Feds had tried to get me to talk, but I refused to say a word. "I did it, Storm." I then explained why.

He whistled. "Well, it's understandable, but I don't know if we can call it *justified*, Scotty. And that's not all." He opened his briefcase and looked into it. "Scotty, there's a whole bunch of other shit they think you're involved in. I know you weren't, but I don't know if we can convince them of that."

"It's Colin, isn't it?" I couldn't keep the bitterness out of my voice.

"Why do you say that?" He finally looked at me.

"Because I am pretty sure he killed Pasha Saturday night. I'm also pretty sure he had Frank kidnapped last night; those two thugs at Mom and Dad's worked for him." *The man who had held a gun to my mother's head had been working for Colin.*

I wanted to throw up.

"Did you talk to Frank?" I asked. "How mad is he?"

"He's pretty mad," Storm admitted. "Apparently, on Sunday night he had gone to get water and was on his way back to the dance floor when he saw Colin walking out of the bar talking on his cell phone. He followed him to a meeting with the two guys, and Colin saw him. They overpowered him and held him at the Bourbon Orleans until you"—he grinned at me—"broke him out. Nice work, by the way."

"Thanks."

"Apparently, Colin's real name is Abram Golden. He's a former Mossad agent, who's apparently gone rogue. He works for the highest bidder. Money is the only thing that matters to him— he doesn't care about politics."

"I can't believe it," I whispered.

"I can't either," Storm said, shaking his head. "He fooled all of us, Scotty. I—I thought of him as a member of the family. We all did."

I wished I could feel something. I just sat there, numb, like I had since I'd been brought in. It was weird. I should have felt *something*, right? Angry? Betrayed? Sad? Heartbroken? Deceived? Something—anything—would have been better than the numbness, the sense that not only could I not feel anything, but I never would, ever again.

"Apparently, he was working for this Kafelnikov person," Storm went on, "to kill Sasha and Pasha—and no one can find Colin. You were the last person to see him. He went out the French doors and just vanished."

"Sasha and Pasha were both dead," I said. "His job was over, and the two guys—the dead ones—he just abandoned them." *No honor among thieves or murderers, apparently.* "What about Angela Blackledge?" That was something I didn't understand.

Storm sighed. "There apparently is an Angela Blackledge, and she does operate a worldwide investigation and security company, but she claims that Abram Golden—or Colin Cioni—whatever— never worked for her, and that she never opened an office in New Orleans. That was his cover, apparently."

"Great." *No career now, no job, no boyfriend. I'd been lied to, manipulated, and Frank's life had been put at risk—hell, my whole family's lives had been put in danger. Colin was long gone before those guys broke into my parents' house. Even if he had wanted to protect us, he was gone and there was no one holding their leashes.*

Why wasn't I angry? Why was I feeling so empty?

"Bring them in," I said. I just wanted the whole thing to be over with.

They questioned me for hours. I offered to take a polygraph. It was pretty obvious to me at first that the federal agents couldn't believe anyone could be as stupid as I apparently was. It took hours to convince them, rather humiliatingly, that, yes, indeed, I was that trusting and naïve and stupid. They finally agreed to drop the assault charge down to a misdemeanor. I would plead guilty and get probation. It meant losing my chance at ever getting a private eye license, but I didn't really care at that point. Finally, it was all over and done with, and I tiredly walked out into the lobby of the police station. All I wanted to do was go home and go to bed and pretend none of it had ever happened. But my night of surprises wasn't quite over yet.

The last people I expected to see were my grandparents.

Papa and Maman Diderot were sitting on a bench in the lobby. Maman's head was down on his shoulder, her eyes closed. He had his arm around her shoulders. She was still wearing the dove gray suit she'd had on earlier that day. Papa, as always, was wearing a three-piece suit of charcoal gray, the vest buttoned over a crisply starched white shirt. I stood and looked at them for a while. They really looked cute, this sweet older couple sitting on a hard wooden bench in the police station, while cops walked in front of them leading disheveled drunks in handcuffs. Papa's pinkish scalp glowed in the overhead lights, and the silver gray hair on either side of his face was combed perfectly. I felt reasonably sure they never expected to spend their Lundi Gras evening in a police station. But, then again, my mom's been their daughter for a long, long time—probably nothing much surprises them anymore. I watched his face, looked at the lines etched into it. I saw the resemblance to Misha around the eyes and wondered if Misha and I had any similar features. I hadn't really thought to look. Maman always said I was the "spittin' image of Papa when he was young," which I'd always found a little distressing. I walked over to them. "Hey," I said, smiling at them. "What are you two doing here?"

Papa stood up and threw his arms around me. He's a little shorter than I am, maybe five seven, and as he's gone gray, the bourbon and fine food has been catching up with him, causing him to develop a bit of a potbelly that looks almost silly over his spindly legs. I was stunned. I couldn't remember the last time I'd had any physical contact with him, and he was holding me pretty tightly. I looked over his shoulder at Maman, who was smiling. She winked at me and then held a manicured finger to her lips. I gave her a questioning look, and she shook her head from side to side. Finally, after what seemed like an awfully long time, he let me go and said gruffly, "You know, son, I've gotten used to meeting your parents at jails, but this is a new one for me." His eyes twinkled a bit. "Not only your mom and dad, but my grandson and his partner? If we're not careful they're going to name a cell block after us." He turned to Maman. "What do you think, dear? Would a Diderot cell block be fitting?"

She shrugged. "God knows we've spent enough time in police stations. Certainly more than I ever thought I would." Her eyes twinkled as she spoke, taking some of the sting out of her words.

I stared at them both and shook my head. Were these my Diderot grandparents, making a joke in a police station? And did he say "my grandson *and his partner*"? Was he actually acknowledging Frank? I was dumbstruck and unable to think of a single thing to say. Finally, I managed to croak out, again, "What are you two doing here?"

Papa sat back down next to Maman and patted her leg. "Storm called us to meet him here. Apparently we need to have a family meeting." He waggled a finger at me and then patted Maman's leg again. "Your grandmother finally came clean with me before we came down here."

I raised an eyebrow and looked at her. Again, she winked at me and shook her head slightly. "I finally told him the truth about Misha. I swallowed my pride and told him about his *son*." She placed extra emphasis on the last word, and it didn't take a psychic gift to know what she meant by that. No word about there having been triplets, nothing about two of them having been murdered over the weekend. Papa didn't need to know any of that, after all, and why not embrace the one son who had survived?

More secrets, more lies.

I gaped at her and opened my mouth to say something, to contradict her, but stopped myself. What was the point in telling him now? Pasha and Sasha were dead; it would only hurt him. And he didn't need to know all that stuff about the Russian mob. He'd feel guilty, even though he'd never known they had existed—feel guilty about abandoning them to their fates in Russia. No, Maman was right. One son was all he needed to know about.

And then I realized that sometimes secrets and lies were really for the best. There was no point in causing the old man pain.

Not to mention Colin's betrayal.

I sat down next to Papa, who patted my leg affectionately. I smiled at him. He was no longer the scary, opinionated, my-way-or-the-highway old grump I'd always seen him as. No, he was just a man who tried to do the best he could with his kids, who made mistakes, but underneath it all, he loved his family. It was all bluster and bark, because that was the only way he knew how to show affection.

I'd never be afraid of him again.

"You're going to be thirty this year," Papa said, with a smile. "And look at you! A licensed private eye, all settled down. I wasn't sure when you dropped out of Vanderbilt, but your Diderot blood is too strong."

"Well, I don't think I'll get to be a private eye anymore, but what do you mean?"

"I was afraid when you dropped out of Vanderbilt you'd waste your life, son." He squeezed my knee. "That's why I cut off your trust, you know. I didn't want you to just be a layabout, like your uncle Bayard." His eyes darkened. My mother's only brother had never worked a day in his life, living off his trust fund and never once using his law degree. He drank a lot and was currently on his third wife. "But you worked, didn't you? I worried about it, you know, worried that you'd wind up living off your parents." He sighed. "I wasn't so sure about the dancing thing, but you managed to make it work."

"What?" (*He knew I'd been a stripper?*)

"I have to say I admired that." He looked at me shrewdly. "No skills, no training, but you found a way to make money and support yourself. I am proud of you, son."

"You're *proud* of me?" My eyes welled up with tears.

"Of course I am, son. I love you." He looked at me as though surprised I could have ever doubted it. "Besides"—he winked at me—"you're the spittin' image of me at your age. Handsome devil."

I couldn't help myself. I started crying. I told myself it wasn't my grandfather's words but the release of all the stress I'd been under since Sunday morning.

"Here now! What's wrong? What did I say wrong, Maman?"

"Oh, honestly, Papa." She opened her purse and handed me a handkerchief. I wiped my eyes. "Has it ever occurred to you that maybe you said something *right* for once in your life?"

"Oh." He put his arm around me and squeezed.

Slowly but surely, everyone came out. Mom and Dad came out first but weren't surprised to see the grands. Mom and Dad each hugged Maman and Papa. I remembered what Rain had said: this wasn't the first time, and the grands certainly didn't think it would be the last time. Apparently, they wouldn't have it any other way. As much as they fought and argued, as much as Mom complained about them, they loved each other and they were family. Papa was proud of Mom and Dad. I could see it in his face as he chatted with them. I just sat and listened, wondering about the craziness of my family. Apparently, Mom came by it naturally, from her parents. Papa was proud of his daughter—her spirit and her passion and following her heart into what he thought were crazy causes—and he supported her even as he disagreed with her.

That, I realized, was what *family* really meant.

Then Frank joined us. Papa clucked over the dark bruise on the side of his face after Mom introduced them. "It's a pleasure to finally meet you, sir," Frank said.

"Can't think why we haven't before." Papa glared at Mom and Dad. "I'm sure *some people* thought I wouldn't welcome you to the family, but anyone who can put up with my grandson is sure as hell welcome in my house."

"Dad—" Mom started to say, but Maman hushed her, and

she settled back on her bench, her eyes glittering. I knew the look; she and Papa were going to have a knock-down-drag-out as soon as they possibly could, he insisting that Frank had always been welcome on Third Street, she insisting he was an old homophobe who wouldn't have them in the house.

Just your typical American family.

Frank hugged me, and I held on to him for longer than was probably necessary. "I love you," I whispered in his ear, and he nuzzled my neck for a moment. "I was so worried. . . ."

He squeezed my hand as Storm escorted Misha out into the waiting area. There was an awkward silence for just a moment, and then Papa stood up and walked over to Misha. He looked tiny next to his hulking Russian son, and then he stuck out his hand.

"I understand our wives convinced you not to tell me who you are," he said gruffly, his voice thick with emotion.

"Yes, sir." Misha's big hand swallowed up Papa's, and then they were hugging, and Misha picked him up off the ground.

He really doesn't know his own strength. They walked off together to a far corner of the room and started talking.

"Venus is inclined to rule it a justifiable homicide," Storm said. "Pending the autopsies, of course." He went on to say that they'd found a high-powered rifle in the killers' hotel room, and they were pretty certain it was the rifle used to kill Sasha. They were running the ballistics. They were Russians, and it probably wouldn't take long to tie them to Kafelnikov's gang. Maman took Storm aside and started whispering to him, and every once in a while Storm would look over at Papa and Misha. Undoubtedly, she was enlisting him in the new conspiracy of silence.

Nobody mentioned Colin's name, which was really a blessing. I sighed in relief. Apparently, it was all over.

I was so tired.

As we walked out of the police station into the crowded streets of the Quarter, I took Frank's hand. "Are you okay?"

He gave me a frigid smile. "I'm fine. Perfectly fine." His jaw clenched. "I am going to hunt him down and kill him."

I stopped. "Frank—I know. I know how you feel." I took a deep breath. "And I understand how you feel. But we can't—we *can't*—do this. We can't let this affect us and who we are as people."

Frank glared at me. "He kept me hostage for two days, Scotty. He's responsible for your uncles' deaths. And"—he choked up—"and I thought he loved us, Scotty. I loved him."

I led him over to the curb and sat him down. He looked crazy in his smeared body paint and ragged sweatpants. "I know, Frank. I know it hurts." But it didn't; I still felt nothing. But I knew it had to be said. "But we have to somehow, someday forgive him for everything."

"I'll never forgive him," Frank said darkly.

I held him for a moment, and he clung to my arms. "Let's go home, babe," I said finally. He nodded, and we both stood up. "We're going to be fine. We still have each other."

He squeezed my hand.

Since Mom and Dad's place was a crime scene—I briefly wondered where their massive stash of marijuana was hidden, but Venus had always known about their habits, so that probably wasn't going to be a problem—I offered them my apartment. "I can just stay upstairs with the boys—with Frank," I said and winced. Mom and Dad wanted to go get some things out of their apartment, and Maman, Papa, and Misha had a lot, obviously, to talk about. So, Frank and I walked home alone.

It had stopped raining, and the ground was slick and wet. The streets were crowded with people, singing, shouting, and laughing. "It's kind of weird," I said as we headed past the cathedral. "I mean, seeing all these people carefree, in costume and having a good time."

Frank shrugged. "Don't you like what I have on?" He pirouetted clumsily and grinned at me.

I laughed and kept walking. I was too tired to really laugh, probably from all of the adrenaline that had ebbed and flowed through my body over the last two days. *Maybe that's why I'm so numb,* I thought. *I'm too tired to feel anything.* Every muscle in my body ached, and all I really wanted to do was take a hot shower and go to bed with Frank. "I'm sorry Mardi Gras turned into such a nightmare," I said out loud.

"Scotty, it's never your fault." Frank laughed. He kissed me on the cheek. "How can you take the blame for any of this?" He gave a bitter laugh. "Doesn't matter whether you bought Ecstasy from Pasha or not—he still would have wound up dead—and all of this would have blown up in our faces." He sighed. "Christ, Scotty, even the jobs were faked."

"I know." I shrugged. "Unemployed again. Maybe they need a dancer at the Pub for tomorrow."

"Oh, no you don't." Frank pulled me into a hug and squeezed me tight. "You aren't going back to stripping. I can move downstairs and we can split the rent. I've got my pension from the FBI, and maybe you can train people again. Or we could get jobs with another agency."

"I don't know. I'm kind of soured on the whole private eye thing," I said, kissing his neck. "But we don't have to decide now. We don't have to decide anything. Let's just try to forget about it all, shall we?"

The fourth-floor apartment felt strange once we walked inside. It seemed quiet and empty. Frank checked the closets; Colin had apparently left everything behind. "I guess we can take this stuff to Goodwill," Frank said, going through Colin's half of the closet.

"I'm taking a shower." I walked into the bathroom. *If that's how Frank copes, let him,* I decided. *But I don't want to think about Colin anymore.* I didn't want to think about him ever again. There was no response, so I stripped off my clothes and climbed into the hot spray. I soaped up my body and luxuriated in the hot water coursing over my aching, tired muscles. All I wanted to do was get into bed and sleep for two or three days. Forget Fat Tuesday—I never thought I would think that—but I just didn't care about missing it.

I just wanted to stay home and hide.

I got out of the shower and dried off, put on a pair of Frank's sweatpants, and walked out into the living room. Frank was sitting on the couch, flipping through the television channels with that angry look on his face. "Frank, let's go to bed, okay?"

"How could he do it to us?" Frank asked. "That's what I don't get. How could he tell us he loved us, how could he have slept with us night after night, spent so much time with us every day, and we never had the slightest idea of who he really was?"

I curled up next to him on the couch and put my head on his shoulder. "I guess we'll never know. I'd like to think he did feel something for us, but . . ." My voice trailed off. "He even fooled Mom. Mom liked him, and she's always right about people. There's a first time for everything, though."

"And the Blackledge Agency thing," Frank went on. "I mean, I checked them out. But he was really smart there, using an agency that really exists. I mean, no one would ever think to check, right?"

"Not in New Orleans. This city's a magnet for con artists."

Frank kissed the top of my head. "Well, let's go to bed."

"No more thoughts about hunting him down and killing him?"

"Okay, I won't do it," Frank replied, his voice hard. "But I can't promise not to think about it."

The High Priestess

*a caution not to speak of that which
must remain secret*

Needless to say, I didn't sleep well.

The bed seemed empty with just the two of us in it, and no matter how much I cuddled up to Frank, or how good his big, strong arms felt wrapped around my waist, I couldn't fall into a deep sleep. My mind just wouldn't let anything go, wouldn't relax, *couldn't* stop thinking. Frank was somehow able to fall asleep—probably from exhaustion—but as much as I hoped his even breathing might lull me to sleep, it didn't happen. I just lay there all night, drifting off for a little while, but then waking up again. Around three in the morning I got very sad and started crying. I held it in a bit, just sniffling a little and letting the tears roll down my face. I didn't want to wake Frank. Angry as he was, I believed that if he saw *me* crying, he'd get even madder than he already was.

And then he'd probably have a stroke. He wasn't far from it.

A couple of times I slipped out from under Frank's arms and went down to my apartment. Mom and Dad were asleep. They always went to bed early on Lundi Gras; Fat Tuesday was the only exception they ever made to their never-get-up-before-noon rule. I smoked some pot, hoping it might help me sleep or at least relax me somewhat. My muscles were all knotted up. I tried to do a reading with my cards. But the Goddess wasn't responsive. I was on my own.

Shouldn't I have known? Shouldn't we have figured it out sometime over the last five months? What kind of psychic gift do I have, if I can go to bed every night with a sociopathic murderer without any conscience and not have the slightest idea? What the hell is wrong with me, anyway? He could have slit our throats at any time in our sleep.

Maybe that was unfair, but I couldn't help thinking that way. But then again, I'd never felt endangered. Not once.

And then I remembered that incredible megawatt smile, the way his face would soften sometimes when I'd see him watching me, or Frank, and I started to cry again.

He couldn't have been acting. He had to have feelings for us. We were more than just a cover story. No one is that good of an actor.

But then that other insidious voice would whisper, *But of course he's a good actor. He wouldn't still be alive if he weren't. He's very good at what he does. Do you really think you're the first person he's ever deceived, fooled, lied to? He leaves scorched earth in his wake, lives destroyed, shattered, ended. How many people do you think he's killed? No, he never loved you and Frank; he was laughing at you the whole time—at your naivete at playing private eye, at your innocence and blind trust.*

I *hated* that voice. Was it any wonder I couldn't sleep?

Around five-thirty I walked out onto the balcony and sat in one of the chairs with a joint. The sun was starting to rise; the darkness of the night was beginning to lighten. The air no longer felt cold and damp. I sat there and smoked the joint, watching a freighter pass by on the river, heading out to the Gulf of Mexico. Down past the turn in the river, coming up toward the city, was a massive cruise ship, and I smiled. Every year, RSVP Cruises has a big boat dock at the foot of Canal Street on Fat Tuesday, disembarking thousands of gay men ready to party. Even as I sat there, Zulu was lining up on Napoleon Avenue in Uptown, and Rex was lining up right behind it. Yet now, the night was peaceful and quiet. I just sat there.

No matter what was going on in *my* life, Fat Tuesday was going to go on like it always does. In a few hours, the streets would be packed. People were probably already out on the parade route, drinking and getting ready. All over the city, alarms were going off, and people were putting on their costumes. All through the Quarter, lights were coming on as people dragged their tired asses out of bed to get ready for the party they were throwing, for the guests who would arrive wanting mimosas and screwdrivers, Bloody Marys and Irish coffee.

Where are you now, Colin? Are you out of the country? On your way to your next job? Are you thinking about us? Or are we already forgotten, just two more on the long list of people you've used and lied to?

I pinched the joint out and walked back inside through the window. I'd only turned on one light in the living room, and as I set the roach in an ashtray, I happened to glance over at the television and caught my breath.

The picture frame on top of the TV was empty.

I got up and walked over to it. I picked up the wooden frame, held it in my hands, staring down at it.

It had held a picture of the three of us in our Halloween costumes, down in the courtyard. Millie and Velma had taken it, all three of us in our harem boy clothes, and we were all laughing, huge smiles on our faces, our arms around each other. It was my favorite picture of the three of us because we all looked so happy, even with Frank's arm in a sling.

He had left his clothes. He had left his toiletries. He had cleared out, taking nothing with him—*except the picture.*

He had to have cared on some level. He climbed the side of Jax Brewery to rescue me back in October. If he didn't care, he could have just left me there to die.

I started crying again, wiping at my face and hugging the

frame to my chest. He *wanted* to remember us. That had to mean
something, didn't it? It wasn't all a lie; we'd meant something to
him. After a few minutes I put the frame down on the coffee table
and went back to bed. Frank was lying on his side, and I curled
up behind him, putting my arms around him. He leaned back
into me, and I closed my eyes.

Fat Tuesday dawned sunny and clear, the sky blue and free of
clouds. The Universe chose to smile on New Orleans, and it was
absolutely gorgeous outside. I'd set the alarm for seven, and when
it went off I reached out and shut it off. Frank sat up, wiping at
his eyes. "Hey," he mumbled at me. We'd talked very briefly before going to bed about whether we were going to participate in
Fat Tuesday and finally had decided to just set the alarm and see
how we felt when we woke up.

"Hey—did you sleep well?" I peered closely at his face. The
bruise was still pretty bad but was starting to fade a bit. If we did
go out, the masks I'd picked out for today would cover up the
bruise.

He shrugged. "Okay, I guess. But I'm wide awake now."

"Do you want . . ." I let my voice trail off.

He threw the covers back and stood up, stretching, the muscles in his back, shoulders, and arms rippling. He was wearing a
gray pair of Calvin Klein boxer briefs that hugged his butt. "You
know something?" He turned and looked at me. His jaw was
clenched again. "I don't want to let that fuck ruin my first Fat
Tuesday."

It's a little late for that, I thought, as I stood up and yawned.
"Why don't you get in the shower? I'll go start some coffee and
get our costumes together—if you're sure."

He nodded. "I'm sure. I don't want to sit around here all day
and just think about it, you know?" He walked into the bathroom. He had a point; I sure as hell didn't want to sit around
sulking all day and feel sorry for myself. I pulled on a pair of
sweatpants and started the coffee, then headed down the back

stairs. Our costumes were hanging in the bedroom closet. Mom and Dad were awake, smoking away in my living room. The entire apartment reeked of marijuana, and I made a mental note to make sure to leave the windows open after they were able to get back into their place. Mom and Dad already had their costumes on. They were going as two of the Ten Commandments; Mom was *Thou shalt not kill* and Dad was *Thou shalt not commit adultery.* They and eight of their friends were going as the complete set. Basically, they looked like slate tablets with the words carved into the front. "How are you doing, son?" Mom asked, offering me the joint she was smoking.

"Good as can be expected, I guess." I shrugged.

"Forget about him, son," Dad said. He tried to give me a hug but his costume wouldn't really let him, so he just rubbed my head. "He fooled all of us, I'm afraid."

"He didn't fool *me*," Mom said. "I knew there was something not quite right about him."

I just looked at her. She had the decency to blush. I walked over and kissed her cheek. "I love you, Mom."

She stroked the side of my face. "Don't let this change you, my baby."

"I won't. I promise." I gathered up our costumes and went back upstairs.

My original idea for the Fat Tuesday costumes had been to go as zebras. We had all gotten square-cut bathing suits with a zebra pattern on them. We'd made hats to go with them, but the body paint was going to be a pain in the ass and I'd decided not to bother with that. Instead, I decided to go with what had originally been intended to be our Lundi Gras costumes. They were a little more elaborate but a little less intensive than the Mercury costumes from Sunday night. I'd gotten David to make each of us a very short pleated skirt that barely covered our butts. Mine was gold, Frank's was green, and Colin's was purple. We had wreaths for our hair that matched the skirts. We also had vests in the same colors as well as capes, and, of course, elaborate matching masks. We were, basically, going as the Spirit of Mardi Gras. As I walked up the stairs, I decided what we'd do was switch them out. Instead of being just one color, Frank and I would mix the pieces so we would be decked out in the colors of the day.

Frank was sitting in the living room when I got back upstairs. I dumped all the pieces of the costumes into an easy chair. He was holding the empty picture frame, and there were tears on his face. "Are you okay?" I asked him.

He nodded and put the frame down, wiping at his face. "Yeah, I'm fine. I'm still mad, though—I don't know if I'll ever not be mad at him." He sighed and stood up. He had a towel wrapped around his waist. "But I'm not going to let him ruin our day—or our lives. He's dead to me now."

"Frank—" I hated hearing him talk like that.

He held up his hand. "Scotty, please."

I pointed at the frame. "He took the picture, Frank. He left everything else, but he took that. Why do you think that is?"

"Don't defend that bastard to me," Frank snapped. "I don't care what he took or what he didn't take. If—and when—I ever see that worthless prick again, I'm going to tear him limb from limb."

"Frank, please." I put my arms around him. "We're both entitled to be hurt and angry—I'm not saying we aren't. And I'm not defending him—there's no way anyone could ever defend what he did." *Pray for a brave heart.* "But life never hands you anything you can't handle. It's *how* you handle it that makes the difference. Now, it would be easy to let this poison us both, change the people we are . . . but I'm *not* going to give him that kind of power over me. I'm not going to be someone else from now on. I'm still Scotty. And you know what else? We still have each other, don't we? And that's the most important thing, Frank. He can't ever take that away from us—*unless we let him.*"

"I know." He nodded, tightening his own grip on me. "I love you, Scotty."

"I love you, Frank." I kissed his cheek. "Now, I'm going to go get in the shower."

When I walked back into the living room, toweling my hair dry, Frank was sitting on the couch. He had on his little green skirt, his green sandals, a yellow vest, and the purple mask was pushed up over his head. He'd laid out the gold skirt, the purple vest, and the green mask for me. Frank had also made me a large cup of coffee liberally laced with Irish crème. The leftover costume pieces were piled in a corner of the room. I just looked at them for a minute while putting on my costume. They looked so sad, so forlorn. When I'd planned these costumes—*no, don't go back there, Scotty. That's a bad place. Don't ever go back there. Just focus on going forward, the here and now.*

Frank whistled. "You are such a hottie, Scotty." He picked up the roach I'd left in the ashtray and lit it, taking a deep inhale.

I stared at him in disbelief. "Frank—"

He gave me a lazy grin. "Now, there's nothing wrong with a little recreational drug use, is there? Seems to me I've heard that before someplace." He offered it to me, and I took it, inhaling deeply.

"Frank, you aren't doing this because—"

He waved his hand. "I'm loosening up, Scotty." He took another hit and started coughing, smoke spewing out of his mouth. "I was thinking while you were in the shower. And you're right. Life doesn't give you anything you can't handle; it's all in *how* you handle it. And I've decided I need to take the stick out of my ass and relax and enjoy my life." He waved his hand. "I've wasted a lot of my life being, I don't know, hung up about things. And I'm going to try to change that. I'm going to try to be more like you." He grinned a little weakly at me. "You're pretty smart, you know that?"

"Are you sure that's a good idea?" I couldn't help but grin back at him. "I mean, I'm hardly a role model or anything."

"I can think of worse." He stood up and I caught my breath. I'd done a great job picking out these costumes. Frank looked like a million bucks. The skirt was a little short, barely covering him in the front. I could see the bottom of his purple thong underneath it. I walked over and tugged it down a little bit until it was low on his waist, showing the deep crevices where his torso met his hips. "Shall we go?" He put his arms around me and planted a deep kiss on my lips.

"You got everything?"

He checked his little camera bag. "Wallet, keys, money. The only thing missing is the Ecstasy."

I gaped at him.

He shrugged. "Why the hell not?"

So, we took a hit each.

We were going to march with the Society of St. Anne. We weren't going to make it to the beginning of the marching parade; I figured we could catch up to it when it crossed Esplanade on its way into the Quarter. The Society of St. Anne is one of the best parts of Fat Tuesday—fabulous costumes, everyone in a great mood, going from bar to bar, drinking and just having a great time. I figured we'd break off from them before they headed down to Canal to catch Rex; Canal Street is too big of a nightmare on Fat Tuesday. We'd hang out at the gay bars.

Frank and I held hands as we walked up Esplanade to Royal. We walked in silence, both of our faces sad and long. I had brought two extra hits of Ecstasy for later. I was starting to feel it a bit—that warm, happy feeling when you just love everything. "I hate to say it, but I'm going to really miss him," Frank said finally as we posed for a couple of tourists who wanted to take our picture. The tourists weren't in costume, but almost everyone else on the street was. I grinned at a group in *Wizard of Oz* outfits. They even had some little people with them dressed as the Lollipop Guild. "The one thing I don't understand—" he broke off.

"What?"

"I don't know," he said glumly, nodding to the tourists as they thanked us for letting them take our picture. "The one thing that doesn't make sense to me is why he stayed here so long. I mean, I know Pasha and Sasha were his targets, and Sasha didn't get here until a few weeks ago, but Pasha had been here for months. Why didn't he just kill him then?"

"I guess there are a lot of things we're never going to know." We started walking again. "Who knows? But maybe—"

"Yeah?"

"Maybe he *did* love us, Frank. Maybe he was here because he wanted to be." I shrugged. "The only thing he took was the picture. Nobody is all bad. I truly believe that. Everyone has good in him. Maybe I'm naïve, maybe I'm just dumb, but I'd like to believe—no, I'm *choosing* to believe—that he loved us."

"You really are something, you know that?" Frank stopped walking and looked at me, a big smile on his face. "I love you, Milton Scott Bradley." He put his arms around me and hugged me.

And I knew we were going to be okay, that we were going to get through it all. We had each other, and that was the most important thing. "I love you so much, Frank."

"Excuse me?"

We pulled apart. A woman dressed as a skeleton with a Richard Nixon mask and holding a big plaster bone in one hand was standing there. "Can I take your picture?"

We put our arms around each other's waists and gave her a big smile.

"Thank you." She turned the camera around so we could see the digital picture.

We looked *fabulous*.

"Happy Mardi Gras!" I called out to her as we walked on, hand in hand.

"This is amazing," Frank commented as a group of people dressed as the Seven Deadly Sins jostled past us, calling out "Happy Mardi Gras" as they passed. "I could never have imagined this."

I stepped on a set of beads and my foot slipped. Frank caught me before I could fall, and I looked down at them.

There was a mixed set: green, gold, and purple beads alternating on the string. There was a medallion face down. I knelt down and picked them up, turning the medallion over. I grinned.

It read "MARDI GRAS MAMBO."

How could I have forgotten? Crazy things happen during Carnival every year. There's just something about it, something that gets in the air that makes people do things they wouldn't ordinarily do. Sure, this year had been a little extreme—well, a lot extreme—but after all, what could you do?

It's Mardi Gras.

I slipped them over Frank's head and kissed his cheek. "Come on; let's get moving. We don't want to miss St. Anne," I said.

There was a crowd milling about at the R Bar on Royal Street in the Marigny. In the distance I could hear what could only be the Storyville Stompers, the marching band that leads the Society of St. Anne. I nodded and said hello to friends—at least people whom I thought I knew. Everyone was in masks. There was a Spiderman, several Wonder Women, a couple of harlequins, Romeo and Juliet, gladiators, witches, and ghosts. It was almost too much for my mind to handle. I was on sensory overload.

"You want a drink?" Frank asked, starting to bounce a little bit. He was starting to feel it.

So was I.

"Just water's fine," I said, taking some deep breaths to keep it under control.

He threaded his way through the crowd and inside the bar.

Life is good, I thought, watching Frank's skirt bounce, revealing just a hint of curved, hard butt. People turned to stare after him as he walked past, and who could blame them? He was gorgeous. *No, life is good. Stay focused on the positive. The Goddess blessed us both by bringing us together, and as long as we have each other, we can handle anything, we can get through everything, and that's what is really important. I have a great family; I have a great guy; I have great friends; I have a great life. I am truly blessed, and that's what we both need to remember. It's not going to be easy to get over it, but as long as I have Frank I can do anything.*

A loud cheer went up from the crowd as the Storyville Stompers came around the corner, and the crowd of costumed people dancing behind them cheered right back. A feeling of joy and peace came over me. Maybe it was the Ecstasy—I can't really say—and when I saw Frank coming toward me with two bottled waters in his hands, I said a quick prayer of thanks to the Goddess. He had a huge smile on his face. I threw my arms around him and we stood that way for a while, just holding on to each other, and I knew I was right. I could handle anything as long as I had him by my side.

Thank you, Goddess. Thank you so much for all of your blessings.

"You were gone a long time," I said, taking the cap off the bottle and taking a swig.

"It's pretty crowded in there—and everybody wanted to know what I have on under this skirt." He grinned at me. "This is so *awesome.*"

"I was a little worried." I put the cap on my bottle and looked at him slyly. "And with your habit of getting kidnapped . . ."

He stared at me for a second and then started to laugh. "You little asshole!"

I was about to say something smartass when someone called my name. I turned and saw David running up to us. He was wearing leather shorts, a leather cap, and boots. He was dragging a sexy Hispanic-looking guy in jeans and no shirt by the hand. "Hey!" He grinned as he walked up. "This is Diego. He just moved here from Dallas."

"Hey," I said, shaking his hand. Diego was at most five feet three, and all muscle—a sexy little spinner. His abs were perfectly cut, and his waist was tiny. "Nice to meet you, happy Mardi Gras, and welcome to New Orleans!"

He grinned at me. "This is crazy!" He looked around, his eyes wide. "It's like this every year? This is so wonderful!"

I just smiled at him.

David leaned over and whispered in my ear. "You would not believe the weekend I've had! What have you guys been up to?"

I looked at him, then at Diego's smiling face, and then at Frank. They were all smiling. I looked around at the crowd of happy, festive people in costume and was filled with joy. There is so much joy in my life, so many wonderful people—how could I stay down? How could I be negative? I am the *fucking* luckiest man alive.

I threw back my head and laughed, putting my arm around Frank's waist and pulling him close to me.

"You wouldn't believe me if I told you," I replied, winking at Frank. "Come on, boys, let's have some fun." I threw my arms out and looked up at the sky. "Happy Mardi Gras!!" I shouted at the top of my lungs.

A loud cheer went up from the crowd, and we all four linked hands and fell into step behind the Storyville Stompers and headed into the Quarter.

They never did catch Colin.

I didn't really think they ever would—he was too good. They found his car at the airport in short-term parking. Apparently he'd gotten on a plane out of the country on Monday afternoon. Best as we can figure, as soon as Sasha was dead, he just hopped into his car and drove to the airport. But on his way, he stopped by the apartment and grabbed the picture of the three of us.

Papa pulled some strings with the licensing board, and both Frank and I managed to get our own licenses. Since the rent on our office space was paid for a year, we decided to keep it, and now we are partners in Sobieski & Bradley. We changed the name on the door, got new business cards, and started over. It was sad cleaning out Colin's desk, but there wasn't really anything in it other than office supplies. He left no real traces of anything behind—but then he'd never really had anything of that nature here.

Storm continues to throw work our way, and so does Millie. We're doing okay with the business, and after Mardi Gras, I was kind of happy to return to some semblance of calm and normality.

Papa doesn't know, to this day, that there were triplets. At first, I wasn't sure it was such a great idea to keep it from him, but Maman finally convinced me. Misha claimed their bodies as the next of kin. We had them cremated, and we spread their ashes in the river. It was a sad moment—all of us gathered there on the Moon Walk. I prayed for them, as I'm sure we all did.

Misha was a little awkward at first as part of the family circle, keeping quiet and not talking much. I talked to him a few times, and he told me stories about his brothers—my uncles—and what they were like as kids. But as time passed, his Diderot blood became apparent, and he started giving as good as he got at family gatherings. He even managed to leave Mom speechless and sputtering once.

He was *definitely* a Diderot.

Frank moved into my apartment, and Millie and Velma rented out the top floor to a group of flight attendants—all male, of course. They just use it as kind of a base, so a lot of the time it's just empty. I did a ritual cleansing before they moved in, just to be on the safe side.

It hasn't been easy for Frank and me, but as more time passes, it gets easier. And we have each other, which is the most important thing. Nobody ever mentions Colin to us—to people outside the family we just say it didn't work out and he moved away. I try to remember the times we had together that were good, when we laughed and joked, and whenever either one of us starts going to that dark place, I just think about the picture. I remember that he took that picture with him, wherever he was going.

It's easy to hate, but it's so much harder to forgive.

I'm not there yet—and neither is Frank. But every day, we pray for the strength to get past our hurt and anger.

And every day, I wake up in Frank's arms and feel grateful. Grateful to be alive, grateful for my family, grateful for all the blessings I have.

And I know someday I'll get to that place where I can forgive

Colin for everything—we *both* will—and we'll be better people for it.

Life never hands you anything you can't handle.

It's *how* you handle it that matters.

And we're going to be just fine.